I0723520

FRIEND ZONED

JENNIFER SUCEVIC

Friend Zoned

Copyright© 2016 by Jennifer Sucevic

All rights reserved. No part of this book may be reproduced in any form or by any electronic or mechanical means, including information storage and retrieval systems, without written permission from the author, except for the use of brief quotations in a book review.

This is a work of fiction. Names, characters, businesses, palaces, events, locales, and incidents are either the products of the author's imagination or used in a fictitious manner. Any resemblance to actual persons, living or dead, or actual events is purely coincidental.

Cover Design by Mary Ruth Baloy at MR Creations

Home | Jennifer Sucevic or www.jennifersucevic.com

ALSO BY JENNIFER SUCEVIC

....

PROLOGUE

....

Sam

It's the light scraping of the windowpane being forced up that has my eyelids feathering open. Not a moment later, a small body slips through the opening before dropping quietly to the floor of my second story bedroom. Cautiously, she treads across the wooden floorboards so as to not wake my parents before toeing off her black chucks and shedding the gray hoodie. When she's in nothing more than a thin pink tank top and a pair of black yoga pants, she moves toward me again. Without a word, I simply hold open the blankets so she can slip beneath them.

I pull the sheet and comforter over her, tucking them around her body. "Nightmare?" It's sleepily that the word falls from my lips into the swirling darkness. Without looking at the clock, I know it has to be well after midnight.

"Yup."

That's all she says and because this is a well-established routine, one we've been doing for about two and a half years, I know it's pointless to push for more. I've come to understand that all Violet needs is for me to chase away the dreams that continue to haunt her. The last thing she wants is to talk about them.

And so I do the one thing I love best, I curve my six foot two frame around her petite body, pulling her against me until we're both comfortably settled. Even though I had been slumbering soundly before her arrival, I always sleep better with her tucked safely in my arms.

An unintentional sigh of contentment falls from my lips as the fragrance of her rosemary mint shampoo hits my senses. I've learned to enjoy this time with her because come morning, when my alarm goes off at six thirty for school, she'll be long gone. Back in her own bedroom about fifty yards away.

And it'll be like it never happened.

Violet doesn't talk much about her parents or the younger sister she lost in a car crash when she was fourteen years old. It's what sent her life spiraling into chaos, forcing her to move in with her grandparents the summer before eighth grade.

But I know the nightmares still claw at her during the darkest part of the night. When they do, she'll scamper up the scarred hundred-year-old oak tree that stands outside my bedroom window with its gnarled root system and thick branches. Since I never know when she'll show up, I leave the window unlatched so she can come and go as she pleases.

Violet burrows into my embrace before a soft sigh, one that echoes my own, leaves her lips before arrowing straight through my beating heart.

"Comfy?" I don't know why I bother to ask. I can tell by the way her body goes lax against mine that she is. Then again, maybe I want to hear her say the words. Maybe I want her to finally acknowledge that when she needs comforting, it's me she runs to. I'm the only one who can keep the nightmares at bay. There aren't many people Violet allows herself to be completely unguarded with. I count myself lucky to be one of the chosen few. Protecting her has become second nature.

More like a reflex.

Again, she sighs in pleasure, "Mmm hmm."

But it's enough.

Enough for now.

"Good. Go to bed so we can both get a little shut eye." Although I would stand guard over her sleeping form until the sun came up in the eastern sky if that's what she needed. If that's what it took for her to get a little bit of rest.

Violet may not realize it, but she completes me in the most basic sense of the word. When she's wrapped up tight in my arms, it's like I can finally breathe again. Which is kind of strange because, before Violet Winterfield entered my life, I never realized that I wasn't sucking in full breaths of oxygen.

This girl is mine. I marked her as my own when I locked eyes on her as she stepped out of her grandparent's navy sedan three summers ago.

As my eyelids droop, she murmurs into the darkness that continues to cloak us, "Don't let go, okay?"

Her words have me pressing my lips against the gentle curve of her cheek before whispering fiercely, "I won't let go, Vi. Not ever."

Chapter One

VIOLET

Sam slides onto the chair parked next to me about thirty seconds after class begins. His jean-clad leg presses up against mine as he settles in. Not taking my eyes off the professor, who has already launched into the lecture for the day, I whisper from the corner of my mouth, "Nice of you to join us, Mr. Harper."

Even though I'm not looking his way, I know he's grinning from ear to ear. I can all but feel it. His smiles are as blinding as the sun. Heat radiates from them in heavy waves. Any minute his warm breath is going to feather across my—

"I had to haul ass all the way from the stadium." He snorts before adding, "Coach scheduled a mid afternoon practice just for the fun of it."

Well...that last comment is debatable. It's early November, and damn chilly out. The Bulldogs have been on an incredible winning streak this season, which means ramped up practices and workout schedules so they can keep their number one seed going into the play-offs. At this point, everyone in their conference is looking to tear them down.

I glance at him, and notice that his dark blond hair is all shiny and wet from the shower he must have just taken. His bright blue eyes spear mine with a sparkle of mischief simmering in them. His cheeks are flushed, and his breathing is just a bit labored.

I'm slammed with the realization that this is probably how Sam looks right after a rowdy bout of sex. Something hot slides through me before settling deep in my core. Not knowing where the hell *that* thought sprang up from, I abruptly shift my body away from his. My brows pull together in bewilderment.

What the heck is that all about?

Not that I want to dwell on what it means, but those kind of pesky thoughts regarding Sam have been cropping up with a disconcerting amount of frequency lately. It's like I blinked one day and suddenly he looked different to me.

That being said, I need these feelings to go away.

Sam and I are friends.

Good friends. And I don't want that to change.

We met when I moved in with my grandparents who live next door to his family. That was eight years ago, and we've been tight ever since. Somehow, we lucked out, both of us choosing to attend Barnett University.

I wanted to stick close to my grandparents since I'm all they have, and Sam plays football for the Barnett Bulldogs. He was offered full rides to play at half a dozen other Division I programs, both in and out of state, but chose to stay local as well.

Needing to refocus my runaway thoughts, I murmur under my breath, "I'm hoping for your sake that you finished up the paper that's due today on the *power of the judiciary over the legislature.*" I keep my gaze focused straight ahead. The last thing I need is to incur the wrath of Dr. Rickets.

"Yup. Freshly printed with references cited up the ass."

I almost snort but rein it in at the last moment. References had better be cited or Rickets will come after you with both barrels blasting. He's flunked people in PS 345- *the Judicial Process* for less. Since Sam and I are both in the pre-law program, we have a lot of the same classes. Although, this is the only one we have together this semester. We end up hunkered down at the library on a fairly regular basis.

Rickets continues droning on as Sam gets his laptop up and

running. After about fifteen minutes, he leans toward me again, breaking my concentration. Unfortunately, laser focus is required because this class takes dry to a whole new and challenging level. "Are you planning to hit the Sigma party tonight?"

I'm on the verge of responding when our professor's sharp voice slices through the stale air of the classroom.

"An answer if you please, Mr. Harper."

My belly drops about eleven stories. Even though I try not to let Sam distract me, I hadn't been aware of a question being thrown out.

Sam, however, doesn't miss a beat. "Within limits, judges do, in fact, make law. Common law is their creation, and statutes require their interpretation. All law must continually be aligned with the Constitution. But at the end of the day, the Constitution means what judges decide it does."

If Rickets is at all impressed by the fact that Sam answered without even blinking, he doesn't let on. Although, by the way our professor presses his fleshy lips together, I'd have to say he's disappointed not to have caught Sam by surprise. He continues lecturing in a monotone voice, biding his time before springing yet another complex question on some unsuspecting student just trying to muddle their way through this class so they can graduate.

Almost leisurely, Sam stretches out his body in the seat next to me. As he does, the bottom of his soft gray cotton T-shirt rides up giving me a distracting view of rock-solid abdominals before I force my gaze away.

I seriously don't understand what's going on with me lately. I mean, it hasn't been *that* long since I've been with a guy. Certainly not long enough to warrant me noticing the taut ridges of my best friend's six-pack.

But I am.

I am *so* noticing them right now.

And that is all kinds of wrong.

"So, you in or out for the party?" he asks.

Annoyed by the unwanted feelings that keep popping up within me, I shake my head before muttering, "Can we discuss this after class? I'm trying to focus here."

The key word is *trying*.

Clearly, I'm having a difficult time with that. Which doesn't make the least bit of sense.

There is no way I should be having these kinds of thoughts about Sam. It feels, I don't know—incestuous.

Sort of.

We've known each other since we were fourteen years old. For goodness' sake, I used to crawl into bed with the guy when we were in high school. Sam was the only one who could chase away the nightmares. That being said, nothing ever happened between us. There certainly weren't any wandering hands during the middle of the night. No copping a cheap feel. No I'll-show-you-mine-if-you-show-me-yours. He would simply hold me in his arms while I slept.

That was it.

Up until recently, I never thought of Sam as anything other than my best friend.

Which is precisely why these thoughts are disturbing on so many different levels.

Unperturbed by my abrupt tone, he shrugs before slouching further onto his chair. "Sure."

Sam has—for all intents and purposes—a photographic memory. So, chit chatting the class period away is no biggie for him. All he has to do is read something once and it's locked in for life. I'm not going to lie, it's annoying to people like myself who have to study their asses off to pull decent grades.

Even though Sam doesn't face the same academic challenges that I do, he lets me borrow that big brain of his anytime I need it. He's pretty great about studying with me or re-explaining concepts that I don't have a firm grasp on.

After another thirty-three minutes, which is precisely three minutes past the end of class, Rickets finally releases us back into the world. People scatter from the room as if they're fleeing for their very lives. Rickets dearly loves a captive audience and is always reluctant to turn them loose when his time draws to an end.

As soon as we clear the door of the classroom, Sam slings his muscular arm around my shoulders as we make our way out of the polisci building. It may be bright and sunny out, but there's a cold north-easterly wind whipping its way through campus. I'm bundled up in my silver North Face coat and Sam is wearing his football jacket.

"I hate this weather," I grumble right before Sam tugs me closer. The guy radiates heat like a furnace. That being said, I can't help but snuggle into his warmth as the wind continues to slap at us with icy cold fingers.

"Better?" His lips are so close to my ear that the husky cadence of his voice sends an unexpected shiver skittering down my spine. My gaze flies to his, praying that the hitch in my breathing has gone unnoticed.

He flashes a brief smile but doesn't seem any wiser to what's going on within me. A little sigh of relief escapes from my lips. I don't under-stand why I keep reacting to him this way. It's disconcerting. Not to mention, embarrassing.

The first couple of times it happened, I shrugged it off as a fluke.

Unfortunately, we're moving past fluke and toward—

Nope. Not going to go there. Because I definitely don't think about Sam like that. Furthermore, I don't *want* to think about him like that.

"Much," I squeak as my heart continues to jackhammer painfully under my breast.

He glances around and asks, "So, where's what's-his-face? Hasn't he been meeting you after class?"

I send him one of those *I-don't-really-want-to-talk-about-it* looks, and he immediately chortles, which isn't a good look on him. "Jeez, Vi, ran another one off already, huh? That was fast. Even for you."

"Eight days," I confirm reluctantly. Which is par for the course where I'm concerned. My relationships have absolutely zero staying power. I've had cartons of milk sitting in my fridge that have outlasted some of these guys.

Which is...yeah...just plain sad.

"I don't know why you bother."

I shake my head and agree with the sentiment. "Me, neither."

"Off to sociology?"

I'm not even sure why he asks. The guy probably knows my schedule better than I do.

"Yup, then I'm done for the day." Although I do have a ton of studying to plow my way through this afternoon, which is pretty standard. There is no shortage of books that need cracking and papers that need writing.

"I have philosophy at one, film review, and then another practice to run through. So, are you heading to that party or what, Winterfield? There's not much else going on tonight." His arm tightens around my shoulders, drawing me closer until I'm able to get a whiff of his cologne. My insides do a little impromptu dance.

That reaction nearly sends me stumbling.

Seriously…WTF?

"After all the parties we missed because of Rickets class, not to mention studying for the LSAT, we've earned it." Trying his best to cajole me into attending, he adds, "Come on, Vi, it's supposed to be a huge monster bash. No one does it better than the Sigmas."

He's not lying about all the parties that have been missed because of writing that paper for Rickets' class and studying for the law school entrance exam, which we took in September.

Hmmm. I have to admit that he makes a damn good argument. Maybe we do deserve to cut loose, if only for a night.

That being said, I still hedge. "I have to see if Mia is up for it, but yeah, we'll probably stop by at some point." Mia is my roommate as well as best friend. We met freshman year in English 102.

You know when you meet someone, and right from the get-go it feels like you've known them your entire life? That's the way it was with us. We fell into an easy camaraderie. Sam is the only other person I've ever clicked with like that. Normally, it takes time for me to warm up and feel comfortable.

But not with Mia.

This is our third and final year rooming together. I'm really going to miss her after graduation. Mia's plans are to move to Philadelphia where her boyfriend, Carter, lives and right now, I have absolutely no idea where I'll end up studying law. Worse, I won't know until the spring when my (fingers crossed) acceptance letters start rolling in.

Sam squeezes me closer so that I'm pressed up against all the hard lines of his body. I hate to admit that my pulse skitters at the contact.

"Cool. Text me when you're heading over," he says.

Ha!

I give him a noncommittal response because I know *exactly* why he wants to nail down my ETA. This is nothing new. Samuel J. Harper considers himself to be my unofficial big brother. Even though I haven't asked him to look out for me, he insists on doing it anyway.

End result—the guy is a major cock blocker.

He could lay off with the whole big scary brother act he's got going on. I'm twenty-one years old and certainly no timid virgin. Sometimes, I have to wonder if he's under the misconception that we're living in Victorian England...

And he needs to safeguard my virtue.

Too late, dude.

Much too late.

What I suspect is that he enjoys frightening off potential suitors.

I almost snort.

Fine, we're talking more like one-night stands. I'm not exactly looking for a life partner at this point. I'm focused on finishing out my senior year of college before heading off to law school.

But still...a girl has her needs.

I should be allowed to blow off steam just like he is. Unfortunately, because of his height and sheer muscle mass, it isn't difficult for him to deter prospective candidates. I've yet to find a dude who will stand up to him. And if they're not willing to do that, then they probably aren't worth my time.

The guy definitely needs a girlfriend to preoccupy him. Maybe then he would leave me alone.

"All right, Vi, I'll catch you later." With that, Sam drops a quick kiss on the side of my face before taking off.

As I watch his long-legged strides eat up the concrete pathway, two girls sidle up next to me. For just a moment, all three of us silently watch Sam's retreating figure until he disappears into the thick crowd.

They sigh in total male appreciation.

The blonde wearing a beanie on her head clears her throat as my eyes swing curiously to her. "We were wondering what the deal is between you and Sam Harper."

I raise a brow.

Yeah, I know *exactly* what kind of intel these girls are after. They want to know if Sam and I are sleeping together. Since we tend to spend a lot of time hanging out, people naturally assume that we are.

I may not be into Sam that way—I'm really not—but I'm well aware of his finer points. He towers a few inches over six feet with a body honed by both football and weightlifting. He's got thick, dirty blond hair and bright, piercing ocean-hued eyes. The real draw, in my opinion, is that he's a seriously nice guy.

One of the best you'll ever meet.

When I moved in with my grandparents, Sam was the only kid who went out of his way to pry me from my shell. We spent that entire summer playing video games in his room, going to the movies, hanging out at the mall, and swimming at the country club his family belongs to.

The blonde's gaze darts to the brunette at her side. "You know, is he your boyfriend?"

Since I recognize them from Rickets' class, and they both seem like nice girls, I decide to let them off the hook. "Nah, we're not together like that."

Surprised by my answer, the blonde clarifies, "You have absolutely no interest in him? Because I don't want to poach someone else's man."

See? I like her even more now. This chick has just solidified her position as the number one girl I'm planning to push in Sam's direction.

"Nope, we went to high school together. We're nothing more than good friends."

With a shake of her head, she reveals a row of bright white teeth. "How are you *just friends* with someone as hot as him?" She stares at me as if I'm crazy.

That's the moment an image of his shirt riding up during the middle of class, revealing those rock-solid abs, nudges its way back into my brain. I clear my throat uncomfortably and force the memory away. "We don't think about one another like that."

Seriously...I don't.

I mean, we don't.

Is it really a big deal if I feel a little zing of attraction between us every once in a while? My guess is that it's completely normal. Certainly nothing to get bent out of shape over.

The brunette elbows her curvy friend before waggling her eyebrows. "Well, her loss is your gain, Allie."

My eyes quickly skim down the length of her.

Long blonde hair and deep brown eyes—check.

The thin, body hugging coat she's wearing shows off a rather impressive sized bust. Another check.

I can't help but smirk, feeling good about what I'm intent on doing. "Actually, you couldn't be more his type if you tried. Here," I decide on the fly, "I'm going to give you his number. Text him and see what happens." Sam seems to favor girls with long blonde hair, big brown eyes, and curvy little bodies.

He is such a typical dude.

Her eyes widen like she just won the lottery. "Really?"

I give her a wink. "Absolutely."

Maybe hooking him up with someone else will put the kibosh on all these strange bursts of attraction that keep zipping around inside me. What I need is for everything to slide back to normal between us. And maneuvering this girl in front of him is the perfect way to do it.

She beams. "Thanks! I'll definitely text him." Shaking her head, she introduces herself, "I'm Allie, by the way." She cocks her head toward her sidekick. "And this is Lanie."

"I'm Violet. Just tell him that I gave you his number. He won't mind at all." I give the pair a little wave. "Okay, well, I've got to hustle to sociology. Good luck with Sam."

"Thanks again!" They wave in return before our small group splinters apart.

My guess is that Sam will appreciate me steering this chick in his direction.

Added side benefit—it gets him off my ass.

Which is clearly a win-win situation in my book.

Chapter Two

SAM

"Dude, I'm curious—when was the last time you got laid?" Dylan pauses for a beat before forging ahead with the conversation. "I'm being totally serious right now."

Sadly, I know he is.

Not bothering to answer, because doing so will only perpetuate the conversation, I glance around the Sigma party. It's as jam-packed and out of control as I suspected it would be. We're talking elbow to elbow crowd, music at an ear shattering decibel, a few games of strip beer pong already in progress, drinks galore from the makeshift bar, and—if my nose isn't deceiving me—a few bowls of pot being passed around. It isn't even ten yet, and this party is just getting started. Although, none of that stops me from zeroing in on Violet like a heat-seeking missile. Even though she's clear across the room, I keep my sights locked on her.

I hoist the beer to my lips and take a swig. "What? You keeping tabs on me or something?"

Because that's not creepy at all.

A knowing brow slides its way across his forehead. "I don't have to. You're coiled tighter than a freaking spring. It's obvious what your problem is. You need to get all that poison out. If you don't, it'll end up messing with your mojo on the field."

I nearly laugh at that.

Fucking poison?

Is he serious?

Stupid question—of course he is.

In an attempt to stifle any more questions or unsolicited advice regarding my current *poison* situation, I shoot Dylan a glare before my gaze bounces back to Violet.

And the asshat attempting to make moves on her.

Just look at him over there.

He's so damn close, he's practically mauling her. And watching him run his fingers up and down the curve of her cheek has me grinding my molars together in silent aggravation. Not a moment later, her lips curve upward before she laughs at whatever the hell he's yammering on about. She may be a good forty feet from me, but I can still tell she's got those damn fuck-me eyes going on.

Yeah...that's not going to happen on my watch.

"Uh oh," Dylan chuckles, "looks like it's time for you to run off another one."

My head snaps toward him.

Finally.

That's got to be the first sensible thing that's come out of his mouth all night. "You're abso-fucking-lutely right." I down the rest of my beer before shoving the empty plastic cup into Dylan's hand. "Good call." Unwilling to waste another minute, I clap him on the shoulder before taking off.

"Dude, I was freaking kidding! Get your pathetic ass back here before you embarrass yourself even further!"

I don't bother with a response. I think we both know it's too late for that. At this point, I'm a man on a mission. And that mission is to get the encroaching usurper away from my girl.

Whether she wants that is totally up for interpretation.

This isn't the first time I've run off some dude and it won't be the last. It's not like I don't understand the attraction. Violet Winterfield is gorgeous. She has long, thick blonde hair and big, whiskey-colored eyes fringed with dark lashes. I'm not even going to talk about the sweet little body she's rocking, because getting a woody at this point in the evening would only further solidify my pathetic status.

And I don't really need that.

My gaze sharpens on them. If I'm not mistaken, the guy looks to be making a move.

The move.

He's on the verge of leaning in and planting one right on her lips. He's inching closer and lowering his face. Her eyelids are feathering closed. People scurry out of my two-hundred-pound way as I barrel through. I have to consciously flex my hands because I want to punch that douchebag in the face for daring to touch what's mine.

Unfortunately, all that will do is piss off Violet. I've learned through trial and error that I can't come in all hot, ready to tear some guy limb from limb.

Nope.

I have to be more subtle than that. Trust me, it's a fine art I've perfected over the years. This guy won't realize what's happening until it's too late.

Some sixth sense must alert Violet to the fact that I'm on the move because her eyes widen as they ensnare mine right before I wedge my way between them, snaking an arm around her in the process.

As I do, everything in me settles. Violet's proximity has a way of doing that. It always has. My life can be a raging mess, but when I'm with her and she's in my arms or I'm just touching her, the world around us quiets to a barely perceptible hum.

It's more addictive than crack.

And I crave that stillness like nothing else.

With a lazy smile tilting my lips upward, I press a kiss against her temple before hauling her closer. With that simple action, I feel my pulse settle. Rational thought seeps its way back into my brain as my tense muscles release. And then I nearly swallow my tongue at the feel of her breast pressed against my T-shirt covered chest.

Damn. That gets me every freaking time.

At the moment, I'd give my left nut to toss her over my shoulder and take her back to my place so I can immerse myself in that gorgeous body of hers for a full, forty-eight hours. I don't even know if that would be enough time. I really don't. I've never wanted anyone the way I want her.

The way I *need* her.

But first things first.

"Hey, babe," I say.

Instead of waiting for Violet to respond, because I know damn well what kind of retort my greeting will elicit, I turn my attention toward the jack-wad whose jaw has slacken at my sudden arrival on the scene. It takes everything I have inside not to snort out a laugh. He looks confounded that the girl he was just hitting on is now in the arms of another dude.

He's blinking his eyes all slow-like as if he's trying to play mental catch up. You can almost see the gears in his head gradually shifting as he processes the fact that his odds of getting laid tonight just plummeted into the single digits. For a split-second, he looks ready to put up a fight before taking a good look at me. I flex my biceps so he won't get any foolish ideas that will end badly.

For him.

In all honesty, I might enjoy channeling some of the pent-up sexual frustration careening through my system by plowing my fist into this guy's face. Even though he isn't going to get laid tonight, neither am I.

His face transforms and I see the moment recognition dawns. "Harper, right?" He shifts his weight from one foot to the other before the irritated look disappears.

I give him an easy smile. "Yup, that's me."

"Dude," he shakes his head apologetically before jerking it toward a now frowning Violet who is still smashed up against my body, "I had no idea this was your chick." Rather hilariously, he shoots her a look rife with silent accusation. "She didn't say a word about it."

Since this is usually the part where Violet will offer up a protest, I tug her closer. "No worries." I smack another kiss against her head. If the low growling noise emanating from her is any indication, then my guess is that she's annoyed that I've managed to foil yet another hookup attempt on her part.

I can only grin evilly at that.

"What do you think your chances are against Miami Ohio this weekend?"

As her no-longer-going-to-happen one night stand questions me about the upcoming game, Violet slides an arm around me before snaking her hand beneath my T-shirt. Under different circumstances, her touch would be entirely welcome, except I know what she's up to. I steel myself as she pinches a chunk of my flesh between her forefinger and thumb before twisting it viciously.

Think massive titty twister minus the titty.

Fuuuuuck!

I hiss out a sharp breath as her fingers dig into me. I can only imagine the considerable damage she's doing to my body. "I think our chances of coming out of it with a win are solid. They're running a tough offense but there are some holes in their defensive game that we'll be able to exploit. Especially since they have a few guys out with injuries. We're operating at one hundred percent, and King is playing the best ball of his life."

By this point, the guy has all but forgotten about Violet as he continues to rapid-fire questions at me. He's talking stats, playoff picks, and bowl games. And hey, I love talking ball as much as the next guy, but Violet is clearly steaming. Not to mention, she's bruising the shit out of my skin.

When I can't take another moment of those brutal instruments of torture, I extricate us from the conversation. Luckily for me, Violet is more than ready to leave now that her evening has been thwarted. My arm is still wrapped around her. I'm thinking about attaching myself to her like a barnacle for the rest of the evening. That way no one else will get ideas in regard to her availability.

Leaning closer, I murmur in her ear, "You can stop pinching me now. I've saved you from the fumblings of that drunken idiot." I wait a heartbeat before adding, "You're welcome."

I know my comment will only crank her up. But I kind of enjoy when she gets all heated up. I like the way her eyes flash with fire and the pulse in her throat thrums. It's fucking hot.

Violet doesn't disappoint. She screeches to a halt, refusing to budge any further. Her dark brows lower over eyes that spark with anger. Her hands bunch at her sides like she's contemplating whether or not to throw a punch.

Like I said—goddamn sexy.

She grits between clenched teeth, "He was *not* a drunken idiot! He was actually a nice guy and you chased him off."

Fine. Maybe he was.

But still...

I give her a considering look before stating the obvious, "He didn't seem to mind that I stole you right from beneath his nose, now did he?"

Violet makes that growling noise deep in her throat again. Damn, but she's adorable when she's all riled up. It makes me want to wrap her up in my arms and carry her out of here. But I don't. She's liable to cause even more physical damage to my person if I were to attempt something along those lines.

"*Sam!*" My name explodes from her lips in frustration. "That's only because you let him think we were a couple!" She throws her arms wide. "Of course, he was going to back down."

Maybe.

Then again, maybe not.

I shrug. "Listen, if I was interested in a chick, I'd pursue her until she told me herself that she wasn't into it."

FYI—Violet has never come out and said that she wasn't interested or into it.

What? I'm just saying...

She rolls her dark brown eyes at my guy logic. "I think you do this just to mess with me."

I'm tempted to shake my head, but don't bother. Violet's a really smart girl but there are times when she can be totally clueless. *Especially* where I'm concerned. She doesn't get that I have feelings for her. That I've *always* had feelings for her. It's like she's put me in some little box marked with big bright colors- *just a friend* and refuses to let me out. After eight long years, it's driving me crazy. Something has got to give. And I don't want it to be my sanity. Because I'm precariously close to snapping.

Short of spelling it out for her, I don't know what else to do. I want this girl so damn bad and yet, here she is trying to hookup with some random dude rather than consider for one moment that the friendship we have could be a solid basis to something more, something deeper, something infinitely more meaningful.

It's on the tip of my tongue to tell her why I'm constantly cock blocking her, but I rein it in at the last second. Instead, I say in my best cajoling tone, attempting to placate her, "I don't want to see you get tangled up with the wrong kind of guy."

For instance—one whose name is not Sam Harper.

Exasperation bleeds through her voice as she huffs, "I wasn't exactly looking for a long-term commitment." She raises her brows before adding, "If you know what I mean."

Fuck yeah, I know *exactly* what she means. Hence my sudden arrival on the scene.

Like I said before—totally clueless. It would be cute if I weren't so sexually frustrated by the situation.

With those thoughts circling around in my head, I pull her into a darkened hallway off the living room where the flow of people is a little lighter and spin her toward me. "So, you're just on the prowl, looking to get laid?" My teeth are clenched. The idea of her doing that pisses me off.

Her dark brows knit together as she stares up at me like I'm stupid. "Well, duh!"

My eyes narrow in response.

Unfortunately, those words are enough to have my junk stirring with the notion that she wants to have sex. There's only one dude who should be buried deep within her tight heat and that's me, goddamn it.

Before I can spit one single word out, she snaps, "What? You're allowed to sleep around, but I'm not?" Her hands settle on the soft curve of her hips as she glares.

Violet would be shocked to know that I haven't hooked up with a chick since the end of second semester last year. And that was only because I was completely shitfaced and trying to fuck Violet out of my system once and for all. Clearly, that didn't work since my main mission in life is to foil any and all of her attempts to get laid.

I found a chick who looked exactly like her—long blonde hair, deep brown eyes, nice soft tits, and I fucked her about six different ways before throwing in the condom and admitting that a paper-thin carbon copy wasn't ever going to diminish the need I have for Violet Winterfield.

And I haven't bothered to hookup since that little unwelcome revelation.

What's the point?

If I have the need to release the *poison,* as Dylan so charmingly put it, then my hand is as good as anything else. If I can't have her, I don't want anyone else.

And that's just fucking sad, man.

I plow a hand through my hair before admitting, "No, of course you can." Unless I'm willing to nut up, my hands are tied. I can't say one word about what she does. Over the last couple of years, I've tried numerous times to clue her in to what I'm feeling. I've dropped hints, given her little touches here and there, held her in my arms, and invaded her personal space. I've even tried kissing her, which is exquisite torture. But it's always the same—absolutely nothing.

Nada.

She's completely oblivious to all my attempts.

A slim brow rises across her forehead. "Then why are you always getting in my way? Is this a joke or something?"

A fucking joke?

Seriously?

I'm ready to go off like a damn shot over here and she thinks this is a joke?

I want to laugh.

Hysterically.

All the while tearing my hair out.

When I finally open my mouth, it's on the tip of my tongue to push out the words once and for all. To let the chips fall where they may. But...if she's not into it, where the hell does that leave us? Would my feelings make her uncomfortable? Would she then avoid me?

I don't think I could stand that.

Instead of purging myself of the truth, I slam my mouth shut before shaking my head.

Yeah, yeah... You don't have to say it.

I already know.

Biggest.

Pussy.

Ever.

Got it.

As if sensing my agitation—but clearly not understanding where it stems from—Violet lays a hand on my forearm before squeezing it. "Look, Sam, I really appreciate you watching out for me, but I can handle myself. If I want to go home with someone at the end of the night, I'm going to do it." As she releases the words into the atmosphere, all of the pent-up anger that had been vibrating within her slowly dissipates.

My hands tighten as I think about Violet getting it on with some asshole that isn't going to treat her right.

"I'm a big girl," she continues. "I can take care of myself. You're so used to looking out for me that sometimes you take it too far." She steps closer before twining her arms around my neck. The soft curves of her body press against all my hard lines. "But you don't have to do that anymore. I'll be careful, I promise."

I have to remind myself to unlock my tightened muscles before snaking my arms around her and hauling her close.

"I love you, Sam. You're my best friend."

Her earnest words have my heart sinking like a heavy stone. Not because I don't want to be her best friend, of course I do. I love that we're friends. That we've stayed close over the years, and nothing has managed to separate us. I love that I'm the first person she turns to when something is going on in her life. But it's not enough anymore. If I'm being honest, it hasn't been enough for a while.

I want more.

I want to be Violet's everything.

This conversation has me wondering if that's even possible. Maybe I've been fooling myself all these years by holding out hope that she'll wake up one day and realize what's been sitting in front of her the entire time.

Me.

Unaware of the thoughts churning in my head, she leans up on her tiptoes before pressing her mouth against mine. Since I have absolutely zero self-control where Violet Winterfield is concerned, I sweep my lips across hers until she hesitantly opens. Even though it's not much, it's more than enough for my tongue to slip inside her mouth and mingle with hers.

For just one moment.

One fucking moment.

Reluctantly, I draw away before it can get weird. Maybe I need to accept that Violet will never feel the same way about me. I'm doomed to be a friend and nothing more.

As she holds my gaze, there's a hint of confusion shadowed within her dark eyes. Like I've thrown her for a loop by slipping her a bit of tongue. The truth is that whenever she presses her lips against mine, I have a hard time resisting the urge to deepen it. So, for a fleeting moment or two, our tongues will touch. Maybe I'm hoping to spark something within her. Or maybe I'm completely masochistic.

At this point, it's anyone's guess.

All I can say is that it hasn't done one damn bit of good.

Those thoughts crash through my head as Violet unwinds her arms from around my body. Uncertainty flickers across her face as she takes a hesitant step away. Her fingers lift, slowly buzzing her lips before her gaze locks on mine.

"I should find Mia. I think we're going to head out soon."

Since there's nothing more for me to say, I murmur a quick, "Sure, okay."

She takes a few steps away before throwing one last glance over her shoulder. "I'll see you later, Sam."

I jerk my head in response and watch her melt into the crowd of rowdy students blowing off steam on a Thursday night. If she plans on leaving this party with another dude, I hope to hell I don't see her do it.

Chapter Three

VIOLET

Sam picks me up from my dorm around eleven o'clock before we head over to my grandparent's house on the other side of town. It's about a twenty-minute ride from campus, which means I can pop over anytime they need something.

Or whenever I'm craving a home cooked meal.

Under normal circumstances, Sam and I will talk the entire way. But that's not the case today. Instead, he's oddly silent. Dare I say contemplative? Even though I don't know for sure, and he certainly hasn't mentioned anything about it, I suspect his mood has something to do with what happened at the Sigma party Thursday night.

It's hardly the first time Sam has run off a guy who's been hitting on me. More like the fortieth. And I'm probably being conservative with that estimate.

So, what's up with the weird vibe?

All I know is that I don't like it.

It makes me feel twitchy and nervous. Two things I never am when we're together. There are only a few select people I can be myself with. Mia, my grandparents, and Sam. With them, I can strip away the protective armor I wear for the world and just be me.

Violet Winterfield.

As I dwell on Thursday night, that kiss nudges its way back into my thoughts for the hundredth time. It's ridiculous because it was hardly anything at all. Certainly not something to obsess over.

So what if he slipped me a little bit of tongue?

Who cares?

It's not like we haven't kissed before.

Hell, Sam Harper *was* my very first real kiss.

It happened in eighth grade at a party in the dingy, cobweb infested closet of Cooper Staub's basement.

Seven minutes in heaven.

And that certainly wasn't the only time we played that game either. It was common with the middle school set. Of course, anything that involved getting your hands on the opposite sex was hugely popular.

After that, we would share little kisses here and there. It wasn't a big deal. Honestly, I've never thought much about it. But *that* particular kiss feels somehow different, and I can't figure out why.

As those thoughts roll through my head, my gaze shifts to him. Unable to stand the peculiar tension that fills the cab of his truck, I blurt, "Is everything all right?"

His gaze darts to mine and his fingers tighten around the steering wheel on his Ford F-150 as we zip effortlessly through late Sunday morning traffic.

"Yeah, everything's fine." His brow furrows before volleying the question back at me. "Why wouldn't it be?"

Unsure how to put my feelings into words, I shrug. This is exactly what I'm talking about. The sudden tension that has cropped up between us isn't normal. Our relationship has always been easy. And now it feels anything but. "I don't know," I admit. "Thursday night, I guess..." Unsure how to proceed, my words trail off as I gulp down my unease.

Without taking his eyes off the road, Sam reaches out and laces our fingers together. "It's all good, Vi." His deep blue gaze pierces mine before he gives me a slightly crooked smile in return. "Promise."

I huff out a breath as all of the thick tension drains from my body, leaving me almost limp with relief. I hadn't realized how anxious I'd become thinking there could be an issue between us. Sam means every-thing to me.

A tiny smile tilts my lips upward. "Okay." I need to put Thursday out of my head and forget about it.

Sam clears his throat. "So, I've been thinking about what you said the other night and you're right."

I arch a brow. "I am?" Well...good. That's exactly what I like to hear. The only problem is that I have no idea what I'm right about.

His gaze stays locked on the ribbon of road in front of him. For some strange reason, I get the feeling that he's avoiding eye contact. Sam is usually so straightforward and forthright. "Yeah, you can hookup with whoever you want, and I shouldn't get in the way of that."

I study our entwined fingers all the while turning his words over in my head. What he's saying should be a relief. Sam has been a major pain in the ass when it comes to my sex life. I swear to God, every time I get close to sealing the deal, he magically appears from out of nowhere and within minutes, I'm going home solo.

Again.

A girl can only take so much vibrator action. There are times when you need the real deal.

"I didn't go home with anyone Thursday night." The comment escapes from my mouth before I can think better of it.

His gaze slices to me before bouncing back to the road. "You didn't?"

Is that a hopeful note tinging his voice or am I reading into this?

And why would it even matter?

I shrug before shifting in my seat. "Just wasn't feeling it, I guess."

"Hmmm."

Before I can put the kibosh on my wayward thoughts, they're pouring from my lips. "What about you?" The breath catches at the back of my throat as I watch him from the corner of my eye.

He doesn't glance my way as he shakes his head. "Nah."

His staccato answer has me racking my brain, trying to remember the last time I saw Sam hookup or go out with a girl. My brows beetle together as I silently turn the question over in my mind. Has he even been with anyone this fall semester? What about the summer? Unless he's been keeping the information under wraps, I don't think so.

As I turn my body toward him, ready to give him the third degree, Sam pulls up to the curb in front of my grandparent's large Victorian. When I was a kid, I used to think it resembled a gingerbread house with its cerulean-blue wood siding and lacy white trim that looked like piped icing around the eaves. Deep purple wooden steps lead the way to an inviting beveled glass front door. There's a gleaming white swing that hangs from the covered porch. A round turret flanks the left side of the house, spearing into the sky. It has a comfy window seat with soft pillows piled on top of it. I used to love curling up there on stormy afternoons or when I needed some alone time. It was the perfect little reading nook. Even though I came to this house under horrible circumstances, I have nothing but happy memories of living here with my grandparents.

Hands down, they are the absolute best. I'm lucky to have them in my life. I will forever be grateful to them for being there when I needed them most. It's one of the reasons I decided to stay and attend Barnett instead of going further away. I even offered to live at home and commute, but they both encouraged me to move onto campus and spread my wings.

I don't realize Sam is still holding my fingers until he gives them a gentle squeeze. The gesture has my gaze arrowing to his.

"Ready?" he asks.

"Yup." I hoist my smile. Even though I still get the feeling there's something on Sam's mind, I decide to put it on the backburner for the time being.

The two of us jog up the front porch stairs like we've done hundreds of times before. Without knocking, I throw open the door and peer around the foyer.

"Hello?" I call out. "Gran? Gramps?"

Sam leans toward me before murmuring loud enough for me to hear, "You did tell them what time we were stopping by, right?" He waits a beat, his voice dropping further, "Because I seriously can't deal with walking in on them getting it on *again*."

With a snort, I elbow him in the ribs. "I thought we agreed to never mention that particular incident again. Do you have any idea how psychologically scarring that experience was for me?"

His eyebrows shoot up, crashing into his hairline. "Yeah, I do because I was subjected to it as well. It still haunts me to this day." He shakes his head as if trying to dislodge the memory.

Yeah, good luck with that, buddy.

I roll my eyes and attempt to put a positive spin on what never should have been heard in the first place. "At least they're still active and in love." I give him a hard poke in those rock-solid abs of his. They're bounce-a-quarter-off tight. "You should be so lucky to have hot sex when you're in your seventies."

All right, so maybe that comment crossed a line.

By like a mile.

Sam winces before muttering, "Jeez, Vi! You saying that is almost as bad as hearing them go at it."

As those grumbled words slide from his lips, my grandmother's voice fills the air as she breezes through the hallway leading from the kitchen to the large foyer. "Violet and Sam, you're here!"

The guy next to me straightens to his full height as I give her a cheerful smile. "Hi, Gran!"

With a pleased expression, she envelopes my body in her arms before giving me a little squeeze. My eyelids flutter closed as I sink into her embrace.

This feeling right here...it's exactly what home feels like. After everything that happened with my parents, Gran was always there with a warm hug and words of comfort. It was together that we made it through our shared grief.

As I untangle myself from her, I glance around the spacious foyer and living room to the left. It's filled with delicate furniture and price-less antiques that have been collected over a lifetime. Most mornings, my grandfather likes to sit in the sun-filled space and enjoy a cup of coffee while perusing the newspaper. Even though he's quite adept at tooling around on the internet, he prefers to read a physical copy. He likes the feel of it in his hands. Every morning, the paper is delivered to the house around six. When I don't find him in his normal spot, a kernel of concern blooms in the pit of my belly. "Where's Gramps?"

Despite her lips tipping up at the corners, I catch the worry that flickers in her hazel-colored eyes before vanishing. "He's upstairs resting a bit." Before I can fire off anymore questions, she turns to Sam and pulls him in for a hug. That's all it takes for a smile to tug at the edges of my lips as I watch Sam get wrapped up in my grandmother's delicate embrace.

An unexpected warmth fills my heart as I stare at the pair. Sam has known my grandparents his entire life. He thinks of them as his own. He'd probably continue to stop by and check on them even if I weren't in the picture.

I can't help but love him for that. Not all twenty-two-year-old college guys would give a rat's ass about the wellbeing of their elderly neighbors. In high school, he would cut their lawn in the summer, rake their leaves in the autumn, and shovel snow from their walkway after each winter storm.

As my grandmother pulls away, she loops her arm through Sam's before turning back to me. "I'm so glad you two were able to find the time to stop by for a visit. The toilet in the upstairs bathroom is leaking, and Edward hasn't felt up to taking a look at it." She beams another smile at Sam.

My brows slide together as the concern returns full force. I don't like to think about anything being seriously wrong with either one of my them. As much as I hate to admit it, they've slowed down over the years. Even though I knew it was bound to happen, it's still hard to accept.

And this is a large, rambling hundred-year-old home in need of constant repairs, upkeep, and maintenance. There are times when I worry that it's too much for them to handle on their own. Even though my grandfather is seventy-five years old, and my grandmother is closing in on seventy-two, I can't imagine them sitting around, languishing in a senior citizen home. It's an issue that will need to be dealt with in the not-so-distant future.

"Is Gramps okay?" I hate the way my heart skips a beat as I give voice to my concerns. Over the past couple of years, he has suffered from a few heart issues. I don't know what my grandmother or I would do without him. It's been the three of us for so long. The thought of him not being around has a thick knot of apprehension forming in the pit of my belly.

"He's fine. Just feeling a bit under the weather. it's nothing to be concerned about." She gives Sam's bulging forearm a little pat. "Otherwise, I wouldn't have bothered you with this."

"It's no problem, Mrs. Winterfield. You know that I don't mind helping out."

She shoots him another grateful smile before reaching up to pat his cheek. "I know that, Samuel. You're such a dear boy. You always have been." Her gaze latches on to mine before adding somewhat coyly, "One of these days you're going to make some woman very happy."

Right...

Forget what I said about coy. There's absolutely nothing sly about her comment or the calculating look she aims in my direction. I almost roll my eyes because what she really means to say is that *I* should nab Sam before some other lucky lady snaps him up.

Have I mentioned that my grandmother fancies herself a matchmaker and is constantly trying to nudge me in Sam's direction? When I was in high school, her machinations used to annoy me. Now, it's more of a running joke between the three of us.

As my gaze returns to Sam, I think my grandmother might be right in her assessment. He'll probably make some woman extremely happy. A tiny prick of displeasure slides through me at the notion before I shrug it away.

Sam's bright blue gaze stays locked on mine. Barely is he able to contain the smile simmering around the edges of his lips. "Oh, I don't know about that, Mrs. Winterfield. I can't seem to find a woman willing to put up with me."

Disbelief settles on Gran's expression as she squeezes his arm again. I'm beginning to suspect that she might be enjoying herself a little too much over there. I can't blame her for it. Even Sam's muscles have muscles. His entire body is solid and well-defined. "I have a hard time believing that! You're such a handsome boy. Not to mention, smart."

She stares at me as if I'm too clueless to realize what I'm missing out on. Unconsciously, my gaze slides back to Sam before settling on his smirking lips. That kiss, the one I keep insisting was completely insignificant, forces its way into my thoughts. A little shiver skitters its way down my spine as I remember what it felt like to have his warm mouth sliding over mine. My entire body stiffens as that image plays through my mind in slow-mo.

What the hell am I doing?

My cheeks fill with heat as I yank my gaze from his and shove that thought away before clearing my throat. "I guess Sam should probably get to it, huh?"

A satisfied smile tugs at my grandmother's mouth. It's like she knows exactly what's running through my brain. "The tools should already be up there, dear."

"All right, then. I'll go up and take a look at what's going on. Hopefully, it'll be an easy fix and we won't have to call a plumber." His brows draw together and his gaze shifts between us as if realizing he's been left out of a private joke. "After that, I need to stop and say hello to my parents."

I jerk my head into a nod before Sam disappears up the curving staircase. We hear his heavy footfalls on the second floor as he makes his way to the bathroom. Once he's gone, my grandmother turns to me with a contented smile.

"It's difficult to believe that Sam is still single." Just in case I hadn't already gotten the hint, she adds, "A strapping lad like that won't stay that way for long."

I can't help the gurgle of laughter that escapes as I repeat, "*Strapping?*"

Her face crinkles with humor. "Back in my day, we used to describe muscular men as *strapping.*"

I certainly can't disagree with her assessment. Sam is most definitely *strapping.*

She lowers her voice before picking up the threads of our previous conversation. "It's surprising that you two have never gotten together. He's the kind of man who would treat a woman right."

I roll my eyes.

Here we go again.

Cue the *Sam is the best guy in the whole wide world* spiel.

It's not like I disagree with her. He's amazing. But there are only so many times I can hear it.

"Gran," I practically groan.

I've lost count of how many occasions we've had this conversation. It must be somewhere around a million. Needless to say, my grandmother adores Sam. Actually, *adores* isn't a strong enough word. And I can't deny that she's probably right in her prediction. Sam would treat any woman he was with like a princess. He's so sweet and caring. There's absolutely nothing douchey about the guy. Which admittedly is a rare find on any college campus these days.

Knocking me out of my reverie, she waves a hand in front of my face. "Oh, don't deny an old woman her pleasure. One of these days, you're going to open your eyes and see what's been sitting in front of you this entire time." Instead of waiting for a response, she hooks her arm through mine before patting my hand affectionately. "You mark my words, Violet. Some girl will snag his interest one of these days and she'll thank her lucky stars to have found such a wonderful young man."

Instead of focusing on the comment, I snort before muttering under my breath, "Old woman, my ass."

Not bothering to chastise me for my language, she chuckles. "Why don't we make lunch for when that strapping young man of yours is finished fixing the toilet."

I give her a dramatic sigh before following her to the sun-filled kitchen.

Thirty minutes later, the four of us are sitting around my grandparent's small round table enjoying the BLT's she just whipped up since they are Sam's favorite. Extra mayo, heavy on the lettuce, one thick slice of tomato, and bread lightly toasted—just the way he likes it. He must have worked up an appetite fixing the leaky pipe. He's already wolfed down two sandwiches and is set on devouring a third. And we only sat down ten minutes ago. Naturally, my grandmother fusses over him the entire time.

I turn my attention to my grandfather and can't help but notice that he looks tired. Maybe even a little pale. He's nowhere near as animated as usual. A prick of concern flares to life inside me. "How are you feeling, Gramps?"

His face creases with wrinkles as he flashes me a smile. "Just trying to shake this bug I've picked up. Other than that, I'm right as rain." He takes a small bite of his sandwich before chewing it methodically. When he finishes, he asks, "And how's my favorite girl doing? Are classes going well?"

I tear off a hunk of bread before popping it into my mouth and nodding. "Everything's fine. Classes are all good."

"Have you thought about submitting applications to any other law schools?"

My grandfather was a district attorney for twenty years and then a circuit court judge for another fifteen. I think he's proud that I've decided to follow in his footsteps just as my father had before me.

Since I'm well aware of the response my answer will elicit, I say offhandedly, "No, I think three schools are enough." I'm leaning toward Barnett for obvious reasons.

In all fairness, the university does have a top-notch law program. I know he'd like me to look further away, but the idea of being more than a three-hour drive from them is tough for me to consider.

As expected, he levels me with a steely look as if he knows why I'm set on continuing my education close to home. "You don't need to stick around here, Violet. Your grandmother and I are perfectly capable of taking care of ourselves. We think it's important for you to branch out and experience life somewhere else. Maybe look at UCLA or Berkeley. How about Columbia in New York? This is a wonderful chance for you to live somewhere you've always dreamed of. Don't squander an opportunity like this by not considering all of the possibilities that are out there." His eyes skewer mine. "You'll only regret it in the end."

You know what I would end up regretting?

Not being there for them when they needed me. Not spending time with them when I could have because I know all too well how short life can be. So, it's highly doubtful I'll regret not moving further away at this point. I have my entire life for that. And honestly, I like living here. This is my home. And my grandparents are the only family I have.

I glance down at the half-eaten sandwich on my plate and shrug in response. This isn't the first time we've had this conversation. And, because my grandfather is stubborn and only wants what's best for me, it won't be the last. A moment later, Sam slips his hand around mine before squeezing it.

When my gaze flickers to him, he gives me a smile in return. That's the thing about Sam, he totally gets me. He understands why I make the choices that I do, and he doesn't try to change them. He accepts and supports me, no questions asked.

"Barnett's a good school, Gramps," I finally say. "Why do I need to live somewhere else when I'm perfectly happy here?"

Given the fact that my grandfather was a cagey lawyer in his day, he's learned when to pick his battles. And clearly this is one he's not going to win. Instead, he turns his attention to Sam and asks, "And what about you, Samuel? What schools did you end up applying to? I imagine you've set your sights on expanding your horizons a little broader than my granddaughter."

The corners of my lips curl upward as my grandfather gives me a little wink.

Sam shoves the last bit of BLT into his mouth and swallows it before guzzling down half his glass of water. "I threw in an application at Barnett as well but I'm also considering Cornell and Columbia."

Looking thoughtful, my grandfather nods. "All excellent schools. I would expect nothing less from you."

"I'm trying to decide if it's worth retaking the LSAT."

"Oh, please." I can't help but roll my eyes at that bit of nonsense because Sam scored a freaking one seventy-two. The first time taking it. The guy is so damn smart, it's almost sickening. That being said, I couldn't be prouder of him. Sam was the valedictorian of our high school graduating class and now, going into his senior year at Barnett, he has a near perfect grade point average.

While academics have always come easily to him, that isn't the case for me. I have to keep myself focused and organized, biting off little chunks and continually working toward my goals instead of cramming or waiting until the last minute. And I definitely can't have Sam sitting next to me in every class, even though that's how we could have arranged our schedules, or I would end up flunking out. The guy barely has to pay attention. Hell, he probably doesn't even need to attend, but he always does. He never misses.

Sam smirks as his deep blue gaze locks on mine. "What?"

"You scored a one seventy-two on your LSAT. I would be throwing a party if I ended up even close to that." I got a one sixty. Not terrible, but not great by any means, which sums up my academic career perfectly. A little better than middle of the road. "If anyone should be retaking the entrance exam, it's me. I don't even know why you're applying at Barnett. You could get accepted at Harvard Law, if you wanted." I'm not kidding about that either. The thought of retaking the LSAT makes a cold sweat pop out across my brow. That test was brutal. I thought my brain was going to leak out of my ears with all the hours Sam and I spent hunkered down studying at the library.

He shrugs before shifting self-consciously on his seat. Sam has never been one to brag about himself, his family, or his achievements. Like everything else in his life, he keeps it tightly under wraps.

And I get it.

There's a lot of pressure on Sam to achieve great things and follow in Derek Harper's illustrious footsteps. Sam's father is a state senator, so it's important for him to keep a low profile and not do anything that will garner bad press. He doesn't go to parties or bars and get shitfaced or out of control. Nor does he sleep around so that his sexcapades end up splashed across those stupid websites that are solely dedicated to the Barnett football players.

Maybe other twenty-two-year-olds would chafe and feel resentful about that kind of pressure heaped on them at such a young age—the stress to conduct himself like he's in his thirties rather than early twenties—but Sam handles it well.

Most people at Barnett, even those who know him, don't realize he's related to the state senator. And that's exactly the way Sam likes it.

"We'll see what happens. I haven't decided where I want to go yet. My dad attended Columbia." He flashes a brief smile. "He's hoping I'll end up there."

"Nothing wrong with that," my grandfather says, "as long as that makes the most sense for you."

His words are a sudden reminder as to the inevitable changes next year will bring. I can't help but think about how different everything will be when Sam heads off in one direction and I go in another. We've been entangled in each other's lives for so long. Not a single day goes by that I don't see or talk to him.

The thought of Sam being somewhere else, living a life without me, sends a little pang of sadness shooting through me. We've been at each other's side for the last eight years. I suppose I'll have to get used to it. I can't see Sam sticking around here for another three years.

Something shifts in his eyes. It's like he knows exactly what's churning inside my head. Needing to shake off the sudden melancholy, the corners of my lips lift into a brief smile before I finish off the chips on my plate.

"I should probably head over and say hello to my parents." With that, Sam rises to his feet. For someone so big, he's agile. "Thanks for lunch, Mrs. Winterfield."

"I should be the one thanking you for coming over here on a Sunday afternoon to fix the toilet. I'm sure you have better things to do with your time."

Sam's smile softens before he leans down and plants a quick kiss on my grandmother's cheek. "It wasn't a problem. I can stop by anytime you need help."

"You don't mind if I hang out here, do you?" I ask.

He shakes his head as if expecting no less. "Nope, I won't be long. Then we can head back to campus."

Even though I love Sam's family, I'd rather spend more time with my grandparents.

And like everything else, he gets that as well.

Chapter Four

SAM

I head over to the Victorian that looks, from the outside, similar to the Winterfield residence. There's a wide lawn that separates our houses. I'm pretty sure my dad would love to move into something newer, grander, and in a more upscale neighborhood but my mom fell in love with this house twenty years ago and refuses to uproot the family.

As I let myself in through the beveled glass front door, I find my mom in the kitchen pouring over an old book of family recipes. My father's silver SUV is parked in the driveway, but he's conspicuously absent. My guess is that he's holed up in the sunroom that he's taken over as an office so he can work from home on the weekends.

Not that he spends much of his time here.

More often than not, he's traveling to the state capital or Washington DC when the senate is in session. Since Dad has been in politics for the last fifteen years, my mom decided it would be easier to give up her nursing job at the hospital so she can be here for me, my younger brother, Gavin, and sister, Arianna. Or Ari, as we affectionately call her.

Once she spots me, Mom does a double take as a smile spreads across her pretty face. "Sam! I didn't know you were going to drop by today. I would have prepared lunch." Her hands land on her slender hips as she gives me a mock frown. "You should have texted."

I nod toward the Winterfield house. "Violet asked if I could stop by and repair something for her grandparents."

My mother's dark blonde brows draw together in concern. "Is everything all right?"

"It's fine. A pipe in the bathroom needed tightening up. It was a quick fix."

My mother and I have the same blond hair and deep, ocean-hued eyes. Where she's more fine-boned, I take after my father. He's tall, broad, and played college football. I was groomed at a young age to follow in his esteemed footsteps. Not only with sports, but in law, and hopefully one day, politics.

"They should have called me. I would have been more than happy to get your father…"

Her voice trails off as one of my brows hikes up across my forehead. I can't see my suit-wearing father wielding a wrench, attempting to fix a leaky pipe in our own house, let alone at the elderly neighbor's next door.

The edges of her lips tremble upward before she finishes that thought, "Well, I could have at least called a plumber for them."

Her offer has a soft chuckle escaping from my lips.

That's *exactly* what she would have done.

She straightens to her full height of five foot seven before coming around the large, white marble island to give me a hug. This place might be old and full of charm on the outside, but it has been completely gutted and renovated inside. It's one of the many concessions my mother made in order to stay in this neighborhood.

She pulls away before asking, "Can I get you something to eat? We can order Chinese if you're hungry."

I shake my head. "Nah, Mrs. Winterfield made us grilled cheese sandwiches after I fixed the pipe." I pat my flat belly. "I'm stuffed."

"Did Violet come with you?"

"Yup. She wanted to stay and visit with her grandparents while I stopped over here. Mr. Winterfield hasn't been feeling well. He must have picked up a bug or something."

Worry creases her face. "I'm sorry to hear that. Maybe I'll pop over tomorrow and check on them."

I can't help but smile at my mom's concern. She cares a great deal about our neighbors, especially the Winterfields. Sometimes it surprises me that she married someone like my dad. It's not that my father is a bad guy but with his work schedule, he's absent most of the time and that leaves Mom on her own more often than not. Even though she's busy, I think she misses working at the hospital. Since Arianna is eleven and in fifth grade and Gavin is fourteen years old and in eighth, she still needs to be around for them. My dad is gone for weeks at a time, so he can't be counted on to help out at home.

That was one of the factors I considered in my decision to stick around and attend Barnett University. Although, I think we all realize that it was Violet's choice to stay that tipped the scale for me. I wasn't ready to relinquish her after high school. I wanted more time.

"I'm sure they'd appreciate that," I say, only now realizing how quiet the house is. It's almost *too* quiet, which is definitely odd. Gavin and Ari usually have friends over and my father, when he's here, is surrounded by staff. Even on a Sunday afternoon. "Where is everyone?"

"Your father is in his office making a few calls and Ari and Gavin are both at friends' houses. They'll be sorry to have missed you. They each brought a friend to the game yesterday." She beams. "They couldn't have been prouder of their big brother and how well the team is playing this year." Then she makes an exasperated noise in her throat. "Now that football is over, Gavin's already chafing at the bit. He can't wait to get back out there and play again. Although he did make the school basketball team this season, so that should keep him busy. But still, that boy is all about football." Her eyes sparkle. "Just like his big brother."

Gavin plays quarterback for the local Pop Warner program. Already he has an impressive arm. I wish I had more time to spend throwing the ball around with him. My dad's time is limited and playing catch in the backyard is low on the priority list.

Making a split decision, I offer, "Maybe I'll try to get back over here during the week so we can run some plays."

Her face lights up at the idea. "Gavin would love that. Both he and Ari miss having you around. You've been so busy lately."

She's not telling me anything I don't already know. "I miss them, too." Then I add because it's the truth, "I miss all of you."

"It's nice that you stayed close and we're able to see all your home games."

My mother hasn't missed one single game this season. Actually, she hasn't missed one ever. Peewee through college. No matter what, I can count on her to be there. Our family has always been her first priority. My father, on the other hand, rarely makes it to more than one or two of my games a season. He's always busy brokering a deal, attending fundraisers, at the state capital, or in Washington, DC.

Especially since his seat is up for reelection next year.

The only time I begin to question whether or not politics is really something I want to get involved in is when I see how much time Dad spends away from his family. It has to be about seventy percent.

Do I really want that for myself?

Not really.

It's not like I have to make any decisions right now. I haven't even been accepted to law school yet. Although, I'm not worried. I've got a three-point-nine GPA and feel pretty good about my LSAT. I know Violet is concerned that she didn't score high enough, but I think she'll be fine.

After what happened Thursday night, I've been thinking a lot about Violet and my feelings for her. In the back of my mind, I always realized that at some point, we would head off in different directions. But I'd been holding onto the hope that maybe she would finally wake up and see how perfect we are for one another.

Thursday night was the slap in the face I needed to finally get it through my thick head that what I've been hoping for all these years isn't going to happen. I need to start focusing on what's best for me and my future and stop worrying about what Violet is doing.

Trust me, that realization is a bitter pill to swallow.

I've spent too many years putting Violet's wants and needs ahead of my own. It's just going to take time for me to make those mental adjustments and stop thinking about the possibility of an *us* and start concentrating on *me*. She's been such an integral part of my life for the last eight years. I'm not even sure if I can turn off those thoughts.

But I have to, right?

There's no longer a choice in the matter.

I can't keep doing this. I need to find a girl who, you know, actually *wants* to be with me. And that girl isn't Violet Winterfield. No matter how much I might want it to be. It's an ugly truth that needs to be accepted.

"I thought I heard your voice."

With a phone in one hand and a stack of papers in the other, Dad steps into the sunny kitchen. His appearance is, as usual, impeccable. Even on the weekend. He's wearing a pair of perfectly pressed tan slacks and a crisp looking light blue button down. This is as casual as he gets. I don't think the guy owns a pair of jeans or ratty old gym shoes. His salt and pepper colored hair is short and perfectly shaped. Every other week, a stylist comes to the house to give him a trim. Unless he's in DC. Then I have no clue what he does. I assume someone comes to his condo to cut his hair.

I tip my head toward our neighbor's house. "I was fixing something next door and thought I'd stop over for a few minutes to see how everything's going."

He nods but already I can tell he's losing interest or at least mentally running through everything that still needs to be accomplished for the day. I think he honestly works twenty-four seven, which is something else I'm not quite sure I want to do.

It's not that he seems unhappy or even burnt out. I think the man enjoys what he does. He flourishes on bringing opposing sides together and hammering out deals that are beneficial to all parties involved. Or hopping on a plane and flying across the country on a redeye. And the constant campaign strategy sessions don't seem to be a problem. He loves holding town hall meetings and speaking with constituents. Instead of buckling under the stress and strain that comes with being a high-profile political figure, he thrives on the pressure. Sometimes I have to wonder if the man has ADHD, because he's constantly on the move, always going from one thing to another. I'm exhausted just thinking about the schedule he keeps.

Once I fall silent, he turns to my mom. "You'll be ready to leave by two?"

She nods before giving me a look. "Another fundraiser."

My mom hates those big fancy dinners, but she's always a good sport about attending because they're unavoidable. It's one of the ways my dad raises money for his war chest.

"How long will you guys be gone?"

"At least four hours," Mom says.

An idea takes shape in my head. "Maybe I'll see if Violet wants to stick around for the afternoon and we can stay with the kids."

"Gavin and Ari would love that. They adore Violet. Especially Ari. She really misses having her around."

"More than me?" I'm teasing of course.

Sort of.

With a smile, she shakes her head. "Never more than you."

"I'll see if she can hang for the afternoon." I slide my cell from my pocket and shoot Violet a text. Within moments, she fires back a reply. She's finished with most of her studying for the weekend, so staying until six isn't a problem.

My attention gets pulled back to Dad when he says, "Mom said the game went well yesterday."

I'm about to give him a condensed version of the highlights when his cell goes off.

With a sigh, he glances at the screen before muttering, "Sorry, I need to take this. It's important." As he answers the call, a smile breaks out across his face as he booms, "Mike! Thanks for getting back to me so quickly." There's a pause before he says, "I know, I know. That's why I thought it was important for us to put our heads together on this one." Another pause. "Do you have fifteen minutes to talk?"

And then he's gone, disappearing back into his office. Both my mom and I hear the door close firmly behind him. He'll probably stay holed up in the study until it's time to leave for the fundraiser. Silently, my gaze slides to hers. For a split-second, she stares down the hallway. A frown mars her normally smiling face.

I can't help but feel bad for her.

It's almost like she's stuck in a marriage which in no way resembles a partnership. Sometimes I wonder if she's satisfied with the choices she's made in life and how everything turned out. Sure, she has three healthy kids, a nice home, and a comfortable lifestyle, but she's married to a guy who is never around. And she gave up a career that I'm pretty sure she enjoyed.

As I stare at her, I realize that this isn't the kind of marriage I want for myself. I don't want to give seventy percent of my time to my career and thirty percent to the person I've chosen to spend the rest of my life with. What sucks is that when I envision my future, it's Violet who I think about. I have to remind myself that it will take time to let go of all the hopes and dreams I've carried around with me and for new ones to spring up in their place.

Violet stays at her grandparent's house for another hour which is exactly when Ari and Gavin are supposed to arrive home. Since Gavin is fourteen and a good kid, he usually keeps an eye on Ari when my parents head out for a couple of hours.

The front door opens with a crash as feet pound against the dark cherry wood flooring. Almost comically, Gavin screeches to a halt when he sees me loitering in the kitchen with the Chinese I ordered for dinner.

"Dude, what are you doing here?" he says.

"Nice to see you too, *dude,*" I say with a smile.

He flips his long blond hair out of his eyes until I'm able to catch a glimpse of his face.

Jeez.

Exactly how long has it been since I've seen my little brother? I swear he's grown at least another inch and his hair now resembles a mop. Albeit a perfectly tousled one, which makes me want to laugh. Only recently has he kicked his personal hygiene habits into high gear.

This is exactly the kind of effect the opposite sex has on guys his age. I know it all too well.

I can't resist lifting my chin toward his head. "Bet Dad loves your hair."

He snorts before folding his arms across his chest. Already I can tell that he's going to be broad just like I am. He might find himself playing defense rather than QB when he's older. Although I hope not. Gavin loves the position, and he has real talent.

A smirk settles across his face. "He hates it, but I'm still not cutting it."

My lips lift.

Good for him.

My dad is all about our public persona and how we look portrayed as a family, which is why he has an image consultant on the payroll. What I can and can not do has been hammered into my head from a young age. Especially during an election cycle. My father would probably shit a brick if I ever pulled some of the crap I hear about from the guys on the football team.

It's why I try to keep a low profile at all times.

Again, I can't help but wonder if politics is the right career path for me. The necessity to be perfect all the time, afraid to make the tiniest mistake or take a misstep, seems exhausting. Not to mention, the pressure of living your life under a microscope.

Dismissing those thoughts, I tell him, "Looks good on you, bud."

He gives me another cheeky smile before catching sight of the white cardboard containers on the marble island.

"Please tell me you ordered kung pow chicken."

I cock a brow. "Have I seriously been away that long?"

He snorts in response before grabbing a plate from the cabinet.

I'm about to ask where Ari is when I hear the front door open and female voices fill the foyer.

"You're staying with us, and Sam is here, too?"

My little sister sounds thrilled by the prospect. It only makes me feel guilty for not returning home more often to see them.

"Yup, you've got us until six o'clock," Violet says.

"Yay!" That exuberant shout is followed up with another question. "Can we give each other mani-pedis?"

"Sure. I thought we could also try out some of those fancy hairstyle videos you were showing me last time."

My chest clenches at the sound of Violet's voice.

A second later, Ari barrels into the kitchen like a locomotive. She's all long legs and skinny elbows. Like my brother, she's grown, too.

Sheesh. The pair of them are like weeds. She all but launches herself at me and like always, I catch her mid-air in my arms, hugging her close until she's gasping for breath in between squeals of laughter.

There's a smile curving Violet's lips as she follows my sister into the kitchen. I can't resist grinning in return as our gazes collide. She loves Gavin and Ari as if they were her own. And I know they feel the same about her. Ari thinks of her as the sister she never had. Even though I realize that no one will ever take the place of Isabelle, Violet's younger sister who died in the car accident along with her parents, I know they have a special bond.

Violet has become an important part of their lives. But that will change next year. I hate how unsettled the notion makes me feel when I dwell on the future. What I hate most of all, is that for the first time in eight years, Violet and I won't be together.

She'll be off living her own life.

And I'll be doing the same.

Chapter Five

VIOLET

"Is there any possibility that you can clear out for the weekend?" With a hopeful expression, Mia pauses before tacking on, "And FYI—I'm making that request more for your sake than my own."

I almost groan because that can only mean one thing. "Carter's rolling into town, isn't he?" My eyebrows rise across my forehead. "And you don't want any witnesses to the depravity that will be taking place for the next forty-eight hours."

The sly look she sends my way is rife with meaning. "I really hope so. Do you have any idea how long it's been? Trust me, you do *not* want to be around for any of that."

Okay, one—*gross*.

And two—damn right I don't.

I made the epic mistake of not finding alternative accommodations for a weekend last year when he crashed at our place. Needless to say, I had a difficult time looking Carter in the eyes the next morning.

Those two are ridiculously loud.

And just when you think it's over and people can catch a little shut eye, they start up again. If nothing else, their stamina is impressive. Halfway through the first night, when I couldn't stand another second of their porn-inspired soundtrack, I ended up dragging my blankets into the commons area on our floor. Although, I couldn't get comfortable on the ratty couch because all I could think about was the amount of jizz I was probably sleeping on.

So no, I won't be sticking around for a repeat performance if I can help it.

Mia and Carter are like an X-rated show waiting to happen. They're constantly groping one another and making out. Clothing spontaneously explodes from their bodies, which is exactly why it's better to get the hell out of Dodge for the weekend rather than hang around like some kind of perv with voyeuristic tendencies.

"Maybe I can crash with Anna," I mutter before pulling out my phone and firing off a quick text. A few seconds later a response pops up.

Sorry, headed home for the wknd. Won't b around.

"What about Sydney?"

I shake my head. "She's not getting along with Ellie again and I don't really want to get in the middle of that." If worst comes to worst, I suppose refereeing for the weekend wouldn't be so bad.

In silence, we rack our brains for another alternative.

She bites down on her lip before throwing out a suggestion. "I guess Carter and I could rent a hotel room for the weekend. I mean, that would be kind of fun."

Neither one of us adds *expensive,* but that's what we're both thinking.

Making a face, I wave a hand and dismiss the idea. "No, that's just stupid."

I can always stay with my grand—

Her voice cuts quickly into my thoughts. "What about Sam?"

Sam?

Well...I suppose I could bunk with Sam and his roommate, Roan, for the weekend. It would be a heck of a lot better than staying here and having to listen to Carter and Mia going at it like a pair of energizer bunnies. Been there, done that. Bought the T-shirt. I have zero interest in a repeat performance.

"Yeah, I'll check with him." I shoot Sam a text.

Smiling like a Cheshire cat, Mia asks, "And how is golden delicious doing?"

Golden delicious.

I can't help but snort out a laugh. That's Mia's pet name for Sam.

Not that he knows it.

When they first met freshman year, she had a massive crush on him. Nothing ever happened between them, but it wasn't for lack of Mia trying. She threw herself at him every single weekend. I have no idea why Sam wasn't interested. Mia is gorgeous with long, thick ebony colored hair. Mossy, green-colored eyes, and an olive complexion that does her Italian ancestors proud. She's also tall and curvy.

Rather strangely, Sam has never batted an eyelash in her direction.

"He's fine."

Mia props her chin up on her hand as she purrs out the next words, "Yes, he certainly is."

Another small laugh gurgles up from my throat as I shake my head. "And what would Carter say if he heard you talking like that?"

She sticks out her tongue in response. "Oh, stop ruining all my fun. I'm always careful not to scream out Sam's name when I'm coming."

"Mia!" I can't help the scandalized note that creeps into my voice. I really hope she's kidding about that. I mean, she has to be. *Right?* Mia loves her boyfriend. They got together two years ago when Carter was a senior. After graduation, he moved to Philadelphia for a civil engineering job.

Hence the sexfest that is currently being planned for the weekend.

My eyes narrow as a grin slides its way across her face.

There are times when I suspect that she says these things solely to get a rise out of me. I've grown used to it over the years, but I don't particularly like when she makes comments about Sam. Secretly, I'm glad they never got together. That would have been weird.

"Like you've never rubbed one out thinking about that sexy bod of his?"

My mouth drops open before crashing into our thinly carpeted floor. "Mia!" Even though I should be used to the over-the-top remarks she makes, heat gathers in my cheeks. "Of course not!"

She levels a knowing look my way before adding a little wink for good measure. "Oh, please, that boy is hotness personified. Can't say I haven't used my battery-operated boyfriend a few times thinking about all those delicious muscles."

When I shake my head, she spears me with a look of disbelief. "Are you seriously telling me that you have *never*, not one damn time, fantasized about him while getting off?"

Again, I jerk my head in denial. "Never."

Technically this isn't a lie. I have absolutely *never* gotten off to thoughts of him. But lately—for some strange reason—I can't stop noticing how good looking he is with all that thick blond hair and those gorgeous blue eyes.

And don't even get me started on that big, broad chest of his.

Plus, he's tall. Not to mention hard.

His body!

His body is all hard and muscly.

For goodness' sake, I have no idea about *that*.

Dwelling on *that* part of him feels like it would be crossing an imaginary line in our friendship. Even if he never found out, I'd still know.

Luckily, his response saves me from the god-awful conversation I've been sucked into while I wasn't looking.

"Well? Don't keep me in suspense. What's golden delicious got to say?"

"*Sam*," I enunciate while skimming over the message, "says it would be fine."

Her smirk turns into a grin that overtakes her face. "I'm sure he did."

I huff out a breath and glare. "He has an extra bedroom because his roommate, Dylan, moved in with his girlfriend." I ground out the words slowly, "So, I'll be staying in *Dylan's* room for the weekend."

Her eyes widen before she flutters her dark lashes. "Of course, you will. Wherever else would you sleep?"

I throw my bags into the backseat of Sam's truck before sliding in next to him. "Thanks again for picking me up."

His hair is all shiny and damp from the shower he took after practice. "It wasn't a problem. This weekend will be fun." There's a slight pause as his gaze cuts to mine. "Are you sure that you don't mind laying low tonight? With a game tomorrow, I need to hit the sheets early."

"Of course not," I tell him.

"If you wanted, you could always head out on your own. Just because I'm making an early night of it doesn't mean you have to."

"No, I'm good," I reassure him again. I'm not really in the mood to go out and party.

His teeth sink into his lower lip as his gaze stays fastened on the ribbon of road beyond the windshield. "I figured we could have dinner and then maybe watch a movie. What do you think?"

"That sounds perfect." This week has been exhausting. Chilling at Sam's for the night sounds good. I'm sure we'll end up going out tomorrow night. Especially if the Bulldogs pull off another win. Then Saturday night will be crazy. And it's not just the team that will be celebrating. The entire university will turn out to help.

"Good."

Once we get back to his place, I dump my bags in Dylan's room before changing into a pair of comfy black yoga pants and a well-loved T-shirt. I pad on bare feet to where Sam is cooking in the small kitchen.

"What are we doing for dinner?" I was thinking we would probably order some take out, but Sam already has a bunch of ingredients spread out on the counter. Eggs, bacon, heavy cream, noodles, parmesan cheese, and garlic.

It looks interesting. Not to mention, fattening. Which I assume means that it will taste delicious since those things seem to go hand in hand. "What are you making?"

He wields a knife in one hand while chopping garlic on a cutting board. "Fettuccine carbonara."

The easy way he flicks his wrist as he cuts up the garlic has me thinking that this isn't the first time he's done it. A pot filled with water boils away on the stove. A large skillet is heating on a burner with chopped bacon.

"Fancy," I say with a smile.

He smirks while continuing with his prep work. "It might sound fancy but it's actually pretty easy. It's something my grandmother used to make."

I nod. "Is there anything I can help with?"

He points to the refrigerator. "Do you mind throwing the salad together?"

"Nope." I head over to the fridge before pulling out lettuce, a cucumber, shredded cheddar cheese, and a bottle of lite ranch dressing. There's a ripe, medium sized tomato already sitting on the counter.

"Croutons are in the cabinet, if you want them."

Who can eat salad without crunchy little croutons?

As I finish preparing the salads, Sam drains the noodles before adding the bacon and garlic. Then he dumps the egg, cream, and parmesan mixture over the noodles before tossing it all together. Impressed with his mad cooking skills, I inhale a huge breath as my tummy rumbles in anticipation.

"Oh my God," I breathe, "that smells *soooo* good!" Other than stopping over to have dinner at my grandparent's house, I don't get home-cooked meals very often.

"Tastes even better," he says with a grin before carrying two heaping plates to the table in the dining room.

I can't wait to dig in. I'm starving. Pasta is one of my favorites. It's total comfort food.

"Do you want a glass of wine with dinner?"

Wine?

My eyes nearly cross. "Yes, please!" If Sam continues to treat me like this, I may never leave.

He brings me a half-filled glass along with a bottle of water for himself before we both twirl noodles around the tines of our forks. As I take my first bite, my eyelids feather closed.

Holy hell...

"Sam, this is seriously amazing!" I'm not kidding either. It's freaking delicious. Cream, garlic, bacon, parmesan, and noodles have to be one of the best combinations in the world.

He nods before shoveling another heaping forkful into his mouth. "I'm glad you like it. Guess it's a good thing you decided to stay over on a carb loading day."

Damn right I am! And *like* isn't nearly a strong enough word for the way I feel about this pasta right now. "I absolutely love it."

We gobble up the carbonara and I enjoy my glass of wine as we talk about everything that happened during the week. Once we're both stuffed, I help Sam clean up the kitchen before we settle on the couch in the living room to watch a movie.

"Where's Roan?" I'm surprised it's so quiet around here and we have the place to ourselves.

Roan King is Sam's roommate, and first-string wide receiver for the Barnett Bulldogs. He's looking to turn pro after the season, and pretty much treated like a demigod around campus. Actually, the entire town treats him that way. About a month and a half ago, he did something that shocked the university.

He got himself a girlfriend.

People went absolutely freaking crazy—by which I mean girls who were holding out some kind of irrational hope that he would fall madly in love with them. There were a lot of unhappy ladies after Ivy Kaster snagged his heart. A few tried sharpening their claws on her.

"He's working at the library. He didn't think he'd be back until ten or so."

A couple weeks ago, Ivy, Roan's girlfriend, auditioned with the Cincinnati Ballet Company and was offered a spot. Since dance was her dream, she decided to drop out of college before the end of first semester. Yesterday, she said her goodbyes. Lexie, Ivy's roommate, couldn't afford to live on her own. So, Dylan, her longtime boyfriend, moved in with her.

I nod toward the spare room they now have available. "What are you going to do with Dylan's room?"

"Liam Garrison is thinking about moving in second semester." He shrugs. "Guess he's having some roommate issues.

"Liam's a really nice guy." It's not like we're best friends or anything, but he's always friendly when we run into each other.

One of Sam's brows hikes up as his gaze sharpens on me. "You think so, huh?"

I give him a small smirk before settling on the couch with my glass of wine. This is turning out to be one of the nicest evenings I've had in a long time. But that's hardly surprising. It's always that way when we're together.

Unable to help myself, I tease, "He's pretty hot, don't you think?"

Before I can blink, Sam nips the half-filled glass of wine from my hand and sets it down on the end table near the couch before attacking me with his fingers.

"So," he drawls, continuing with the torture, "Liam Garrison is hot, huh?"

A high-pitched squeal flies from my mouth as his fingers dance along my ribcage. When I'm finally able to push the words out, they're screechy and breathless. "Did I actually say that?" I attempt to wiggle out of the firm grasp he has on me, but he holds tight, refusing to let go. Those damn fingers of his seem to be everywhere.

"Yeah, I'm pretty sure that you did."

Gasping for breath, I finally admit, "I was kidding! Now stop tickling me!"

Instead of ceasing the torture, he continues to move his hands over my sides until I'm to the point of peeing in my pants. "Nope. I don't think I will." Finally, when I can't stand another second, he hauls me into his arms and holds me against his chest as I fight to catch my breath. We sit like that for a long moment.

And it feels...*good*.

Really good.

I'm reluctant to admit that it feels better than anything else has in a long time.

I squeeze my eyes shut, and attempt to turn my thoughts in a different direction. The last thing I need is to allow my imagination to meander down this road again. *Especially right now*. But I can't seem to help myself. As I inhale a breath, the woodsy scent of his cologne assaults my senses, making me almost dizzy with it. All I want to do is inhale another lungful.

What the hell is wrong with me?

I honestly don't know where all these strange thoughts keep coming from.

This is Sam we're talking about.

Sam!

Not some random dude I can crush on without repercussions. Sam is my best friend. One of the greatest guys I have ever met. The last thing I want to do is mess that up with fickle feelings and out of whack hormones. He's not a casual acquaintance I can avoid around campus after a hookup. We're in this relationship for the long haul. I need to get my body under control and remember that.

It's only when he clears his throat that my eyes pop open. I really hope he didn't notice me trying to inhale a whiff of him. How embarrassing would *that* be?

His voice turns gruff. "If you're done drooling over Liam Garrison, maybe we can get on with the movie?"

Even though I don't necessarily want to, I pull out of his embrace because I know it's the right thing to do. What's weird is that it doesn't necessarily *feel* like the right thing. I don't like these little sparks of attraction that keep flaring to life within me. All they do is knock me off balance and leave me feeling confused about our rela-tionship.

Sam uses the remote to find a list of movie channels before scrolling through them at breakneck speed.

When an oldie but goodie catches my eye, I jump up and point. "That one!"

He flips back a few channels before a deep groan slides from his lips. "Really?" Then he whines like a little boy trapped in a man's body. "Do we *have* to watch that again?"

I can't help the smile that spills across my face. "Yup, that's the one." I'm practically chortling with delight.

After a few silent moments, Sam arrives at the realization that this isn't a winnable war for him and grumbles under his breath, "Fine, but you owe me."

Ha!

I owe him nothing.

I've been subjected to way too many freeze-your-butt-off-in-the-stands football games to ever owe him for anything. And he knows it, which is precisely why he capitulated so easily.

I laugh as the opening credits for *Sixteen Candles* roll across the screen. Even though it's a movie from the eighties, I love it. We're talking total cult classic. I've lost track of how many times I've forced Sam to sit through the film. It's enough that we can easily parrot the lines back and forth to one another which makes the movie more enjoyable.

Even though he was groaning only moments ago, I think he secretly likes it as much as I do. I mean, come on, it's hilarious. With a contented sigh, I pick up my glass of wine before settling on the couch and nestling close to his body.

Out of nowhere, I'm slammed with the realization that my grand-mother is right. Sam *is* perfect boyfriend material. I suppose it is kind of surprising that he hasn't had more of a steady girlfriend throughout the last six years. He's handsome, smart, athletic, and so sweet that you just want to kiss the hell right out of him.

Okay, let me clarify that statement—*I* don't want to kiss the hell right out of him. But I can certainly understand why other girls would.

He's a seriously nice guy. And he's a good friend. Not only to me, but to everyone he allows into his inner circle. I'm not talking about the groupies or people who want to hang around with him because of his football status. If Sam considers you a friend, there's nothing he won't do for you. The guy is loyal to a fault.

It's kind of weird now that I think about it. He's gone out with girls here and there, but the relationships never seem to stick. It's like he's not into them. Maybe he's just focused on academics and football.

Sam could easily have his pick of women on this campus. And yet, I rarely see him with anyone. More often than not, he ignores the girls who compete for his attention. Sometimes I wonder if he realizes how much ass he could be getting on a daily basis.

In that regard, he's different than Roan, Liam, and Dylan. Before Roan got together with Ivy, he was definitely a player. Dylan was pretty much the same way before dating his longtime girlfriend, Lexie. But Sam has never been like that. He's never been into easy hookups or casual one-night stands. I'm not saying he hasn't had them, but it doesn't seem to be a way of life for him like it is for some of his teammates.

"Question," I suddenly pipe up before finishing off my second and final glass of wine for the evening. I'm not drunk by any means, but I do feel pleasantly buzzed. I'm content to be snuggled up against Sam on the couch in his apartment on a Friday night watching one of my favorite movies.

"Answer." His arm is casually slung around my shoulder as his body heat seeps into me. It's probably a good thing that I'm only wearing a thin, cotton T-shirt, otherwise I would be sweating bullets. Instead, his warmth feels good. I'm tempted to burrow closer.

Sam chuckles when I swat at his chest. "What? I thought we were playing word association."

Not bothering to respond, I forge ahead with my question. I can't be the only one who sees how awesome he is. "Why don't you have a girlfriend?"

His eyes widen before settling on me as the movie continues to play in the background. "*What?*"

It's like I've totally thrown him off by broaching the subject, which is strange because we talk about everything. No topic is off limits between us.

The alcohol careening through my system gives me liquid courage to figure out the answer. Sam is such a great guy. Any chick would be lucky to have him. "Why hasn't some girl locked you down already?"

His brows lower as he stares silently at me like I'm a complicated algebraic equation that needs to be methodically solved step by painful step. When he doesn't utter a word in response, something propels me to keep pushing.

The longer he holds my gaze, the more my body prickles with awareness. It almost feels as if the air between us has become heavier. Or maybe it's all in my imagination. Maybe two glasses of wine were a little too much. All I know for certain is that the breath I inhaled is now trapped in my lungs and there's nowhere for it to go. His eyes are fathomless. I feel myself getting ensnared in their dark, bottomless depths.

"You're just so perfect," I finally murmur, "sometimes it's hard to believe you're still single." I shake my head, remembering the chick who approached me. At the moment, I can't remember her name. "Oh, I forgot to mention that I gave your number to a girl from Rickets' class the other day."

"You did *what*?"

I freeze as he snaps out those three little words.

Why does he seem angry about it?

It's carefully that I repeat, "Um, yeah. Last week after class, a girl came up to me, wanting to know if we were together—"

"What did you tell her?" he asks, cutting me off as his gaze continues to pin mine in place. It's the oddest, yet most exhilarating feeling I've ever experienced.

Only now do I regret bringing up this entire line of questioning. Although, it's much too late to backpedal. "Umm, I told her that we were friends."

Because that's exactly what we are, right?

So why is he staring at me like that?

I inhale a breath before tripping over myself in my haste to explain. "She was totally your type."

One brow arches. "I have a type?"

Is he being serious?

I snort and roll my eyes. "Well, duh." Every girl I've seen him with is a carbon copy of the one before her. Although, there's nothing unusual about that, lots of people have a physical type they're attracted to.

"And what would that be?" he asks.

A prickle of nerves dance down my spine at the softly spoken question. It takes a moment for me to push out the answer. "Long blonde hair, big brown eyes, soft curvy body." I cup my hands in front of my chest. "Big boobs," I mutter as if he doesn't know.

A strange expression settles over his face before he admits, "Yup, you've nailed it. That's *exactly* the kind of girl I go for."

Air rushes from my lungs as I release a shaky laugh. "Well, I've been your best friend since middle school. I know what you like."

It's slowly that he strokes the blond stubble covering his chin. "I guess you do."

I blink and suddenly it feels as if his face is closer than it was a few moments ago. Which is...odd. My heart picks up its pace, pounding a bit harder at his nearness. Sam fills my entire line of vision, eclipsing everything around us until I'm only aware of him. The whole sexy package.

Shit...I didn't mean to think that.

Although, it's totally true. From his blond hair and blue eyes to full lips and muscular body, Sam is sexy. That's the one word that keeps popping up in my head. It must be all the alcohol rushing through my system that makes his gaze feel almost hypnotic in its unwavering intensity.

The tension rachets up between us until it feels explosive.

It's a relief when something happens on the television screen, drawing my attention away from Sam. After a second, he too, becomes ensnared in the plot and characters.

The odd pressure crackling in the air gradually dissipates as we both laugh. Even though we haven't been watching the movie, we know it so well that hearing one line can send us into peals of laughter.

Neither of us pick up the thread of our previous conversation as we settle onto the couch and watch the rest of the film in silence. After about ten minutes, I scoot toward Sam. He wraps his arm around my shoulders and pulls me closer until I can rest my head on his chest. A small sigh of contentment escapes from me as I settle against him. Even though things got strange there for a moment or two, it's all back to normal now.

And that's exactly where it needs to stay.

"What'd you and Violet end up doing last night?"

Roan gives me a little shove before waggling his dark eyebrows like the immature asshole that he is. If I was hoping the whole Violet-spending-the-weekend-at-our-place would go unmentioned—it's not going to happen.

"And I'm guessing it wasn't each other either since you were both sacked out in separate bedrooms by the time I made it home."

Pulling out his pads, Dylan smirks before sitting down on the wooden bench to get ready. Game time is set for noon. We're playing Akron today. It's another big one.

What the hell am I saying?

At this point in the season, they're all big. We're gunning for another championship and bowl game. With it being my senior year, you bet your ass I want to go all the way. Some of these guys will be playing for Barnett next year or entering the NFL draft in the spring. They're football careers will continue, but for me, this is it. After this season, I'm done. So, I need to give it my all. Every damn thing I've got.

You'd think these two would have their earbuds in, cranking some tunes, getting into the zone, gearing up to kick a little ass.

Nah. Why would they want to do that when they could spend some time busting my balls?

Dylan eyes me speculatively. "Still no movement on that front, huh?"

I glare, hoping that's answer enough. Clearly, the Violet situation isn't something I want to discuss. Especially with them.

Unfortunately, he doesn't take the hint. "Hey, I've got an idea—why don't you stop being such a pussy and put it out there already?"

Great. Just what I need—more unsolicited advice.

Hauling my shit out of my locker, I spend a few minutes taping up my wrist because it's been bothering me lately. But not enough to stop playing. The damn thing could be falling off my arm and I'd still be out there on the field.

"Dude, you need to face facts, you've been friend zoned." Dylan shakes his head all sad-like. "And once that happens, there's no coming back. It's impossible to move back into the—*I'd-like-to-fuck-you* zone." His expression morphs into a shit eating grin. "Not that I would know anything about what you're going through."

Rarely do I listen to the bullshit that spews from Dylan's mouth, but this time, I think he might be on to something. That being said, there is no way I'm going to mention that Violet is now trying to set me up with other chicks. These two would have a field day with that. I almost fell off the couch last night when she'd admitted to giving my number to some random girl.

I mean...*really?*

She's seriously trolling the campus on my behalf? Does me getting laid really require a group effort?

Unbelievable.

The situation between us is much worse than I originally suspected. In my limited experience, when you're into someone—even a little bit—you don't attempt to fix them up with other people.

I grind my back molars together and refrain from saying a word. At this point, I need to evict Violet from my head and focus on kicking Akron's ass today. That, at least, is something I can control.

To a certain extent.

"Your name might as well be *Samantha* for all that girl notices. Does she even know you have a penis, albeit a teeny tiny one, dangling between your legs?" Dylan continues.

My glare becomes ferocious.

Tiny dick, my ass.

But you know what?

In all honesty, I have no idea if she realizes that I'm a dude or not. Once in a while, there's a flash of heat between us but it's not enough for me to act on. I don't want to totally hang myself out there unless I'm reasonably sure she feels the same way. Otherwise, opening myself up could turn out to be nothing more than a suicide mission.

And I'm no Kamikaze pilot.

Not where Violet is concerned.

Unable to stop myself, the question tumbles from my lips before I can rein it in again. "And what exactly would you do if you were in my situation?"

Roan folds his arms over his chest as a smirk settles across his face. "I wouldn't know anything about that either, dude. I've never been friend zoned before. Most chicks can't wait to jump my bones."

The bastard is right about that.

I arch a brow and remind, "Huh. That's funny, because I don't seem to recall Ivy wanting to jump right into bed with you."

His smirk turns into more of a slow grin. "Nope. And that's all I'm going to say about that."

I shake my head. I never thought I'd see the day when Roan King settled down with one chick and yet, that's exactly what has happened. Even though they're living in separate cities, it's obvious that Roan is in love with Ivy.

The sad thing is—that's *exactly* what I want. A relationship. I'm tired of being out there on my own. Tired of the hookups. And the groupies that are always hanging around. Sometimes you can't tell who likes you for you and who's in it for the status you bring to the table. Some of the guys get off on that. They don't give a shit as to why someone wants to screw them. They're just happy to soak up all the attention and adoration.

But that's not me.

It's never been me.

And the fact that I want one specific girl doesn't help matters either. I've tried to forget about Violet, putting her out of my mind, and moving on. It's not like I haven't dated other women. But no matter who I'm with, I can't resist comparing them to her. And once that happens, it's all downhill from there.

Like a freaking bullet train. Then the relationship ends and I'm back to where I started—alone and pining for a girl who is oblivious to my need. As much as I hate to admit it, Violet was spot-on in her observations. I hadn't realized that I'm constantly hooking up with girls who look exactly like her.

It's pretty messed up.

And it's not helping matters either. None of these girls will ever be Violet Winterfield. It's like I'm constantly setting myself up for failure. These females are nothing more than a paper-thin version of the one I really want.

Seriously, how freaking pathetic is that?

That was more of a rhetorical question...

Unfortunately, I'm aware of the answer.

"Why don't you nut up and tell her how you feel? Let the chips fall where they will." Before I can even open my mouth, Dylan tacks on, "Don't get me wrong, I like Violet. She's a cool chick, but how much longer are you going to wait around for her to get with the program? Enough is enough, man. It's time to shit or get off the pot."

As ineloquent as his words are...they're difficult to disagree with. Maybe I need to take Dylan's advice and tell her how I feel. Whatever happens, at least I'll have an answer. Then I can move on instead of being stuck out here in no-man's land for the foreseeable future.

With all of his sage advice churning in my head, my gaze settles on Dylan. I suck in a deep breath and admit, "I think you might be right."

His eyebrows rise. "I am?"

As painful as it is to admit, I nod my head. "Yup, in a rather shocking turn of events, what you've said makes perfect sense."

He tilts his head as his eyes narrow. "It's not really *that* shocking."

Roan shakes his head. "No, dude, it's *completely* shocking." He roots around in his locker. "In fact, I need to write this day down, so I don't forget."

Dylan flips us the bird before walking away. "You guys are assholes."

For the first time all morning, I grin.

Truth.

Around nine o'clock that night we all head to O'Brien's. It's a little dive bar a few blocks from campus where a lot of college students hang out. Well, the ones who are twenty-one or, at the very least, have a decent fake ID. The rest stick to campus and the inevitable victory parties that will take place up and down Greek Row. It seems like all of Barnett has turned out to help celebrate. Even if you're not a football fan, it's as good as any excuse to get together with friends and have a few drinks.

I'm happy for the guys, happy their last year playing together is turning out to be a season for the record books, one they'll remember for the rest of their lives. Hell, I think everyone at Barnett will remember it.

Sam is a first-string left tackle. It's his job to protect the QB's blindside on passing plays and counter-act the pass rush of defensive ends. The only reason I know that is because I've spent more than my fair share of time with my ass in the bleachers, hollering at the top of my lungs, cheering him on. And today, Sam totally did his job. Akron never got close to touching Liam Garrison.

Last year, Sam considered entering the NFL draft. Unfortunately, he ended up injuring his wrist junior year. Even though he continues to play through the pain, I know that has a lot to do with him not looking to continue with the sport. He's focused on law school and pursuing a career in politics.

Once this season ends, Sam's football career will be over with it. My guess is that graduation will be bittersweet for him. He's been playing ball with these guys for the last four years and some of them will enter the draft in the spring. Like Roan King. It's all but certain that he'll get snapped up by a professional team.

I'm not sure what Dylan will end up doing. Like Sam, he's suffered a few injuries over the years. I know he wants to play professionally, but there hasn't been as much interest surrounding him as there is for Roan and Liam. While the dark-haired QB is a junior, I've heard he'll stick around and play next year even though he could technically enter the upcoming draft.

As we push through the doors, the bar is already jam-packed. The lights are low, and the music is vibrating off the walls. At the back of the bar, a few tables have already been pushed together and some of their teammates are sitting around and enjoying a beer. As usual, there are a ton of scantily clad girls hovering around the guys.

Ugh.

Jersey chasers.

There is never a shortage of them vying for male attention.

We find open seats and settle on them. Sam is to my left and—

"Hey Violet, how are you doing?"

I smile at Liam Garrison. Even though it's still early, groupies are already buzzing around him, trying to secure his attention for the evening. Instead of checking out all the available talent, his gunmetal gray eyes stay locked on mine.

"I'm good. Congrats on the win today. That was an awesome forty-yard pass to Roan in the third quarter."

"Thanks." He grins, flashing bright white teeth. "I knew there was some good luck coming from the stands today."

Liam Garrison is gorgeous in a completely dangerous kind of way. He looks more like a rock star than a clean-cut athlete. He's got short mahogany-colored hair. It's shaved close on the sides and spiked up on top, styled in a fauxhawk. Tattoo sleeves run down the length of both muscular arms. Colorful ink peeks out from beneath the collar of the black Bulldogs T-shirt he's sporting.

Am I curious as to how much of his body is covered in ink?

Guilty. And I'm certainly not alone in that curiosity. He's the bad boy of Barnett football. And the girls go freaking wild for him.

I roll my eyes. "Oh please, who needs luck when you've got talent?" And tons of it. He has an amazing arm. A real cannon.

Liam gives me a flirty wink. "I love a girl who knows what she's talking about."

A smile tugs at the corners of my lips as I shake my head. I've known Liam since he was a freshman rookie player and he's always been a flirt. Apparently, nothing has changed in that regard. Sam slides an arm across the back of my chair before leaning around me to give Liam a silent chin lift in greeting. The QB's smile widens as he hoists a brown bottle of beer to his lips and takes a long swallow.

The waitress—who already looks harassed by the thick crowd—stops by to take our order. Not having to fight your way to the bar for a drink is one of the many perks to being with a table full of hot college athletes.

"What do you want, Vi?" Sam asks.

With all these bodies pressed together, the temperature is already rising in the room. I shrug out of my jacket and throw it over the back of my chair. "Beer is fine."

When the waitress glances at Sam, he orders drinks for both of us. I can't help but notice the way her gaze lingers on him before she takes off. The tiny spark of jealousy that flares to life takes me by surprise. Knocked off balance by the emotion, my attention slides to Sam to see if he's checking her out as she makes her way back to the bar. Instead, he pins me in place with his steady blue gaze. Something indefinable settles within me at that knowledge.

What the hell is up with that?

I've never felt territorial where Sam is concerned. Half the time, I'm trying to hook the dude up, so he'll stop cock blocking me every chance he gets. These strange feelings that have taken root are seriously freaking me out. I thought if I gave it enough time and ignored them, they would fizzle out.

But that has yet to happen, and I'm beginning to wonder if it ever will.

When our liquor arrives, I grit my teeth as the pretty brunette with a shoulder length bob focuses way too much attention on Sam. Normally, Roan and Liam are the big draws. That's not to say Sam isn't good looking. He's just quieter. Instead of seeking out the limelight, he shies away from it. He's happier to hang back, allowing his teammates to be swamped by all the female attention.

I know part of that is because he worries about things ending up online and affecting his father's reputation. Opponents would snap that shit up and use it against his dad in a heartbeat.

But this girl isn't overlooking Sam at all. Her sights seem to be locked on him, which is kind of pissing me off. Does she not see that his arm is draped across the back of my chair?

Is she blind? Or does she just not care?

Believe it or not, I run into those kinds of girls all the time. Hell, they're more than happy to join the pair of you for the evening if that's the only way they can sleep with an athlete.

Freaking jersey chasers. Some of them have zero self-respect.

Irritation pounds through me as her gaze continually darts to him as she passes out our drink order. When she slides past us, her hand brushes over Sam's bicep. Even when her fingers trail lightly across him, he doesn't glance her way. It's like he's totally oblivious to the fact that she's attempting to flirt with him.

Instead of giving her the attention she craves, his gaze remains focused on me. A shiver of awareness shimmies down my spine when he closes the distance between us, his warm breath feathering against my ear.

"I know that look," he says. "What's wrong?"

Flustered by the possessiveness rampaging through my system, I pick up my beer and lift it to my lips before downing most of the contents. I'm trying to buy some time since I have no idea how to respond.

It's not like I can tell him the truth.

That I feel...

That maybe...

Crap.

There's no way to deny what I'm feeling.

It's jealousy.

At this very moment, hot spikes of possessiveness are careening through my veins like fire. Sam would probably laugh his ass off if I told him what was going on. I can't imagine how awkward that would make everything between us. Nothing ruins a friendship faster than unrequited lust.

The worst part is that I don't want to feel this way about Sam. I don't want to look at him any differently or be sexually aware of him. I don't want my breath catching when I'm close enough to inhale a whiff of him or to fantasize about that rock-solid body of his. And I certainly don't want to feel this gut-wrenching jealousy when another girl flirts with him in front of my face.

I don't want any of it.

"Nothing's wrong," I mutter before slamming the bottle down on the scarred table in front of me.

Even though I'm doing my best to avoid eye contact, his narrowed gaze continues to carefully search mine. It's like he's attempting to pick through everything I'm so desperately trying to hide. Sam knows me well enough to realize that I'm not being truthful with him.

He glances toward the back door of the bar. "Let's go outside and talk for a few minutes."

Oh, hell no.

The last thing I want to do is discuss the situation. For the love of all that's holy, I'm not even sure what *the situation* is yet. What I know is that if he presses me hard enough for answers, I'll cave. Like a cheap stack of cards.

I can't lie to him.

I've *never* been able to hold anything back from Sam. I can't help but blurt out the truth when I'm in his presence. It's terrible. Even his mom, Beth, knows better than to confide in me when it has anything to do with Sam.

Don't even mention the birthday surprise I managed to mess up a couple of years ago. I've yet to live that one down with his family.

Instead, I do my best Jack-in-the-Box impersonation by popping out of my chair, nearly knocking it over in the process. "Let's dance."

Yes—dancing.

Loud music.

Lots of quick paced movements.

Elbow to elbow crowd.

Zero opportunity to converse.

Or—more than likely—interrogate me until he's gotten to the bottom of my odd behavior. FYI—Sam will one day make an excellent trial lawyer. He's good at asking questions and ferreting out the truth. *Especially* where I'm concerned.

One brow climbs across his forehead. When he doesn't rise to his feet, I grab his hand, attempting to haul him up. Which is a fruitless effort on my part. The guy is all muscle. Like two hundred and some pounds of it.

"Hey, if Harper isn't interested, I'd be more than happy to—"

Liam doesn't get a chance to finish that sentence before Sam is shooting out of his seat. His fingers tighten around my hand before towing me onto the dance floor. As my gaze catches Liam's, I notice his eyes simmer with barely suppressed humor. It's not lost on me that Liam is doing his damnedest to get a rise out of Sam.

What I don't understand is why.

Luckily, the tune is upbeat and fast-paced. It's exactly what I need. I don't think I could handle the feel of Sam's arms wrapped around me right now. Not with the way my body is buzzing with awareness. All of my emotions feel strangely close to the surface.

Instead of focusing on that, I lose myself in the music as it spills from the sound system. Within moments, we're both throwing our hands up in the air and when the chorus plays, we pretty much scream the lyrics in each other's faces with huge grins spilling across our faces.

See?

This is exactly what normal feels like between us. Just us goofing around. Having fun. Being silly. Not whatever weird bullshit that was back there. Those feelings have been totally messing with my head lately and I'm tired of it. Jealousy has no place in our relationship. At least it never has before. So, it doesn't make sense why it would start now.

Three songs later, and the dance floor gets even more crowded with writhing bodies pulsating to the heavy beat. Even some of Sam's teammates are out here shaking their asses, which means there are tons of groupies in skimpy shirts over barely contained breasts and teeny tiny skirts shaking theirs as well.

Ugh.

That I can do without.

But where the team goes, the jersey chasers follow.

That's just the way it is.

As that song ends, a slower one begins. People scatter from the dance floor in search of liquid refreshment as my gaze slices to Sam. For a brief moment, I contemplate my options.

Head back to the table?

Stay frozen in place like a deer in headlights?

Indecision keeps me rooted in place.

As he opens his mouth to say something, a girl wedges her way in between us. She gives me a friendly smile before turning big brown eyes to Sam.

Wait a minute...I know this girl. She's the one I gave Sam's number to.

"Want to dance?" she asks him.

He shifts his weight from one foot to the other as his attention slides to mine before bouncing to the pretty blonde standing between us.

"Umm..." His voice trails off.

"I'm Allie. The one who texted you after the game today." She tips her head toward me before giving him a wide smile. "I hope you don't mind that Violet gave me your number."

His brow rises as his gaze slices to mine. In the blink of an eye, his expression becomes shuttered. I have no idea what he's thinking.

Which is odd. I always know what's going on in Sam's head.

But not this time.

The three of us stand there as the music continues to play. The dance floor has cleared out except for a dozen couples who are now wrapped up in each other's arms, swaying intimately to the beat. I should head back to the table before the situation can become anymore uncomfortable. Unsure what to do, I take a hasty step in retreat, only wanting to flee. Sam's gaze holds mine captive as I take another step backward.

Right into someone's hard chest. Almost immediately, strong fingers wrap around my upper arms to stabilize me.

Sam's blue eyes go flat as a husky male voice whispers in my ear, "How about that dance, Violet?"

Without turning, I know whose embrace I've become ensnared in.

Even though Sam's gaze continues to pin me in place, I watch as Allie throws her arms around the blond tackle. Liam turns me in his arms before his hands grip my waist. As my gaze catches his, a spark of humor dances in his eyes.

We sway to the music for a few silent beats before he asks, "What's up between you and Harper?"

Hmmm. That's an excellent question. I wish I knew.

I clear my throat and tell him what the truth should be, "We're just friends." What I'd like to know is when that became a lie.

Liam tilts his head as if assessing the truth of my answer. I have the strangest feeling that he doesn't quite believe me. Although, that this point, I'm not sure if even *I* believe me.

"Is that so?"

The directness of his gaze knocks me off kilter. "We've been friends since eighth grade," I add as if that will somehow legitimize my response.

He nods before tugging me so close that I can feel all of his hard lines. Liam has to be a little over six feet tall. Compared to most of the other guys on the team, he's leaner, which makes perfect sense since he's a quarterback.

And, yeah—he's definitely hot as hell.

But it does nothing for me. For some reason, there's only one guy who fills my thoughts. And he happens to be dancing next to me with another girl in his arms.

"Are you sure there's nothing going on between you two?" he questions again.

"We're just friends," I repeat. Although I have to wonder who I'm more intent on fooling—him or me.

"Good. Then there isn't a reason for us not to go out, right?"

My wide gaze snaps to his as my feet stutter to a halt. "What?"

A smile spreads across his handsome face. "You heard me. I'd like to take you out sometime."

By the way his lips quirk at the corners, I'm guessing my facial expression says it all. "Like on a *date?*"

His eyes spark with silent laughter. "Yup."

It feels like my brain has stopped working and I blurt, *"With me?"*

In all the years that I've known Liam, not once has he ever directed any interest my way. Don't get me wrong, he's always been friendly. But he's never acted in a way that would lead me to believe there's any attraction between us. None of the guys on the team have ever hit on me. They treat me like Sam's little sister. As if there's an invisible no-fly zone around me.

He snorts. "Yeah, *you.*"

I'm not going to lie—I'm having a difficult time wrapping my head around this one.

My brows furrow. "Why?"

Liam Garrison could have his pick of women on campus. He leaves a trail of broken hearts in his wake. Unlike Roan King, he's actually been known to have relationships. Which only makes him a more highly sought out commodity. Sure, he'll enjoy a one-night stand from time to time, but there are girlfriends sprinkled in there as well.

And yet, knowing all this, it's on the tip of my tongue to decline the unexpected offer.

When I don't respond, he pulls me close enough for his warm breath to feather across my ear. Playfully, he wheedles, "Come on, Violet. It's one date. No pressure and all fun." He draws back enough for his gaze to lock on mine. "Promise."

I don't know what to do. Is there a reason I *shouldn't* go out with Liam?

Not really.

And Sam isn't an acceptable excuse either since we're nothing more than friends. Maybe this is exactly what I need. Maybe going out with another guy will get my mind off him.

It can't hurt, right?

"Okay," I hear myself agreeing.

"Great."

When the song comes to an end, I quickly step out of Liam's embrace. Relief floods through me as I do. Unconsciously, my gaze searches the surrounding vicinity for Sam.

But he's nowhere to be found.

And neither is Allie.

Chapter Nine

VIOLET

It's after one in the morning when we finally decide to call it quits for the night. Even though we're heading out, there's a rowdy bunch who decide to stay and close down O'Brien's. To show us how lame we are for leaving early, they boo us on the way out.

Loudly.

With a grin, Roan gives them a one fingered salute in response. As we drive back to the apartment, I can't help but notice that Sam is quieter than usual.

Once home, I wait until Roan disappears inside his room to Face-Time Ivy before hesitantly asking, "Is something wrong?"

The strange vibe that keeps reverberating between us is now back in full force. It sucks all the oxygen from the room, making it almost impossible to breathe. Already it feels as if our relationship has shifted. No matter how hard I try, I can't seem to get a firm handle on the situation.

And that frightens me. I'm not good with change. I'd prefer our relationship stay the same. Just friends. No weird vibes messing up what we have going on between us. No thoughts of what Sam feels like beneath his shirt or...

Smells like.

Without answering, Sam heads to the fridge and grabs a water. He quirks a brow before silently holding out a bottle for me. As I step into the dimly lit kitchen and take the cool plastic container from his hand, I wait for his response.

I need to know that we're good.

Solid.

Unshakable.

That this sudden weirdness isn't going to end up ruining our friendship. I don't know what to make of all these strange feelings that keep bubbling up to the surface. All I want is for everything to slide neatly back into place.

"Nope," he says. "Everything's fine."

It's what I was hoping to hear but does nothing to settle the anxiety simmering in me. For some reason, I don't believe him. He seems on edge. Almost as if there's frustrated energy pumping through his system.

And that's not like him. Sam is one of the most chill guys I know.

Before I can question him further, he scrubs a hand over his face. "I'm really beat. I'm going to hit the sack, all right? We can talk more in the morning."

Unsure what to do, I nod and watch him walk away. The door to his room closes softly and I find myself alone in the kitchen.

An hour later, I'm in bed and staring sightlessly at the ceiling. Even though I'm tired, I can't seem to fall asleep. I toss one way before turning in the opposite direction. All of my thoughts are focused on Sam. On our friendship and what's happening between us. I keep combing over my memories, trying to pinpoint when our relationship shifted. But there isn't one specific moment that sticks out in my mind. It's more like a gradual evolution. One I had no idea was happening until it was too late.

Fed up with all the angst rolling around inside me, I throw off the covers. Maybe Sam is awake, and he's plagued by the same thoughts.

Is there a reason why we can't talk this out like two rational adults?

We're friends. Best friends. We have been for a really long time. We've never had a problem opening up and being honest with one another.

That's what friends are supposed to do, right?

Talk everything to death?

Exactly.

It's quietly that I pad down the short hallway before gently tapping on his closed bedroom door. When there's no response, I knock a little louder before carefully pushing it open and tiptoeing inside.

As I slink closer to the bed, my gaze slides over him in the darkness and my mouth turns cottony. Sam is lying on his back, one brawny arm thrown over his eyes. His chest is bare. Moonlight pours in through the unadorned window, throwing light and shadow across his sprawled-out form.

My muscles lock in place. It's as if I'm paralyzed to do anything other than stand over him.

Like a total creeper.

I don't think I could stop my hungry gaze from licking over every sinewy muscle if I wanted to. Which, quite frankly, I don't.

He's breathtaking.

Big and yeah...strapping.

So freaking strapping.

It's not like this is the first time I've seen Sam without a shirt on. We used to spend our summers at the country club pool, swimming all day and hanging out under the hot sun. I've seen Sam in swim trunks and nothing else plenty of times. But catching sight of him like this has something hot rocketing to my core where it explodes like a firework. I'm transfixed by the sight of him.

The urge to reach out and stroke my fingers over all that brute male strength is so overwhelming that I have to clench my fingers in order to stop what every instinct inside me is screaming to do. I feel like such a perv standing over him like this and ogling him while he sleeps.

Is this seriously what I've been reduced to?

Apparently so.

Because here I am.

Almost savagely, I gnaw at my lower lip wondering when the hell I began to think about Sam like this. When did I notice what a gorgeous body he had? Or how attractive all that thick blond hair was? Or the way his bright blue eyes cut right to the heart of me?

I swallow thickly as those thoughts echo through my mind.

Leaving me completely breathless.

Yup, this is bad.

I shake my head, attempting to loosen those dangerous thoughts before they can do permanent damage. Sneaking into Sam's room so we could talk was a mistake. Thank God, he's still asleep. He has absolutely no idea that I'm lurking around in his room. I can tiptoe out of here before crawling back into my bed and forgetting this ever—

"Vi?" His voice is all thick and raspy as if coated with sleep. It strums something deep inside me. "What's going on?" He blinks groggily before propping himself up on his elbows. My heart skips a beat as his gaze fastens on to mine. "Is something wrong?"

Crap.

Even though he can't see it, my cheeks heat with embarrassment. I scramble around for a plausible explanation. Unfortunately, my brain has gone on a temporary hiatus and I have no idea when it might start to function again.

"I, um..." there's a pause, "couldn't sleep." I sound like a moron as I stutter out those words.

His brows knit together as he struggles to wake. He blinks a few more times before his gaze runs over the length of me. That's when I remember that I'm wearing a hot pink tank top that leaves little to the imagination and cotton panties.

My first thought is to cover myself, but I resist the urge. A few weeks ago, feeling self-conscious in front of Sam wouldn't have even crossed my mind. Over the years, there have been dozens of times when I've changed in front of him without thinking about it.

"Why not?" Is it my imagination or has his voice dropped a few octaves? Every once in a while, his gaze flicks to mine before straying downward.

I can't help but wonder if he likes what he sees.

Oh my God!

Did I seriously just think that?

I need to get out of here before I do something stupid. Something

I'll end up regretting in the morning. Something that will do irreparable damage to our friendship.

"Sorry I woke you. Like you said earlier, we'll talk in the morning." It's hastily that I take a step in retreat, only wanting to escape before I can become any more of a bumbling fool. "All right?"

Sam throws off the covers before swinging his legs over the side of the bed. "Come here, Violet."

His voice is deep and gravelly. It's so commanding that I instantly halt in my tracks. Another shiver of desire slides through me like warmed honey. Unsure what to do, I hesitate near the door while deciding if I should ignore him and make a quick break for it.

"*Violet.*"

My eyes flare as his voice whips out again, startling me from my indecision.

"What?" I squeak that one word into the darkness as tension crackles like electricity around us.

"*Come here.*"

When he holds out his hand for me to take, I don't stop to think about the ramifications. I close the distance between us until his fingers can slip around my smaller ones. It's slowly that he tows me toward him. With one final tug, I tumble into his arms. His body is all warm and hard as I find myself held securely on his lap.

"Tell me what's going on."

I give my head a little shake. What am I supposed to say?

I'm barely able to think straight with his arms wrapped around me and my bottom nestled against his hard thighs, let alone string together a few passable words to make a plausible sentence.

One of his hands rises to stroke my cheek. I'm not sure what to do with all these out-of-control emotions careening around my system. They're so disconcerting. For a moment, I squeeze my eyes tightly shut and try to regain some sense of equilibrium. I have to clench my thighs together to stifle the desire coursing through me.

"Look at me, Vi," he orders.

My eyelashes flutter open before my gaze locks on him. Almost desperately I admit, "I don't know what's going on anymore." I'm confused and afraid to admit the truth. I've never felt like that with Sam.

His body stills beneath mine. "What do you mean?"

"It feels..." my words trail off.

I suck in a quick breath and realize that I'm standing on the precipice.

Do I tell him what's *really* going on?

Or do I continue to tamp down these feelings and pretend they don't exist?

What's the saying—fake it until you make it?

Although I'm pretty sure they didn't mean it like this.

"What? What does it feel like?" Even though his words are gentle, I hear the underlying thread of tension running through them. The very same tension that seems to rear its ugly head more and more often between us.

Tension that feels strangely like—

"Different," I whisper hesitantly.

Does he feel it, too?

The way it swirls around us, ratcheting up until it's almost impossible to breathe?

His brow furrows. "Different in a bad way?"

No, this doesn't feel bad. But it does feel scary. Kind of like we're taking a giant leap into the unknown.

I shake my head.

Neither of us say anything more on the subject.

He breaks the heavy silence that has fallen over us when he shifts me around in his arms. "Do you want to sleep here tonight?"

It's not a question I have to think about. I want to be with him. I want to feel his arms banded securely around me. What I don't want is to dwell on the reason for it.

"Yeah."

As we settle on the bed, he rearranges our bodies. His front is curved around my back as one arm curls protectively around my body. All of the restless energy that has been clawing to get out, instantly quiets as he anchors me securely to him in more ways than one.

After I moved in with my grandparents, I would have nightmares.

Unexpected flashes from the accident that haunted me for years afterward. The only person capable of chasing them away was Sam. Whenever I would jolt awake from one in the middle of the night, I'd crawl out my bedroom window and into his. He would rouse as soon as I dropped to the floor before lifting the covers so I could slide quietly beneath them. It's as if he knew, even then, exactly what I needed. He would hold me in his arms like this and somehow, I was able to sleep through the rest of the night. In the morning, before either of our families woke, I'd sneak out of his house and back to my own.

That went on for years.

It was during our senior year of high school, when Sam started going out with a girl from our class, that I stopped going over to his house. I forced myself to not rely on him so much. Even though we were best friends, Sam didn't belong to me.

Not really.

Being with him like this has all those nostalgic feelings of comfort and security hurtling to the surface. I've had my fair share of boyfriends over the years, but none have ever been able to give me the same feelings of safety that Sam so easily rouses within me.

It leaves me to wonder if anyone else ever will.

Chapter Ten

VIOLET

I stretch, fighting my way out of the best sleep I've had in months. As soon as I do, three things hit me at once.

One—I'm not alone.

Two—there's a warm palm cupping my breast.

And yeah, it feels good.

Three—I'm pretty sure there's a boner nestled against my backside.

That's all it takes for my eyes to pop wide and I'm instantly awake, wondering what the hell happened last night and why I'm blanking on it. As I inhale a sharp breath, I hit rewind and try to figure it out.

I remember going to O'Brien's and having a few drinks. Although certainly not enough to get blackout drunk.

I danced with Sam and then Liam.

We were booed out of the bar as we left.

Sam was more quiet than usual on the drive home.

I tossed and turned, trying to find sleep.

Nerves prickle along my skin because it's all starting to come together now.

I creeped into Sam's room so we could talk.

I'm going to hazard a guess and say that it's Sam's hand palming my boob and his erection pressed against me. Air gets clogged in my throat as I listen to his deep, rhythmic breathing.

All right. It appears that I've managed to dodge a major bullet here because—thank you Lord Jesus—Sam is still sleeping soundly, which means that he has no idea what's going on.

That morning timber is absolutely normal.

It's no biggie.

My body stiffens as he grinds his thick cock against the cotton barrier of my panties. I bite down on my lower lip to stifle the whimper of pleasure that is desperately trying to escape. It takes everything inside me not to wiggle my ass against him in response.

Exactly *how* am I going to extract myself from this situation without waking him?

That's the million-dollar question.

Everything already feels weird and tense between us. This incident will only send us careening over the cliff into awkward-ville and I'm in no mood to make a pit stop there. What I need to do is get us back to the land of normal. All this strange sexual tension flaring to life between us is beginning to drive me nuts.

I almost wince when his hand gently squeezes my breast as if he's testing the weight in his palm. A deep growly noise rumbles up from his chest as his erection slides against me again. And damn it—*damn it* —my nipples have stiffened into hard little points that are begging to be played with.

What I need to do is hightail it out of here ASAP.

Thank goodness it's Sunday and Carter will be heading back to Philadelphia. I can escape to my dorm and put some much-needed distance between us until I can firmly wrangle all of these thoughts and feelings back under control again.

I lay stiff as a board listening to the steady sound of Sam's breathing. As I'm about to detach myself from him, Sam's hand meanders from my breast down my ribcage before skimming south of the border. His fingers are on the verge of breaching the elastic band of my panties when I rocket out of bed before hitting the door that leads into the hall.

"Vi?" His voice is all groggy, like he's trying to shake off the thick cobwebs of sleep.

"Yeah?" I'm panting like I've just run a marathon. My heartbeat jackhammers painfully against the wall of my chest. I need to get out of here before I self-combust.

"Where are you going?"

"I'm, ah," I jerk my thumb toward the hallway, "heading back to my room."

I can't help but glance over my shoulder as he rolls onto his back, stretching out on the queen-size mattress. With a gulp, I notice how his muscles flex and bunch. Unconsciously, my gaze roves over the tight ridges of his abs until they get to—

My mouth tumbles into a shocked *O* of surprise when I see how the sheet has tented below his waist.

Holy crap.

His boner is enough to send me scurrying from the room like a virgin on prom night.

————

Two hours later, we're sitting in a diner about a block away from Sam's apartment. They serve the best breakfasts here all day long. Naturally, this place is packed after the bars close. Can't say I haven't been here a few dozen times myself.

Sam appears unruffled by what happened this morning as he swallows down half his glass of orange juice before setting it in front of him.

I wish I could be that nonchalant. Instead, I'm having a difficult time meeting his blue-eyed gaze from across the table. My face feels hot and as much as I wish it weren't the case, I'm completely turned on. No matter how hard I try, I can't stop thinking about the thick erection pressed deliciously against me this morning.

Shit.

Not deliciously. It was definitely not delicious.

Or big.

Or...gulp...*thick.*

As much as I hate to admit this, I'm kind of a girth girl. I'll take thick over long any day of the week.

Damnit. These thoughts aren't helping matters one bit. In fact, they're only making it worse.

Much worse.

As those memories swirl unwantedly through my head, I shift on the red vinyl covered booth. There's an ache that is starting to throb insistently between my—

"Vi?"

My gaze slices from the paper straw wrapper I'm wadding up into a tight little ball before unwinding, flattening, and doing it all over again. As I sit across from Sam, I'm nervous and twitchy. And I hate it. This isn't the kind of relationship we have.

"We never finished talking last night," he says.

My muscles tense when I think about picking up the threads of our previous conversation.

No, we hadn't gotten around to that. I'd been so comfortable in his warm embrace, that I'd immediately fallen asleep.

And then I'd woken up refreshed and—

Turned on since there was a lovely boner snuggled against me and a warm palm cupping my breast.

I seriously can't believe those thoughts just flitted through my head.

In the eight years that we've been friends, I have *never* imagined what sex with Sam might be like. Not ever. We've always been *just friends*. He's had girlfriends. I've had a long string of ill-fated boyfriends that were doomed for failure from the get-go. And we've both hooked up with other people in the interim.

It has never been weird between us.

No crackling sexual tension.

No thoughts of *what if* clinging to my subconscious.

The cold light of day has me wondering if it's nothing more than a disastrous idea to open up this Pandora's box. Everything already feels strange and awkward. Unstable. As if our entire relationship is suddenly careening out of control and there's not a damn thing we can do to stop it. Openly expressing those ideas will only make it worse.

Because there will be no turning back.

But right now...*right now* we can ignore what's happening and pretend it's not there. And maybe, if we pretend hard enough—long enough, it'll all just go away without us having to deal with it.

He regards me steadily, waiting for an answer. My shoulders stiffen. Already I can tell that he's not going to let this go. Maybe he feels it too...the weirdness that has cropped up between us, suffocating the easiness we've always taken for granted.

As I open my mouth to respond, someone slides into the booth next to me. His hip hits mine, nudging me over further. I blink in confusion, realizing that Liam has joined us.

His dark hair is styled into its trademark fauxhawk and he's wearing a black leather jacket with a soft-looking gray Henley beneath it. His dark wash jeans hang low on his taut hips and he has on a pair of black leather boots.

"Hey." Oblivious to the simmering tension, his gaze bounces between us before refocusing on me. "You two don't mind if I join you, do you?"

I peek at Sam from beneath my lashes and rein in the sigh of relief that threatens to escape. "Of course not."

Sam remains silent as Liam settles against the vinyl booth before grabbing a menu to peruse. I get the distinct feeling that he's not happy about Liam crashing our breakfast. Even though the atmosphere is more strained, I'm glad the conversation Sam and I were about to delve headfirst into has been aborted for the time being. It's yet another bullet that has been dodged this morning.

Sheesh. Since when has my relationship with Sam felt like a minefield that has to be carefully navigated?

Never.

That's when.

What I need is to take some time and think about everything that has been going on between us before Sam and I sit down and hash things out. And clearing out of Sam's apartment will definitely help with that. I think a bit of distance will do us both some good. Maybe it's what we need to get our relationship back on track again. At this point, that's all I can hope for.

The waitress comes over and Liam orders a coffee along with eggs, bacon, hash browns, and pancakes.

Before tacking on a side of fruit.

And two slices of lightly buttered wheat toast.

When Sam and I stare at him with raised brows, he says by way of explanation, "I'm starving. Haven't eaten a thing all morning."

"Clearly." I can't help but laugh.

Liam and Sam discuss the game yesterday and what plays need to be tightened up before the next one. As their conversation continues, the tension slowly ebbs. I sit back, sipping my orange juice as I listen to them discuss the away game next weekend and the first-string offensive tackle who sprained his ankle yesterday and his chances of getting back onto the field by Saturday.

Which, apparently, aren't good.

By the time our breakfast is served, everything feels almost normal again. Maybe I can chalk all of this up to a strange few weeks. And my relationship with Sam will simply slide back to the way it's always been.

Because that's what I want...isn't it?

Chapter Eleven

SAM

"Are you ready to go?" I want to hustle Violet back to the apartment so we can sit down and talk about what's going on between us. This conversation has been a long time in coming and it finally seems like she might be ready to have it.

I also want to get her away from Garrison.

Goddamn mother fuc—

"I'm going to run to the bathroom before we leave, all right?" Violet says, forcing Liam to slide from the booth so she can shimmy her way out. I'm all too aware of the way his hand trails over her arm, all in the guise of helping her up.

Yeah...nice try, pal. I know exactly what you're up to.

The fact that Garrison nods at her like she's talking specifically to him makes me gnash my teeth together in aggravation. The dude is completely oblivious to the fact that he hijacked my breakfast. Then he stands in the middle of the aisle and watches her hips sway back and forth as she disappears toward the back of the restaurant. By the time Liam sits his ass down, I'm tempted to leap across the table and wring his damn neck.

His eyes slice innocently to mine. There's just a hint of a smirk sliding its way across his lips.

I'm going to be completely candid about this—I like Liam. I really do. He's a phenomenal QB and in the two years I've known him, he's been a decent guy. He's not some freaking prima donna out on the field like some QB's I've played with. Nor is he a head case. I've unfortunately run into that as well. Hell, it looks like he might even be moving into Dylan's old room because of his current housing situation.

And I'm cool with that.

Although, at the moment?

I'd like to knock the piss out of him for the way he keeps eyeing up Violet. What the fuck is that about? Up until last night, he's never shown one damn bit of interest in her.

Unperturbed by the hard-edged glint shining in my eyes, he nods toward where she was last seen. "She's a great girl."

His casual comment makes my hands tighten beneath the table. When I can't hold it in a moment longer, I snap. "Dude, what the hell are you doing?"

One dark brow slants upward as he smirks. "What are you talking about?"

Grrrr.

My eyes narrow as my temper ignites. I'm beginning to think this whole act is deliberate, just to piss me off. Which would be pretty fucking stupid considering that it's my job out on the field to protect him.

During a game, I have no problem taking someone down. But rarely have I been moved to the point of violence. That's not my style. I'm not a hot head. I'm always cool, calm, and in control of my feelings. Plus, it's been all but pounded into me that I need to continually rise above the fray. I can't do anything that will reflect poorly on my father or his political career. It's probably why I enjoy football so much. It's an outlet. I can knock people around and it's perfectly acceptable.

Hell, I'd go so far as to say that it's encouraged.

But that doesn't mean I can't be riled up when the occasion calls for it. Back in high school, I punched some asswipe in the nose who was giving Violet a hard time. Needless to say, no one bothered her after that.

Did I catch a shitload of trouble from my father?

And his image consultant?

And his PR dude?

Yup. But it was totally worth it. And furthermore, I would do it again if necessary.

In all the years I've been playing football, I've never experienced the urge to lay out one of my own teammates.

Until now.

"I'm talking about Violet." My teeth are tightly clenched as I force out the words. "What the hell are you doing?"

Even though I'm practically vibrating with tension, he shrugs like we're just sitting around shooting the shit. Instead of answering my question, he says, "Did she tell you that I asked her out last night?"

Everything in me stills. "You did *what?*"

His wide grin grows. It's getting more difficult to hold myself back and not take a swing at him. "I asked if I could take her out sometime."

My eyes are so narrowed, I can barely see. Of course, I can barely see through all the damn smoke pouring out of my ears. Over my dead body will he take her out!

Garrison is a player.

Maybe not like Roan used to be.

But still...

He's enough of one that I wouldn't want Violet anywhere near him. Even if I didn't have feelings for her, I still wouldn't want them together. I'll be damned if I allow him to get his hands on her. He'll just mess her up.

When I'm finally able to wrap my lips around words, I grit them out succinctly, "And what did she say?" Barely am I holding on to my temper by a thread.

He flashes a lazy grin. "She's totally into it, man. Just have to pick a time and place."

My shoulders collapse as I mutter, "No shit."

He straightens before folding his hands in front of him on the table as he eyes me steadily. The smile disappears from sight. "Any reason why that shouldn't happen, Harper?"

Why that dirty little son of a—

"Okay, I'm ready to go."

Before I can say anything—hell, before I can blink, Liam slides out of the booth and invades Violet's personal space. "What are you up to for the rest of the day?"

She looks startled by the question. "Oh. I was planning to do a little studying later this afternoon."

He cocks his head toward the entrance of the diner as I sit there like a dumbass and watch him make a play for my girl right in front of my eyes.

And what do I do?

Nothing.

Abso-fucking-lutely nothing.

"I've got my bike with me, how about I take you for a ride? I'll have you back in plenty of time to get your work done."

Indecision flickers across Violet's face as she gnaws at her plump lower lip before her gaze drifts to me. We stare for a silent heartbeat. It's like I'm paralyzed. Unable to do anything that will put a stop to this madness.

And even if I weren't, what am I supposed to do?

Tell her that she can't go?

If she wants to spend time with Liam fucking Garrison, who am I to tell her no? It's not like she's ever hooked up with any of my teammates before. By unspoken agreement, all the guys pretty much steer clear of Violet.

It's quietly that she asks, "Do you mind if I leave with Liam?"

Fuck.

I jerk my shoulders into a tight shrug before mumbling, "Nope. Not at all."

You bet your damn ass that I'm pissed at Garrison. But you know what? I'm angry at myself for not doing something to put a stop to this impromptu date.

After another moment of scrutiny, she turns to Liam who is grinning like a Cheshire cat. I'm seriously going to pound the crap out of him next time we're on the field. Or better yet, I'll let him get the piss knocked out of him by the other team. I don't give a damn if he's our first string QB. The guy is going down.

"Great. I've got an extra helmet on the back of my bike, let's go."

When his gaze slides my way, a taunting smugness fills it. "I'll catch you later, man."

He tows her out of the restaurant before I can say or do anything else. Violet's soft brown eyes catch mine one last time before she disappears through the doors and into the sunshine.

I scrub a hand through my hair before digging around in my wallet and throwing a few bills onto the table.

Would you like to guess who got stuck paying the check?

I'll give you a clue—it's the same chump whose ass is sitting alone at the table.

I swear to God, when I get my hands on that little shit, he's going to rue the day he looked sideways at Violet.

That's a fucking promise.

Chapter Twelve

VIOLET

"Does that feel all right?" Liam asks, tucking my long hair behind my ears before carefully pulling the helmet over my head.

I give a quick nod and in return, he gifts me with a lazy smile.

There is no denying it, Liam Garrison is a hot guy. The man oozes sex appeal through his pores. It's ridiculously intoxicating. That being said, I'm not quite sure what I'm doing here with him. And part of me feels like crap for walking out on Sam. Maybe I should have said no to Liam's offer and headed back to the apartment with the blond football player.

But then we would have ended up discussing last night…and the weeks leading up to it. As far as I'm concerned, that's just another bullet that has been dodged. It's not a conversation I want to engage in until I have a better handle on my feelings. For the time being, I'll avoid Sam by spending a little time with Liam. I can grab my stuff from his apartment later and head back to the dorms.

Liam instructs me to climb on behind him until I'm straddling the bike. Once I'm seated, he grabs my arms before wrapping them around his middle.

"Hold on tight," he says.

My tongue darts out to moisten my dry lips. "Okay."

Without warning, the motorcycle roars to life and we take off, zipping through the tree-lined streets near campus. After a few minutes, my muscles loosen, and a smile stretches its way across my face as the wind whips past us. All of the issues that have cropped up with Sam gradually fall to the wayside.

I can't help but enjoy the feel of the wind as I press against Liam. Even though it's mid-November, and the sun is bright and shining, there's a definite chill to the air. There's something freeing about being on the back of a motorcycle.

Especially when you're clinging to a hot guy for dear life.

For the next thirty minutes, we wind lazily through the busy city streets until he pulls up in front of a battered cream-colored brick building on the east end of town. Liam parks the bike and cuts the engine before climbing off.

My legs are rubbery from the vibrations, and they nearly buckle as I hop off the seat. His arms slide around me before that can happen. I stare at the rundown single-story pool hall we're parked in front of. When my gaze bounces back to him, a grin simmers around the corners of Liam's lips as if he's able to read my mind.

He nods toward the place. "Do you play?"

I snort. "Once or twice."

Or just once.

"Don't worry, I have no problem instructing you as to the proper way to sink a ball."

Why that sounds so dirty, I have no idea.

The devilish glint that lights up his gray eyes tells me the comment came out sounding exactly the way he intended it to.

Five minutes later and we've peeled off our jackets. I take a peek at my surroundings, it's difficult not to notice that the inside of this place is just as derelict and forlorn looking as the outside. There are ten pool tables scattered throughout the space. Sunlight pours in through the grimy windows as neon-colored beer signs blink from the walls.

A few older men are parked at the bar, glasses of beer in front of them as they watch whatever sports program is playing across the TV screen. Since it's barely noon on a Sunday, I'm wondering if they're diehards from the night before or beginning their day with a little hair of the dog that bit them.

Liam grabs a pool stick from the stand on the wall and inspects it carefully before handing it to me. I take hold of it, wondering if I should examine it as well. Although it's not like I'd know what to look for.

He picks out another one for himself before racking the balls on the table. Once he lifts the triangle, they stay in place and his gaze settles expectantly on me. "You want to break?"

My brows draw together as I decide how to go about this. I must look as lost as I feel because he chuckles and leans his stick against the wall before sauntering toward me.

Liam gives me a wink. It's one that should make my pulse skitter. Oddly enough, it doesn't.

"Come here," he says. "I'll show you how to do it."

He moves behind me, wrapping his arms loosely around my body as he positions the stick against my fingers so the wood can slide easily back and forth between them.

Even though this has nothing to do with sex, the purposeful movements have me thinking about other things that were sliding against me only a few short hours ago. My mouth turns cottony as I gulp and push the memory away before it can invade my brain.

"Okay," he says as his warm breath feathers against the outer shell of my ear, "just like this." His chest presses against my back as he pushes my upper body forward until I'm hovering over the rectangular-shaped table. "Spread your legs a bit wider."

The husky command whispered near my ear should leave my breath hitching.

It doesn't.

"That's it," he continues.

I focus on the stick and the white ball I'm aiming for as the slim piece of wood moves easily through my fingers.

"Are you ready?" he asks.

With a nod, I take aim at the white cue ball, hoping it will crash into the triangle of colorful ones, scattering them across the green felt. I'm not completely clueless about pool. I know that if I sink either the solid balls or the striped ones, that will be my color for the rest of the game.

"Nice and easy, baby," he murmurs, "nice and easy."

My stick strikes the white ball which propels it into the triangle of colorful ones in the middle of the table. They scatter in every direction.

Instead of retreating and giving me some breathing room, Liam continues to stand behind me. His arms are loosely wrapped around my body and my back is pressed against the steely strength of his chest. We watch the balls roll across the green felt before settling. The red number three slides into the far-right pocket. As it does, I turn and grin at him.

"See?" he says with an easy smile. "You're a natural."

Rather unattractively, a snort escapes from me. "Let's not get carried away. I think it was more beginner's luck." But it's kind of fun. Especially since we pretty much have the place to ourselves. Other than the guys at the bar, the pool hall is empty. Over the next hour and a half, we play three games.

Even though this is kind of a date—sort of—I'm not nervous around Liam. It feels more like two friends hanging out. Easy and relaxed. Low key. There's absolutely no pressure at all. No thick tension that leaves the nerves prickling uneasily at the bottom of my gut.

The only one I've ever felt that way with is Sam. The realization has my thoughts drifting back to him. For the first time in my life, our normally easy relationship feels full of complications and pitfalls. And then there's the weird sexual tension that vibrates between us whenever we're together.

After a while, Liam grabs a couple of Cokes from the bar. Since I'm intent on avoiding the entire Sam situation at his apartment, I'm more than happy to start another game. Not that I'll ever be a pool shark, but I'm holding my own against Liam. Or maybe he's just letting me think I am.

It doesn't matter. I'm having fun.

Liam breaks, immediately sinking two solid-colored balls. When he's finished with his turn, his gaze flickers to me. "So, you and Harper go way back, huh?"

I assess the table carefully, studying the placement of the striped balls before deciding which one would be easiest to knock into a pocket. I may not win the game, but that doesn't mean that I don't want to sink as many of them as possible. "Yup. We met in eighth grade when I moved in with my grandparents. Our families are neighbors and we've been friends ever since."

With my stick in hand, I take aim and hit the green striped number fourteen and then the red striped eleven. I flash him a smug smile when both balls end up exactly where I intended them to.

Which is inside a pocket.

Any damn pocket.

His lips curve in response as he pushes away from the wood paneled wall where he's been lounging. Silently, he studies the table before taking aim. "Have you two ever hooked up?"

Even though he never glances up from the green felt, my gaze flies to him.

If you had asked that question a month ago, I would have died laughing because I couldn't imagine feeling sexually attracted to Sam.

Clearly that's no longer the case. But there's no way I'm going to reveal the truth to Liam. "Nope. We've always been friends."

And we're still friends. Although it feels different now. Unwanted memories from last night crash through my mind. I can't help but remember the hot licks of jealousy that arrowed through me as the waitress made cow eyes at Sam. Or trailed her fingers over his bicep.

Grrrr.

I have to shake my head to clear it of all those unwanted thoughts. Liam glances up and captures my gaze right before sliding the stick easily through his fingers. The white cue ball knocks into both the yellow number one and the green number six. Both find their way into a pocket.

"Lucky shot," I mumble. Although it probably isn't luck at all. Liam is good at the game. *Really good.*

As his lips curve into a smug smile, his dimples flash and wink. Is there no end to his hotness? And why isn't it doing a damn thing for me?

"Just keep telling yourself that, sweetheart."

His words have me sticking out my tongue in response.

"Be careful," he warns lazily as his gray eyes sparkle, "I just might get ideas."

I can't help but snort.

For whatever reason, I don't think that's the case. There isn't any sexual tension simmering in the air between us. Not like there is with a certain someone else.

Two more turns and the game ends. Liam wins three times, while I win once. As I grab my jacket, ready to take off, his gaze settles on me. It's almost as if I'm being silently assessed. For what, I have no idea. When I give him a questioning look, his eyes narrow. After we leave the pool hall, he removes the black helmet from the back of the bike and places it over my head.

He hesitates as his gaze searches mine. Before I can ask what's wrong, his face lowers to mine. The breath catches at the back of my throat. Because of his notoriety with the ladies, I expect him to be forceful and take control of the situation.

The kiss turns out to be nothing like that.

It's gently that his lips sweep over mine before settling on them. As the caress unfolds, it's slow and leisure. Almost as if we have all the time in the world to explore one another. The unhurried way his mouth slides over mine has my eyelids feathering shut as I open to him.

This is exactly what I need.

Someone to take my mind off Sam. And who better to do that than the much sought-after quarterback for the Barnett Bulldogs?

Sexy-as-sin Liam Garrison.

If anyone can get me to forget about what happened this morning in Sam's apartment, it would be him, right?

So, I'm going for it. I'm going to totally let this happen. As far as I'm concerned, it *needs* to occur. It feels like my friendship with Sam depends on it.

All right, that's a lot of pressure I'm heaping on to myself. I need to dial it down a few notches and chill.

Liam's tongue slips inside my mouth to mingle with my own. There is no tentativeness in the way he strokes it against me or the way his fingers curl around the back of my neck, holding me in place while he explores every inch of my mouth.

It goes without saying that Liam knows how to kiss. As the caress unfolds, I can't help but think that this experience is quite pleasant. Unfortunately, that's all it is.

Pleasant.

There aren't any sparks or fireworks.

It's just...*nice.*

Nothing more.

Nothing less.

I'm certainly not mindless with the desire he's carefully stoking to life inside me.

When Liam finally breaks away, a thoughtful expression mars his handsome face. His gray gaze searches mine before he releases a puff of breath. The sound is chock-full of regret.

"Yeah, that's pretty much what I was thinking, too," he says.

Huh?

My brows draw together as his strange comment rattles around inside my head. Before I can ask what it means, he's pulling the black helmet over his head and hopping onto the bike. And then we're taking off, flying back toward campus.

Chapter Thirteen

VIOLET

When I make it back to the guy's apartment, Sam is nowhere to be found and Roan is walking out the door. He's hitting the library for some research and won't be home until after dinner. It's probably not a good sign that my first reaction is relief.

Now I can throw all my stuff into a bag and get the hell out of here before Sam returns. Then, from the relative safety of my dorm, I can take a few days to think about what's going on between us. I'm hoping that with enough time and distance, these feelings will simmer down and—

My phone dings with an incoming text.

I grab it and scan the message.

Crap.

Carter is going to stay for another night.

My belly flips in response to that bit of unwelcome news. All I want is to make a clean get away before Sam returns and forces me to discuss all the issues that have sprung up between us. That's the last thing I want to do. Doesn't he understand that avoidance is the best possible tactic at this point?

Every time he popped into my head today, my mind circled back to the morning wood he was grinding against me.

And how much I liked it.

Yeah...we definitely need distance. Just a little bit of space so our relationship can slide back to normal. The only way that's going to happen is if I clear out of here and get back to my own place.

Damn Mia and her loud-ass boyfriend!

All right, they're both loud as hell.

As much as I would dearly love to tell her to forget it, I can't. Mia and Carter don't get to see each other very often, so how can I crash the little lovefest they've got going on over there?

I just can't do it.

And I'm certainly not sleeping in the commons area on our dorm floor again.

I guess that means I'm stuck here until tomorrow. That is if Sam is cool with it. If not, I could always crash at my grandparent's house. Although, since I don't have a car, I'll have to catch the bus to get across town.

As all of this rolls around in my head, a key is jammed into the door. My heart stutters in response as a sweaty looking Sam walks into the apartment. Even though it's about forty-degrees outside, he's wearing long gray athletic shorts and a black T-shirt that has the sleeves ripped off. He's holding a Barnett Bulldogs sweatshirt in one hand and a large plastic water bottle in the other.

Unable to move, I stand motionless. As his gaze slices to mine, I give him a tentative smile. My heart thuds heavily against my chest as air gets trapped in the middle of my throat. When he gives an answering nod in response, everything in me loosens.

For whatever reason, I thought he might be mad that I took off with Liam after breakfast. That doesn't appear to be the case. Although, when it comes down to it, there's no reason for him to be angry that I'm spending time with another guy.

I shift, already feeling the thick tension as it settles over us. The easy camaraderie that has always been a part of our friendship is nowhere to be found.

Sam goes to the fridge and grabs an orange Gatorade before twisting off the top. He guzzles down half the bottle in one fell swoop.

Transfixed by the sight, I can't help but stare at the way his throat works as he takes long swallows of the beverage.

That really shouldn't be so sexy.

Like at all.

He's just drinking Gatorade, for goodness' sake.

And yet, here I am totally staring. Possibly drooling. Almost nonchalantly, I swipe my fingers across my lower lip just in case. I think I might be losing it. What other rational explanation could there be? Lusting after Sam feels all kinds of wrong.

Maybe it's for the best if I avoid the entire situation and stay with my grandparents. I can spend some quality time with them. But then I'm stuck riding the bus and it'll take more than an hour to get there. Not to mention getting back to school tomorrow morning with all my crap in tow.

Unsure what to do, I scrub a hand over my face as an internal debate wages within me.

"Is something wrong?" he asks.

My gaze snaps to his as he leans against the kitchen counter before finishing off his drink.

"What?" I clear my throat because that came out sounding more like a croak.

"Was there a problem with Garrison?" His thickly corded muscles tense. His arms bulge and flex as the question whips from his mouth. All of the sudden, he looks pissed as hell. "I'll kick his damn ass if—"

I shake my head. "No, nothing like that." He thinks this has to do with Liam? Thank goodness for that.

As he studies me from across the small space, his expression turns hesitant. "Everything go all right with that?"

I shrug. For some reason, I don't want to discuss the time I spent with Liam. It's not uncommon for Sam and me to discuss the people we're seeing. Normally, we don't hold anything back. Now that I think about it, I suspect it might be one of the reasons why neither of us have had a lasting relationship.

"Yeah," I say. "He took me for a ride on his bike and then we played a few games of pool."

Sam's brows draw together as he folds his arms across his chest.

The way he stands with his legs spread a couple of feet apart, muscles tensed, and head cocked shouldn't look so sexy. And it certainly shouldn't have my panties flooding with heat either.

"You don't play pool," he says.

I give him a wan smile, wanting whatever is happening to my body to simmer down and dissipate. "Guess I do now."

An unintelligible sound rumbles up from deep within his throat. "If there's not a problem with Garrison, then what's going on?"

I nibble at my lower lip before reluctantly admitting, "Mia wants to know if I can stay here for another night. Carter is going to stick around a little longer than expected." It would be in everyone's best interest if Sam kicked my ass to the curb. I wouldn't even question it. I'd just grab my stuff and get out of here before anything else happened.

Instead, his eyes narrow and his dark blond brows draw together as if he doesn't understand. "Why would that be a problem?" His expression is one of confusion, which is good. It means that whatever is going on between us is purely one-sided.

It's *my* problem.

One he's blissfully unaware of.

All of the anxiety careening around inside me dissolves at the realization and I almost smile in relief. "It's not." Then I toss in, "I don't want to be in your way."

He rolls his eyes like I said the stupidest thing ever. "Seriously? Why would you even think something like that? Plus, we have the spare room. It's not a problem at all." For a moment, his gaze searches mine as if he's trying to get to the bottom of what's going on inside my head.

Good luck, buddy. Not even I know what's going on in there.

"You're always welcome here," Sam says. "You never have to ask."

Since I don't want to act any weirder than I already am, I nod my head in acceptance.

It's one more night. What can possibly happen in twelve short hours?

Absolutely nothing.

I'll hole up in Dylan's old room with claims of studying my little tushie off, then I'll hit the sack early, and clear out even earlier in the morning.

It'll be fine.

"I'm going to head over to the dorms and pick up a few things." Another outfit, clean underwear, and a few books for class tomorrow.

"Here." He tosses his keys at me. "Just take the truck."

I catch them midair. "Are you sure?" It's not like I haven't driven his vehicle before, but still...

"Yeah, Vi, I'm sure. What are you going to do? Trek across campus loaded down with stuff?" He shakes his head like I'm making a big deal out of nothing. And maybe I am. Who knows anymore? "Just take the truck and then we'll figure out what to do for dinner. Okay?"

Yeah, that sounds good.

And you know what?

It almost feels as if everything has slid back to the way it should be.

"Thanks. I'll be back in about thirty minutes."

"All right, I'm going to jump in the shower." As he slides past me, I find myself trying to catch a whiff of him as he heads toward his bedroom. He should smell all gross and disgusting from working out.

He doesn't.

"I'll see you in a little bit," I call after him.

With his keys in hand, I head for the door. By the time I get to his pickup parked in front of the building and pull it into gear, I realize that I forgot my dorm keys.

Crap.

I slip back into the parking space and turn off the truck before jumping out and heading into the apartment. Using Sam's key to open the door, I fly inside. As I turn the corner into the short hallway that leads to Dylan's bedroom, I realize the bathroom door is wide open.

I stumble to a halt when my gaze lands on Sam as he's drying his hair with a towel.

Naked.

He doesn't have one stitch of clothing on.

Or a towel to cover him.

Unable to move a muscle, I stand transfixed. An odd sort of paralysis takes hold of me as my gaze licks over every exquisite inch of him.

And he is, without a doubt, exquisite.

I knew Sam was ripped. He works out religiously and has been playing football for fifteen years. I've caught sight of him without a shirt on lots of times. Just this morning, for instance. Not to mention, last night. My gaze had lingered on his broad chest before dropping down to his—

Gulp.

And there it is.

He isn't hard.

Another gulp.

Not like this morning. His thick cock lies there, nestled between those tree-trunk sized thighs of his. Even though he isn't stiff, his size is still impressive.

I'm pretty sure I just gasped.

Or moaned.

Or emitted some kind of sound because he lowers the towel from his face as his blue gaze locks on my wide one. Surprise flashes in his eyes. Neither of us say one damn word.

Not.

One.

Damn.

Word.

I'm held totally immobilized by the sight before me. My brain is firing off commands—*close your eyes! Run! Turn away!* But my body isn't receiving the signals. I'm stuck standing here slack-jawed like a sheltered virgin who has never seen a penis before, which is the furthest thing from the truth and yet, I'm still gaping.

This is definitely not one of my finer moments.

All Sam has to do is reach out and slam the door in my face. Then the horror currently taking place would be over. Instead, he stands there, gaze holding mine.

No, that's not quite right.

It's not just *holding* mine.

More like *blazing* with heat and intensity and—

Oh, God.

Don't do it.

My gaze drops to his long thick...*erection*.

When the hell did *that* happen?

All of a sudden, he's rock-hard.

Rock.

Hard.

My mouth turns cottony as I stare at his gorgeous cock.

Holy shit.

Did I seriously just think that?

"Violet."

The low growl emanating from deep within his chest has my gaze snapping to his. Even though my throat is drier than the desert, I gulp. I've never seen his eyes flash with such intensity. It's enough to have me breaking free from the stupor that has fallen over me.

That's when my fight or flight response kicks in. I turn tail and flee the apartment before racing down the steps as fast as my feet will take me. Since his keys are still clasped in my hand, I jump back inside the pickup and throw the gear into reverse before peeling out of the parking lot.

Holy shit.

I just saw Sam with a massive boner.

And all I could do was stare in total fascination.

This is bad.

Really, really bad.

Chapter Fourteen

VIOLET

When I find the courage to slink back to the guy's apartment, it's well after midnight. Everything is dark and silent. I don't realize that I'm holding my breath until it rushes out in relief. There's no way I could face Sam right now. I'm embarrassed by my own behavior. Instead of turning away when I saw him, I stood there and gawked at his cock like a perv.

His very *hard*, very *thick* cock.

I really need to stop thinking about that. It's one thing to feel it nestled against my ass in the wee hours of the morning, separated by at least two layers of clothing, and quite another to catch a glimpse—all right, way more than a glimpse—up close and personal. If I had to, I could probably render a fairly accurate description to a sketch artist.

Or pick it out of a line up.

This is terrible.

And we certainly aren't going to talk about how I was tempted to get even more up close and personal with his erection either.

Unfortunately, I've been unable to think about little else since the incident occurred.

Why can't I laugh the entire episode off? We should both be able to do that. For all I know, he already has. Sam shot me a text earlier, but I couldn't bring myself to respond. I needed time to pull myself together again. All I want to do is shake off the uncomfortable situation and move on. And yet, that feels impossible. Our entire relationship seems to be teetering on the brink of disaster.

For a good hour or so, I debated the merits of grabbing some stuff from the dorm and crashing with my grandparents, but there are books I need in Dylan's room. Plus, I still have Sam's truck.

I can't hijack his vehicle, now can I?

Well...maybe I could.

If I puss out now, things will only get weirder than they already are. And I don't want that to happen. So, I've come back to face the music but that doesn't mean I'm not relieved to face it tomorrow morning rather than tonight.

This has got to be like the fourth bullet I've dodged today.

I don't even know anymore. I've lost count.

Quietly, I tiptoe into the bedroom I've been staying in before locking the door behind me. As I do, everything in me collapses. All I want is to dive under the covers, squeeze my eyes tightly shut, and fall asleep. Maybe when I wake up in the morning, this whole cock incident won't seem nearly as bad as if feels.

I wince. Now I've mentally dubbed it *the cock incident*.

Perfect. Just perfect.

I quickly change before hopping into Dylan's queen-size bed. Any other night, I would wash my face and brush my teeth. Maybe even take a hot shower. But not tonight. Nope. There is no way I'm going to chance another run-in with Sam. I'll scrub everything extra-hard in the morning.

As I slide beneath the covers, I release a puff of air and close my eyes. This day feels like it lasted forever. Hopefully, when I wake up in the morning, I'll realize that what transpired between us wasn't such a big deal after all.

So what if I saw his cock?

Who cares?

I mean, we're both adults. It's not like I haven't seen half a dozen other ones before. Although, it's definitely been a while since I saw one that was so long and thick.

As that thought settles within me, I flip over onto my side and desperately try to dislodge the image from my mind. His erection had risen from a nest of dark blond curls. And then there had been those heavy looking ba—

My eyes snap open.

What the hell am I doing?

No...seriously?

I throw myself onto my other side before huffing out a frustrated breath. After a few minutes, I pound my fist into the pillow, attempting to even out the fluff.

No more thinking about Sam's girthy cock.

Goddamn it!

Sam is my friend. My *best* friend. Next to my grandparents, he's all I have. I'm unwilling to risk our friendship over a bit of sexual attraction. Not only would that be shortsighted, but it would also be stupid. There is no way you can have sex with someone and remain best buddies afterward. It doesn't work that way. I have a terrible dating track record. I'm barely friends with the guys I've slept with. Sure, they're nice enough when I see them out and they're trying to get inside my pants, but other than that?

Not so much.

I refuse to risk our eight-year friendship for a roll in the sheets.

When fifteen more minutes creep by, it becomes apparent that I won't be able to stop thinking about what happened with Sam. Not that anything actually happened because it most definitely did not.

Know what's even worse than not being able to stop thinking about the massive erection he had been sporting?

That my panties are now soaked. I'm so turned on that I can barely think straight. My clit is throbbing to some imaginary tempo.

Pulsing, pulsing, pulsing...

When my fingers slide their way inside my panties, I don't bother to fool myself about what's going on. I know *exactly* what has stoked the flames of my desire to such a fevered pitch. And it has nothing to do with Liam Garrison's kiss earlier this afternoon.

Honestly, I haven't even thought about it.

Not one damn time.

Now that I've committed to this little self-love session, I slide my panties down my legs before kicking them off under the covers. Then I squeeze my eyes shut and widen my thighs, groaning at the first flick of my fingers over the smooth flesh before zeroing in on my already throbbing clit.

I don't remember how long it's been since I've felt this horny.

Even though I try to fantasize about someone else—*anyone else*—my mind keeps circling back to Sam. And the way he held me in his arms this morning. His palm cupping and squeezing my breast. His heavy erection pressing against my panty-covered ass.

With a little more pressure, my fingers work my flesh faster with quick, circular strokes. My legs fall open as I arch off the mattress. A moan escapes from between my parted lips as I caress that little bundle of nerves.

Oh, God. I'm going to—

"Vi?"

A soft knock on the bedroom door has my eyelids flying open and my heart nearly seizing. But my fingers don't stop. I'm too damn close. My body is strung tighter than a bow, and I am literally *aching* for release.

I grit my teeth and bite out a response. "Yeah?" The word sounds low and forced. I should stop touching myself while he's standing outside the door, but I can't. It feels way too good. And his deep voice only turns me on more. I have to bite my lip to stifle the little whimper that is trying desperately to escape.

"Open the door so we can talk."

Oh, hell no!

That is *so* not going to happen.

Even though I'm horrified by the idea of him seeing me like this, my fingers keep moving. Circling. I'm so slippery, and it feels so damn good. Especially when my fingers buzz lightly over my clit. My teeth sink deep into my lower lip in an effort to keep everything bottled up inside.

"No," I gasp. As much as I fight to keep my voice level, it's not. "We'll talk tomorrow."

As soon as those guttural-sounding words roll off my lips, the door handle rattles. I can almost imagine Sam with his hand wrapped around the knob as he attempts to get inside. For some strange reason, that image morphs into one where he's slowly pumping his hand over his thick erection as I watch.

Thank freaking God that I had the foresight to lock the door.

"Let me in, Vi."

That image is all it takes for me to shatter. And this time, I'm unable to choke back the low moan of pleasure that escapes.

"Well, you sure are here bright and early."

My grandmother pulls me in for a warm hug as I step inside the sunny kitchen.

I shrug, and say with an overly cheerful smile, "I've missed you guys, and thought I'd swing by for breakfast."

Those words have her lips tilting up at the corners. "Aww, you're such a sweet girl." In the very next breath, she adds, "You should have brought Sam with you."

Yeah...there's no way that was going to happen. Even the thought is enough to leave me wincing. I couldn't get out of the apartment fast enough this morning. As soon as I heard Sam and Roan take off for their workout, I threw my things into a bag and flew out the door.

Kind of like an escape convict fleeing the scene of a heinous crime.

After last night, there was no way in hell I was sticking around for their return. As much as I would love to hash all this out with Sam and get our friendship back on track, I can't do it right now. My emotions are all over the place.

If everything were normal between us, we could sit down and laugh our asses off about this. But...

I just can't do that.

Not after last night. Not after seeing him standing there naked. His body had been so big and beautiful. Those thick slabs of muscle all gleaming wet with droplets of water. I'd stood there immobilized, staring at him, wanting to lick all the moisture from his body. Not to mention, stroke my hands over all those solid ridges.

Then later that evening—him knocking on the door while I'd been touching myself. And fantasizing about him. About that hard body. His erect cock. The way he'd rattled the door handle, attempting to get inside.

Had he realized what I'd been up to?

Could he hear me?

No matter how hard I tried, I just couldn't stop all the pent-up pleasure from escaping when I'd orgasmed. There had been bite marks on my lower lip where my teeth sunk into the plump flesh in an effort to stifle the cries.

It hadn't worked.

As much as I hate to admit it, him standing outside the door, demanding to be let inside had only made the situation hotter. When I finally came, I'd practically saw stars, it was so damn intense. And that hasn't happened in I-don't-know-how-long. Actually, I don't think I've ever made myself come that hard.

Unconsciously, my hands rise to my cheeks. They feel like they're on fire.

"Hun, you doing okay?" A small frown mars my grandmother's face as she glances over at me. "You look flushed."

Ugh.

How am I going to look Sam in the eyes again, let alone be in the same room with him without dying of total embarrassment?

I have know idea.

"I'm fine," I mumble before settling at the table. I need to stop thinking about this before I burst into flames. "It's nothing."

Her brows pinch together in concern. "Hmmm. Maybe you're coming down with something." She goes to the refrigerator and takes out a half-gallon jug of orange juice before pouring a tall glass and placing it in front of me.

No amount of vitamin C is going to fix this mess.

"Drink up," she instructs. "I don't want you to get sick."

Then she's off to the cabinet, rifling through the contents before finding whatever bottle she's searching for. Airborne. She sets the huge container of gummies in front of me. "You better take these back to school with you. Can't be too careful about all those germs flying around."

Instead of arguing, because I know a losing battle when I see one, I agree. "Okay." Better for her to think that, than suspect the truth.

She places her hands on her slender hips. "Why didn't Sam come home with you? I miss seeing his handsome face around here."

A puff of displeasure escapes from my lips. I was hoping she would forget about that line of questioning. Guess I should have known better. Gran may be climbing into her seventies, but the woman has a mind like a steel trap. Worse, she can ferret out a lie within minutes of it rolling off my tongue. I'll have to play this one cool. There is no way I want to discuss the *cock incident* with her. Or has it now been more appropriately dubbed—*the cock/rubbing-one-out incident?*

I'm tempted to bang my head against the table to loosen those thoughts from my brain.

Before I can do that, my grandmother lays a palm across my forehead. "You're looking flushed again, sweetie. Maybe you should lie down for a bit and I'll call the school and tell them that you're not feeling well. You can stay here and take it easy for the rest of the day."

For the first time all morning, my lips twitch. I really love my gran. She's the best. "No, that's not necessary."

Concern flares in her soft, hazel eyes. "You need to take better care of yourself, Violet. If you run yourself ragged, you'll wear yourself down and end up catching something."

"I'm fine," I say, attempting to reassure her again. "You don't have to worry about me."

She makes a noncommittal noise in her throat as if she doesn't believe me. My grandmother has always been overprotective where I'm concerned, and who can blame her? She lost her only son, daughter-in-law, and granddaughter in a car accident eight years ago. Beside my grandfather, I'm all she has left.

So, I get it.

I feel the same way about them. Without my grandparents, who would I have? That thought brings a boulder-sized lump of emotion to my throat, making it impossible to swallow.

The answer to that question is *Sam.*

Next to my grandparents, he's the most important person in my life and right now, we're having...*issues.* I don't really understand what's going on between us. All I know is that it's making our relationship feel awkward.

To the point where I've gone into avoidance mode.

Since I have no idea how to fix this problem, I'm left to wonder how our relationship can survive. The feelings I've developed for Sam keep steamrolling over me when I least expect them to.

It makes me wonder if we'll ever be the same again. Will we ever just be Sam and Violet? Best friends? Completely platonic? Can-talk-about-any-and-everything and nothing affects our relationship?

I don't have an answer to that. And that's scary considering how important he is to me.

As all of this churns in my head, my gaze returns to my grandmother and the concern written clearly across her face. Guilt hits me like a swift punch to the gut for not being straight-up with her. The last thing I want to do is let her think that something is wrong with me when there's not. Especially when my grandfather hasn't been feeling well lately.

As she cracks two eggs and scrambles them in a pan, I decide this is as good of a time to come clean as any. It might even be a relief to tell someone what's really going on. For obvious reasons, I can't talk to Sam about this. And Mia is tied up with Carter.

Figuratively, not literally...I hope.

Gran is the only other person who might understand the situation. She knows how special my relationship with Sam is. Surely, she'll be able to see how foolish it would be to jeopardize our friendship.

That being said, there is no way I'm telling her about cock-gate or me getting off with him standing outside the door last night. There are some things that can't be discussed with a grandparent, and this is definitely one of them.

"Sweetheart, you better take some of that Airborne right now. You're looking positively feverish."

"I'm not sick, Gran." I inhale a deep breath. "It's something else."

She stands at the stove with a spatula in hand as her gaze holds mine. "Oh?"

This is more difficult than I expected. I focus on my half-filled glass of orange juice before deciding to drink some down. Maybe the vitamin C will help boost my courage.

"It has to do with Sam," I mumble, barely loud enough for her to catch. Although my grandmother has excellent hearing, so she picks up on my words without any problem.

Her face creases with worry. Ugh...I am killing this poor woman with my ineptness. "What happened to Sam? Is he all right? Is there something we can do to help?"

"No, I mean Yes..." Oh, for the love of all that's holy, I don't know any more. "Maybe."

"Well, that certainly clears things up." A small smile tips the corners of her lips as I torture myself. "Thank you."

A weak chuckle escapes. Why does this have to be such a mess? All I want is for everything to go back to the way things were before. That's what would be best for everyone. Then we could just be Violet and Sam, like we've always been. There wouldn't be any of these tangled feelings to muck things up.

"I don't know, Gran." I pause, drawing in a deep breath and attempting to calm my nerves. Admitting how I feel shouldn't be so scary. "I'm really confused right now."

She slides the scrambled eggs onto a plate before setting it down in front of me and taking a seat at the table. "Can I assume this confusion has something to do with Sam?"

Relief rushes through me that I didn't have to voice the words out loud. I shovel a forkful of eggs into my mouth. Between bites I say, "I think my feelings for him are changing." My belly trembles as I give voice to the truth.

Gran is quiet for a long, contemplative moment. When I begin to wonder if she'll respond, she asks, "And that's a bad thing?"

Fork poised midway to my mouth, I nod my head. Doesn't she understand what a catastrophe this is? "It has the potential to be."

It would ruin our friendship.

"Sam is a wonderful boy, Violet." She shakes her head as if I'm doing a simple arithmetic problem and she's stumped as to how I continually arrive at the wrong answer when the right one is so obvious. "Why would you think that? Ever since you two found each other when you were fourteen years old, you've been thick as thieves. I've never seen two people better suited to one another than you and Sam."

I shovel in another bite and point the empty fork at her. "That's *exactly* why this feels like a disaster waiting to happen. He's my best friend, and I don't want to ruin our friendship over feelings that probably won't last."

Just as she opens her mouth, I cut in sharply, "Even you have to admit that I'm not the poster child for successful and long-lasting relationships." With a snort, I add, "I'm more like the kiss of death."

She places her hand over mine and gives it a gentle squeeze. "Maybe that's because you haven't found the right guy."

"Maybe there's no such thing as *the right guy*," I fire back.

She quirks a brow. "The right girl then? Because if that's the case, I'll have you know that your grandfather and I are quite progressive thinkers on the subject."

Caught off guard by the question, I can't help but dissolve into a fit of giggles. It feels so good to laugh about something. "No, that's not the issue, but I'm glad to hear you're down with the LGBT movement." I shake my head and sigh, "I don't know what the problem is, Gran. I never seem to click with any of the guys I'm with. I end up," I shrug, "losing interest in them, I guess."

There always comes a point when I realize that I'm wasting my time, and I'd rather hang out with someone who gets my jokes. Someone I'm totally in sync with. Someone I can be myself around.

I grimace as those thoughts roll through my head.

Jeez.

Only now do I realize that I've been sabotaging every relationship because I'd much rather spend time with Sam than get to know someone new. Or maybe the guys I pick aren't able to live up to the guy I already have in my life.

Ugh. This situation is much worse than I originally suspected.

With a tilt of her head, Gran scrutinizes me. "Are you going to tell me what happened with Sam to send you running back here so early in the morning?" One brow arches across her forehead as she patiently waits for my response.

Nothing *per se* has happened. Sam hasn't done or said anything. I'm not even sure if he realizes there's a problem. For all I know, I've blown this whole situation out of proportion.

These feelings are beginning to affect how I feel when we're together and I hate that.

I hate that I act differently around him.

I hate these little sparks of jealousy that flare to life within me.

Or that I now look at him in a different way.

Or that I can't stop thinking about him.

When the hell did I become so obsessed with Sam Harper?

Now that I've uncovered more of the truth, I realize the shift in our relationship has been a long time in the making.

Reluctantly, I admit what I can no longer hide. "My feelings have changed where Sam is concerned. It's been happening for a while. I didn't realize it, or maybe I didn't want to acknowledge it to myself. It's like I can't even look at him the way I used to. And I don't know what to do about it." I gulp before forcing out the rest, "Do I sit on it, and hope that it's just a phase? That everything will go back to the way it was? Or should I act on these feelings?" When I finally run out of steam, I stare anxiously at my grandmother in hopes that she'll have a sage piece of advice to dole out because right now, I need it.

I'm all but drowning in my confusion and self-induced misery.

Silently, she pulls me into her arms before gently rubbing my back with comforting strokes. "Now, was it so hard to admit that you have romantic feelings for Sam?"

The woman is kidding, right?

"Umm, yeah," I murmur against her shoulder, "it was." What this means is that nothing will ever be the same between us again. I realize it, even if Gran doesn't. Not all change is good. Sometimes you end up losing the people you hold dearest.

With a chuckle, she admonishes, "No, it wasn't." There's a pause before she continues, "You've always been a brave girl, Violet." Gran pulls away enough to search my eyes. "But not with love. You've spent the last eight years safeguarding your heart and I can't really say I blame you for it. You've already lost so much. I understand why you'd be reluctant to experience any more heartbreak."

The softly spoken comment sends a rush of hot tears to my eyes.

She's right.

The loss of my parents and younger sister was soul crushing. Maybe I did build walls around my heart as a way of protecting myself. Sam, however, has always been the chink in my armor. He snuck past all my defenses when we were still kids. I trusted him from the beginning and not once has he let me down. He's always been there to protect and hold me close.

His friendship isn't something I take lightly or for granted. No matter how long I live, there's no way I'll find another friend like Sam. Our relationship is rare. Precious. And I would be a fool to let it slip through my fingers over fickle feelings of attraction. I've experienced that firsthand. True friendship is difficult to come by.

"At some point, you'll have to decide if your feelings are worth taking a chance on. Love is always a gamble, sweetheart. But finding that person, *the right one*, is always worth the risk."

Maybe she's right.

But I also know that some things are just too important to gamble away.

I bump open the door with my hip and heft my bags into the suite. I can't deny the sharp shafts of relief that pump through me. Distance and perspective are exactly what's needed right now.

With a quick glance around, I catch sight of Mia sitting on the couch in the living area we share.

When she remains silent, lost in her own thoughts, I call out, "Hello!"

Her head swivels toward me before a ghost of a smile curves her lips. "Hey, girl. Thanks again for clearing out for the past couple of days, I really appreciate it. I hope everything was cool with Sam."

Yeah...we're not going to discuss that situation at the moment.

Or possibly ever.

"It was fine. How did your visit with Carter go? Did you guys have a good time?" Before she can answer, I throw up a hand. "If you're going to tell me that you two never left the room and it was just one long marathon of sexy times, I'd rather not hear the gory details, thank you very much."

The forced smile stays glued to her lips. I thought for sure that would get an exaggerated eye roll or maybe even a chuckle. *Something.*

Instead, she says, "Yeah, it was nice. I feel bad for kicking you out of the suite for three days. I owe you big time."

I've known Mia long enough to realize that something is off with her behavior. I drop my bags by the door to my room before settling on the chair next to her. "Is everything okay?"

After having Carter all to herself for a long weekend, Mia should be flying high. Or is she missing her boyfriend already? Like me, Mia will graduate in May. I know living in different cities has been a challenge for the couple, but she only has one more semester to go and then they'll be together again.

Silence falls over us and it only rachets up my growing concern. Just when I wonder if she'll answer, Mia murmurs, "We went out for dinner last night and Carter proposed."

Shock reverberates through me. All I can do is stare as those words sink in.

Proposal.

Carter and Mia.

Marriage.

"*Holy shit*!" I jump off the chair and hurtle myself at my bestie before proceeding to squeeze the life out of her. "Congratulations! I can't believe this! You must be so excited!"

It's only when her body remains stiff that I untangle myself from her. As our gazes collide, air gets trapped in my lungs.

"I," she gulps, "I told him no."

My eyes widen as I repeat, "*You said no?*"

"I had to." Her tone turns defensive. "Come on, Violet, I'm twenty-two years old! I haven't even graduated from college yet. I have no idea what he was thinking by asking me to marry him." She tosses her hands up in the air. "I mean, he never even brought up the subject before last night. Never bothered to ask if that's what I wanted or was ready for."

My expression sobers. I'm almost afraid to ask for more details. "What did you tell him?"

"That I was nowhere near ready to get married." Even though I hear her giving voice to the words, I can't believe they're actually coming out of her mouth.

Carter proposed.

And Mia said *no*.

It feels like I've entered the Twilight Zone.

"What happened after that?"

She blows out a long breath as moisture gathers in her eyes. It takes effort for her to blink it away. Mia isn't an overly emotional person. In the years that I've known her, rarely have I seen her moved to the point of tears. And it breaks my heart to see it now. "He was," she pauses before forcing out the rest on a broken whisper, "*upset*. He asked if I wanted to break up."

"Did you?" Mia and Carter have been together for two years and in the blink of an eye, they're talking about breaking up?

What the hell is going on here?

How does something like that happen?

She gives her head a slight shake. "No. I told him that I want to marry him someday, just not right now. If I'm being totally honest, probably not for a while. I'm not in any hurry to tie myself down. We have the rest of our lives for that. Why do we have to rush into it?" Her hand drifts to her forehead before she rubs her left temple as if there's a massive headache brewing there.

"Was he okay with that?"

My guess is that he wasn't. How could he be?

"No, it ruined the rest of the night. Even though I tried to pretend everything was fine, it wasn't. He barely spoke to me after that. I was hoping it would be smoothed over by the morning, but he was still quiet when he headed home." Mia shrugs as if she genuinely has no idea what the future holds for them.

There's no way Carter would want to lose Mia over this. He adores her. They're perfect for each other. "I'm sure he needs a little time to work everything out in his head." I bite down on my lower lip before adding, "He's probably embarrassed that you turned him down."

"Yeah, well...he shouldn't have blindsided me."

"Have you spoken to him at all?"

She shakes her head as guilt flickers across her expression. "He texted after he made it home, but that's it." Sorrow fills her big green eyes, and my heart goes out to her. "I'm going to let things settle for a few days and then I'll give him a call. Make sure we're okay." Mia's attitude doesn't surprise me. She's a very cut and dry, no-nonsense kind of person. Emotional upheavals are not her thing.

"I'm sure everything will be fine. Carter loves you."

Even though she nods, doubt is etched across every line of her face. "I don't understand why he thought it would be a good time to propose. It doesn't make any sense. It's not like I was hinting around at a ring or picking out names for our kids." She twists her fingers together in her lap. "I want to focus on finishing school and launching my career." Mia is one of the lucky ones, she spent the last two summers interning for an IT company not far from where Carter lives, and they've already extended an offer for full time employment after she graduates. "Maybe go to grad school in a few years. I want to be established in my career before I even think about any of that other stuff."

"You did the right thing. It would have been so much worse if you'd actually said yes and then tried to break it off later."

The color drains from her face. "When he pulled out the box, I just sat there, completely frozen," she admits quietly. "My heart sank. I wanted to jump up and tell him to put it back in his pocket and we could pretend it never happened."

"I'm sorry," I say softly. "I can't imagine how hard that must have been."

"Yeah, it sucked. What hurt most was how distraught he was." She swipes at the wetness shining in her eyes. "You should have seen the look on his face when I said *no*."

I reach out and slip her fingers into mine before giving them a gentle squeeze. "It'll be all right. He just needs some time to get over it."

"I hope so, Vi. I really do love him. I just don't need to be a child bride to prove it."

I can't help the gurgle of laughter that escapes from my mouth. "Definitely not."

After a few moments, she changes the subject. "Did you and Sam have a good time this weekend?"

"Yup." Even though I try to keep my expression blank, there must be something that gives me away.

Her eyes narrow. "Hmmm. Why don't I believe you?"

I shrug. "Dunno."

"You know what I think?"

I shake my head. Although, I can guess.

"I think something happened this weekend."

Heat floods into my cheeks. "Nothing happened," I mumble.

"Oh, my God! You're blushing!"

Ugh. She's right, my face is definitely heating up.

When I remain silent, she wheedles, "Come on, you know you want to tell me."

No, I don't. There's a part of me that wants to forget everything that occurred this weekend.

I shake my head before muttering in an offhanded manner, "It's nothing really."

This only makes her chuckle more. She's practically rubbing her hands together with anticipation. "How about you tell me what it is, and I'll be the judge of that."

Her comment leaves me groaning.

Instead of revealing the real issue that had me hightailing it out of Sam's apartment at the crack of dawn this morning, I say, "I went out with Liam yesterday."

Her eyes nearly bulge out of their sockets as she stares in disbelief. Her flummoxed expression brings a smile to my lips. "*The* Liam Garrison? As in the QB for the Bulldogs? Hot, tattooed, motorcycle-riding Liam Garrison?"

I roll my eyes. "Is there another one?"

She shakes her head. "And just how did *that* come about?"

Rather matter-of-factly, I recount what happened. "Yesterday morning, Sam and I ran into him at breakfast, and he asked if I wanted to spend a few hours with him." I pop my shoulder at the end of the story.

"Sheesh...you're gone for a few days and I miss everything." She pauses before inhaling a breath. "Did he have his motorcycle with him?" Mia clasps her hands and shakes them at me. "*Please, please, please* tell me that he had his motorcycle."

I can't help the smile that springs to my lips as I nod.

"*And?*" She leans forward, drawing closer. "What happened then?"

"We drove around the city for a while and then stopped to shoot some pool."

A tiny smirk settles across her lips. "And how did *golden delicious* take that?"

"*Sam,*" I emphasize, "was fine with it."

My mind tumbles back to yesterday morning and the look on his face when I walked out of the restaurant. All right, so maybe he wasn't *completely* fine with it. But he certainly didn't tell me not to go. We all know how overprotective Sam can be. His reputation as a cock blocker has been well-earned.

A grin tips the corners of her lips. For the first time since walking in this afternoon, my roommate looks more like the Mia I've grown to love over the last three years. She waves a hand. "Oh, I'm sure he didn't mind at all that you took off on a motorcycle with one of his hot teammates." Her shoulders shake with silent laughter. "I bet he helped you onto the back of Liam's bike and gave you a condom so you could practice safe sex before telling you to have a great time. Am I right?"

"Of course not," I say with a snort. "You know how Sam is. He's more like an annoying big brother."

Mia shakes her head. "Jeez, Vi. It's almost cute how oblivious you are."

I frown. No one has ever accused me of that before. "No, I'm not."

"Where Sam is concerned? Yeah, you are."

Instead of asking what she means, I brush off the remark and redirect our conversation away from Sam. He now feels like dangerous and murky territory. "Anyway, there's nothing between Liam and me. He kissed me and—"

She doesn't give me a chance to finish the sentence before pouncing. "He kissed you! Liam Garrison actually *kissed* you?" She looks dangerously close to swooning.

"Um, yeah." I fold my hands in my lap and add, "It was nice—"

"His kiss was just...*nice*? That's it? Liam Garrison gave you a ride on his motorcycle, took you to play pool, and then kissed you, and it wasn't anything more than *nice?*" Her voice rises with each word.

I nod before shrugging. "It was nice. Nothing more, nothing less."

"That's seriously disappointing." There's a pause. "Was he bad at it?" Almost immediately she shakes her head. "No—that seems impossible. He's way too gorgeous to be bad at making out."

"No, the kiss was fine." My mind turns back to yesterday. "It just wasn't anything special. There was zero chemistry between us."

Her lips slant down at the corners. "*Definitely* disappointing."

I nibble at my bottom lip because I have a decision to make. Do I tell her what happened with Sam?

Or keep it to myself?

I could really use Mia's advice regarding the situation. I know what my grandmother said, and there's a part of me that thinks she might be right. But still...the prospect of opening up to Sam and telling him that my feelings have changed is a scary one.

What if he doesn't feel the same way?

Or what if he's into it and then we fizzle out a month—or even ten months—later. I'll still end up losing my best friend. The one person I can always count on. It's a huge risk.

As I gnaw at my lower lip, Mia's eyes narrow. She's like a bloodhound that has picked up a scent. "I get the feeling there's more." She pauses before demanding, "Oh my God, what else could have possibly happened? It was literally three days!"

I hedge. "What makes you think anything else happened?" I shouldn't even bother with subterfuge. I'm no good at it. I have zero acting chops.

She swirls her pointer finger at me. "Because you've got that look on your face." Her eyes narrow in an assessing manner before she adds, "It's that *I-don't-want-talk-about-it* look. Just do us both a favor and spill your secrets. Otherwise, I'll have to beat them from you, and I don't have the energy for that."

There's no way Mia will allow me to slink away without revealing every juicy detail. I shake my head before resting it in my hands and groaning, "A lot happened and none of it was good."

"Yes," she murmurs, "I can see that. Now tell me *exactly* what happened with *Sam*."

My head pops up and my gaze cuts to hers only to find a knowing smile wreathing her face. "Why do you think this has anything to do with Sam?"

"Because it's been a long time in coming. You two are ridiculous."

I blow out a steady breath. "I've probably mentioned before that when we were younger, I used to crawl through Sam's window at night and sleep in his bed, right?"

"Yeah." She drawls out the word so that it sounds more like *yeaaaahhhhhh*.

"Well, things felt a little weird between us at the bar Saturday night and I couldn't sleep, so I went to talk with him and ended up sleeping in his room."

Her mouth tumbles open. Before she has a chance to rapid-fire questions at me, I cut her off. "*Nothing happened between us.*"

The way her body deflates has my lips twitching with humor. "Well, that's a damn shame."

Ignoring her grumbled words, I continue, "When I woke up in the morning, he was pretty much wrapped around me."

She scoots a little closer before propping her chin up on her hand and gazing at me with wide eyes. "Go on. This is just starting to get interesting."

"His hand was on my boob and—"

"Yes, *yes!*" She looks on the verge of falling off the couch.

Even though no one else is around, I drop my voice. "His erection was pressed up against my backside."

She squeezes her eyes tightly shut and whispers, "Please tell me you put that morning wood to good use."

I shake my head. "Once he started grinding it against me, I freaked and got the hell out of there."

Her eyes pop open as she stares at me before smacking a hand against her forehead. "Are you being serious right now?"

"Umm, yeah. Although, I don't think he remembers because he was sleeping." I pause. "I'm pretty sure he was sleeping. He was breathing really heavy. Anyway, I left as quickly as I could. When he came out of his room two hours later, he was dressed and asked if I wanted to grab breakfast." I shrug. "Everything seemed normal." Well, as normal as it's been between us lately. "While we were out, we ran into Liam and I ended up taking off with him after breakfast."

Mia stares at me as if I'm an exotic specimen smeared across a microscope slide. "Huh."

I draw in a breath and decide to come completely clean. I've gotten this much out. There's no point in holding in the rest.

"When I came home a few hours later, I got your text about spending another night at Sam's place. He had just come back from working out and said I could use his truck to pick up a couple more things. I was about to pull out when I realized that I didn't have my dorm key. So, I went back inside to get it. When I got to the apartment, Sam had just finished with his shower." I glance at Mia and notice every muscle has gone rigid as she waits with bated breath. I force out the rest. "Let's just say that he had a towel." I pause. "But he was using it to dry his hair."

We stare at each other, neither of us uttering a word. Mia folds her lips around her teeth as a smile tries to break free. Now that I have roughly twenty-four hours separating me from the incident, my lips tremble as well. Almost as if on cue, we burst into laughter. Gut pinching, belly aching, can't-stop-if-I-tried laughter.

Oh God, it feels so good to laugh about this.

We're both dying when I gasp, "And then he got another erection while I was standing there gawking at him!"

She swipes at the tears in her eyes before nearly chortling, "Oh, I just bet he did!"

I shake my head and force out the rest, "Here's the worst part—"

Mia shrieks, "There's a *worst* part?"

"Of course, there is! After catching him naked, I bolted from the apartment. When I came back eight hours later, Sam and Roan were both sleeping. So, I snuck into Dylan's room. But I couldn't stop thinking about him sliding his erection against me when we were cuddled up in bed together that morning. And—"

I seriously can't believe I'm about to share this with Mia but here it goes, "I rubbed one out."

Heat stings my cheeks as I finish off the story. "Just when I was about to come, he knocked on the door, wanting to talk!" I shake my head, still unable to believe that it actually happened. Just in case she doesn't understand the full picture I'm trying to paint, I add, "*I came with him standing right outside the door! Like right outside it*! I couldn't stop myself!"

Mia looks completely shocked and yeah, just a bit impressed—thank you very much, as she dissolves into another fit of giggles. "Good for you! I have to say—I seriously didn't think you had it in you!"

That makes two of us.

Laughter bubbles up in my throat as I admit, "It was such a good orgasm!"

I should really stop talking now. This is total overshare. Which I tend *not* to do. But honestly, this is Mia, and I can tell her anything and she won't judge me for it. That's one of the reasons I love her to pieces. She's a great friend. The absolute best.

She swipes at her eyes again as a grin lights up her face. "I really have to thank you."

The muscles in my stomach hurt from all our shared humor. "For what?"

"For telling me about this. You have no idea how much I needed a good laugh."

"Anytime," I say with a smile.

Because you know what? I needed it, too.

"All right, finish the story. What happened after you came with Sam standing outside the door? Did you let him in so he could finish you off?" A hopeful expression lights up her face.

I roll my eyes. Does she really think I'd do that? "Hell, no."

She waves a hand. "Let me guess—instead of finally talking everything out, you ran away again."

The girl knows me well.

I glance away. "Yeah. I snuck out around seven in the morning when they left to workout and had breakfast with my grandparents."

She resettles against the back of the couch. "What are you going to do about this, Vi?"

I groan and shake my head. "I have no idea. Part of me wants to tell him that my feelings have changed, and the other part just wants everything to go back to normal. I don't want to lose Sam as a friend, and we all know that I suck at relationships."

Mia scoffs. "You don't suck at them." She pauses before adding, "You're kind of like Goldilocks...you just haven't found the right fit yet."

"What makes you think Sam is the right fit?"

"What makes you think that he's not?" she counters in return.

Chapter Seventeen

VIOLET

For the next two days, Mia's words roll around like marbles in the back of my head. On Tuesday, I deliberately dawdle on my way to Rickets' class so that I'm late. Not by much, certainly not enough to incur his wrath, but just enough so that there's no time for Sam and me to delve into any meaningful conversations.

During the entire class period, all ninety tortuous minutes of it, his leg continually brushes up against mine. Every time it does, a little burst of awareness shoots through my body, making it impossible to focus on the lecture.

At one point, I wonder what it would feel like to climb that big body of his like a tree. Those thoughts make me squirm uncomfortably in my seat, attempting to alleviate a bit of the pressure forming between my tightly clenched thighs.

Once class is wrapped up for the day, Sam pounces, asking if I want to grab a coffee and talk. Instead of manning up and hashing things out with him, I make up some lame excuse as to why I have to haul ass across campus.

I really hate to admit this but...I rubbed another one out last night thinking about Sam.

All right, fine. Twice. I'm a total deviant.

In light of the current situation, I've decided to make one last ditch effort to salvage our friendship and keep everything from changing. I need to find someone who can take my mind off Sam. I'm talking about a good old-fashioned hookup. I'm beginning to spend way too much time alone in my room, if you catch my drift.

Carpal tunnel syndrome has become a very real fear.

Which is why Mia and I have our asses planted in a booth at O'Brien's. Sure, it's a Wednesday night. And it's not exactly as hopping as it would be on a Friday or Saturday evening, but there are still a fair number of people out enjoying themselves.

Upon closer inspection, there are a decent number of prospects. I'm guessing the NHL game on the big screen TV behind the bar has a little something to do with that.

All I need is one guy who can take my mind off Sam. One guy who can distract me long enough for things to simmer down and slide back to normal. It has to be someone who can get my hormones snapping to attention like a certain someone else with bulging biceps, a wide chest, bright blue eyes, sexy blond hair, and a thick co—

I wince.

I really need to stop thinking about him like that. It's going to ruin our friendship. Not to mention, I've never masturbated so much in my life.

With my head on a swivel, I scope out the local talent, attempting to find a target to lock on. Mia takes a sip from her ice-cold mug before cocking a disinterested brow my way. "You sure this is a good idea?"

Of course not. But it's the best I've got at this point. For most of the ride over, Mia encouraged me to be honest with Sam.

There's no way I'm ready to deal with those kinds of ramifications. If that makes me a puss, so be it.

So, I'm going with option B.

Option B is all about finding a distraction for the evening. Or longer. It's really the only viable alternative, when you think about it. I either find someone who can take my mind off Sam, or I screw up the best relationship I've ever had because I want to jump his bones.

A whole bunch of times.

Mia thinks option B is destined for failure. She's being a real negative Nancy about the situation. I probably should have asked someone else to be my wingwoman for the evening. She likened this expedition to craving a huge, juicy, double-decker burger with the works loaded on top, but deciding to settle for a crappy, three-day old, convenience store hot dog instead.

And maybe she's right.

Maybe I *am* settling.

Sure, of course I want that burger. I'm all but *starving* for that damn burger. But, for obvious reasons (ie- that burger is my best friend), I can't have it. So, I've decided to go for that crappy, three-day old, convenience store hot dog instead because it will take my mind off the juicy burger I'd rather sink my teeth into.

But you know what?

Maybe that crappy-ass dog will end up surprising me. Maybe I'll actually feel somewhat satisfied after consuming said dog. I mean, anything can happen, right? Or maybe it'll make me so violently ill that I'll end up puking my guts out. Either way, I won't be thinking about that burger, now will I?

So, win-win.

In one thirsty gulp, I down half my beer. Or as I like to call it —*liquid courage* before eyeing up my prospective candidates for the evening.

With a sly smile, Mia points to someone loitering at the bar. "I think bachelor number one over there is right up your alley."

Either she's mocking me and has found a guy who I would never go for or...she's found someone who looks exactly like Sam. We're talking six feet tall, short blond hair, and a hard body. Don't even get me started on those well-defined shoulders.

I know *exactly* what Mia is up to by picking this guy. He hits a little too close to home.

My narrowed gaze swings back to my friend. She raises a brow in silent inquiry. Yup, it's definitely a trap. One I'm going to steer clear of —thank you very much.

I shrug and sit back in the booth. "He's not really my type."

Actually, he's *completely* my type.

She rolls her eyes. "Oh, please." Instead of arguing, her attention returns to the bar where a good number of guys are watching the hockey game.

"All right," her gaze scans the general vicinity, "how about him?"

I focus on bachelor number two, already knowing it's not going to happen. He does nothing for me. But beggars can't be choosers. It's not like I'm picking out my future husband here, right?

This is nothing more than a distraction.

I guess he's kind of okay looking—if I squint real hard. This is just a guess, but I probably weight more than he does. And that thin pedophile mustache he's rocking has seriously got to go.

I think we'll keep that one on the backburner for now. "Nah. He doesn't..." my voice trails off.

"Look like Sam?"

My gaze narrows before cutting to her. "No," I lie, "that's *not* what I was going to say."

"But it's what you were thinking," she chides sweetly.

Fine, so maybe it was. But I certainly don't have to admit that to her. The last thing I need to hear is yet another rendition of—*I-told-you-this-was-a-bad-idea*. "No, he's just a little too *lean* for my tastes."

She snorts before taking another drink of her beer. "Whatever you say." Then she perks up. "How about that guy over there?"

My gaze slides to bachelor number three. I'm pleasantly surprised to discover that bachelor number three has potential.

You know what I like best?

He doesn't look anything like Sam and I'm one hundred percent sure he weighs more than I do. Plus, he has wavy chestnut-colored hair. I'm trying to imagine what it would feel like to tunnel my fingers through it. On closer inspection, it's doubtful I could penetrate the helmet hair he's got going on because he's using more product than I am.

Whatever. That's not important.

I focus on his eyes. They're definitely not a piercing blue. From what I can tell, they look to be a nice rich brown. Dare I say soulful? Yeah, I'm going with soulful. Added bonus—he's muscular. Okay...in that regard, he sort of resembles Sam. So, sue me, I like well-built men.

Or *strapping,* as my grandmother would say.

Is there necessarily any pinging action going on?

Nope. But I'm pretty sure I can work with this.

Unwilling to waste any more time, I slide from the booth. "Wish me luck, I'm going in."

"You don't need luck, you've got great tits. Just thrust them out. It gets 'em every time."

I snort at her advice because, well…there's some truth to the statement. Not the part about me having great tits, but just having tits in general. If you thrust them out, picking up guys becomes ridiculously easy.

I'm a woman on a mission as I stride toward him. When I'm a couple of feet away, his gaze collides with mine before sweeping over the length of me. He must like what he sees because his mouth curls up at the edges.

It's almost criminal how easy it is to pick up men.

Instead of gloating, I school my features and give him a flirty smile as I tuck a stray lock of hair behind my ear. "Hi."

"Hey." His gaze never deviates from mine as he hoists a bottle of beer to his mouth before taking a long swig.

I'm detecting a definite air of interest here. This guy just might be a keeper. For tonight, anyway. I clear my throat before introducing myself, wanting to get the preliminaries out of the way. "My name's Violet."

"Nice to meet you, Violet. I'm Nick." As those words leave his lips, his gaze darts over my shoulder before he tacks on hastily, "And this is my girlfriend, Bree."

I'm sorry. Come again?

A tall, slender woman wraps her arms around his neck. Nick shifts his weight before giving her a peck on the lips. Bree glares at me before grabbing the sides of his head and forcing his mouth to hers. Then she proceeds to maul him.

I'm guessing this is my cue to leave.

Sheesh. All the guy had to say was—*not interested.* Those two little words would have had me moving on to bachelor number four.

Whoever the hell that is.

With a roll of my eyes, I spin on my heels and stalk back to our table. My gaze lands on Mia. Her shoulders are shaking. I can tell that she's three seconds away from busting a gut. A barely contained grin wreaths her face.

My eyebrows lower in response.

When I'm finally close enough to the table, I say with a sigh, "Go ahead and let it out."

That's all it takes for Mia to lose it. She laughs for a good three minutes before her chuckles subside.

"It wasn't *that* funny," I grumble.

"Actually, it was. You should have seen the look on your face when he introduced his girlfriend! It was priceless, Vi. Completely priceless." She glances over in their direction again before shaking her head.

I can't help but look as well.

Yup, they're still going at it.

After thirty more minutes, I've drained another beer and have approached two more guys who—if you can actually believe it—are more interested in watching the game on TV than striking up a conversation with yours truly.

And trust me, I've been thrusting out my boobs the entire time.

Nada.

I stare glumly at my empty mug. "Picking up guys is more difficult than it appears."

As those disheartened words leave my lips, Mia dissolves into another fit of giggles. "For you, yes. I really should be videoing this. It would make a hilarious GIF."

"You suck as a wingwoman," I mutter.

"You suck at picking up dudes," she tosses back.

I can't exactly argue with that, now can I? Apparently, I do suck at picking up guys. Who knew?

This night has turned out to be a complete bust.

"I'm going to the bathroom," I say, feeling deflated. Once there, I take care of business and reapply my lipstick.

As I return to the table, a guy loitering at the bar catches my attention. Before I can think better of it, I beeline toward him. With his back to me, I'm able to see the broad set of his shoulders.

Right there, I know he has potential. And he's tall. I like that, as well.

I peek at Mia and notice that her face is glued to her phone.

Good. The last thing I need is her making a video of my most humiliating fails.

Because she would do it.

My gaze slides back to the guy. I'm not really able to see much more of him because he's wearing a ball cap. I have no idea what he looks like, but so far, I'm intrigued. And I'm desperate with nothing to lose and everything to gain. This night hasn't gone the way I anticipated. Once again, my attention settles on his sexy shoulders. The sheer width of them is breathtaking.

And then I feel it. A little zing of attraction.

I almost pump my fist in the air.

See? I knew this was the right approach to take. I just had to be patient.

The way his tight, gray T-shirt stretches across all that broadness has my mouth salivating. I weave through the people standing at the bar before squeezing myself in next to him. I'm about to tap him on the shoulder when he turns and meets my gaze.

"Hey, Vi."

My eyes widen as the sexy smile disappears.

Oh, for fuck's sake.

"What are you doing here?"

If Sam registers the shock and dismay in my voice, he doesn't say a word about it. He tips his head toward Mia who is still sitting in the booth with her phone. "Mia texted that you guys were here to catch the game. I was just ordering a beer before joining you."

"She did, huh?" My narrowed gaze slices to my traitorous ex-friend. She looks up and gives me a wide grin along with a wave.

"Yup."

Something trembles at the bottom of my belly as I glance at Sam.

"I'm surprised you're out on a Wednesday night. I thought for sure you'd be home studying."

Yeah, studying probably would have been a lot more productive than what's happened here.

"Just felt like grabbing a beer," I mutter before nodding to the big screen TV on the wall, "and, you know, watching the game. I, ah, thought it might be fun."

I don't even know who's playing tonight. Or any other night, for that matter.

Sam raises a skeptical brow. My guess is that he sees right through my paper-thin lie because I don't follow hockey. It's doubtful I could name one player from the league.

He nods toward the booth. "Mia said she was going to head home but that you wanted to stay and hang out a bit longer. So, I thought I'd swing by and keep you company."

"She said that?" It's official. I'm going to kill her.

Sam smiles as if he knows I've been avoiding him and has finally found a way to thwart me. He grabs his beer off the counter with one hand before wrapping the other around my fingers and tugging me across the bar. I rack my brain, trying to figure out how I'm going to extract myself from the situation. Spending time alone with Sam is definitely not a good idea. Especially right now. As we arrive at the table, Mia scoots out of the booth before grabbing her purse. A sly smile hovers around the edges of her red-slicked lips.

"I'm going to get moving," she announces. "There's some homework I need to finish up."

Narrowing my eyes, I grit out, "Thanks so much for calling Sam. That was super thoughtful of you." I hope she sees the murderous glint shimmering in my eyes.

Damn Mia, and her interfering ways.

Her grin intensifies. "No problem, sweetie." She points a finger and wags it between us. "You kids have fun tonight, but not *too* much fun." And then she skedaddles away before I can think of a reason to detain her.

Silently fuming, I watch her saunter out of the bar as Sam settles onto the side of the booth Mia vacated. There's nothing else for me to do but slide in nervously across from him.

My attention falls to the empty mug in front of me before slicing to him. Energy snaps and sizzles in the air between us as our gazes collide. Unable to withstand the connection, I drop mine back to the table.

"Vi?" My name comes out sounding low and gravelly as I slowly run my finger over the rim of my mug. "Did you really come here to watch the game tonight?" His expression remains shuttered. I have no idea what he's thinking.

Air gets trapped at the back of my throat as I stare mutely. I don't think he believes me. It probably doesn't help that the TV is all the way across the bar, and from the angle I'm sitting at, I can barely see it.

"Ummm..." My voice falters before I murmur almost questioningly, "Yes?"

His eyes narrow before he reaches out and nabs my fingers. His hand practically swallows up my smaller one. The feel of his warm flesh over mine has an unexpected shaft of desire arrowing through me. I swallow thickly and attempt to shake it off.

This shouldn't be happening. We're supposed to stay strictly within the friends zone. That's the way it's always been. Screwing with that— all right, bad choice of words— *messing* around with that is a disastrous idea.

"You don't sound altogether sure."

I shift restlessly before raising my gaze. "Does it really matter?"

His eyes take on a hard-edged glint before he responds gruffly, "Yeah, it does."

"Why?"

For a long stretch of time, his blue depths bore into mine. Even though the game is on, music pours through the sound system around us. It changes from a fast-paced beat to a slower one. Before I can blink, Sam slides out of the booth. His fingers are still clasped around mine, almost as if he'll never let them go. And right now, part of me doesn't want him to.

"Where are we going?" I ask.

"To dance."

"What? *Now?*" I glance at the floor. The bar isn't very crowded. "There's one other couple out there."

"So?" He shrugs.

By this point, we've reached the area and he's tugging me toward him. When he finally wraps his arms around me, I know I'm in deep shit. They feel like home. They always have.

I think that might be part of the problem.

It only takes a few moments before my muscles loosen and I'm melting into him. My head settles against his wide chest as I inhale his woodsy scent. His lips press close to my ear. As his warm breath feathers over my flesh, it sends a tidal wave of sensation scampering down my spine.

Just as my eyelids lower, he whispers, "Did you come here looking to get laid?"

"*What?*"

He presses his mouth against my ear before carefully enunciating, "*Did you come here looking to get laid?*"

I gulp and force out the lie. "Of course not."

That's *exactly* why I came here.

It doesn't escape me that the reason I need to get laid is currently holding me in his arms, pressing me close to his body, until I'm almost dizzy with the intoxicating scent of him.

Maybe Mia is right, and I need to be straight with Sam. How much more of this can I take before shattering into a million jagged pieces?

The thought of laying myself bare scares the crap out of me. Unsure what to say, I chew my lower lip before reluctantly admitting the truth. "Yeah, I did."

His arms tighten as his face hovers closer. All I'd have to do is turn my head a fraction to the left and my lips would align perfectly with his. Something clenches in my core at the thought of his mouth sliding over mine.

"Why?"

Instead of turning my head, I keep my face angled away before squeezing my eyes tightly shut. It feels as if I'm perched on the edge of a cliff, moments away from descending in a terrifying freefall where I will—more than likely—land with a painful splat.

This is *Sam* we're talking about here.

My best friend.

The one guy I can be completely open and honest with. He knows me. He knows the *real* Violet Winterfield. He sees what others don't. He always has.

"Vi?" Hearing my nickname roll off his lips has my eyelids springing open for a second time. My teeth sink into my lower lip, wanting to force the words out, but I'm still unable to take that final plunge into honesty.

"What do you want me to say," I whisper, my voice trembling with nerves.

His mouth drifts closer to my ear. Chills sluice down my spine as a groan attempts to break free from my lips. I'm so turned on right now and he's doing nothing more than holding me.

"The truth. I want you to tell me what's really going on."

There's no way I can do that. I just...*can't*. Something indefinable has spiraled out of control between us and I have absolutely no idea how to rein it back in again.

Even though Sam isn't being rough, it still feels as if he's trying to break me down and get at the truth. He's doing everything possible to get me to admit what I'm feeling. If I were smart, I'd step out of his embrace and put a little distance between us. Just enough so I can breathe without inhaling him.

"Sam," I groan as his lips nip my earlobe.

"What?" Tiny shivers gallop across my flesh as his warm breath feathers over me.

Argh.

I can't think straight when he does that. His lips meander down the column of my neck. Instead of putting a stop to this madness, I tilt my head, allowing him greater access. My legs feel all wobbly, like Jell-O. Any moment, I'm going to collapse into a gooey pile on the floor.

Then his mouth is back at my ear. "You need to understand one thing, Violet." He pauses, his presence scrambling all of my thoughts. "If you go home with anyone tonight, it's going to be me."

/ Chapter Eighteen

SAM

I've had enough. Whether Violet realizes it or not, we're done playing games. If she thinks for one damn moment I'm going to stand by and allow her to go home with a random dude, she's out of her mind.

That's not going to happen.

Up until Sunday, our relationship had been teetering precariously on the edge of *something more*. Waking up with my arms wrapped around her, my morning wood pressed against her backside, and my hand palming the generous curve of her breast, forever tipped the scales. There's no turning back from that. I couldn't rein in my desire even if I wanted to.

I owe Mia big time for shooting me a text and clueing me in to what was about to go down. Even though she never mentioned what they were doing here, I had my suspicions. With the last few days ratcheting up the sexual tension between us, and her subsequently avoiding me, it was only a matter of time before Violet attempted to diffuse the situation.

I should have realized she would try something like this.

Can you believe it?

The girl was actually trying to fuck me out of her system. I almost laugh. Hell, if she'd bothered to ask, I would have been happy to tell her that it wouldn't work. I've tried enough times to know.

If Violet wants to ride a cock, it's going to be mine.

That's just the way it is.

With deliberate movements, I drag my lips across the delicate flesh of her neck. I want this girl in the worst possible way. I always have. I've never craved anyone the way I do Violet. The last few days have taken a toll on both my self-control and patience.

At the moment, I'm fresh out of both.

We're done tiptoeing around what's happening.

"Did you hear me?" I growl.

Her body trembles in my embrace, and I tug her closer until she's able to feel my hardened length pressed against the soft contours of her belly. I want her to understand what she does to me.

All of her supple curves drive me crazy. I'm desperate to sink inside her body because I know it will be nothing short of nirvana. I've dreamt about it for years. Hell, the first time I got hard and jerked off were to thoughts of Violet. Snapshots I had tucked away in the back of my mind.

A whimper escapes from her, and it sends me careening over the edge until I'm frantic with the need to taste her, touch her, drive myself inside her.

Even though it feels impossible, I keep every urge I have to drag her out of here tamped down. It took a couple of days for me to realize what was going on between us. That she was fighting it, fighting her changing feelings. Violet is afraid to let go. I need to convince her that this is worth taking a chance on.

I press a kiss against the corner of her mouth. "If you want to fuck," I say in a voice that sounds as if it has been dredged from the bottom of the ocean before pressing another caress to the other side, "you'll fuck me."

Her muscles go lax. I can't tell if she's going into shock at the dirty way I'm speaking to her or if she's turned on by the words pouring out of my mouth.

Or maybe it's a combination of both.

When I stroke my mouth across hers, she parts her lips in silent invitation.

All right. Good. I'm going with the whole *turned on* theory. And yeah, maybe a little shocked, as well. But mostly, turned on.

That I can work with.

"You're done running from me," I tell her. When she remains silent, I nip at her lower lip with my teeth until she gasps. When I release the plump flesh, I notice her eyes are dilated with pleasure and lowered to half-mast. It's the sexiest fuck-me look I've ever seen, and it's the exact expression I want on her face when I drive my dick inside her.

My narrowed gaze never relinquishes hers. "You're done avoiding me."

For years, I've dreamt about all the ways I wanted to take her. Fast fucking that leaves us both breathless. Slow, sensual screwing that has us falling just a little bit more in love with each other. I want her on all fours, legs spread, gorgeous pussy perfectly displayed. I want her sitting astride me, taking my dick deep in her body so I can palm her breasts while she rides me. I want to watch her tits bounce with every upward stroke I take.

I want it all. I want to have Violet every possible way there is.

And make no mistake, I *will* have her.

Even though I know she wants me, I hear the threads of fear weaving their way through her voice. "We shouldn't..."

She still doesn't get it. *This* is going to happen. It's a done deal. It was never going to end any other way than with her in my bed, in my life, in my heart.

Unable to help myself, I laugh. Pained chuckles that are scraped raw with need. Desire that has been patiently held in check for the last eight years. Her startled gaze cuts to mine. "Do you have any idea how much I want you? Or how long I've been waiting for you? *For this?*"

She shakes her head and I find myself leaning toward her until my forehead can rest against hers. Our gazes stay locked, and the world around us falls away.

"Way too fucking long," I tell her. "I'm done waiting for you to play catch-up."

Another protest tries to fall from her lips. "I—"

"I know you don't," I say, cutting her off.

Her tongue darts out to moisten her lips, and the movement leaves me groaning as desire slams through me. Attempting to wrap her head around this, she tries again, "You never said anything."

I shrug. "You weren't ready to hear it."

If I'd tried to start something in high school, or two years ago, or even six months ago, she would have shut me down. It would have made everything awkward. I know Violet. It's only recently that she's become aware of me as something more than a friend. If she thinks for one moment, I'm not going to press my advantage, then she's out of her mind.

"What makes you think I'm ready now?" she asks.

I draw away enough to meet her gaze. The sexual haze filling them has cleared. Challenge fills her dark depths. I give her a look so rife with heat, I'm surprised it doesn't singe her alive.

My lips find her ear. "Tell me what you were doing locked away in your room Sunday night."

For a second time, I pull away so that I can watch every emotion as it crashes across her delicate features. Violet has the most expressive eyes. Open and completely unfettered.

With me.

I've noticed that as well.

She lowers her guard with me.

Except lately.

They flare wide with surprise. Mortification shines in them as well.

I almost shake my head.

Doesn't she realize how hot that is? The idea of her touching herself, getting off, and I'd been no more than eight feet away?

It drives me insane to think about.

The silent admittance written across her face makes me wish that I'd been a little more persistent when attempting to get into her room that night. My arms tighten around her before I rumble with all the pent-up sexual frustration surging through me. "I could hear the little moans falling from your lips." Even thinking about it has my balls drawing up against my body, aching with the fierce need for release.

She gulps but remains silent. It becomes obvious that I've knocked her off kilter. Maybe that's a good thing. Maybe that's exactly what needed to happen.

Her mouth tumbles into a stunned little *O*.

I close the distance between us before running the tip of my nose along the curve of her jaw. "Who were you thinking about when you were touching that sweet little pussy of yours?"

She whimpers and sinks her teeth into her lower lip, remaining stubbornly silent. Doesn't Violet realize that I'm going to break down every last defense until she admits her feelings to me?

My fingers strum along her ribcage. "Hmmm?"

"Sam..."

"Yeah, baby?" I press a kiss against her temple. "Were you thinking about my hard cock? Did you imagine what it would feel like to have me stroking you with it?"

When she doesn't respond, I place my fingers under her chin, leaning in until my lips can ghost over hers. With leisure movements, my tongue darts out to lick at the sugary sweetness of her mouth.

Damn, but I bet she tastes amazing everywhere.

And I plan to find out.

That knowledge settles the restless need rampaging within me. Otherwise, I'd be moments away from tossing her over my shoulder and carrying her out the door.

I need to slow this down. My tongue slips inside her parted lips until it can mingle with her own. The little whimper she emits only spurs me on, but I refuse to rush this.

One song ends and another starts up, and still our mouths stay fused together. She's locked in my embrace and I'm not letting go any time soon. Her soft curves are pressed against all my hard lines. Need claws its way through me from deep inside, but I tamp it down, keeping the beast under control.

I've waited too long to blow it now by pushing her too far, too fast. There are times when I think I understand Violet better than she knows herself. And what I realize is that she needs to be seduced. Cajoled. I need to prove this isn't a mistake. *Us* being together isn't something she needs to be afraid of. It feels so natural for our friendship to deepen, to morph into something more.

I've spent my entire life waiting for this moment.

And tonight, the wait is over.

Chapter Nineteen

VIOLET

Sam backs me up against the door to my bedroom as we stand in the common area of my suite. His body cages me in as his lips linger over my mouth. But he never quite touches me.

More like teases.

It only makes me want him more than I already do. All I want is to feel the firm pressure of his mouth sliding lazily over mine again.

And the things he whispered in my ear...

Holy hell.

I thought I'd burst into flames on the spot. Who knew that Sam could talk so dirty or that it would totally turn me on?

My panties are completely drenched, and my clit is throbbing with a life all its own.

My hand rises to the collar of his T-shirt before fisting it with my fingers. I want to drag him closer until I don't know where he ends, and I begin.

In this moment, all I want is for him to touch me. To touch me like I've fantasized about. To touch me like I've been touching myself all the while imagining it was him.

"Sam," I groan as those thoughts tumble through my head.

His lips slant a bit to the left before pressing a kiss against the corner of my mouth. "What, baby? Tell me what you need. I want to hear you say the words."

I whimper as desire surges through me. "You," I whisper. "I want you."

Some distant part of my brain is shocked that this is occurring. Almost like I'm going to jerk awake and realize that it's nothing more than a sexy dream. Are we seriously moments away from crossing the imaginary line that has always held our relationship in check?

Who am I kidding?

We crossed that line a few days ago when I woke up snuggled in his bed with his hand sliding over my body and his erection pressed against my backside. Our relationship shifted at that point. I just couldn't bring myself to admit it. I couldn't admit that I wanted Sam. I was too afraid our relationship was changing, evolving into something more.

Something new.

Something different.

But I'm done being scared.

I'm done running away from him.

And from myself.

Carefully, he nibbles the curve of my jaw before trailing down the column of my neck. I can't stop the whimper that escapes. It's like he knows exactly how to touch me. He knows what will send me careening out of control.

With my back pushed up against the door, I scrabble around for the handle before grasping the knob and turning it until the door pops open and we find ourselves tumbling inside the dark space. Sam wraps his arms around me as we stumble toward the twin-size bed shoved against the far wall. As we fall onto the mattress, Sam lands on top of me but his weight never crashes onto mine.

A giggle escapes from me as he draws away.

"Are you okay?" he asks.

"Couldn't be better." And damn, if that isn't the truth.

Heat flares in his bright blue eyes. Now that he's stretched out on top of me, I feel the hardened length of his erection nestled against my core. His gaze holds mine captive as he flexes his hips. Air gets trapped in my lungs as his cock slides along my cleft. I can't help but widen my thighs until I'm able to cradle his girth. Until I can feel the drag of him as he thrusts against me.

"Does that feel good, baby?" His voice drops. I can tell he's hanging on by a thread and I love it. Love that I do this to him.

Another low moan of need escapes from me. What he's doing feels amazing. How long has it been since I've had sex? At least a few months. But this is way more than that. This isn't an itch that needs scratching.

Because this is Sam.

My best friend since eighth grade.

It's the same fourteen-year-old boy who helped pick up the shattered pieces of my heart before putting me carefully back together again after my family died. His friendship made everything easier when I started at a new middle school, in a brand-new town. He took care of me, looked out for me, and helped me navigate a world filled with teenage pitfalls.

Through it all, I was always his first priority. I never understood that until now. Tears prick the back of my eyes as the realization dawns on me.

"Vi," he growls.

His lips ghost over mine. Back and forth until I feel a scream building up in my lungs. Until everything in me coils so tight that it's possible I might self-combust. When I can't take another moment of this sweet torture, his mouth finally closes over mine, caressing my lips with gentle strokes that are my undoing.

I open, wanting to feel the sweep of his tongue deep inside my mouth. I think about all those little kisses we've shared throughout the years. It's like they were all leading up to this cataclysmic explosion.

And I never saw it coming. I must have been blind. Or maybe, like Sam claimed, I wasn't ready to accept it.

I think back to the way Sam's gaze would follow me. He was always watching. Or the way he would constantly cock block me. I'd thought he was looking out for me, but now I realize it was so much more than that.

I have no idea how long his mouth continues to stroke over mine. All I know is that I want him so much that it becomes painful.

He pulls away before whispering, "Tell me what you were doing in your room Sunday night."

I can't think when he's sprawled on top of me. The way his dick strokes my core. It whips me in to a frenzy of emotions that ricochet dangerously inside me. His lips tease mine, making me crave so much more than what he's giving me. My mind grows fuzzy. My nerve-endings are over-sensitized by the way he stokes my body to life.

What was the question?

"Hmmm?"

His voice turns rough, more demanding. "I want you to tell me what you were doing alone in your room."

Oh...Sam really needs to move on from that. Clearly, he knows I was masturbating while he was on the other side of the door. Why do we have to talk about it? When I refuse to answer, his lips feather gently across mine. Over and over until I'm mindless with the taste of him.

"Tell me," he urges.

The demand has the dreamy haze clearing from my eyes. His gaze burns into mine. The need to escape from it pounds through me and I squeeze my eyes tightly shut.

"Vi," he whispers, "don't shut me out. Look at me, baby."

If it were anyone else asking, I don't think I could do it. Hesitantly, I crack open my eyes only to find Sam's face hovering over mine. The heat and desire blazing from his blue depths almost takes my breath away.

"Tell me what you were thinking about." His voice is low and husky, filled with yearning.

Unsure, I hesitate. Do I keep denying what happened even though he knows the truth?

Or do I lay myself bare and give him exactly what he's asking for?

I realize that I want to give him everything.

"You." I admit. "I was thinking about being in bed with you that morning. About the way you were holding me, and the feel of your thick cock nestled against me. I haven't been that turned on in a long time."

He groans before rolling his hips, flexing them against mine. The movement sends a shockwave of pleasure arrowing through me. "Do you have any idea how fucking sexy that is? I could hear the breathy little moans you were making. I wanted to break down the damn door and fuck you until you were screaming my name."

Those wicked words leave my clit aching as I squirm beneath him, attempting to relieve just a fraction of the pressure. Now that the floodgates have been opened, it all comes pouring out.

"It made me so horny to imagine that you were running your hands over me. Even though I knew you were right outside the door, I couldn't stop touching myself. When you said my name, I came so hard. It felt so good to let go." Better than anything else ever has.

That's the moment I realized I was screwed.

Figuratively, not literally.

He rolls his hips against me again as I teeter on the brink. Even though we're both clothed, I'm close to splintering apart.

"Show me." His words are low and gruff, almost as if they've been scraped raw.

And so damn sexy. They shoot clean through me, straight down to my—

"*What?*" My eyes flare wide. Is it possible that I misunderstood him?

He can't possibly want me to...um...*you know*.

"Show me how you were touching yourself, Vi."

How insane is it that I'm so turned on? I've never felt this kind of desire course through me. It wouldn't take more than a few flicks of my fingers to have my body falling apart.

But.

And it's a pretty big *but*.

Touching yourself feels...*private*. Something you do behind closed doors. When you're alone. By yourself.

See the trend here?

I've never thought of masturbation as a spectator sport.

As if silently trying to convince me, he flexes his hips against mine.

His hard length slides home. Lovely little shards of pleasure ricochet through me at the contact. I can't stop the moan that escapes from my lips.

"Please, baby? I stood outside your door, imagining how beautiful you would look with your legs spread wide, stroking yourself to thoughts of me." He thrusts again. "I want to watch you touch yourself."

How can I possibly say no when he makes it sound so...

Sexy.

That thought alone has my clit pulsing a steady beat.

Sam takes my silence for acquiescence and rolls to the side. For a moment, I stay still and gather my courage. Touching myself in front of him feels wildly intimate. Even though I'm nervous, I want to do this.

My fingers fumble as I sit up and strip off my top. I draw in a deep breath before starting on the jeans. It takes more than one attempt to flick open the button. When I'm down to nothing more than my bra and panties, I chance a peek in his direction. His gaze slides over my exposed flesh, singeing every inch of me.

The look on his face is reverent. It has the breath catching at the back of my throat. How did I fail to recognize these feelings for so long?

"You're so damn beautiful, Vi."

He makes me feel beautiful. The way his gaze burns over me. The rough scrape of his voice as if it's a battle to keep himself in check. The tight coil of his body, poised to devour me in one tasty bite.

The way his attention stays riveted, patiently waiting for me to remove the rest, gives me the confidence I need to unsnap my bra. As I do, the straps slide down my arms before resting at my elbows. The cups nearly fall off my breasts. I watch his face as I pull the delicate material away from my chest before tossing it to the floor. I hear his swift intake of breath and see the way his fingers clench so as not to reach out and touch me.

As my heart thumps against my chest, I unfold my body and lower myself to the pillows. There's a tiny scrap of fabric that covers me. His gaze slips from my naked breasts, down my ribcage, before traveling over the curve of my belly, to the panties still covering the part of me that throbs for him.

Everything in me stills. I've never seen Sam look so heated before. So turned on and full of longing. It's a heady sensation to realize that I do this to him.

I inhale another ragged breath before hooking my fingers into the delicate fabric at my waist and shimmying it down my hips. My gaze stays fastened to him, wanting to see every expression as it flickers across his face.

The way his heated gaze licks over my mound sends hot spurts of desire careening through my system. I lay motionless and allow him to look his fill.

With unhurried movements, he leans toward me and presses a gentle kiss against my mouth before pulling away. Instead of touching me, he settles on his side with his head propped up by his hand, as his attention rakes over me.

Usually, when I'm naked with a guy, he's naked as well. I've never stripped off my clothes while someone lie fully dressed next to me, down to the tan timberlands laced on his size twelve feet.

It's unexpectedly sexy.

His gaze is worshipful as it slides over me, lingering on the tips of my breasts and the patch of curls between my thighs. Silently, he watches every move I make. Every rise and fall of my chest. It leaves me feeling strangely powerful. Almost like I could bring this two-hundred-and-twenty-pound guy to his knees by spreading mine.

The only sound that fills the room is our heartbeats and the harsh breath that falls from our lips as the moment lengthens between us. It's slowly that I allow my legs to fall open as one hand trails from my ribcage, down the curve of my belly, to the top of my pubic bone where my fingers hesitate. As much as it turns me on to watch him, I close my eyes.

To do this—*really do it*—I need to forget that Sam is here, watching me. That he knows every caress of my fingers is driven by thoughts of him. Even with my eyelids shuttered, I'm aware of his presence. I hear the harsh sawing of his breath.

Even at this point—feeling self-conscious—I know it won't take much. All I have to do is think about the way his erection was sliding against me a handful of moments ago. Or the way he looked in the bathroom, moisture clinging to his ripped body as he dried his hair after stepping out of the shower. The sexy cut of his abdominals and the way his cock had elongated, stretching to its full length, as we stared at one another.

A whimper slides from my lips as I think about the heat that had flared to life inside me. I'd been held spellbound by the sight of him. What I'd really wanted to do was close the distance that separated us before stroking my hands over his rigidly held muscles. I had wanted to sink to my knees and hold his stiff length in my hands as I licked the velvety tip with my tongue before sucking him deep inside my mouth.

The ache between my thighs intensifies, pulsating before my fingers are able to glide over it. The anticipation gathered inside me is almost my undoing. So badly do I want to slide them over my aching clit.

But I don't. Not yet.

I hold off until the throbbing turns unbearable before allowing my fingers to slide through the curls above my lower lips. Sam's breath catches as I run my fingers through the wetness that has gathered around my swollen flesh. A little moan of pleasure breaks free as I do. Unable to resist any longer, I graze my fingers over that tiny bundle of nerves. Unconsciously, I widen my legs and stroke my slit.

No longer am I aware of Sam beside me, taking up most of the room on the bed. All I can focus on is the tantalizing build of intensity that has coiled deep in my core. Climax is only a few strokes away, and I want it so badly. I'm greedy for the pleasure that is cresting inside me.

With purposeful movements, my fingers skate over my soaked flesh. Circling around my center before dipping inside. Pleasure spikes within me as I drag my fingers over my sensitive clit. Once, twice, three times.

I can't help but wonder what it would feel like to have Sam's mouth on me, his tongue lapping greedily. Spearing and driving inside me.

My body is strung impossibly tight as my back arches off the mattress and an orgasm streaks through me. As I cry out Sam's name, his lips crash onto mine in a kiss so possessive that it steals my breath away. His thick fingers join mine, touching and stroking as I gasp out my pleasure.

Even after the last remnants of my orgasm subside, his fingers don't stop moving. They continue to dip inside me, sliding through my wetness, grazing over my clit.

I've never felt anything like that before in my life.

It was...*amazing*.

He kisses me as his fingers sink inside my heat. His tongue thrusts in much the same way I imagine his thick cock would. Even though I've just come, and I should be satiated, I'm not.

I want him.

I want to feel his hard length inside me, filling me to completion.

"That was beautiful," he murmurs. "Absolutely beautiful."

As I open my eyes, our gazes lock. He brings his fingers—the same ones that had been buried in my body—to his parted lips before drawing them inside his mouth. His eyelids feather closed as if tasting the most decadent dessert.

Heat instantly flares back to life within me as I watch him.

Oh my God...that probably shouldn't be so hot.

But it is.

It so is.

Chapter Twenty

VIOLET

The entire time we sit in Rickets' class, Sam has my fingers ensconced in his own as if for safekeeping. As if I might disappear if he relinquishes his hold for even a split-second. There's never a moment when he isn't toying with them or stroking his thumb against the sensitive flesh of my palm. It would be distracting if it weren't so cute.

It's been over a week since the night at O'Brien's. I have to say, it's been pretty amazing. I keep waiting for the bottom to fall out. I keep expecting to feel itchy or antsy or whatever-it-is-I-start-to-feel before I decide to cut and run.

That has yet to happen.

My state of happiness is disconcerting. Almost as if everything is right in the world. I'm flooded with an overall feeling of wellbeing, which is scary.

I've never felt this kind of contentment course through me. Certainly not over a guy. It's odd how such a subtle shift in our relationship has made me feel complete. Unexpectedly settled in a way I couldn't have dreamed possible. It's like a missing puzzle piece has been maneuvered into the spot where it always belonged.

Even though we've been together for a week, Sam and I still haven't slept together. To be clear about the reason for that situation—it's

Sam's doing. Or *not* doing, as the case may be. I was ready to do the deed after that whole let-me-watch-you-get-off-to-thoughts-of-me encounter.

The kicker that sent me careening over the edge was watching him lick my cream off his fingers. The animalistic pleasure that stole over his face as he sucked every last drop was my undoing.

Hot damn.

I have to press my thighs together as heat and need flare to life between them. *Again.* Me getting turned on at the most inopportune of moments has become my new normal.

Much to Sam's delight.

And my unending chagrin.

The man enjoys keeping me on the edge and flexing his newfound sexual power in my face. He's taken years of pent-up sexual frustration and is hellbent on tormenting me with it. The sultry gazes he sends in my direction. Or the way he strokes his hands over my body. The downright dirty things he whispers in my ear. The way he describes in bone-melting detail all the delicious things we're going to do to one another. He paints vivid images inside my head. I can all but taste them.

His words alone are capable of igniting a raging inferno in my panties.

Not that I'm complaining, but I'm horny as hell all the time. My clit throbs to life as soon as I catch a glimpse of Sam. Or hear the deep timbre of his voice. Or feel the slow slide of his fingers against my heated skin. Or see him after he's stepped out of the shower and is wearing a pair of body-hugging black boxer-briefs. My nether regions have now been trained like one of Pavlov's dogs with Sam being the dinner bell.

It's maddening.

More absurd is the way he revels in it.

A few days ago, we were studying on the third floor of the library and he wouldn't stop shooting these heavy-lidded, smoldering gazes across the table at me. After about thirty minutes of trying to refocus my attention back to the book I was attempting to read, I finally told him to knock it off because I couldn't concentrate.

Without another word, he bolted out of the chair and dragged me off to a distant corner of the stacks. Then he yanked my back against his chest and shoved his hand down the front of my jeans until he could bury his fingers deep inside my wet heat. It only took five pumps of his hand before I was getting off. With my head turned toward him, his lips devoured mine, swallowing down every guttural groan he wrung from my body.

Know what's even worse?

At the time it was happening, when his fingers were stroking me and I knew I was going to come in a blaze of glory, I didn't give a damn who saw or heard me.

At that moment, I could only focus on greedily taking every single ounce of pleasure he was willing to dole out. I honestly don't understand what this man is doing to me. I've never been into public exhibitionism before. And yet, he could have done whatever he wanted, and I would have let him.

It's terrible. Not to mention scary. And completely exhilarating at the same time. I've never wanted another man the way I crave Sam. I keep trying to rationalize it. I mean, come on—this is *Sam* we're talking about. The guy I've been best friends with for the last eight years. Up until about a month ago, I never thought about him in a sexual manner. Then I blinked my eyes and did a complete one-eighty where he was concerned.

Now I can't look at him *without* thinking about sex.

Without wanting him.

It's like an addiction. I am *completely* addicted to Sam Harper.

A gurgle of laughter almost escapes from me at the absurdity of that statement.

Before I know it, Rickets is dismissing class, and I couldn't even tell you what the topic of today's lecture was. Sam and I talk as we leave the building. Already his arm is slung around my shoulders and he's drawing me toward him, pressing a kiss against the top of my head.

Sam has always been affectionate, but now it's even more so. And I love it. I want to revel in it. He's like the sun pouring light down upon me and, rather unexpectedly, I find myself opening up to all that brilliance.

As we reach the fork in the pathway, Sam stops before wrapping both arms around my body and drawing me close. There's a spark of contentment shining in his blue depths. I think that sentiment is reflected in my own gaze. Never in a million years would I have thought it could be like this.

Our friendship has allowed a natural easiness to flow between us. It's the foundation for which this new relationship is being built. I've never experienced that before. There's something infinitely deeper and more profound between us. A new level of intimacy that we're only now able to unlock and explore.

"I'll see you after practice?" he asks.

A smile spreads across my face. The plan is to do a little studying and then stay the night at his place. If I'm lucky, maybe I can seduce the guy into finally giving it up. I almost snort as that thought tumbles through my head.

I'm beginning to suspect that he wants me to beg for it.

Like *that's* going to happen.

Oh, who am I kidding?

Of course, I'll beg for it. I want Sam in the worst way possible. And maybe I owe it to him for waiting so patiently.

With his fingers tucked beneath my chin, Sam brushes his lips across mine. I love the way he kisses me. It's always thorough. As if he wants to take his sweet damn time. When he pulls away, I'm pretty sure there's a glazed look in my eyes. He gives me a smug smile before throwing in a wink for good measure and taking off. For one bemused minute, I can't resist watching him stride away. My gaze fastens onto his tight backside as a sigh of satisfaction slides from my lips. He really does have one fine ass.

"Clearly, you two aren't *just friends* anymore."

Jerked out of my happy bubble, my gaze flies to the girl who has sidled up beside me.

Allie. Right. I gave her Sam's number a couple weeks ago in an attempt to hook them up.

Her tone leaves me wincing. I clear my throat, unsure what to say.

"Sorry about that. We really weren't anything more than friends at that point. Had I known this was going to happen, I wouldn't have encouraged you to text him."

She tilts her head and sizes me up before nodding. Her expression softens, becoming one of friendliness before she shrugs. "It's cool. As much as I hate to admit it, you two look good together." With a snort, she adds, "The guy can't keep his hands off you."

I can't help but beam.

Allie rolls her eyes before jabbing me in the side with her elbow. "All right, knock that shit off. You've unfortunately taken one of the good ones off the market. It's kind of slim pickings around here, if you know what I mean."

A gurgle of giddiness bubbles up from my throat. "Sorry, I'm not trying to be obnoxious about it."

Her eyes narrow. "You need to try harder."

Even though I make every attempt to school my features, it ends up being a useless endeavor. This must be what relationship happiness feels like.

"You can make it up by passing along some inside information on a few of the other football players."

My mind whirls with the possibilities before locking onto one in particular. "I might have someone for you."

"Now you're talking." She links her arm through mine. "Come on, I'll walk with you to class, and you can tell me all about him."

Chapter Twenty-One

VIOLET

Even though the building is closed for the evening and everything is dark and silent, I pitch my voice low in case the janitorial staff is hanging around. "Should we be here?"

What if there are surveillance cameras capturing our every move?

That thought leaves me gulping before my eyes search the corners of the echoing hallway we're currently sneaking down.

All right, fine...I'm the one sneaking.

Think *Mission Impossible* covertness. I'm pulling from all three movies at this point. Sam, of course, is simply walking beside me with a sexy-as-all-hell saunter. Like it's no big deal that we're prowling around the athletic center after hours.

"As long as we don't get caught, there's nothing to worry about."

The comment has me skidding to a halt. "You're joking, right?"

His lips lift into an adorable smile that, under normal circumstances, would melt my heart and flood my panties with heat. At the moment, my nerves are too jacked up for melting or flooding of any kind.

Which is a shame.

"It'll be fine, I promise," he chuckles. "Now, come on."

He nabs my hand and tows me down the darkened corridor. My heart jackhammers painfully under my breast. I am a self-proclaimed rule follower. I've never been into breaking them. Hence my decision to study law.

"You realize that if we get caught, we'll have a record for breaking and entering, which could mean no law school?" At this point, I would be ecstatic to get out of here before we trip a silent alarm system.

For all we know, campus police are already on their way over to arrest us.

His fingers tighten around mine before he shakes his head as if I'm a baby for considering the ramifications of our late-night jaunt. "You need to settle down. Nothing is going to happen. And we didn't break in, all right? I have a key."

"That might be so, but I'm guessing that key isn't supposed to be in your possession."

"Stop asking questions," he whispers. "The less you know the better. It's called *plausible deniability*. Remember that."

"Great," I mutter under my breath, "what are we even doing here?"

"You'll see, now shush and follow me."

Even though I'm tempted to flee, I give serious consideration to his words. This is Sam we're talking about here. He would never do anything that would get either of us in trouble. If there's one person I trust implicitly, it's him. Nothing will ever change that.

A moment later, he pulls open a door and the scent of chlorine teases my nostrils. "Are we—"

Before I can get the question out, he pulls me to him before snaking his arms around my body and smacking a kiss against my lips. "No more questions."

He holds me captive for a heartbeat before setting me free. Then he's towing me through the men's locker room until we're pushing out another set of doors that lead to the Olympic-sized swimming pool. Even though the lights are off, one entire wall is floor-to-ceiling windows that allow bright moonlight to filter in and shimmer off the water.

Sam tugs the shirt over his head, revealing perfect washboard abs before throwing it onto the wooden bench by the locker rooms. His fingers hover over the button of his cargo pants before sliding it free from the hole and shoving the material down his thighs.

My gaze takes a leisure tour of his body. All those chiseled lines. The dark blond hair that arrows sharply down his lower abdomen before disappearing inside his boxers. The play of sinewy muscle as it stretches across his chest has all the saliva drying in my mouth.

He's beautiful.

Is it wrong that I want to nip at all that rock-solid strength before licking every inch of him?

Cue the panty flooding.

His socks get thrown into the growing pile of hastily stripped off clothing as I enjoy the impromptu show I'm being treated to.

"Come on, Winterfield, you gonna join me in there or watch from the sidelines?"

Indecision flickers through me.

Am I seriously going to do this?

Am I going to strip down and jump into the campus pool after hours?

Before sound judgment can swoop in and interfere, I whip the long-sleeved shirt over my head, and toss it on top of his discarded pile of clothing. Then I wiggle out of my shoes before pulling off my socks.

As I shed my clothes, a smile curves Sam's lips. The way his gaze tracks my every movement is sexy. No one has ever made me feel so wanted. No one has ever breathed life into the need that surges restlessly through my body.

When I'm down to my bra and panties, Sam stretches out a hand for me to take hold of. "Come here, beautiful." His voice turns gruff, strumming something in the pit of my belly.

His fingers ensnare mine as we move closer to the water. With our toes curled around the edge of the tile, we gaze at the smooth surface.

"Ready?"

I suck in a breath and nod.

"One...two...*three*!"

Our hands tighten as we arrow through the clear liquid, touch the bottom, and push off before rocketing to the surface. As we bob in the water, a grin lights up my face as a bubble of giddiness explodes within me.

"I can't believe we're doing this!" I whisper.

Sam bridges the distance between us and captures my lips with his own. They're cool and damp as they sweep across mine.

For the next thirty minutes, we splash around as silvery moonlight pours over us. Even though our voices are pitched low, they echo off the cavernous walls. There's something magical about being in the pool alone at night.

I shutter my eyelids and relax, allowing my body to float as the water gently rocks against me. I can almost feel the worries that have been eating at me fall away, gradually sinking to the bottom of the pool.

I've spent the last three and a half years at Barnett, steadily working toward my degree, so I can move on to the next phase of my life. But now that it's here, within striking distance, I'm dreading it. Unlike Mia, I have no idea where I'll be next year. I don't have a job lined up and I'm not jumping into a career. I'm applying to more schools so I can one day practice law. The reality of the situation is that I won't know if I'll be accepted to any of them until the spring.

What will happen if I get rejected?

My LSAT score of one-sixty is good, but not great. Coupled with my three-point-five GPA, there's always a possibility I'll be rejected. I don't have a backup plan in place if the worst-case scenario comes to fruition. And it's a little late to change majors at this point. For the time being, I'm stuck.

The question of what I'll actually be able to do with a pre-law studies degree if I don't end up going to law school is something I can't stop dwelling on. It's the million-dollar question right now. Or maybe I should say—the one-hundred-and-sixty-thousand-dollar question since that's what my education at Barnett has cost.

My guess is that it won't be worth much. I'll be stuck working a minimum wage job while trying to figure out plan B. After four years of hard work and student loans, that's depressing as hell.

Sam is lucky. With his LSAT score and GPA, he doesn't have

anything to worry about. He's a shoe in for all the schools he applied at. Any of them would be lucky to have him. He's going to make one hell of a lawyer someday.

I'm startled out of those thoughts when strong fingers wrap around my ankle and tow me through the water. A heartbeat later, Sam's handsome face peers down at me. A smile curves his lips. It's a slightly crooked one that I've seen a million times over the last eight years.

I've always found it endearing. Now I find it something more.

A shiver of excitement bolts through me as I hold his gaze.

"What are you thinking about?" he asks.

Sam has always been so good at picking up on my moods, allowing me to talk out my issues without necessarily trying to fix them. "Law school," I admit reluctantly before tacking on, "how next year will play out."

He slants a brow. "So, nothing too heavy?"

His lighthearted words have my lips lifting at the edges. "Nope, not at all," I agree.

We fall into silence before he says, "You know everything will work out, right? You're not going to have any problems getting into the schools you applied at."

I shrug. You never know what the applicant pool will look like for a certain year, and how you'll stack up against the competition. My score and grades are good, but they're not outstanding. I don't think I could have worked any harder.

Not knowing what the next step will be is scary. Maybe I won't get a chance to take that next step toward a future I've always dreamed about. Maybe I'll be one of those people who gets left behind. It makes me physically ill to think about everyone else moving forward while I'm stuck scrambling, trying to figure out my next move.

I squeeze my eyes shut. "I just want to know where I'll be next year and what I'll be doing. It'll be a huge relief to have everything finalized."

One way or the other.

He leans over and presses his lips against mine. As I open my mouth, ready to deepen the caress, he pulls away. Not far, just enough so that I can feel his warm breath drifting across my lips. Just enough to leave me yearning for more. Eyelids fluttering open, I find his blue depths piercing mine.

"Everything will be fine, Vi. You need to relax and stop worrying about the future."

I almost snort. Sam has no idea what it's like to work your ass off academically. And the grades I'm pulling, they're not exactly stellar. I work hard just to earn B pluses and A minuses.

"It's so easy for you," I admit. "You've never struggled in school the way I have." Ever since I've known Sam, he's breezed through everything. Academics have never been a challenge. Even when he loaded up on AP classes junior and senior year in high school, I don't think he expended any more energy than before. I took two AP courses each year, and had to hunker down, carefully plowing my way through the material. And I was still overloaded and overwhelmed much of the time.

He brushes his lips across mine until my breath catches at the back of my throat. "I know," he acknowledges, "but look how well you've done. I don't think you'll have any problems getting into Barnett. And you should be fine for Loyola and Purdue. You need to relax, baby."

Baby.

My heart spasms with pleasure at the endearment. I love how easily the word rolls off his lips. As if calling me that is so natural.

"I hope you're right."

"Let's wait and see what happens over the next couple of months. You're not alone in this, Vi. Whatever happens, I'm here, and we'll figure it out together."

His softly spoken words have my heart expanding with all the love I have inside for this man. He's right. I'm not alone and hearing him say it makes me feel better. No matter what happens, Sam will be at my side. And together we'll figure out the future.

Another silence falls over us as we bob in the water. I close my eyes, content to enjoy the moment. I want to take it in and savor it. My mind drifts for a while. When I open them again, Sam is at my side. His gaze rakes over the length of my body before settling on my breasts.

I glance at my chest and realize that my nipples are straining against the delicate fabric. The heated way he stares makes my body buzz with anticipation. It only takes one look from him to stoke everything to life inside me.

I reach around my back and unhook the clasps of my bra before sliding the straps down my arms and throwing it onto the side of the pool. It makes a slapping sound as it hits the tile. I relax again, floating next to him as he admires the view.

His lips descend, covering one stiffened peak before sucking it deep inside his mouth. Need spirals through me as I arch my back. With a popping noise, he releases one rosy-tipped breast. His face hovers over mine as his fingers pluck at my nipples. Heat coils deep within my belly. A whimper of pleasure escapes from between my lips as he plays with my body. There's nothing rushed about the way he touches me.

"Do you know how long I've been waiting for this? For you?"

Even though he continues to touch me in a way that drives me crazy, the sexual haze clears from my eyes.

"I'm sorry," I whisper. "I didn't know." Sometimes I wonder how I could have been so blind. When I think back on it now, I'm able to see his need so clearly.

"You don't have anything to apologize for." His gaze sears mine. "You were worth the wait, Vi."

I reach up, trailing my fingers over the hard angles and planes of his face. There's a bit of stubble that covers both his chin and cheek. His bright blue eyes are focused on me. I think they've always been focused on me. Almost like tunnel vision. I'm only sorry it took me so long to realize what was right in front of my face all these years. Sam has always been my best friend. With the exception of Mia, girlfriends have come and gone from my life, but Sam has always been, without fail, a steady constant.

I never want to lose that.

Or him.

I come to my feet and wrap my arms around his neck, pressing my naked breasts to his chest. With our mouths scant inches apart, my gaze cradles his. "It might have taken time for me to catch up, but I'm here now and I'm not going anywhere."

As his lips ghost over mine, a tidal wave of anticipation floods through me. I couldn't want Sam any more than I already do.

"Damn right, you're not."

And then his lips are crashing onto mine.

I'm swept away on the feel of him as his tongue plays havoc inside my mouth. I'm lost to the sensation of his thick arousal pressing against my core, making everything inside me dilate with pleasure.

His hands slip down my naked back, disappearing inside my panties until he's able to cup one round cheek in the palm of each hand. He pulls me closer until we're skin to skin.

Sam groans as I shift against him, trying to relieve the aching pressure growing inside me. "You need to stop doing that," he mutters thickly as his lips caress a trail down the column of my neck.

A moan falls from my mouth.

I want him.

Right here.

Right now.

Under the silvery moonlight that pours in through the windows.

"Why? Doesn't this feel good?" When I'm wrapped around him like this, it feels nothing short of blissful. And I know *exactly* what would make it feel even better.

"It's too damn good," he growls as his tongue laps at my throat, bathing the pulse with his tongue.

"Is there really such a thing?"

When he pulls away, the intensity is enough to scorch me alive. With a deliberateness, he rubs his lips across mine.

Once, twice, three times.

"Listen, baby, when I finally have you, it sure as hell isn't going to be in a pool."

His words leave me groaning as frustration pounds through my system.

Humor simmers in his voice as he says with faux sympathy, "Awww, is someone feeling impatient and horny?" It scrambles my senses when he nips at my neck.

All this waiting is killing me. It's all I can think about. I'm consumed with thoughts of Sam and his hot body. I'd like to give him a taste of his own medicine. I want him as frenzied as I am. When he holds me close, his hands palming my ass, I grind myself against him.

It feels so damn good.

Even though I'm tempted to close my eyes and enjoy each sensation as it spirals through me, I keep my gaze locked on his.

Sam grits his teeth as his blue depths leap with fire.

I rock my hips against him again. "Don't you want me?"

"You know I do," he growls.

A moan slips free from me as his covered cock grazes my clit at just the right angle. Unable to help myself, I bow my back as he holds me against him. My eyelids drift shut as pleasure ripples through my entire being. It's like throwing a stone into a calm lake and watching the way rings spiral outward.

I'm so close.

From grinding.

Sad, but true.

My back bends as everything in me tightens. My teeth sink into my lower lip as all that delicious—

"Oh, no you don't!"

His harsh words slice through the sexy haze clouding my brain as he drops me to my feet. My mouth falls open as my eyes widen.

I can't believe he just did that!

As our gazes clash, Sam leans forward and gently nips at my lip. His eyes hold mine captive. The heat within them snaps and sizzles, clawing at me with their barely harnessed need.

"The next time you come," he growls, "it'll be while riding my hard cock."

That being said, he takes my mouth in a punishing kiss. One that is so demanding, I can't help but surrender under the firm pressure of his lips as they rove over mine. His tongue plunders my mouth. It's only when a whimper escapes from me that he pulls away. His gaze sears mine as my tongue darts out to lick at my now tender lips.

"Do you understand?"

Even though my core aches for release, I give him a tight nod.

I've never seen this side of Sam before.

Assertive.

Demanding.

Forceful.

I hate to admit it, but it only makes me want him more than I already do.

Chapter Twenty-Two

SAM

Our hands are all over each other, frantically stroking and exploring as we burst through the apartment door. Now that we're together, I have this insatiable need to touch Violet. Whether it's holding her hand, kissing those plush lips, or cocooning her body with my own, I crave that physical connection.

No...not *crave*. *Crave* isn't nearly strong enough of a word.

I *need* it.

Like oxygen for breath.

I need Violet.

Even if we're sitting in class, I need the intimacy. The reaffirmation that this is really happening between us and isn't a dream I'm going to startle from.

At this point, I'm chalking up all these out-of-control feelings to this being a new relationship. At least, I hope that's what it is. I've waited so damn long for her to see me as something more than a friend. And now that she does, I need my hands on her all the time. Violet Winterfield is like a drug pumping wildly through my veins.

All I want to do is pull her into my room and have my way with her. Holding back has been torture. Even though I've been vibrating with the intense need careening through my system, I didn't want to rush her into bed. Instead, I've tried to give Violet time to acclimate. The last thing I want is for her to have regrets.

Once I have her, she's mine. I won't let go of her anytime soon.

But that didn't mean I couldn't drive her crazy with my touch. The downside is that I'm making myself just as freaking nuts. The thought of burying my cock deep inside her soft pussy has tormented me since she ended up in my bed two weeks ago.

Who am I kidding?

I've been dreaming about her for years.

Years.

As the sound of voices hit me, I realize we aren't alone.

Damn.

I rip my gaze from Violet only to find Roan, Dylan, his girlfriend Lexie, and Liam all sitting around in the living room. Dylan and Liam are focused on gunning down zombies in some post-apocalyptic world.

There's a round of greetings as we make our way into the living room. Exactly how long do we have to stand and make small talk before I can drag Violet off to my bedroom?

Is there a protocol for something like this?

Two minutes?

Five at the most?

I've given her nine days. That's more than enough time to process what is happening between us and change her mind.

Thank fuck that hasn't happened.

Violet is mine. And tonight, I'm claiming what's mine.

Dylan chooses that moment to break into my one-track thoughts of seducing Violet. "Hey, you don't mind if Liam crashes in my old room, do you? Shit is getting intense over at his place."

I shrug. As far as I'm concerned, Liam is welcome to stay here. He's just not welcome to eye-fuck Violet. As long as we're clear about that, everything should be copasetic.

As Liam's gaze meets mine, a wide grin slides across his face. Then his attention shifts to the girl at my side. I frown and haul her closer, so he doesn't get ideas. I really am going to beat the piss out of that guy one of these days.

"Hey, Violet," he says.

A shit eating smirk curves his lips.

Oblivious to the tension that radiates off me in thick waves, she returns the smile. I hate that he took her out and spent time alone with her. I don't think she has feelings for Liam, but I still find myself getting jealous.

It's ridiculous. Trust me, I know it is.

I find it difficult to rein in the possessiveness he rouses inside me when it comes to Violet. The funny part is that I've never felt territorial over a girl before. This is a first. But what else would you expect?

This is Violet we're talking about. I've wanted her for way too long to let sanity get in my way. Maybe after we sleep together, I'll be able to relax a little bit.

Then again, maybe not.

"Hi, Liam," she says.

All right, enough with the chit chat.

I send a scowl in Garrison's direction before hauling Violet into my room and slamming the door shut behind us.

With a smile trembling on her lips, she cocks her head toward the living room. "You don't want to hang out with your friends for a while?"

Wild horses couldn't drag me back out there. "Nope."

That's all I say before stripping off my still-damp shirt. Her gaze falls to my chest and her pupils dilate. I love the fascination she has with my body. I don't think I'll ever get used to the way she looks at me. The way her gaze licks over me, the tick of her pulse as it picks up speed, the way her breath hitches, coming out just a bit quicker. It all means that she likes what she sees. When she stares at me like that, it feels as if I could conquer the world. I've spent years waiting for her to view me as something more than a friend, and now she does.

I can't help but bask in it.

And use it against her every chance I get.

Now that I have her all to myself, some of the testosterone surging through my system begins to drain, and I'm able to slow this down. With unhurried movements, my fingers settle on the button of my cargo pants before flicking it open. Her attention is pinned to me as she sheds her shirt and jeans until she's standing before me in her bra and panties.

I'm tempted to fall to my knees and worship all those amazing curves. I love running my hands over her skin. Violet has no idea how gorgeous she is. Every once in a while, she'll complain about needing to shed a few pounds. I honestly don't understand what she's talking about. Her breasts are full, and I love the way her hips flare. Her tummy is firm but there's a hint of softness to the curve of it.

I have no idea how many times I've jerked off while fantasizing about her lush body. She's the only one I think about. It's been that way since freshman year of high school. What's about to happen tonight has been a long time in coming.

Unable to hold back any longer, I stalk toward her. My hands cradle her face before raining kisses on her swollen lips. As my tongue strokes against hers, I reach around and unfasten her bra. When it slides down her arms, I break contact and slip the material free before tossing it over my shoulder.

"You're so beautiful, baby," I murmur.

Without another word, I pick her up and carry her to the bed before laying her out on top of the covers. Goddamn, but this girl is gorgeous. Ever since I first laid eyes on her, Violet has always been mine. And I'm going to make sure she stays that way.

I hook my fingers into the elastic band of her lacy panties and tug them down her hips. She lifts her legs and kicks away the flimsy fabric. And then she's totally bare. Sharp shafts of need shoot through me. I pause as my gaze slides over her, taking in every dip, curve, and contour of her body. My attention drifts back to her face, and I can't help but wonder if she's nervous. After tonight, nothing will be the same again.

It's on the tip of my tongue to ask if she's certain about this. Before I'm able to force out the question, her lips curve into a smile. She raises her hand and curls her index finger, beckoning me forward.

If that wasn't enough of an invitation, she allows her legs to fall open. A groan rumbles up from my chest as my attention arrows to her pussy. It's so pink and lush, just waiting for my lips and tongue. I'm reminded of what it felt like to dip my fingers inside her tight heat before licking them clean.

She's truly stunning. And mine, I remind myself as possessiveness streaks through me.

With record speed, I remove the boxer-briefs and kneel on the bed. I've dreamt about this moment at least a thousand times but nothing can compare to the real thing. Her thighs widen as I move my shoulders between them. My gaze stays fastened to her core as my hands settle on her thighs, spreading her impossibly wide. I want to lick every inch of her. I want to hear her whimpers of pleasure when I drive my tongue deep inside her body and suck her delicate clit into my mouth.

When I'm done with Violet, she'll never think about another guy again. I'll be all she needs. Just like when I kissed her earlier, my mouth ghosts over her lower lips. She trembles beneath me as the warmth of my breath drifts across her silky flesh.

Once.

Twice.

Three times.

I want her to ache for what only I can give her. Her fingers tangle in my hair as I nibble at her flesh.

She arches. "That feels so good."

Damn right it does.

I don't think I've ever tasted anything as delicious as Violet. I could eat her up all night long. When her muscles tighten and a moan slips from her mouth, I know she's close. I press my lips against her pussy before moving up her body. There's a dazed look in her eyes as my length settles against her heat.

Her breath catches and her gaze stays locked on mine as I slide deep inside her body. Only when I'm buried balls deep do I pause and hold myself still.

Fuck me. I don't think I've ever felt anything as good as this. Her inner muscles clench around my hard length. Already I know that I won't last long. How can I when I've dreamed about this moment for so long?

"You feel so good, baby," I grit between clenched teeth. It takes everything I have inside not to fuck her hard the way I want to.

When I'm back under control, I pull out before plunging back inside again. Our bodies fall into a natural rhythm. Maybe we've never done this before with each other, but like everything else, there's an easiness to it.

Her hands drift down my back, her nails raking across my flesh. The little bit of pain mixed in with all that pleasure is what sends me skyrocketing over the edge. As a groan falls from my lips, she spasms around me and we come at the same time.

When stars burst behind my eyelids, I know that nothing will ever be the same again.

For either of us.

Chapter Twenty-Three

VIOLET

Faint wisps of sunlight filter in through the unadorned window. My eyelids feather open, taking in my surroundings. Sam's body is curved around mine. The man radiates heat like a furnace, and I find myself kicking away the covers before burrowing closer to him.

Instead of waking, his breathing remains deep and even.

Dawn is just breaking across the eastern horizon. Pink and purple color paints the canvas of morning sky in bright hues. Even though I'm exhausted, a smile of contentment settles across my lips.

Last night was amazing.

I don't think I've ever been loved quite so...*thoroughly*. And I have the sore muscles to prove it. Stretching, I test them out.

Yup, deliciously tender.

As I turn in the warm circle of his arms, my gaze settles on his face. Even when he's deep in slumber, and those brilliant cerulean-hued eyes aren't able to pin me in place, Sam is still devastatingly handsome.

My gaze roves over all the carved angles and planes of his face. The slightly crooked nose he broke in high school. Those gorgeous lips that are capable of giving so much pleasure.

Who would have ever suspected?

All the girls he's been with over the years tumble unwantedly through my head. I can't help but wonder if he made love to each of them with as much tenderness as he did to me. I have to tamp down the jealousy because I have no right to feel that way.

Refusing to think about it, I continue cataloguing each feature. He has a sculpted jawline with just a bit of sexy stubble covering it. And then there are those ridiculously long lashes that are feathered against the chiseled bones of his cheeks.

Sam is downright gorgeous.

It's not that I didn't realize it before, I've always been aware of his physical attributes. But it's only within the last month or so that I've become aware of him on a different level. I have always loved Sam as a friend. I still do. But it's deeper now. More meaningful.

For the first time in my life, it feels as if everything has fallen perfectly into place. Being with him fills me with an absurd amount of giddiness. I don't know what to do with all this joy. It almost feels like it's too much for the confines of my body.

Even though I would love nothing more than to lie here for the rest of the day, wrapped up in the warm comfort of Sam's embrace, I need to use the bathroom. Carefully, so as not to disturb him, I untangle myself from his arms before slipping into one of Sam's T-shirts and my underwear so I can leave the room.

I bring the soft cotton to my nose and inhale the masculine scent. My heart spasms at the thought of being cloaked in something that is his. This thing between us feels crazy, but it's a good kind of crazy.

Not more than a few minutes later, I slip back inside the room and close the door behind me. As my gaze settles on the bed, I'm struck by the sight of Sam sprawled out across the queen-size mattress. The breath catches at the back of my throat as I stand rooted in place, unable to do anything more than eat him up with my eyes.

He's rolled onto his belly and one brawny arm is thrown above his head. His face is turned toward the window as the first rays of morning light slant over his handsome features. My gaze roams appreciatively over the broad set of his shoulders, down his well-built back, to his tapered waist before sinking to the high, tight curve of his ass. My pulse quickens as my gaze licks over that area before moving down muscled thighs that are smattered with dark blond hair.

It seems unbelievable that Sam Harper is mine. Has *always* been mine. I almost shake my head at the notion of him waiting patiently for my clueless ass to play catch up. Thank goodness he saw what I couldn't.

I want to hold onto this moment for the rest of my life.

This is the beginning of *us*.

The beginning of something beautiful.

The delicate unfolding of a wonderful new phase in our relationship.

The need to capture this moment arrows through me. Not overthinking it, I swipe my phone from the bedside table before backing up and squeezing his body into the tiny frame of the screen. It takes a moment to focus before I snap him from the perfect angle. After the photo has been taken, I set the phone on the nightstand and climb back into bed.

As soon as I do, he rolls onto his side and wraps his arm around me before hauling me close enough for all my soft curves to align perfectly with his hard lines. Contentment pulses through me as I fall asleep again.

Chapter Twenty-Four

SAM

With a couple of hours to kill in between class and practice, I make a quick trip home to see my parents. It's a little after two in the afternoon when I walk through the front door.

"Hello?" My raised voice echoes off the hardwoods that run through the first floor. Since it's early, I know my sister and brother are still at school. Gavin is on the eighth-grade basketball team, so he won't be home until four, which is around the time my sister, Ari, gets off the bus from elementary school.

"Mom," I call out again, wondering where she is.

After a moment, I hear footfalls coming up from the basement. I go to the door and pull it open as she appears with a few stacked boxes in her hands.

"Hi, sweetie!" She gives me a quick peck on the cheek before sweeping by. "This is a surprise." Concern flickers in her eyes as her brows slide together. "Is everything all right?"

"Yup, it's fine. Just thought I'd stop by and see how everything is going."

When she doesn't respond, I point to the containers in her arms. "Do you want some help with that?"

"Nope, I'm good."

I trail after her as she walks into the formally appointed dining room with its ornate crystal chandelier and Doric columns. Both were added at my father's request. The gleaming wood table in the center of the room can easily accommodate fourteen guests. At least twice a month, Dad likes to host an evening of drinks along with a catered dinner for some of the more influential members of the community. I've been required on more than one occasion to suit up in a tux to help grease palms.

I don't hate it.

But I don't love it either.

The worst I can say is that by the end of the night, my cheeks ache from all the forced smiles. Plus, I have to bone up on the local, state, and national political scene, which is a job in and of itself. My dad's people usually give me a cheat sheet of talking points to discuss.

Since I've been knee-deep in classes and football, Dad hasn't requested my presence of late. If I'm serious about following him into politics, it's something I'll need to be comfortable with. At least look comfortable doing.

What I've learned over the years is that appearances are everything.

Luckily, nothing needs to be decided right now. For the moment, I want to enjoy the bubble Violet and I have created around ourselves. I don't want to do anything that will jeopardize it. After years of waiting patiently, I finally have the girl of my dreams. I'm happier now than I've ever been in my entire life.

Maybe it's crazy, but I feel invincible with Violet by my side.

After she hefts the boxes onto the dining room table, Mom settles a hand on her slender hip. "So, you stopped by during the middle of the week for no reason?" Her eyes narrow as she studies me. "Is something going on at school that I should be aware of?"

I flash a smile. "Nope. I just wanted to check in with you."

That's enough to have her brow smoothing out and a small smile curling the edges of her lips upward. "Aww, aren't you sweet."

I point to the plastic bins she dragged up from the basement. "What are in the boxes?"

She pats one of the lids. "Just some paperwork from when I was working."

"Oh?" My mom quit her job over a decade ago. I can't imagine why she would be schlepping all this up from the basement.

With a sheepish smile, she admits, "I was thinking about going back to the hospital." Quickly she adds, "You know, when the kids are in school. It would be just a few days a week."

"I think that's a great idea." If Mom wants to get back into the workforce, then that's what she should do. I know there's a lot around here to keep her busy, but there isn't a reason she can't do both. Plenty of women do.

"Really?" She seems genuinely surprised by my reaction. "You do?"

My smile broadens. "Yeah, of course. Why not?"

With a shrug, her gaze slides away. Her voice lowers before she confesses, "I haven't spoken to your father about it yet. I know he thinks it's important for me to be here for Gavin and Ari. And I do as well. But they don't need me the same way they used to. I'm not as busy as I once was when you guys were younger. I thought it might be nice to get back into nursing again." As soon as those words leave her lips, she tacks on, "It's just an idea I'm mulling over."

"Mom, I think you should definitely look into it."

We stare at each other for a moment before she gives me a full-fledged smile. Relief fills her eyes. "Thanks, Sam. Your encouragement means a lot to me."

My mom has always been there to support everything I've done. Hell, I wouldn't be who I am today without her. She was tough when I needed it and always there with words of encouragement. "You deserve to do whatever makes you happy."

Hastily, she cuts in, "My family makes me happy. All of you. I couldn't be prouder of how the three of you are turning out. We've raised wonderful, kindhearted children."

"*You've* raised wonderful kindhearted children," I say quietly.

Her gaze holds mine as she nips her lower lip with her teeth before reminding me, "Your dad is a good father. He's always been there when we've needed him."

I'm not sure what propels me to challenge her words, but they're shooting out of my mouth before I can stop them. "Has he?"

She straightens her shoulders as the smile falls from her pretty face. "Unfortunately, work takes him away from his family, but he genuinely believes in what he's doing. That's why it was important that I step away from my career and be here, because we knew there would be times when he couldn't be." Her gaze searches mine. "I hope you understand that, Sam. Everything he does is for us."

Remorse fills me. It was never my intention to upset her. It's carefully that I try to navigate the conversation we're embroiled in. "I know, but you're the one who's made most of the sacrifices. All I'm saying is that I think it's great you're looking to get back into nursing. That's it." Although privately, I do think my question is valid. My dad is gone at least seventy to eighty percent of the time, leaving Mom here to handle everything on her own.

Instead of pressing the issue, she accepts my words at face value and gives me a hint of a smile. "We'll see." Her focus drops to the boxes as she runs her fingers over the lid. "If I'm going to apply for my state license, I'll need to go through some of my old coursework."

Now that we're once again on safe terrain, I say, "I really hope it works out."

She shrugs as if it's no big deal, but I know better. I can see how important this is to her along with the excitement of getting back into her career. "We'll just have to wait and see what happens. I had lunch with an old colleague a few days ago, and he said there were a number of opportunities available at the hospital. He gave me the name of someone in human resources that I can contact for more information. Maybe I'll set up an appointment when I'm ready to move forward with the process."

"That sounds like a good plan."

Her smile wavers and uncertainty flickers in her eyes. "I'm not sure what your father will think about all this."

Air leaks from my lungs because I think we both know how he'll react. Not that I necessarily believe it, but I don't want to dampen her spirits. "Who knows, maybe he'll surprise you, and won't mind as much as you think he will." I really hope for her sake, that turns out to be the case. If she wants to go back to work, she should be able to do it. Everything in their marriage—and this family—shouldn't have to revolve around my dad and his schedule.

The pensive expression remains for another moment or two before disappearing. "Maybe. We haven't spoken about me going back to the hospital for a while. He's so busy gearing up for this election season."

I nod. Although, that's nothing new. Even though the election isn't until next November, strategy meetings are already underway. And it'll only continue to gear up.

"Sam?"

My gaze snaps back to hers. "Yeah?"

She clears her throat. "Please don't mention this conversation to him right now. He's got enough on his plate with everything going on. This is nothing more than a fact-finding mission. After looking into everything, I might decide it's not what I want."

"I won't say a word." Mom shouldn't be afraid of what my father's response will be. She shouldn't have to ask permission to go back to work. Unfortunately, I know what she's trying to convey even if she doesn't necessarily want to say it out loud.

She'll see what kind of commitment going back to school or studying for her license will be, and the kind of hours she can work, and that will determine whether or not she moves forward with the process.

Which sucks.

But I don't tell her that.

I can't.

I really hope that when she decides to discuss the situation with my father, he shocks the hell out of both of us and is supportive.

Instead of continuing the conversation, she changes the subject. "I stopped by and checked on Edward the other day."

"Oh?" My breath gets clogged in my throat. I realize that both of them are getting up there in age, and he hasn't been feeling well lately. For Violet's sake, I don't want to see anything happen to either one of them. "Is everything okay?"

"I think so." She tilts her head as her brows pinch together. "I told

Alice to call if she needed anything, and that I would stop back in a day or two to see how they're doing."

"I don't want Violet to lose anyone else." What I hate is how powerless I feel to protect her from that occurring. My natural instinct is to wrap Violet up in my arms and hold her tight. I want to keep her safe from everything that has the potential to hurt her.

That's all I've ever wanted to do.

Mom's eyes soften. "I take it that everything is good with Violet?"

One side of my mouth hitches. "Yup." And that's all I'm going to say on the subject.

Her brow arches as her smile turns into more of a knowing grin. "So," Mom says smugly, "she's finally come to her senses, huh?"

And on that note...

"Hey, would you look at that," I don't even bother glancing at the clock on my phone, "time to get back to school." I turn on my heels and head for the front door.

"Say hi to Violet for us!" she calls after me, her soft chuckles following me out as I step onto the porch.

Chapter Twenty-Five

VIOLET

Mia knocks on my partially opened door before sticking her head inside. "Hey, Caroline and Maddie are ordering pizzas, are you interested in splitting one?"

Pizza sounds amazing. Plus, I'm in desperate need of fuel for energy. It feels like I'm running on fumes. I've been bogged down most of the day studying for tests and making a last pass through a six-page paper due in sociology on Thursday.

"Count me in, I'm famished. I think my stomach has started to eat its own lining."

"Okay...great." Her mouth hitches at one side. "About the pizza, not your stomach consuming itself. Should I get our usual? Pepperoni with extra cheese and an order of garlic knots?"

"Definitely." My tummy rumbles in agreement.

"Fine, I'll let them know." She disappears out the door and down the hall.

Ten minutes later, I'm having a difficult time concentrating with pizza on the brain. I push away from my desk before heading out to our common area where Mia is sitting with her Kindle.

"Reading something good?" I ask.

She flashes me a slight smile before setting the device on the table next to her. "I'm juggling about three different books right now." Her voice deflates. "With all of these computer programming classes, it's nice to turn my brain off and escape for a while."

My brows draw together. I'm not used to hearing this kind of tone from Mia. "Are you doing okay? You seem kind of off."

She jerks her shoulders before glancing at her fingernails. Or what's left of them. They look as if they've been chewed to the pulp, which is a clear indication that Mia is stressing about something. Even though she hasn't said much about it, I know things haven't righted themselves with her boyfriend.

After a few silent moments, she blows out a breath. "I haven't talked to Carter for a couple of days. He's not returning my calls or texts." Her gaze lifts to mine, and I see the hurt and worry swimming around in her green depths. She drops her voice before admitting, "I don't know what to do anymore."

"I'm sorry, Mia. I wish you would have said something about it sooner." Then again, maybe if I weren't so wrapped up in Sam, I would have noticed her melancholy without her having to spell it out for me.

"We're supposed to be moving in together after graduation, and he's barely talking to me. I took the job in Philadelphia so we could be in the same place again. What am I supposed to do?" Her troubled gaze holds mine.

"I'm not sure," I admit, racking my brain for an answer. It's not like I have a ton of relationship experience to draw from. In fact, I'm the last person who should be doling out advice on how to keep a boyfriend. I'm more skilled at losing them. "If he's avoiding you, then maybe you need to take a road trip to Philly. Then you two can sit down and talk about what's going on."

"Maybe." She nods before picking at her thumbnail. "It's just surprising that he's handling the situation like this. I know things were tense when he left, but I thought with enough time, everything would smooth itself out. That hasn't happened." She flicks her attention to me before whispering, "Maybe this is it for us."

No way!

Unable to believe what I'm hearing, I shake my head in protest. "Go see him. Force Carter to talk to you and get this figured out." I don't want to see their relationship crumble over him proposing and her not being ready to take that next step.

How ridiculous is that?

"Yeah, well," she says with frustration tinging her voice, "it's hard to talk to him when he won't answer my calls." Her brows draw together before she adds, "He's being childish about the whole thing. He needs to get over it and move on."

I shrug. "Maybe he's embarrassed."

She levels a hard look in my direction. "He shouldn't be. It's not like I *don't* want to be with him, it's more a matter of bad timing. I'm not ready to be engaged." Her gaze skewers mine. "I love him more than anything and I want to be with him, but he's making it difficult."

"I know. He probably needs to hear you say that."

A wave of exhaustion rolls over her, and her head falls back against the couch cushions as she stares at the ceiling. "I don't know...maybe you're right. Maybe that's the only way I'm going to get through to him. With finals coming up in a few weeks, I don't have the time to run off and reassure his damn ass."

I give her a slight smile. "Relationships can be a pain. No question about it."

She picks up her head until her gaze can lock on mine. One dark eyebrow slinks across her forehead as she smirks. "Oh? Is that so? I can't believe there are already problems in paradise with golden delicious."

"There aren't any problems with *Sam*." I refuse to acknowledge her little pet name. Now that Sam and I are officially together, I know she uses the endearment to needle me.

"I know. You two are totally sickening." Her head falls back onto the cushion again as she sighs, "Once upon a time, my relationship was like that, too."

I roll my eyes. "Oh, please. Why do you think I have to get the hell out of Dodge whenever Carter rolls into town?"

Her lips twitch. "Those were the good old days."

She lifts her head for a second time. "It took long enough but I'm glad you two are finally together. This is the first time in three years that I've seen you with someone you *actually* want to be with."

The comment throws me off guard. "What do you mean?"

"I don't know. All of the other guys you've been with," she pauses, "you never really seemed into them. Kind of like you didn't give a damn if they were there or not."

Hmmm. I guess she's right about that. They were nothing more than a distraction. Short lived ones, at that. I was never upset when those relationships stalled or flat lined. More than half the time, I was the one pulling the plug, ready to move on.

What I have with Sam feels different from anything I've ever experienced before. I care about him, and what happens between us. The depth of love I have for him is almost frightening in its intensity.

"I'm glad you're happy, Vi. You deserve it." She gives me a wink. "Looks like you finally found your perfect fit, Goldilocks."

A small chuckle escapes from me because it's true, Sam fits me perfectly. Never in a million years would I have guessed that we could be so happy in a relationship.

There's a knock on our door as eight girls crash into our suite with four boxes of pizza, three bags of garlic knots, and a chopped salad before settling around our small living room area. They find places to hunker down on the floor and couch as box lids are thrown open and the intoxicating aroma of pizza fills the air.

I'm devouring my second slice of pepperoni when Maddie says with a smirk, "I heard you're knocking boots with Sam Harper. I thought you two were *just* friends. Not friends with benefits."

I glance around and notice that her comment has ensnared everyone's attention. A few of the girls look stunned by this new development while others tell me that they saw it coming from a mile away. And one, Caroline, asks how long we've been doing the deed.

More questions follow. *Is it any good? Is he hung like a horse? Is it the best sex I've ever had?*

Jeez.

The nerve of these nosy-ass girls.

Instead of answering, I stuff my face with pizza. At the rate I'm going, I'll end up devouring the whole pie single-handedly.

"You're so lucky. That boy is such a hottie." Caroline gives me a wink before adding, "Be sure to send him my way when you're done. I would love to get me some of that."

Giggles erupt, and a few of the girls echo the sentiment.

Even though I should brush off their chatter, irritation ignites inside me. They're discussing Sam, and his body, as if he's a piece of meat.

The conversation lasts for another five minutes while they dissect, in great detail, every body part until I'm blushing with embarrassment. All right...so maybe in the past, I've been guilty of rehashing some of the finer details when I've been with a guy, but I can't bear to do that with Sam.

And I certainly don't want to hear any of them do it, either.

Thankfully, it doesn't take long for the conversation to morph into a hotly contested debate regarding which Barnett football player is the hottest. After a ridiculously elaborate discussion, they're still unable to reach a general consensus.

Each girl has a favorite.

It's only when the pizzas have been demolished, and all of the football players have been thoroughly dissected, do voices finally settle and peace once again reigns over the land.

Sheesh.

You would seriously think these girls were discussing world politics or global warming by how fiercely debated some of these exchanges were.

Once the conversation turns to the men's lacrosse team, I excuse myself to use the bathroom. I have zero interest in listening to them break down the lax players in the same manner they did the football team.

And I don't want them asking anymore in-depth questions about Sam. For the time being, I want to keep our relationship all to myself. What we do is private, and the last thing I need is a bunch of girls wanting to know how he is in bed.

When I finally make it back from the bathroom, Caroline holds my phone in the palm of her hand. Four girls are crowded around her, staring at the screen. As I move further into the room, they simultaneously glance up. A weird feeling creeps down my spine as they continue to stare.

A sly smile mars Caroline's face as she holds out the phone. "Sam just called." She clears her throat as two of the girls glance at each other, not even bothering to hide their grins. "I didn't think you would mind if I answered it."

Giggles erupt as I pluck the phone from her outstretched hand. I really shouldn't have left it sitting on the table when I walked out of the room. That was stupid.

When I have the phone safely back in my possession, Caroline jumps up and dumps her plate into the garbage can. Within a few minutes, the place empties, and Mia and I are left with our box of half-eaten pizza.

A strange feeling washes over me. Like something just happened but no one wants to fill me in.

I glance at Mia, wondering if she feels the odd energy as well. "Kind of weird how everyone cleared out so fast."

Mia holds my gaze for a moment before it skitters away. "I think everyone is just bogged down with studying." She swipes her Kindle from the end table near the couch before tossing the words over her shoulder, "I've got to hit the books."

With that, she leaves me standing alone in our living room.

Even though her words confirm what I was thinking, the feeling in the pit of my belly still feels like something is off. But what? Instead of delving deeper, I decide to let it go. I have to finish proofreading my sociology paper and then get through a few chapters for Rickets' class.

But first things first.

I need to hear Sam's deep voice. I love the feeling of anticipation that skates through me when we talk. It's kind of hilarious, considering that I've spoken with Sam on the phone for years, and have never felt this kind of eagerness.

"Hey, babe," he says, picking up on the first ring.

I love that, too. The endearments that fall so easily from his lips. They strum something deep inside me.

"Hi."

"Heard you ordered some pizza. Did you save a few slices for me?"

I snort. "Sorry, you'll have to fight Mia for the leftovers." And I would seriously advise against doing that. She's like a barracuda when it comes to Peppino's Pizza.

He sighs. "Nah, not worth it. She'll only end up winning."

Damn right she will. There's no way in hell she'll part with a slice. Not even golden delicious has that kind of power. Thank goodness she didn't divulge her little pet name to the girls. I would have seriously killed her.

Switching gears, he cajoles in a voice that arrows straight to my core. "Any chance I can talk you into spending the night?"

By the way his tone dips, I know *exactly* what he has in mind. And it doesn't involve sleeping either...

The ache that flares to life between my thighs has me mentally going over the chapters I need to plow through. It's at least a couple hours worth. If I'm lucky. As much as I would love to see Sam tonight, I don't think it's going to happen. After listening to almost half the girls on my floor discuss his finer points, I have the strange urge to mark my territory.

I should feel embarrassed by such a ridiculous—not to mention primitive and jealousy-driven—impulse, except...well...I don't.

Sam is mine, and I want everyone to know it. Especially some of these girls who think they'll be partaking in my leftovers.

Not going to happen, bitches.

As those thoughts crash through my head, I flop onto my bed, and stare up at the ceiling all the while cradling the slim phone to my ear. "I wish I could, but I have too much studying to do. I'll probably be working until one or so."

"You could study over here," he wheedles, "I promise to make it worth your while."

"*Exactly* how will you do that?" Even though I know damn well how he'll do it, I love hearing him talk dirty to me.

When he chuckles, his voice turns low and gravelly. "Baby, you know *exactly* what I'm going to do to that sweet little pussy of yours."

My thighs automatically clench, and I can't help the moan that falls from my lips. Because yes—I can imagine all the delicious things he would do.

"I need to taste you, Vi. I haven't had you on my tongue in at least forty-eight hours. Come on, baby. Study over here. I'll leave you alone...for a while."

I groan. My clit is throbbing an insistent tempo. "Yeah, we've tried that before. Remember? All you do is distract me."

He snorts in response. "If kissing you and running my fingers over your body is now considered *distracting*, then I'm guilty as charged."

"Of course, you are," I quip, "which is exactly why I'm staying put. I'll spend tomorrow night over there. I promise."

"You're such a killjoy." He sounds like a petulant, two-year-old who hasn't gotten his way.

"Killjoy, my ass!"

Those words have him growling, "You don't even want to know what I'd like to do to that gorgeous ass of yours."

I shoot up on my bed before screeching into the phone, "*Sam*!"

"I'm just saying..." his voice trails off.

His laughter makes me think that he's just fooling around, but who knows with him. Sam has a lot more kink than I ever suspected.

And God help me, I like it.

A lot.

Although, what he's talking about...I'm not too sure about *that*.

"You can get those ideas out of your head right now, buddy," I huff, barely able to keep the amusement from invading my voice.

"Aww, come on, babe," he pleads, continuing to chuckle. Sometimes I think Sam enjoys fucking with me.

Both literally, and figuratively speaking.

He loves talking dirty. A huge grin will light up his face whenever he manages to shock me.

I shake my head even though he's unable to see me do it. "I'm hanging up now. And when I speak with you tomorrow, I don't want to hear any more ass talk. Got it?"

He grumbles before muttering, "Got it." Then his tone changes, becoming more serious. "Night, babe."

"Night, Sam."

I can't help but smile as I hit disconnect and settle in for a few more hours of studying.

Chapter Twenty-Six

SAM

If I didn't know better, I'd think people were craning their necks, attempting to catch a glimpse of me as I hurry my ass across campus. What I can't figure out is if it's all in my imagination, or if something is legitimately going on.

Even though there are about twenty thousand students on campus, I'm not anonymous. Barnett is a huge football school. All of the players are well-known. Even third stringers have clout around here.

And I'm no third stringer.

That being said, I've never commanded this kind of snap-your-head-around attention before.

I don't like it.

Girls point and smile as I book past them. Some wave, and a few blush when eye contact is made. Then there are the others. Ones who are more brazen, who give me wolfish grins as their gazes run down the length of me. I have half a mind to stop and ask what the hell is going on, but I don't because I rolled out of bed late this morning. I was too cranked up after that phone call with Violet to fall asleep last night. So now, I'm trying to hustle my way across campus to make my nine o'clock class on time.

Five minutes later, I slide into my usual seat at the back of my

Environmental Law and Policies class. Somehow, I manage to make it on time. With a huff of breath, I pull my laptop free of its case and fire it up. The back of my neck prickles with awareness. Almost as if somebody is staring holes into me. I swear that half the students are chattering more than they were when I first walked in. And the professor has just started to lecture.

Seriously, what the hell is going on?

I glance around and notice that it's mostly girls who are pointing and whispering. A few attempt to catch my attention. And the looks they're giving me...

It's like I'm naked or something.

I swear one of them just licked her lips.

All slow-like.

No lie.

I mean, what the hell is *that* about?

I'm not Roan King or Liam Garrison, and I have zero problem with that. I've never *wanted* or, better yet, *needed* that kind of notoriety. Usually, I try to fly under the radar. I was treated to countless lectures before leaving for college about everything I did being a direct reflection upon my father (yada-yada-yada). And because Dad expects me to follow in his political footsteps, it's been pounded into my head that I can't do anything that will haunt me later in life when I'm trying to make a name for myself.

I've seen firsthand how political opponents and the media salivate over the most outlandish pieces of gossip. I've also seen what they do to Roan. Shit gets made up about him all the time, and there's not much he can do to stop it. Stories get twisted and turned until they don't even resemble the truth.

For those reasons, I don't have Facebook, Instagram, Twitter, Snapchat or anything else that will leave behind a social media trail. Once that crap is out in the world, the potential for damage is there forever, always dogging your heels.

Since I'm interested in environmental law, and could see myself practicing it one day, I try to focus on the material being discussed. But I'm distracted by the three girls off to the side who keep staring at me. Every time our gazes connect, they offer up hopeful smiles.

It's disconcerting. I've never spoken to any of them before.

All of a sudden, they're trying to catch my attention?

In the middle of class?

It's just plain weird.

Ignoring them, I continue taking notes, answering questions, and contributing to the discussion when I feel I have something worthwhile to add.

But still...that strange feeling that has been gnawing at me ever since I stepped foot on campus this morning won't go away. By the time class is dismissed, I'm twitchy and irritated. I want to know what the hell is going on because something is definitely up. It's like I've been left out of some epic joke.

Or, worse, I'm the butt of it.

As I jump to my feet to leave, the three girls who have been glancing my way the entire hour, block my escape. They stare with shy grins plastered across their blushing faces.

When I remain silent, the redhead standing in the middle clears her throat. "Um, we were wondering if you would sign our pictures." That's when I notice each of them clutching a sheet of paper in their hands. But I'm unable to make out what the image is.

My brows snap together as irritation simmers in my voice, "Sign your *what*?"

The dark-haired girl next to the redhead jumps in. "Our pictures." She gives me a look like I should already know what she's babbling about. "Will you autograph them for us?"

That uneasy feeling in the pit of my gut multiplies. I sling my backpack over my shoulder, impatient to distance myself from them. "Sorry, you have me confused with someone else."

That's when the redhead shoves a thick, glossy sheet at me. I have no other choice but to glance at it. As I do, the floor disappears from beneath my feet.

What the hell is this?

My brain blanks as I continue to stare. The image can't be real. It has to be photoshopped or doctored or something crazy like that.

Except...

Except that's my bed.

In my room.

And I'm naked.

As in *I-have-no-fucking-clothes-on*.

My brain keeps telling me this has to be some kind of elaborate prank, but I realize with gut-wrenching clarity that it's not. This photo isn't a mistake. It's real. Because that's me. And that's my bed. Those are my fucking sheets crumpled around my thighs. And there's my bare ass right smack in the middle of the damn shot. My mind races, attempting to come up with a plausible explanation for what I'm staring at. How the hell could something like this happen?

Who did this?

My gut clenches as my brain spins out of control. Only one person comes to mind.

I crush the picture in my hand and give all three girls a scowl. It's dark enough to have them retreating. As I'm about to walk away, I rip the other two pictures from their hands.

"Hey!"

"Those are ours!"

"Dude, we just wanted you to sign them for us!"

Without responding, I ball my hands before stalking from the room and then the building. Anger and hurt swirl through me, threatening to suck me under.

I can't believe this.

More than that—I can't believe *Violet* would do something like this.

The rest of my shit-for-day doesn't go any better than it began. Only now, Violet is trying to frantically reach me. Her messages fill up my voicemail box. Even though I don't answer, she continues to text.

But I can't deal with her right now. In fact, I don't want to deal with *any* of this bullshit. By the time I drag my ass to football practice later that afternoon, I'm impatient to get out on the field and pummel the shit out of someone. I'm so pissed off. People have been hooting and hollering at me all day long.

Those fuckers on the lacrosse team just couldn't resist throwing a bunch of wisecracks my way. Of which many had to do with, yeah, you guessed it—the crack of my ass. I'm fed up with it. There's a massive tension headache brewing at the base of my skull.

It's only a matter of time before my parents catch wind of this. My father has a whole crew working around the clock, trolling the internet and social media sites for anything that has the potential to damage his campaign. My father is extremely proud of his untarnished reputation. There aren't any skeletons hidden in his closet. At least, none that his opponents have found.

As I push my way through the locker room doors, I yank out my earbuds. It was the only way I could drown out all the people catcalling my name. If I hadn't tuned it out, I would have totally lost my shit. And this situation is fucked up enough without me adding to it by going off the deep end.

As I drop my bag onto the bench, my eyebrows lower, and a growl of displeasure rumbles up from my chest as I catch sight of an eight-by-ten picture of my naked ass taped to the locker. I grab the photo, ripping it down before crumpling and hurtling it clear across the room.

Fuckers.

Ignoring the guys who are already getting into their gear, I focus on pulling out my pads and suiting up.

From the corner of my eye, I catch Dylan and Roan walk into the room before heading in my direction. Their lockers flank mine. I swear, if either of them makes one joke about the situation, I will unleash the fucking beast I keep locked up tight. Just because I seem easygoing and amicable doesn't mean I'm weak or can be messed with.

That's a misconception.

An erroneous one at that.

If anything, it only makes me more dangerous. Do you realize how much self-control it takes to keep your temper in check? To not lead with your fists when that's what you'd prefer to do?

Losing your temper is ridiculously easy. There's no self-discipline involved. And that's not me. It's not who I was raised to be. I was taught to be clearheaded and think before acting. To not allow raw emotion to guide me. To carefully weigh my actions as well as the consequences.

Using your anger to propel you forward as a motivator takes strength of will and character. This is the first time in my life that I've ever felt close to losing control over my emotions.

What cuts even deeper is that I wouldn't be teetering on the brink of a meltdown if Violet weren't involved in this fiasco. After years of patiently waiting for her, she's finally mine. I had assumed she would protect our relationship.

I was wrong.

This picture feels like a blunt-edged knife stuck in my heart. Even though I've thought of little else all day long, I still can't wrap my mind around the fact that she did this to me.

Frustration pounds through me as I rake my hand through my hair. If one word erupts from their yaps, all hell will break loose. I've been pushed to the limit today. One measly syllable from either of them, and I'll lose it all over their damn asses.

As they settle next to me on the bench, Roan clears his throat. "You all right?"

I jerk my head into a tight nod, not wanting to discuss the photograph or anything else that has to do with the clusterfuck I now find myself embroiled in.

Both remain silent as we gear up. But that doesn't stop two sophomore assholes from bellowing out a few choice comments. Pissed off, I throw down my helmet and straighten my shoulders. If I have to beat the shit out of a couple loudmouths to get them to shut up, I'll do it.

At this point, I'm aching to use my fists.

As I walk past Roan, he stills me with a hand to the shoulder. Since this has been one hell of a messed-up day, I let the pair of them knock a few heads together instead. Within moments, all of the noise dies down until the locker room is as silent as a church for Sunday services.

When Liam pushes his way through the door two minutes later, I know there's going to be issues. The moment his gaze falls on me, a wide grin spreads across his face. "Hey, nice ass shot, Harper. Very artistically done. Didn't know you had it in you."

"Shut the fuck up, Garrison," I growl.

Like I want to hear any shit from him?

Liam chuckles before shrugging like my words are nothing more than water off a duck's back. "What's the big deal? I thought it was hilarious."

I don't bother to respond. Liam and I are teammates, but he

doesn't know dick about my life. Most these guys don't, which is exactly the way I like it. In this locker room and out on the field, I just want to be Sam Harper. Not Senator Derek Harper's son.

When I fail to respond, Dylan snaps, "It's not funny."

Roan shoots Dylan a look before dropping his voice. "Does your father know?"

I shake my head. That's one conversation I've tried not to dwell on.

The smirk on Liam's face turns questioning. "Why would his parents find out? It's not a sex tape. Just chill and go with it, dude."

Dylan shakes his head before muttering, "Don't you know who his father is, dumbass?"

Liam raises a brow before glancing my way with more interest. "Should I?"

"Does the name *Senator Derek Harper* ring any bells for you?"

Liam's eyes widen before slicing to Roan for confirmation, as if Dylan might be fucking with him. Apparently, their solemn attitudes are enough to convince Liam that it's the truth.

"Seriously?" He scratches his chin as his gaze holds mine.

I give him a tight nod in response.

"Isn't he running for re-election soon?" Liam asks.

"Yup," I bite out.

Already I know that the media will have a field day with this. And I will never hear the end of it. The thought of Gavin or Ari seeing the photograph leaves a knot of queasiness sitting in the pit of my gut.

"Sorry, I had no idea," he mutters.

I shrug. Harper isn't an uncommon surname, so I'm usually able to avoid being linked to my dad. I could have easily chosen to attend an out-of-state school, but when Violet decided on Barnett, I wanted to stick close as well. When a dull ache throbs to life behind my eyes, I massage my left temple. I still can't believe she did this to me.

Mind officially blown.

Liam grabs his pads from the locker and starts to strip down before suiting up. "How did this happen? Who leaked the photo? Was it some pissed off ex-girlfriend?" His eyes settle on mine as he waits for an answer.

I really wish this had been a pissed off chick with an ax to grind. I could deal with that. But it wasn't. I've spent more time inspecting the picture, hoping to find something that would prove that it's a photo-shopped piece of garbage. It's not. In the upper corner of the picture is the brown leather messenger bag Violet carries around with her. I'd recognize it anywhere.

It's only then that I notice Roan and Dylan have stopped what they're doing and are staring at me. They want to know who fucked me over. Even as I open my mouth, the words stick in my throat. I do the only thing I can, and shrug my shoulders, refusing to say anything at all.

"Do you know who did this?" Roan asks.

I jerk my head into a tight nod.

"What does Violet have to say about it?" Dylan questions. "I'm sure she's pissed as hell."

Something in my expression must give me away because Liam sucks in a harsh breath. "No fucking way, dude." He shakes his head in disbelief. "Violet wouldn't do something like that to you."

My narrowed gaze cuts to his. A day ago, I wouldn't have thought so either. More than that, it pisses me off to hear him defend her like he knows anything about Violet at all. He doesn't know dick.

As soon as I'm suited up, I walk toward the metal doors that lead to the field. I can't sit here for another moment as this shit circles viciously through my head.

I need a grueling practice to kick my ass.

I need to turn it all off.

For just two damn hours.

Then, when I've cooled down and can think clearly, I need to figure out what I'm going to tell my parents because it's not a matter of *if* they find out.

It's a matter of *when*.

Chapter Twenty-Seven

VIOLET

My heart sits in my throat. He won't return any of my calls or text messages. It's not like Sam to ignore me. In all the years I've known him, there has never been this kind of stereo silence between us.

The more time that slips by, the more anxious I become. I just about died when I woke up this morning and saw that picture. The picture *I* snapped when he was sleeping has now been splashed across Instagram and Facebook, not to mention a few websites that are solely devoted to the Barnett football players. In case I hadn't already seen it first thing this morning, a ton of people thoughtfully forwarded the picture to me.

I could only sit and stare in horror.

I mean...*I took that picture.*

It had been private.

Meant solely for me.

Sam hadn't even been aware that I'd snapped it. Which, yeah, makes this situation a bazillion times worse.

So much worse.

No matter how long I sit here racking my brain, I can't figure out how it ended up online. How the hell did someone get their hands on it? Did I somehow, inadvertently, forward it?

I...I don't think so.

It's not like my phone was ever lost or stolen. It's been in my possession the entire time. I *always* have it with me. I blink my eyes and stare down at the slim device in the palm of my hand. I can't remember a time during the last few days when I didn't know exactly where it was.

This doesn't make sense.

And it's not like I showed anyone either.

Mia raps her knuckles against my door before hesitantly poking her head inside. "Are you awake?" From the somber tone of her voice, I can tell that she's seen the photograph. It's like she's reconfirming—without actually saying a word—that this is a huge freaking deal.

Probably all of Barnett has seen that damn picture by now.

Including Sam.

Thick waves of nausea swirl through my belly. Any moment, they'll shoot up like a geyser.

"Yeah," I rasp. It still feels like I'm in a state of shock. Like this is nothing more than a nightmare I'm going to jerk out of with a pounding heart and a shitload of relief.

Do you know what the first thing I'm going to do once I wake up is?

Grab my phone and delete that stupid picture. I'm going to wipe it off the face of this earth. I never should have snapped it in the first place.

Obviously, I realize that now.

Only it's too late because this isn't a dream I'm going to magically wake up from. The unfortunate reality is that I took a naked picture of Sam without his consent or knowledge, kept it on my phone, which has now been leaked to the Barnett University student body.

And Sam won't answer any of my calls or texts. There's suddenly a wall of silence between us that I'm unable to penetrate, which means that he's aware the photograph is out there and that I'm the one who snapped it.

Mia pushes the door wider before slinking in and settling gingerly on the edge of my bed. "Have you seen it?" Her words might be arranged into the format of a question, but they're not. I'm sure she can surmise from the look of utter devastation on my face that I'm still reeling from impact.

I nod as moisture gathers in my eyes. I've been trying to hold back the tears ever since I realized Sam was ignoring me. Knowingly declining my calls. Sending them to voicemail because he has no interest in speaking with me.

The deep well of sympathy in Mia's green eyes has the dam bursting, and the salty wetness desperately searching for an escape route.

This is a big fucking deal. Sam's father is going to blow a gasket when he finds out. And it's my fault. I did this. All because I had wanted to capture a moment. Something that felt infinitely precious.

"Have you spoken to him yet?" she asks, interrupting the whirl of my thoughts.

I shake my head.

That only makes everything a thousand times worse. Sam has that unique ability to settle everything inside me. It's always been like that. Maybe it's because he was the first real friend I made when I came to live with my grandparents after the accident. Or that we've been inseparable for the last eight years. Or that he's the one person I can count on to help me, no matter what life throws my way.

He's my person.

"I've tried texting and calling but he's not answering." My gaze latches onto hers as if it's a lifesaving device. "He always responds. No matter what," I whisper.

"Maybe he's in class?" Even though she's trying to be positive, we both know that's not the reason. Sam would still shoot me a text.

"He knows, Mia. He has to know by now."

How could he not?

I found out about it before I even rolled out of bed this morning.

Her teeth sink into her lower lip before she reluctantly nods. "I'm sorry, Vi."

A bitter laugh escapes from my mouth. If there's anyone who has something to be sorry about, it's me. Not her. I'm the one who created this mess. "Thanks, but this doesn't have anything to do with you. I shouldn't have taken the picture." I shake my head. "I don't know why I did it. He was sleeping and..." I pause before admitting the worst part. "He didn't even know I took it. I never told Sam that I had a naked picture of him on my phone." Heat stings my cheeks as I acknowledge those words out loud. It only slams home the gravity of the situation.

Of what I've done.

She squeezes her eyes tightly shut before burying her face in her hands. "Oh God…"

I sit up and slip my arm around Mia before rubbing slow circles across her back. I don't understand why she's so upset but I appreciate her concern and her friendship. And Mia has always been a good friend.

"This is my fault," she admits. Her voice sounds strangely thick. As if it's clogged with emotion. What I don't understand is why she would say something like that.

Her fault?

That's ridiculous. Of course, it isn't. I shake my head. Mia is completely blameless in this. Unfortunately, it's clear who the asshole in this situation is.

And that would be me.

"This isn't your fault. I took the picture, and I shouldn't have." With a shake of my head, I mumble, "I just wish I knew how it got leaked."

Mia sucks in a deep breath and lifts her head. "Last night, when we ordered pizzas, and all the girls were here…" her voice grows reedy before trailing off.

I sit up a bit straighter and frown. "What about it?"

All I remember from last night is feeling irritated with the way they were talking about Sam, dissecting him as if he were a piece of meat. And then telling me to slide my leftovers their way when I was done with him.

I'm sure they're all drooling over that damn photograph.

A fresh wave of misery crashes over her expression as she bites her lip. Her behavior is odd. Normally, Mia is so forthright. She never beats around the bush when something needs to be said, which is both a blessing and a curse.

My gaze sharpens on her. On the guilt swimming around in her eyes. She's all but drowning in it. An odd prickle of unease slithers through me as my heartbeat picks up speed.

I thought maybe she felt bad about the situation, but now I realize there's more to it than that, which is exactly when it hits me.

Like a locomotive barreling through my brain.

Last night when we ordered pizzas with the girls, I'd needed to get away for a few minutes after their discussion of Sam, and I'd left my phone on the table. When I'd returned, Caroline had the slim device cradled in the palm of her hand. They had been smirking and giggling. And then they'd scattered like rats fleeing a sinking ship. A weird prickle of unease had settled in the pit of my belly, but I'd brushed it off.

Eyes widening, my hand flies to my mouth as I bite out, "You *knew* she looked through my phone?"

I can't believe this!

My mind somersaults. Bile rises in my throat until there's a good possibility I'll be sick.

She shakes her head before her shoulders slump. Her voice is thick with regret. "I wasn't paying attention and I thought they were looking at something on Caroline's phone. It wasn't until you came back from the bathroom and she handed it to you that I realized it was yours they'd been messing around with."

"*Mia!*" I groan, "She must have forwarded the picture to herself before spreading it all over campus!"

"I know," she whispers. "I'm so sorry, Vi. I was talking with Sasha about a class and wasn't paying attention to what they were doing."

My body shakes with anger. "You realized they'd been looking at my phone when she handed it back, right?"

Guilt flickers across her face before she drops her gaze to her fingers, which are twisting in her lap. "Yeah, but—"

"Why didn't you say something right away? I could have gone and... and..." I swallow down the thick lump of emotion that has settled in my throat. "I could have at least talked to her about it!"

Our gazes lock and her body deflates, almost as if it is folding in on itself. "I'm sorry."

I can only stare.

Her apology isn't good enough. It won't fix the irreparable damage that has been done.

"I had no idea what they were looking at." Her tongue darts out to moisten her lips. "After I realized what happened, it didn't seem like such a big deal. I thought they were playing a stupid prank." Her eyes plead with mine for understanding. "Or resetting a ring tone. Something stupid like that."

Laughter bubbles up in my throat. If Mia had given me the heads up, there's the possibility that I could have done something about it.

My temples throb with a headache as I collapse against my pillows. My mind spins, trying to figure out what kind of damage control can still be done. Sam won't even talk to me. He has to know I'm the one who took the picture, which means he probably assumes I put it out there for the world to see.

My heart seizes at the painful realization.

When Mia opens her mouth again, I throw up a hand to cut her off. I can't deal with her right now. "Can you leave?"

"*What?*" Her eyes widen as her mouth tumbles open.

In the three years that Mia and I have been friends, we've never gotten into a fight or even had a disagreement. More often than not, we find ourselves on the same side of an issue. I've never had a girlfriend like her before. Over the years, I've grown to trust her implicitly.

And now that trust has been broken.

Honestly, I have no idea if Mia telling me about what happened last night would have made any difference in how the situation played out. But I would have appreciated the opportunity to get in front of it. As much as it would have sucked, I could have spoken to Sam and prepared him for what was coming so that he wouldn't have been blindsided this morning.

Whatever I'm feeling, it has to be a thousand times worse for him.

It makes me nauseous to think about his naked picture being out there, circulating around campus. Women gawking and drooling over it. Glimpsing something so private and beautiful. Something they have absolutely no right to look at.

Exhaustion fills my voice as I push out the words. "I want to be alone right now. I need to figure out what I'm going to do about Sam."

This is such a fucked-up mess. And I have no idea how to make it better. Sam won't return my calls or texts.

Even though I refuse to look at Mia, I hear the thick tears she's attempting to choke back. Very rarely have I seen her cry. Not even through all the Carter drama has she broken down and bawled. She's always so strong and clearheaded. Mia is all about perspective. About looking forward and not dwelling on past mistakes.

Life is too short.

That's the motto she lives by.

"Vi...I'm really sorry." She reaches out and grabs my hand, squeezing it tightly with her trembling one. "I should have told you right away. I had no idea this would turn into such a shit storm."

I slip my fingers free of hers before repeating, "I know. I just want to be alone right now. I need to figure out what I'm going to do."

How I'm going to explain everything to Sam.

How I'm going to get him to forgive me.

At this point, that might not even be possible.

I might have already lost him.

"If you think it'll help, I'll reach out to Sam. I'll tell him what happened." Her voice wobbles as she fights back the tears that fill her voice. "I'll tell him this is all my fault."

Her husky words have the sharpest part of my anger draining away because, at the end of the day, Mia isn't responsible for what happened. I am. I did this by taking a very private picture of Sam without his consent and leaving it carelessly on my phone where anyone could find it.

"No." I suck in a ragged breath and force my gaze to meet hers. "You should have told me what happened, but I'm the one who's responsible. I took the picture and left it on my phone. I shouldn't have snapped it in the first place." Emotion gathers in my eyes. I can't help but shake my head at my own stupidity. You hear about this kind of thing happening all the time. Someone gets their hands on private pictures and leaks them onto the internet. "I'm such a dumbass."

"No, you're not," she says softly. "You made a mistake."

I shake my head. She's wrong. This is so much more than a mistake. A mistake is when you order a sandwich with mayo and the waitress brings it out with mustard.

That's a mistake.

"I used really bad judgment and invaded Sam's privacy," I choke out. "I was careless with a picture I had no business snapping in the first place. That's so much more than a mistake."

"It's not like that, Vi," she says softly.

"Yeah," hysteria bubbles up in my throat, "it's *exactly* like that."

After a few uncomfortable moments of silence, Mia sighs before rising to her feet. "If there's anything I can do to help, let me know."

Her words are met with a deafening silence because I have no idea if there is a way to repair the damage I've inflicted.

And that scares me more than anything.

Chapter Twenty-Eight

SAM

Even though the entire first floor is lit up, the house itself is eerily silent as I slip inside my family's home. This has been one hell of a long-ass day. Fending off comments, and the determined girls who chased after me to sign their photographs, is the most messed up thing that has ever happened to me.

By the time I got to practice, I wanted to work myself over so I could stop thinking about all this bullshit.

And Violet.

For the life of me, I can't wrap my brain around why she would do something like this. If I didn't know better...if her bag wasn't in the shot...if I didn't remember the morning we woke up naked in my bed... I could easily conjure up another plausible explanation, but I can't.

It was her.

After inspecting the photograph carefully, I'm certain that it happened after the morning we made love for the first time. The memory now feels tainted.

I still haven't returned any of her calls or text messages. It's killing me to avoid her. And yet, I can't bring myself to speak with her. Not yet. Not right now. Not when I'm still feeling this raw and exposed.

And confused.

And yeah...pissed off.

Not in a million fucking years would I have ever associated any of these emotions with Violet. I love her. I've *always* loved her, and she's gone and—I don't even know what to say.

She's gone and broke my fucking heart.

What the hell had she been thinking?

I step into the foyer and pause, attempting to gather myself. What needs to be dealt with is going to suck major ass. Laughter brims on my lips. That's such an understatement.

For about the umpteenth time today, my phone goes off, signaling an incoming text. I palm the device and glance at the screen.

Violet.

Again.

Even though it pains me to do so, I ignore it. I need to give the situation more time to settle before I can deal with her. I want to be clearheaded when we sit down and talk.

As much as I would love to do the same with my family, that's not possible. There is no way I can ignore them. I've been avoiding their calls and texts for the last two hours.

And now I've run out of time.

When I'm done taking care of this, I can focus on Violet, and what's going to happen between us. If I'm being honest, the situation is more devasting than what's about to go down with my family. My world has revolved around her for the last eight years. She's my heart and soul, and I can't imagine my life without her in it.

I straighten my shoulders and move quietly toward the kitchen. Only now do I hear the soft babble of voices. With every step, it feels like I'm walking toward certain death. I draw in a deep breath before clearing my throat and making my presence known. My parents are sitting around the kitchen table with two of my father's senior advisers. Josh is in charge of PR. He's the one who sat me down and lectured me before I left for college. My gaze falls to the other guy. I have no clue what he does. Although clearly, it has something to do with image. Or he wouldn't be here at this time of night.

I force my gaze to my father. Anger radiates off him in thick waves. I shift uncomfortably under the full weight of his icy glare. It's been a long time since I've felt like a recalcitrant child in the presence of my parents. With gritted teeth, I wait for the heaviness of his wrath to hit me full force.

My father continues to glower at me before biting out my name. "*Sam.*"

I jerk my head in acknowledgement. My gaze reluctantly slides to my mom who sits rigidly next to my father. All color drains from her face as disappointment shines from her eyes. I feel like a real piece of shit for being the one to cause her a moment of heartache. She has enough BS to deal with from my father. She doesn't need it from me.

Josh rises to his feet, as does the guy next to him, before awkwardly clearing his throat. This entire situation feels brutal.

"We'll leave the three of you to talk." His gaze skims over me before bouncing back to my father. "Give me a call when you're finished, and we'll discuss what options can be employed to deal with the situation." He shifts his stance before tacking on, "Jeff and Victoria are already looking into what can be done in regard to damage control."

Damage control.

Fucking great.

There are people—*my father's people, no less*—who are feverishly working to clean up this mess as we speak.

The stiff nod Dad gives in response is barely perceptible. After that, Josh and the other guy exit the kitchen as if they're trying to escape the suffocating tension that now blankets the room. For one wistful moment, my gaze trails after them. I want to scrub a hand through my hair, but I don't. It's so quiet that, even from the kitchen, we hear the front door open before firmly closing behind them.

With my hands stuffed into the pockets of my jeans, I lurk at the threshold. Never in my wildest dreams—or nightmares, as the case may be—did I imagine just such a scenario. I really didn't. Maybe I'm naïve. I've tried to be careful about what I do, who I hang out with, who I allow myself to get close to. The fact that Violet—my best friend, the girl I've been in love with for the last eight years—is the one who put me in this untenable position, seriously fucking kills me.

But I can't dwell on that, or her right now. Not when I have to try and explain the fallout to my parents who are livid.

As soon as my father is certain that his underlings have vacated the premises, he tears into me. It's not like I expected any less. The entire way over, I'd prepared myself for the worst. This is a big deal, and I know it.

The words explode from his lips in a tirade.

"*A picture? A fucking naked picture? How the hell could you let something like this happen?*"

"I'm sorry." Instead of telling them the truth—that I know absolutely nothing about it, that I'm as shocked as they are—I hear myself say instead, "It was a private picture. I don't know how it ended up online."

It would be oh-so-easy to throw Violet under the bus and pin any and all wrongdoing neatly on her. To tell them that I didn't know a picture existed until it was being shoved in my face this morning but... I find myself unable to do it. Even though the smartest move I could make would be to absolve myself of any and all culpability, I refuse to do that. As pissed off as I am at Violet, the need to protect her is far too ingrained to do anything else.

For a long moment, my father stares at me like I'm the biggest moron that he's come across in his forty-some years on this earth. And yeah, I pretty much feel like a dumbass right now.

My words sound lame, even to my own ears.

I almost cringe when laughter falls from his lips. He shakes his head from side-to-side before tossing his hands up in the air. When he slams them down again, the table trembles. My mother flinches but remains silent.

"Are you really that stupid? We've only discussed this kind of thing a thousand times!" His face turns thunderous. "*Nothing* is fucking private in our world! There is no such thing as *privacy* when you are a public figure! Pictures *always* get leaked. It's not a matter of *if*. It's a matter of *when*. You know this!" He spears a finger at me. "I know you do because I'm the one who drilled it into that thick skull of yours."

He scrubs a hand over his face as if he's trying to tear the flesh off his bones. "Please tell me there's not a video or something else out there waiting to surface."

I draw my rigidly held shoulders back and straighten to my full height as Dad continues to glare. It's a bitter pill to swallow. I've never done anything to disappoint either of them. "Of course not!"

"*Of course not*," he mimics under his breath, "how could I ask such a thing?" He turns to my mother before shaking his head. "Clearly, there's nothing to be concerned about, Beth. I mean, it's not like there's a naked picture of our son floating around out there for the world to see." Sarcasm drips from every word as he scowls.

Heat blisters my cheeks as my hands bunch uselessly at my sides.

Mom lays a tentative hand on my father's stiff forearm as she attempts to quietly soothe him. "Derek, please..." her voice trails off as if she's unsure how to make the situation any better.

"*What?*" His voice rises, and my mother winces before withdrawing her fingers. "Are you really going to sit there and tell me this isn't a big deal? That it'll blow over or die down in no time at all? That it won't end up affecting my campaign? Or that I won't be standing in front of a crowd, trying to discuss my plans for the next six years in office, the impact I want to make, the fucking *legacy* I want to leave behind, but will instead find myself fielding questions regarding the morality of my own *son*? Of our entire *family*, for that matter?"

Those questions hang suspended in the air for a painful heartbeat before crashing to the floor and shattering into a million pieces.

"In a few weeks, it'll be forgotten," she murmurs. "That picture could have been much worse."

Fury ignites in my father's eyes before he grounds out, "Do you realize that I have never had anything tarnish my reputation? *Nothing*," he annunciates each word as his gaze lands squarely on me again. "Until now." There's a pause. "I've spent my entire life in public office, that's over twenty years, and not once have I ever had my good name dragged through the mud. My morals and ethics have never been called into question." He leans toward me as if he's moments away from lunging. "And do you know why that is?"

Since this is more of a rhetorical question, I keep my trap closed. There isn't a correct answer that will squelch the fervor building in his eyes. It needs to run its course. The only thing I can do is stand there and take all the shit he throws at me.

"I contemplate every decision I make. I consider the company I keep. I'm constantly weighing the consequences of my actions." He stabs a finger at me. "Clearly, that's not something you've been doing!"

"Dad—"

"Don't you fucking *dad* me. We're way past that now!" As he roars the words, spittle flies from his mouth. "Don't you get it? Everything you do affects me! *Everything!*"

My shoulders slump as I force myself to hold his gaze. "I know," I admit. "And I'm sorry." I draw in a breath before allowing it to leak from my lungs. "What do you want me to do?"

He shakes his head, still looking disgruntled. "Josh and Mark are dealing with it as we speak. We'll get the websites that are posting the image to take it down immediately or face legal ramifications." As the brightest parts of his anger recede, exhaustion sets in. It seeps into both his eyes and voice. I see it in the way his broad shoulders slacken, as if he's carrying the weight of the world on top of them.

Another wave of regret crashes over me for causing this shit storm.

His gaze pierces mine before he reminds ominously, "But it's out there, Sam. It will *always* be out there. And that's something you'll have to live with for the rest of your life."

Chapter Twenty-Nine

SAM

Even though it feels like I've been put through the wringer today, I have one last stop to make before I can drag myself home for the night. No matter how bad I suspected it would go with my parents, it exceeded expectations and ended up being ten times worse. The idea that I'm what tarnishes my father's otherwise spotless political reputation makes me feel like a real piece of shit.

That's the first time I've ever skulked out of my own house. All I want to do is head back to the apartment, crawl into bed, and crash for a solid fifteen hours. I want to avoid everyone until this thing blows over.

But I can't do that.

I need to talk with Violet.

I need her to do the impossible and make what happened today—what she did—somehow okay.

Today has been the longest we've ever gone without speaking. What's worse is that Violet is the one person I turn to when I need sound advice or someone to listen. She's the one I wrap myself up in when I want to forget about the rest of the world.

Without her...I feel like I don't have anyone.

Since she's come into my life, Violet has been my everything. The one person I trust above all others. Today she broke that trust. She crushed it beneath the heel of her boot before grounding it into a fine pulp.

Fuck.

I really wish that I was making a mountain out of a mole hill, but that's not the case. Not after the day I've had. Not after the shit I've endured. There aren't many people who you can be yourself with. I might only be some twenty-two-year-old college dude, but even I know that. With Violet, I can strip away all the layers, all the pretenses, and just be Sam. Not Sam Harper, Senator Derek Harper's son. Or Sam Harper, the Barnett Bulldogs football player.

I'm just Sam. Violet's best friend. Her boyfriend. Her lover.

And now...

I don't know.

How do you come back from something like this?

Once I'm at her dorm, I step onto the elevator. As I wait inside for the door to close, four girls crowd in after me. Even though I have a ball cap pulled low over my forehead, recognition shines brightly in their eyes. My jaw tightens as they smile and giggle all the while ogling me from across the tightly enclosed space.

As much as I want to verbally snap at them, I rein it in. The last thing I need to do is lash out and have *that* end up online as well. Instead of making eye contact, I stand stone-faced and stare straight ahead.

Their intense scrutiny crawls over me. It leaves me feeling agitated and pissed off all over again.

As soon as the doors slide open, I shoot out of there like my ass is on fire. I'm not even a full step away before I hear their laughter ring out in the hallway. They can't even be bothered to wait for the doors to close behind me. Thank fuck they didn't shove a copy of that freaking photo under my nose for me to sign.

With my shoulders hunched, I keep my head down and walk through the narrow hall to her room. Everyone I pass turns to stare in my direction.

Once at Violet's suite, I rap my knuckles against the door and wait for her to open it so I can get out of the hallway. My jaw aches from being tightly clenched. Ten seconds turn into twenty and then thirty without an answer. I knock a little louder this time before jamming my hands into my pockets and shifting from one foot to another.

"Sam?"

I swing around and find a pale-looking Violet standing a couple feet away. Normally, the first thing I'd do is haul her into my arms. My lips would descend, sliding possessively over hers, encouraging her to open so I could sweep my tongue inside her mouth. I would be wondering how long I'd have to wait before hustling her off to the bedroom so we could be alone.

There is no better feeling in the world than being buried balls deep inside her soft pussy. The way her body convulses around mine, milking my hard cock of every last drop is addictive.

The first time we had sex, it felt like coming home. There was this sense of rightness to it. Inevitability. As if I had been waiting my entire life to make love to this one woman.

A chill slithers down my spine. As our gazes lock and hold, I realize that I'd been unconsciously clinging to a glimmer of hope that she was innocent in all this. As I search her eyes, that hope dies a painful death. Guilt and shame are written clear as day across every line of her expressive face.

The realization is soul-crushing.

Like a kick in the balls.

This girl is the love of my life. Even at fourteen years old, I knew she was the one for me. In all the years that I've been Violet's friend and longed for more, I never could have imagined there would come a day when I wouldn't want to be near her, wouldn't want to breathe her in, wouldn't want to reach out and stroke my fingers over her soft skin. I wouldn't want to bury myself deep in the heat of her body. Or take refuge from the world in her arms.

But that's how I feel right now.

Shards of bitterness and anger slice through me. The pain cuts so deep that it's a wonder I'm still able to suck in oxygen. Or that I'm able to stand upright when all I want to do is crumble to the ground at her feet.

Remorse swims around in her chocolaty-hued eyes as she averts them before jamming the key into the lock. Somewhere in the back of my brain, I notice the way her fingers tremble as she pushes open the door. Almost hesitantly, she swings around to face me. "Do you want to come in so we can talk?"

I jerk my head into a tight nod. Now that I'm here, I have no idea what to say. It's clear from her reaction that she took the photograph. Honestly, I don't even know if I want to hang around and listen to her explanation. It won't change a damn thing.

Nothing will.

I wait for her to walk inside before silently trailing after her. My hands stay shoved in my pockets. I think we're both thrown off by the way I keep to myself. Her movements are stilted as she sets her bag down on the couch in the small common area in the suite.

Even though Mia doesn't appear to be home, we head to the privacy of her bedroom. Once inside, she settles on the edge of the bed before her gaze lifts to mine. Instead of dropping down next to her, I grab the chair from her desk and turn it around so I can face her.

The tiny spark of hope in her eyes dims as I continue to keep my distance. Violet may not realize it, but it kills me not to reach out and touch her. I want to hold her in my arms and make this all go away.

"Sam," her voice is scraped low and hollowed out with enough regret to leave me wincing, "I'm so sorry."

I search her eyes and shake my head, trying to wrap my mind around what could have possessed her to do something like this. "You took that photograph?" Even though I know the answer to that question, it seems like the easiest place to start.

"Yeah..." She draws air into her lungs before forcing it out again. "The morning after we first slept together. I got up to use the bathroom. It was early and you were still sleeping. When I came back, you were lying there uncovered and you looked," her words falter, "you looked so beautiful and all I could think about was trying to capture a sliver of this moment so I could hold onto it forever." Her fingers twist in her lap. It's a telltale sign of the nerves that are eating away at her.

"I didn't think about the ramifications of what I was doing. I just got my phone and snapped the shot." She glances away for a heartbeat before forcing her gaze to mine. "I'm so sorry about what happened."

I pull off the Barnett Bulldogs ball cap and plow my fingers through my hair. Out of all the bullshit excuses I expected to hear, that wasn't it. My brows draw together. "Did you post it?" How did that image—the one she made sound meaningful—end up online before being shared about a thousand times?

"Of course not! I would *never* do that." She shakes her head and says a little more fiercely, "That picture," her cheeks pinken, "it was for me." She swallows down the thick emotion clogging her throat. "And... and I realize how wrong that was. I shouldn't have invaded your privacy like that."

I shake my head. "If you didn't post it, how did it end up all over the place, Vi? Do you know how many women shoved that photo in my face, wanting me to sign it?"

She winces as the color drains from her face, leaving her ashen.

I know my voice is escalating, and that I'm frightening her. I can tell by the way she shrinks away from me.

Just another fucking first for us.

She gulps in another breath and rushes to explain. "Last night, we ate pizza with a bunch of girls from our floor and I left my phone on the table when I went to use the bathroom. I didn't even think about bringing it with me. When my cell rang, Caroline answered it—"

That's when it slams into me that I'm the one who called Violet.

"I guess she looked through some of my stuff. She found the picture and forwarded it before sharing it with the others." Her shoulders collapse. "I guess it spread from there."

She rises to her feet and hesitantly bridges the distance that separates us before dropping to her knees in front of me. Her gaze never relinquishes mine as I stare down at her. "You have to know that I would never intentionally hurt you. I'm sorry this happened. I shouldn't have snapped that shot of you." She shakes her head before laying it in my lap. "None of this would be happening if I hadn't done it."

As tempted as I am to thread my fingers through her blonde hair, I don't. I can't bring myself to touch Violet right now. Everything in me is conflicted. It's a war of emotions, thoughts, and feelings. Then there's the exhaustion from everything that occurred over the course of this fucked-up day.

It's almost unfathomable that twenty-four short hours ago, my life felt pretty damn perfect. And now it's falling apart at the seams. I can't bring myself to reach out and touch the one person who means more to me than life itself.

When I fail to respond, she whispers brokenly, "Sam? Please talk to me. Say something."

All I can do is stare blankly at her. I don't have the words. In the end, there's nothing I can say to make the situation better. She shouldn't have snapped the picture. It was careless. And you certainly don't leave that kind of image on your phone. You're just asking for trouble.

And here we are.

Fucking waist deep in it.

"I should have told you about the picture. I should have shown it to you that morning."

For the first time, I wonder if it would have made a difference. Would I have had enough sense to tell Violet to delete the image?

I don't know. Unfortunately, in a situation like this, hindsight is twenty-twenty. Pain flares to life behind my eyes. A headache that has been eleven hours in the making.

"Do your parents know?" she asks, interrupting the whirl of my thoughts.

"Yeah." I don't want to rehash that conversation. Another wave of exhaustion hits me like a Mack Truck. I want to be done with this goddamn day, and forget it ever happened. I want to hit rewind or delete or something to get us back to where we were twenty-four short hours ago.

She picks up her head and meets my gaze. Her eyes shine brightly with unshed tears. "I'm sorry," she whispers brokenly. "Sorry I did this to you. I wish there were something I could do to make it better."

I wish there were something to make the whole damn thing go away. But that's wishful thinking and we both know it. "There's not. It just has to blow over." I drag in a ragged breath and mutter, "I should head back to my place. There's work I need to finish up." How the hell I'm going to concentrate is beyond me.

Misery wafts off her in suffocating waves. "Okay…"

Emotion flickers across her expression. I get the feeling she wants to say something more but ends up holding it back, which is probably for the best. At least right now it is. At the moment, I don't have any answers. I just need to get through this and see what happens. And then maybe…

Maybe we can move past it.

But I need time.

And space.

Violet scrambles to her feet as I head for the door to her bedroom. "Sam?"

I glance at her and hesitate before reaching for the doorknob. It doesn't feel like we have anything more to say. And that's just another kick in the balls as far as I'm concerned.

Her voice is thin, almost fragile sounding, when she finally asks, "Are we going to be all right?" The oxygen in the room disappears as I hold her gaze.

What do I say to that?

I guess the truth.

"I don't know," I admit reluctantly.

Instead of pleading or even arguing, Violet nods her acceptance.

When I close the door behind me, a soft sob escapes from her. As much as it breaks my heart, I keep walking.

Chapter Thirty

VIOLET

We're fifteen minutes into Rickets' class, and Sam has barely spoken more than four words to me. Actually, more like three. Without meeting my gaze, he dropped down onto his usual seat and said—*hey, what's up?* I responded with—*not much,* and that was it.

I'm not sure what I expected when shit hit the fan over that photograph, but this wasn't it. I'd thought he would eventually come around, and understand I made a mistake. That hasn't happened. Our relationship has shifted so dramatically in the course of a week that it is no longer recognizable.

And I have no one to blame but myself.

The loss of his friendship has been the most brutal part of it all. I never realized, even before we started going out, just how intertwined our lives were. Okay, yes, I did...but it's even more than I originally suspected.

I miss Sam on so many levels. Without him, I feel empty and lonely. He's been a big part of my life over the last eight years. After I lost my parents and sister, Sam was there. Instead of filling the void they left behind, he carved out a little niche all his own. He's become one of the most important people in my life.

And now he's gone.

At this point, I would be glad to simply have my friend back.

I've sent him a few texts but haven't gotten much back in the way of responses. More like *yes* or *no,* and that's it. At least he's not totally ignoring me. It's a small consolation. I've been too scared to push for more interaction.

Once our ninety-minute class is over, I pack up my things, wanting to get out of there as fast as I can. Normally, Sam and I walk out together with his arm slung across my shoulders.

Since I know that won't be happening, I don't bother to wait around. It hurts too much to sit close to him and yet feel a million miles apart. And there's nothing I can do to make it better. I've asked, and the response is always the same—*nothing.*

I slide past him and mumble a quick goodbye before hightailing it from the classroom. If I had been harboring any hope that he'd stop me, maybe suggest we sit down and talk things out, they're quickly crushed as I disappear through the door.

My heart aches as I leave the building behind. I can't help but wonder if Sam and I will be able to mend our fractured friendship. It's impossible to imagine my life without him filling it. I've cried more this week than I have in a long time. Not since my parents died.

I understand that he's embarrassed, and his family is angry. I get it. I shouldn't have taken the photograph. I wanted to capture something beautiful and all it did was kill our relationship.

The sharp ringing of my phone knocks me from those depressing thoughts. It's always difficult when I come from seeing him because it's a reminder of what I've lost.

As I grab the cell from the pocket of my leather bag, my grandmother's photo pops up on the screen. Guilt slices through me because I haven't called them in a couple of days. Normally, I check in on a daily basis but with everything that's going on, I haven't felt like talking. Especially since I know Gran will sniff out the lies in a matter of moments, and there's no way I can tell her why Sam has distanced himself from me.

I hit accept and force a cheerful note into my greeting. "Hi, Gran. What's up?"

It takes a moment for the call to connect, and her voice to come over the line. I'm about to say hello again when she says, "Violet?"

The way my name trembles sends my belly into freefall. "What's wrong?" Fear grips my heart like a tightened fist.

"I don't want to upset you, but I'm at the hospital with your grandfather. They think he had a heart attack."

I don't realize that my feet have stopped moving until someone knocks into me from behind. The girl shoots me a dirty look before maneuvering around my frozen form.

"Are you sure?" I lock my knees, afraid that if I don't, I'll fall to the ground.

"He's being checked out right now. As soon as I know more, I'll give you a call."

Even though she can't see me, I shake my head. "No, I'm coming over there right now, Gran." There's no way I can focus on sociology knowing that my grandfather is at the hospital and might have suffered a heart attack. The possible diagnosis sends an icy chill shooting down my spine.

"Violet, I know you have class in less than an hour. I don't want you to miss it." She draws in a deep breath as if trying to steady herself before pushing out the rest. "Your grandfather wouldn't want that either. Just stay put until we know what's going on."

"I'll email my professor," I assure her, "it won't be a problem." Honestly, I don't give a rat's ass if it is. My grandparents are everything to me. They're all I have left in this world. If they need me, then I'm going to be there for them.

End of story.

She doesn't argue, which only proves that she wants me at the hospital with her. "All right."

"I'll be there as soon as I can." My mind whirls, attempting to figure out the logistics. "It's going to take me at least twenty minutes to get over there. If you hear anything before then, let me know right away."

"I will, sweetie." Relief floods through her tone. "Thank you."

I disconnect and rack my brain, trying to figure out how I can get across town to where the hospital is located. Mia is in class, but I know she keeps a spare set of keys in the drawer of her desk. I shoot her a text and let her know that I need to borrow her car before hustling my way across campus to the dorms.

When I'm about halfway there, someone shouts my name. Since I don't recognize the voice, I keep moving. I don't have time to stop and shoot the shit right now. I need to get to the hospital and find out what's going on with my grandfather.

"Violet!"

At this point, I'm practically jogging down the cement path when strong fingers wrap around my arm and halt my movements. I spin around, surprised to find Liam. Concern is etched across his handsome face.

He tilts his head and narrows his eyes as they sift through mine. "Are you all right?" If he wasn't detaining me, I would be long gone.

"Liam," as his name slips free from my lips, I realize how close to tears I am, "I can't talk right now, I have to go."

His dark brows furrow. "What's going on?" Almost gently he asks, "Is this about Sam?"

I shake my head.

For the first time in a week, that damn photograph isn't consuming my every waking thought. I almost want to laugh. Or cry. Maybe a little of both. All I know is that I've got to get out of here. "No, my grandfather was taken to the hospital. They think he might have had a heart attack. I'm sorry, but I really need to go." Any moment, I'm going to fall to pieces.

And I can't afford to do that. I have to keep moving.

There's barely a pause in our conversation when he says, "Come on, I'll drive you there." He nods toward the lot that's about a block away near Adler Hall. "My bike is parked over there. I can get you to the hospital in less than ten minutes."

I contemplate the offer for all of two seconds before succumbing. It'll be so much faster on Liam's bike. "Are you sure you don't mind?" I have to practically run to keep up with his long-legged strides.

"Does Sam know what's going on?" He fires off the question as we push past people and make our way to the parking lot.

Even when his gaze settles on me, I keep mine focused on the path.

"No, my grandmother just called." With the current state of our relationship, I wasn't going to bother him with it.

As we reach the paved lot, Liam points to the first row, and I see his shiny black bike parked in a space.

"Do you want to give him a quick call before we take off?" he asks.

I drop my gaze and shake my head. "No."

Uncertainty flickers across his face but he doesn't push the issue. Instead, he pulls the black helmet from the back of his bike before gently placing it over my head much like he did the afternoon we spent together.

Once I wrap my arms around his upper body, the bike roars to life and we're shooting out of the parking lot before winding our way through traffic. Liam is right. It takes about eight minutes for us to reach the hospital. Luckily, we make all the lights. And the ones that turn yellow—I squeeze my eyes shut as we barrel through them.

As soon as he cuts the engine, I hop off the bike and unbuckle the helmet. Liam's fingers brush mine, knocking them aside. Only then do I realize that my hands are shaking.

With the helmet now removed, he asks, "Do you want me to come in with you?" His gunmetal gray gaze pierces mine. There's a tenderness in them that catches me off guard. In that moment, I realize that if I wanted Liam to stay with me, he would do it.

"No, I'm okay." I give him a slight smile. I appreciate him dropping everything to get me here so quickly. For all I know, he missed class.

Liam Garrison is a really good guy. He's usually smirking or fooling around, but when I needed someone, he was there for me—no questions asked. And he certainly didn't have to be. It's not like we're good friends. "Thanks for dropping me off."

He tugs me closer and wraps his arms around me before dropping a kiss against the top of my head. "I hope your grandfather is all right." Then he says, "Give me your phone."

I untangle myself from him and dig out the cell from my bag before handing it over. He taps my screen and his phone buzzes in response.

"There. Now you have my number. If you need anything else, just call. I can pick you up later if you need a lift back to campus."

Gratitude explodes inside me. "Thanks again for everything."

"It's not a problem, Violet."

I give him a quick kiss on the cheek before rushing through the sliding doors of the hospital. Unsure where to go, I stop at the front desk and explain why I'm there. I'm given directions to a waiting room. There are a few twists and turns down a sterile looking hallway before I spot my grandmother sitting in a chair, nursing a small cup of coffee.

My heart spasms as I hurry toward her. "Gran? Have there been any updates?"

Her gaze swings to mine before she shakes her head. She sets her coffee aside and rises to her feet before engulfing me in an embrace. Even though fear continues to pump through me, her thin arms have a way of offering comfort, just like they did when I was a child.

After a few silent moments, we break apart. Our hands remain clasped as we sit down.

Now that I'm here, I release a pent-up breath. "What happened?"

Gran shakes her head as if she can't believe that we're sitting in the hospital waiting room, having this conversation. That a few hours ago they were at the breakfast table, starting their day just like they've done thousands of times before. "I should have realized something was wrong when he told me that he was going upstairs to lie down for a while. He thought it was just a little heartburn. So, he took an antacid and assumed it would pass. A little while later, he started having chest pain. When the pain got worse, he came downstairs and told me what was going on." Exasperation colors her tone. "Can you believe he actually told me not to call an ambulance? He thought I was overreacting." With her lips pressed into a tight line, she shakes her head. "Of course, I called right away. Didn't even think twice about it."

"Thank goodness that you did. He shouldn't have waited so long to tell you what was going on."

"He's a stubborn man, Violet," she says with a huff.

I give her a slight smile because she's right. My grandfather is ridiculously stubborn.

"We arrived about thirty minutes ago." She blinks away the moisture from her eyes. "I have no idea what's going on. They haven't said a word."

"Everything will be fine, Gran." I rest my head against her shoulder. "They're taking good care of him."

After twenty more minutes, I'm ready to climb the walls. In fact, I've been pacing for at least ten of them. I can't sit still for another moment or I'll go crazy. As I swing around, my gaze collides with concerned blue ones.

Sam.

It feels as if all of the oxygen has been sucked out of the room. As we stare silently, all I can think is—*thank God*.

Thank God, he's here.

I have the urge to fling myself as him. Instead of doing that, I tighten my hands.

We're in such a weird place. This limbo where I don't know if we're even friends. I hate it. Hate that I fucked us up beyond repair. Above all else, Sam has always been my best friend. He's the one person I turn to when I need comfort and support. If something amazing happens, he's the first one I want to share the news with. Or, if I want to chill out and watch a movie, Sam's the person I want to be snuggled up against.

Despite the state of our relationship, he still came to the hospital. That knowledge alone has my heart cracking wide open.

"What are you doing here?" I whisper.

His bright blue gaze never releases mine from the intensity of their hold. "Liam filled me in."

Before I can push out anything more, he turns to my grandmother and quickly closes the distance between them before wrapping his arms around her. My heart bursts with even more love as he murmurs something in her ear before giving her a kiss on the cheek.

Unsure what to do, I stand there awkwardly, rooted in place as I watch them, silently wishing that he would take me in his arms, too. That he would offer me the same kind of comfort.

I clear my throat. "You didn't need to come here. Aren't you missing class?"

"I talked to my professor. It's taken care of." Almost dismissively, he adds, "You don't need to worry about it."

I gulp back the thick tendrils of emotion that threaten to choke me. "Thank you."

As a heavy silence falls over us, my grandmother rises to her feet. "I'm going to check with the front desk and see if there's any news."

My focus stays fastened to her as she walks down the corridor. When my gaze meanders back to Sam, I'm startled to find him watching me. A rush of nerves scamper down my spine.

I hate this.

The awkwardness that is now our relationship.

In silence, he closes the distance that separates us before taking me into his arms. Only then can I squeeze my eyes shut as my head settles against his chest.

I've missed this so much.

I've missed him and how affectionate he is.

Always so generous with his love and friendship.

With his time.

I miss everything about this man.

I never realized how solidly the last eight years bonded us together. Maybe I shouldn't be so surprised. He's been my best friend, my confidante, my family. This last week without him has left me reeling, feeling lost and aimless. Adrift. I find myself wanting to text him over the littlest things. There have been hundreds of times when I've pulled out my phone and started typing in the words before remembering that we aren't really talking.

"Are you doing okay, Vi?" As the warmth of his breath slips over me, his question leaves a thick lump sitting in the middle of my throat. Not able to get the words past it, I nod in answer.

"Edward will be fine," he reassures quietly.

I don't know if my grandfather will be all right. And Sam doesn't know it either. More than anything, I want to believe him. Only when I hear it from the doctor, will all the tension in my chest loosen.

"I really hope so."

With his arms wrapped around me, he presses another kiss against the top of my head. It's like he knows exactly what I need. But then again, Sam has always known.

I just took it for granted.

"Why didn't you call me yourself?" His voice lowers, turning gruffer. "Why did I have to hear it from Liam?"

Unsure what to say, I shrug.

The answer is obvious. If everything were normal between us, he would have been the first person I called.

When I remain silent, he draws away. Not far, just enough to search my gaze with his own. When I glance away, his fingers slip gently under my chin before turning it so that I have no other choice but to meet his stare.

"No matter what's going on between us, you should have called and let me know what happened. With enough time, we'll work through our issues. *This* has absolutely nothing to do with that."

It's difficult to hold back the tears that fill my eyes as I nod in understanding.

Almost fiercely, he tugs me back into the warm comfort of his embrace where I nestle against him. As I inhale a deep breath, Sam releases me before slipping an arm around my waist. He anchors me against him as my grandmother walks back into the room with a man in a white coat.

There's a look of relief etched across her face as her gaze locks on mine. Her lips lift a bit as if to say—*he's okay, everything is going to be all right*. My muscles loosen in relief. Almost to the point where I think my legs might buckle. Sam's grip tightens around my waist.

When I glance up at him, he gives me a wink as if he could somehow predict the future.

As the doctor introduces himself, giving us the details of what happened, I drag a breath into my lungs before slowly releasing it back into the world.

I can't help but realize how lucky today turned out to be.

Chapter Thirty-One

VIOLET

"Are you sure there's nothing else I can get for you before I take off?" I flutter around my grandfather like a high-strung butterfly, smoothing down blankets as I go. Even though he finds the attention unnecessary and most likely annoying, I'm powerless to standstill. I'm so relieved that he's back home again.

He rolls his eyes and repeats his now standard refrain, "I'm fine, Violet. Stop fussing over me like I'm a child. It was just a little heart attack."

I have to choke back a biting response.

Just a little heart attack.

Ha!

The man needs to realize that he shaved a decade off my life with his *little heart attack*. Thank God, he's okay. For the most part. What happened could have been a lot worse. So yeah, I'm going to fuss around him a whole hell of a lot. Guess he'll have to suck it up because I won't be backing off anytime soon.

"And you don't need to stay at the house either. Your grandmother and I are perfectly capable of taking care of ourselves. We've been doing it for seventy-some years. You should go back to the dorms. Back to your life."

Doesn't he realize that he *is* my life?

That I'll do whatever it takes to ensure his health is back on track? We're talking daily walks, maybe a little yoga or tai chi at the local YMCA, and super smoothies filled with plenty of antioxidants and vitamins.

Instead of arguing, I humor him. "I will, Gramps. Don't worry about it. I'm just going to stick around here for a bit longer and then I'll head back to the dorms. I haven't missed any classes and I'm getting all my work done. Everything's fine."

I've been staying with them for the last week, commuting back and forth to school. Honestly, I think I'm here more for me, than them. After that scare, I feel the need to stick close. I like seeing firsthand that he's on the mend and getting stronger every day. And I certainly don't mind running errands or driving my grandfather to appointments when I'm not at school.

It's also a lot quieter around here. I've had plenty of time to sit and think about my relationship with Sam. About everything that unfolded between us this last month. The rollercoaster highs and lows. The realization I've come to is that I'm completely in love with him. It might have taken me a while to see him in that light, but now that I have, I've fallen hard and fast.

More importantly than that, I've come to the conclusion that I need him.

I *need* him in my life.

I *need* him to be my friend.

And if that's all we'll ever be, then I can accept it. What other choice do I have?

I knew this dating thing was never going to work out between us. I totally fucked it up, which is exactly what I do when it comes to relationships. I'm no good at them. Over the last week, Sam and I have miraculously found our way back to one another. It's still tentative but at least we're talking. Things are gradually falling back into place.

And that's exactly where it needs to stay.

With enough time, the weeks we spent together will eventually fade from both of our memories, becoming nothing more than a blip we'll forget about.

It's safer that way.

Sam is the one person I can't afford to lose. And if we're just friends from here on out, there's zero chance of that happening.

It makes perfect sense.

My phone chimes with an incoming text message. I don't have to pull it out of my pocket to know that Sam is on his way over to pick me up. I've tried to tell him that I could take my grandparent's car back and forth to school, but he insisted on driving me himself.

Which is fine. I've missed spending time with him, and the only way things will get back to normal is if we continue to move forward and pretend those few weeks never transpired.

I press a light kiss against my grandfather's forehead. "I'll see you when I get back later. If you guys need anything while I'm gone, just have Gran call or text, all right? I should be home around three."

His hand cups my cheek before the corners of his lips pull up into an affectionate smile. "You're a good girl, Violet."

I can't help but return the tender look. "Love you."

"Love you, too."

I snag my messenger bag from my bedroom before jogging down the stairs and swinging into the kitchen where my grandmother is making breakfast. She made me a plate of eggs and wheat toast bright and early this morning. It's just one of the many perks to staying at the house with them.

"Okay, I'm heading out," I tell her.

She glances up from the eggs she's scrambling. "Are you sure you don't want to take the car? Wouldn't that be easier?"

"Sam is already on his way. Plus, what happens if you need it?"

She nods. "Please be sure to thank Sam properly for us. He's been so helpful throughout all of this."

I grab a banana from the bowl of fruit on the counter before shoving it in my bag for later. "I will, Gran."

Sam has been amazing. And his mom, Beth, comes over every afternoon when I'm at school to check on my grandfather and answer any questions Gran might have. I know it makes her feel better to have someone with medical experience living so close.

I hate to admit it, but it's a relief that Beth pops over when I'm not around. I've yet to see either one of Sam's parents since his photo ended up plastered all over the internet. I have no idea if they're aware that I'm the one who took the picture or not.

It doesn't escape me that I'm a total coward for not owning up to the truth. I've known these people for eight years. I've eaten countless dinners at their kitchen table and been invited over for numerous holiday parties. They've always included me in everything, to the point of giving me birthday and Christmas gifts. Beth is, in some regards, like a surrogate mother to me. Sam's entire family has always been kind, generous, and accepting.

And this is how I repay their kindness?

By taking a naked shot of their son and carelessly allowing it to end up in someone else's possession to be distributed like party favors to everyone on campus.

I wince at the ugly image as Sam pulls into the driveway. As I slip from the house, I hustle to his truck and pull open the door before sliding in next to him. Once I'm belted in and he's pulling out onto the street, silence settles over us. It's not one that's uncomfortable or oppressive, but it isn't the easy camaraderie we've shared in the past.

What I've come to realize is that I don't have to let what happened ruin our relationship. I can salvage what's left. Sam pretty much said that we would work everything out between us. I just have to be patient. Hopefully, with enough time, we'll get back to the place we once were.

After a few miles, I clear my throat and broach a topic that I don't necessarily want to discuss. "Are we okay?"

His gaze cuts to mine before one side of his mouth hitches into a slight smile. "Yeah, Vi. We're okay." He sounds more like his old self than he has in a while.

Relief rushes from my lungs because it's the first time he's admitted that since the *incident* happened. It's a gigantic weight lifted from my shoulders. Or maybe my heart. I can finally breathe again.

"Good." I nibble at my lower lip and force myself to ask, "How is everything with your parents?"

He shrugs.

As he makes the simple gesture, I realize how much I've missed running my hands over his muscles. I bite back a sigh as that thought pops into my head. If we're going to be friends, then I can't allow myself to think like that. It's difficult—if not impossible—given how physically aware of him I am.

"All right, I guess. There hasn't been too much in the way of fallout. Dad is waiting to see what happens. He's concerned that his opponent will use it as ammunition once the race is underway."

It makes me gut sick that I'm the one who caused problems with him and his parents. Or impacted his dad's reelection efforts. Sam has spent his entire life flying under the radar, always shying away from the spotlight. It sucks that my careless actions have thrusted him unwillingly into the center of it.

Even though I'm unsure how he'll react, I reach out and tentatively take hold of his hand before squeezing it in my smaller one. "I'm sorry that what I did affected your family. I wish there were something I could do to make it better."

For a moment, his gaze flickers to mine. "You don't have to apologize anymore. It was an accident. Everything with my family will be fine. Just give it time to settle. All right?"

I glance away and stare pensively out the window.

"Vi? Did you hear me?"

Not looking at him, I say, "Yeah, I got it."

There's a beat of silence before he asks, "Then what's the problem?"

I force out a puff of air and admit, "That week without you...it really sucked." My gaze slides to him as he focuses on the ribbon of road beyond the windshield, easily maneuvering through the heavy traffic near campus. "Your friendship means everything to me, and I don't want to do anything to jeopardize it again."

His fingers tighten around mine. "I just needed some time to work through what happened."

"Yeah, I get that. I hate myself for putting you in that kind of position. I really do. This week with my grandparents has given me a lot of time to think. About us...our friendship...and what happened." I suck in a breath and force out the rest. "I think it's best if we go back to being just friends."

A deafening silence fills the cab of his truck as I shift on my seat.

Just when I think he won't respond, he asks, "Is that what you really want, Vi? For us to be just friends?"

No!

It takes everything I have inside to keep the word trapped inside as I force myself to say, "I think it's better that way."

In the eight years we've been friends, we've never had a problem. We never went for days without talking or texting. And yet, in less than a few weeks of us being together, I almost singlehandedly destroyed our relationship.

It seems like that would be the safest route for us to take.

With his bright blue gaze trained straight ahead, he doesn't say another word. My guess is that Sam sees the wisdom of my decision.

Then we can go back to being Violet and Sam.

No pressure.

Just friendship.

The way it was always meant to be.

Chapter Thirty-Two

VIOLET

Mia pokes her head around the corner of the door and glances in my room. "Hey, how is your grandfather doing? It's been a few days since I've seen you."

"He's better! It's a lot of resting right now, which is driving him crazy. I guess there's only so much CNN a person can watch." I open a drawer from my dresser to grab a few shirts to take with me. "There's no reason he shouldn't make a full recovery."

"That's great." She moves further into the room and plops herself down on my bed. "Any plans to move back to the dorms?" There's a beat of silence. "I've missed having you around, Vi. It's way too quiet without you."

My lips lift. "I'll be back in a few days. I want to make sure Gramps is doing all right."

She nods. Mia understands how important my grandparents are to me. She's been invited over for a ton of dinners and has visited during summer breaks. "You can take my car back and forth if you want. It's not like I need it during the week."

It probably would be easier if I used Mia's vehicle. I feel bad that Sam has been carting my ass around. Every time I suggest getting to and from school on my own, he shuts down the conversation. Plus, I like being with him. I hope the more time we spend together, the quicker our friendship will slide back to normal.

To what it once was.

When we were friends.

Just friends.

When I was oblivious to his feelings for me. When my heart didn't beat solely for him.

Unfortunately, with all the quiet time I now have on my hands, I find myself dwelling on the weeks we spent together. The memories refused to be banished. For my own sanity, I have to stop remembering what it felt like to have his hands all over my body. Or the way his fingers would sink into my hair as he held my head in place for a bone-melting kiss.

Or how he—

I shake my head to dislodge those dangerous thoughts before they can take root.

"How are things with Sam?" It's like she can sense the direction my mind has swerved.

Not wanting her to scrutinize my expression, I go to the closet and grab a sweater to toss in the duffle bag. "They're fine."

I don't want to discuss Sam. It still feels too fresh. As much as I want our relationship to be the way it used to, it's not. We're both trying so hard to be normal again. But the thinly veiled tension is still there, wafting around us.

Time, I remind myself. It's just going to take time. I have to be patient. Those two sentences have become my mantra.

Even though I give Mia an overly bright smile, she sees right through it. "Is it?"

"Yup, we're totally good." I pause and force out the rest because it needs to be said. And I need to accept it, no matter how difficult it is. "We've decided that we're better off as friends."

Her dark brows slide together as she watches me from her perched position on my bed. "Oh?"

It's like ripping off a Band-Aid. I have to do it quickly. "It just didn't work out." I pop a shoulder, hoping that she's buying the bullshit I'm trying to sell. "You know how it goes."

Even though I try to keep my expression free from all the hurt and regret that swirls around inside me, Mia sees right through it. "Oh, honey, I'm sorry." She nips her bottom lip with her teeth before asking, "Was it because of the picture?"

I drag in a deep breath before expelling it from my body and zipping up the bag. I need to get out of here and away from her questions. I'm nowhere near ready to do an autopsy on our relationship just yet.

"That was a big part of it," I reluctantly admit.

This isn't my first breakup. More like my hundredth. I should be an old pro at it by now. At moving on without a second thought. But this time is different.

Sam is different.

"It's better this way." Even though I keep repeating the words, I don't believe them.

Yet.

I don't believe them *yet*. It's going to take time and patience.

"I'm really sorry about the whole photograph fiasco," she says. "I should have been paying more attention to what Caroline was doing."

Caroline.

Grrrr.

It's hard not to grit my teeth every time I think about her. And the havoc she created.

I tracked her ass down a few days ago and we had some words. More like some not so nice words, to put it politely. She apologized for stealing the picture from my phone, but the damage is done and there's not a damn thing that can change it.

"For what it's worth, I thought you two were really good together."

Instead of responding to the comment, I jerk my head into a nod and keep my hands busy.

Then she adds another dagger through my heart. "You seemed really happy with him."

A rush of tears pricks the back of my eyes, but I blink them away, refusing to let them fall. What matters most is that Sam and I are gradually finding our way back to one another.

"It's better this way," I repeat stoically.

Maybe, if I'm lucky, there will come a time when I actually believe those words.

Chapter Thirty-Three

VIOLET

"You've been awfully quiet lately," Gran comments. "Everything okay at school?"

I throw a fleeting smile over my shoulder as I finish washing up the dishes in the sink. "Yup, everything's fine."

Even though I've turned back toward the soapy water, I feel my grandmother's warm hazel gaze on me as if assessing my words for the truth. Last week, I casually broke the news that Sam and I had decided to part ways. She had looked surprised before asking a few questions about the demise of our relationship. Instead of being forthright, I'd shut down the conversation before it could spiral out of control. I realize that she's trying to help, but there is nothing that dulls the pain of this breakup. It's like a throbbing wound that refuses to heal. I expected after a solid week of moping, the ache would have subsided by now.

It hasn't.

It still feels raw and surprisingly tender, which is ridiculous. It's not like we were together for that long. Losing Sam shouldn't feel like such a crushing blow.

Lost in thought, I stare out the window above the sink. My gaze roams over the tree-lined backyard until it lands on a small, huddled form sitting on the neighboring swing set.

My brows pinch together as I stare. I've been staying with my grandparents for more than a week, and this is the first time I've caught sight of Ari. The way her head hangs forward, as if she's staring at her shoes, makes me wonder if something is wrong.

"I know you don't want to talk about what happened with Sam," Gran murmurs, "but maybe you two need to try and work things out. Give your relationship another chance."

Air leaks from my lungs as I focus on the small, blonde girl rocking back and forth on the swing. Instead of responding to her comment, I grab a dish towel before drying my hands off. "Ari's in the backyard. I'm going to go over and say hello."

Gran spears me with a knowing look. One that tells me that I'm not fooling her for a second as she scoops chocolate chip cookie dough onto a silver tray before popping it into the oven. Unconsciously, I hold my breath and wait to see if she'll drop the conversation.

With a sigh, she says, "Let her know that the cookies will be done in about ten minutes if she wants to stop over and have a few."

A grateful smile lifts the corners of my lips. "I will."

I grab my jacket off a hook in the back hall, and zip it up before opening the door and stepping outside. The temperature has to be hovering around thirty degrees. I shove my hands deep inside my pockets and walk toward Ari. She must be freezing. Her jacket is thin, and she doesn't have gloves or a hat to ward off the chill.

As the wind whistles past my ears, I wish I'd grabbed a hat and some warm mittens for her. Instead of turning around to get them, I keep moving across the yard. Even when I'm no more than a few steps away from where she sits, Ari doesn't glance up or acknowledge my presence.

I take hold of the yellow chain link swing and lower myself onto the plastic seat. Cold seeps through my jeans, and a little shiver dances its way across my flesh.

"Hey, Ari. Is everything all right?"

She glances at me. Her bright blue eyes—ones that remind me so much of Sam's— pierce mine. I give her a slight smile because it's obvious from the bleak expression marring her usually smiling face that it's not.

The slight shrugging of her slender shoulders is all the response I get.

I push against the ground with my feet until the swing arcs gently back and forth. "Do you want to talk about it?"

Her gaze drops back to her feet as she shakes her head.

"All right," I say, "you don't have to tell me what's going on. Would you rather be alone? I can always head back inside."

Maybe I can't force her to talk about what's bothering her, but I can shoot Sam a text and let him know that something is going on with his sister.

She shakes her head, but still doesn't open up and tell me what's going on. Five minutes slide by as we sit on our swings, allowing them to glide back and forth. The wind whips over us, blowing her long blonde hair so that it tangles around her shoulders. The growing silence only gives me more time to dwell on her brother. Lately, he's all I think about. Sometimes—

"My parents have been fighting a lot lately," she says quietly.

A pit settles at the bottom of my belly. As much as I hope their arguments have nothing to do with the picture of Sam, my guess is that it does. Throughout the years, I've spent a lot of time at our next-door neighbor's house, and I've never known Senator and Mrs. Harper to have disagreements. They never even bicker.

"I'm sorry, Ari." I rack my brain for a way to comfort her. "Most parents fight from time to time. It doesn't necessarily mean there's anything to be worried about."

"I know." She nibbles at her lower lip. "But they've never fought like this before. It's been going on for more than a week."

My heartbeat hitches at her words.

When I fail to respond, she glances at me. Her dark blonde brows draw together. "Is something wrong with Sam?" A thread of concern weaves its way through her young voice.

My fingers tighten around the plastic-coated chains as I shake my head. I can't help but wonder if she's overheard their discussions or if this is more of a hunch on her part.

"Sam is fine," I reassure her before adding, "and he wouldn't want you to worry about him."

"I Facetimed him yesterday. He seemed...I don't know," she shrugs, "sad, I guess." Again, her gaze searches mine. "He's usually smiling and laughing. He likes when I video chat with him, but yesterday he didn't seem very interested in talking. When I asked him why he was down, he said that he had to go and that we'd talk later."

A thick lump of emotion forms in the middle of my throat. "I think he's got a lot going on with classes and football. That's all. You know how much he loves you."

The edges of her lips curve slightly. "I really miss him. He usually stops over to visit or have dinner with us, but he hasn't been able to do that lately."

"Oh." He picks me up and drops me off every day for school. I had just assumed he was stopping by his house. Sam has always been close to his family. For him not to drop by when he's in the neighborhood can only mean that Ari's right.

There's a problem between him and his parents.

"I think Dad is mad at him, but no one will tell me why." Her questioning gaze spears mine again. "Do you know why he would be angry with Sam?"

I suck in an icy breath as the words stall in my throat. What am I supposed to say to this eleven-year-old girl? It's obvious that they don't want Ari to know what's going on, which means that it will only cause more problems if I tell her the truth.

No matter how much I might want to explain what happened, it's not my place.

Although, I don't want to lie to her either. It's a crappy position to be in. What sucks even more is that I'm the one who created the situation. Ari and her parents might not realize it, but I do. I'm the one responsible for the discord that is taking place within their tight-knit family.

"Yeah," I finally admit, "I do."

Her dark blonde brows shoot up so quickly that it's almost comical. Except nothing feels funny at the moment. The toes of her shoes dig into the earth as she halts the swing and jerks it toward me. "Tell me!"

"I'm sorry, sweetie, I can't." I reach out and nab her cold fingers before giving them a squeeze. "I wish I could."

Her face falls before bitter disappointment brews in her blue depths. I'm almost taken aback by the hot licks of emotion roiling within them. Ari is usually so good-natured, so even-tempered. She's sensitive and sweet. In a lot of ways, she reminds me of her older brother.

Above all else, Sam is protective of the ones he loves. Even though Ari doesn't understand what's going on, I have to shield her from the truth because I know that's what Sam would want me to do. He wouldn't want her to find out about the picture.

A blistering heat fills her voice as she snaps with all the pent-up frustration coursing through her eleven-year-old body, "Why won't anyone tell me what's going on? I'm not a baby anymore! I can handle it!"

There is nothing I can say that will diffuse the anger vibrating within her. But maybe there is something I can do to improve the situation.

I can talk to Sam's parents and tell them what transpired. I can make sure they understand that Sam had nothing to do with the photograph. That he didn't even know of its existence until it was splashed across the internet.

A sliver of dread snakes its way through my body.

The thought of waltzing into their house and confessing that I took a naked photo of their son that was later stolen from my phone and made public makes me sick to my stomach.

But what other choice do I have?

I caused this mess. It's only right that I take responsibility for it.

Especially if it will help Sam and his family move beyond it. The last thing I want is for his parents to be angry with him over something he didn't have any knowledge of. I can't allow Sam to continue avoiding his family because of a mistake I made. Only now, in speaking with Ari, do I see how much my error in judgment affected all of them.

How can I allow that to continue when it's in my power to do something about it?

Even though I wish Sam had told me what was going on with his parents, I'm not surprised he chose to keep it silent. We might not be back to the kind of friends we once were, but Sam has always felt the need to shield me from the aftermath of my own stupidity.

As much as I'm dreading it, I understand what needs to be done. I suck in another breath before forcing it out slowly and attempting to settle the queasiness swirling inside me. I squeeze her fingers to draw her attention back to me.

"No one thinks you're a baby, Ari. The issue is really sensitive. I need to talk with your parents. What I have to tell them will hopefully straighten out what's going on. I know it's hard, but can you just trust me on this?"

The pissed off expression is still there as her gaze stays locked on mine.

I've known Ari almost her entire life. I met her when she was three years old. I played with her on the swing set we're sitting on. Dozens of tea parties were held in her pink and white decorated bedroom using delicate miniature porcelain cups and saucers. I'll refrain from mentioning all the times we coerced Sam into attending. I adore Ari. There's nothing I wouldn't do for her. She's a sweet girl and after losing Isabelle, I've come to think of her as a younger sister. If there's a way for me to help her, to help Sam and his family move past this ugliness, I need to do it.

No matter how humiliating or painful it will be.

"Gran just put a batch of chocolate chip cookies in the oven. I bet they're done by now. Why don't you go over and have a few while I talk with your parents? I know she'd love to see you."

Ari presses her lips together before reluctantly nodding. "Fine." There is zero enthusiasm in her voice.

We rise to our feet before she takes off toward the backdoor of my grandparent's house. When she's about half a dozen feet away from me, she swings around.

Her gaze locks on mine as one side of her mouth hitches. "Thanks, Violet."

I give her a strained smile in return.

As Ari disappears through the back door, I square my shoulders and trudge to the Harper's yellow Victorian. With each step that brings me closer, the knot in my belly grows.

I have no idea if what I'm about to do will help the situation with Sam's family. But if there's a way for me to make it better, then I have to try. I can't allow his parents to blame him for something he had no part in.

Chapter Thirty-Four

VIOLET

"Violet! Wait up!"

I swing around and spot Allie trucking toward me from out of nowhere. When she's close enough, one hand snakes out and fastens around my upper arm. The way her fingers bite into my flesh has me wondering if everything is all right.

She looks a little crazy.

All right, maybe more than a little.

A frenzied light fills her deep brown eyes.

I'm tempted to retreat, but her grip is solid. For the time being, I'm stuck.

"Oh my God, have you seen the picture yet?" Not only are her eyes bulging from their sockets, but she's vibrating with pent-up excitement. I've never seen her like this before.

Not that I know Allie all that well, but this isn't her normal demeanor. She's usually more chill. Clearly something big is going on.

My belly nosedives ten stories as I notice the way she's clutching her phone. Dread rushes through my body as I wait for her to drop whatever bomb is about to roll off her tongue. Even though I know it's impossible for there to be another photograph of Sam circulating around campus, that's the only thought crashing through my brain.

Honestly, part of me doesn't want to know what's going on. I don't think I can deal with anymore fallout. I really don't. I've barely recovered from the first shit storm that hit a few weeks ago. "No," I say slowly, "What are you talking about?"

Oh God, oh God, oh God.

Please don't let it have anything to do with Sam.

The fervor in her eyes grows. "*This!*"

She shoves her phone screen in my face. It's so close that I'm barely able to focus on it. I nip the slim device from her fingers before reluctantly taking a peek. Air gets clogged in my throat. After a long moment, I blink and the image swimming before my eyes takes shape.

Holy.

Crap.

Those are the only two words my brain can lock on.

Because I can't—

"I know, right?" Allie sounds almost gleeful. Like she just found out that she won a million dollars. And it's Christmas. Right on her birthday.

I shake my head, unable to rip my gaze away from the small screen cradled in the palm of my hand. It's like a horrendous traffic accident I can't help but stare at.

"My plan is to get that sucker printed off on a twenty-by-sixteen glossy posterboard and then hang it directly above my bed." As she gazes at the sky, a soft smile tips her lips upward as if she can already see it. I'm trying very hard not to imagine what Allie might do alone in her bed all the while staring up at that picture.

She interrupts those disturbing thoughts by screeching at the top of her lungs, "*Can you believe they did something like this?*"

Nope. I really can't.

I wonder if Sam has seen the photograph yet. Better yet, I wonder if the Bulldogs football coach has caught wind of it. I'd hate to be in the locker room when he realizes what his star players have been up to. Sam got his ass chewed out when the head coach found out about the photo circulating around campus.

I believe the lecture entailed—making better choices, private moments remaining private, and why people feel the need to document things that shouldn't be documented in the first place.

The difference is that Sam's photo leak hadn't been deliberate.

This on the other hand?

This is totally intentional.

I mean, come on—of course it is!

There are about fifteen players standing in the buff on the fifty-yard line of the football field. Their backsides are facing the camera. All you see are brawny shoulders, strong backs, tapered waists, chiseled butt cheeks, and muscular thighs.

Did I happen to mention that they're buck naked in the shot?

My wide gaze slides to Allie.

A smile curves her lips upward.

Wide-eyed, with child-like wonderment, she asks, "How did Santa know this was exactly what I wanted for Christmas?"

Laughter gurgles up from my throat. There hasn't been a whole lot to chuckle about over the past few weeks, so it feels nice to do it now.

My gaze drops to her phone again. I have the sneaking suspicion that Roan and Dylan are behind this stunt. It's their asses that are front and center.

Along with Liam Garrison's.

Which is, admittedly, a rather nice looking ass.

Chapter Thirty-Five

VIOLET

I glance around the already crowded bar and ask Mia for the third time, "Are you sure you don't want to hang out at the dorms? We can have a movie night. I'll even let you pick." When her expression doesn't change, I add, "We'll order pizza. My treat."

When she doesn't make a move from the table we're parked at, I realize that I'm stuck at O'Brien's for the duration.

"I am so not in the mood for this," I grumble.

I would much rather be at home, sitting around in comfy clothes, and stuffing my face with pizza all the while lamenting my idiotic stupidity for the millionth time. Unfortunately, Mia has other plans, which include getting shitfaced.

"Don't care," she replies. "I need this." She hoists the brown bottle to her lips and proceeds to drain roughly half the contents in one thirsty gulp before slamming the bottle down onto the table. "Desperately."

Mia's love life has nosedived right before exploding into a fiery ball of flames. After a week of silence from Carter, she told him that she was coming to visit. His response was to pull the plug on their two-year relationship with some lame-ass excuse about needing time apart so he could get his life figured out.

They are now officially on a break.

How do you go from proposing marriage to the supposed love of your life to stomping all over her heart and ending a two-year relationship?

I have no idea. But that's what happened. My heart goes out to her. She's obviously gutted about the entire thing, and I can't blame her for it.

I understand that Mia needs a night out and a chance to cut loose. She needs to forget about her ex, if only for a few drunken hours.

I hope for Carter's sake, he comes to his senses sooner rather than later. Mia isn't the kind of girl to sit around and mope. She'll give herself the weekend to be all sad bastard before picking herself up and moving on with her life. I've seen her when something goes wrong or doesn't work out the way she expected it to. Instead of getting angry or frustrated, she chalks it up to experience, and figures out a different path to take.

Tonight, however, is definitely for wallowing. This is emphasized when Mia flags down the waitress so she can order another bottle of beer even though she hasn't finished the first one.

"So, tell me—what's going on with golden delicious?"

I narrow my eyes. She knows how much I hate it when she refers to Sam like that. "Nothing."

We're friendly, but it's not the same. I have no idea if it ever will be again. And that knowledge is like a knife slicing through my beating heart.

"Okay," she continues, "what are you going to do about it?"

I wince at the steely note that enters her voice. Mia may be taking time to mope about her situation with Carter, but apparently my time has run out.

This isn't a conversation that I want to delve headfirst into. Especially with her. Instead of answering, I lift my drink to my lips and take a sip, hoping that when I fail to respond, she'll get the hint and move on.

But she doesn't.

Have I mentioned that Mia can be annoyingly persistent when she wants to be?

It's not a good quality.

I shift on my chair. "What can I do? We're just in this..." My voice trails off. I don't even know what kind of place we're in right now. "It's just weird. Things aren't totally back to normal, but at least he's talking to me."

That's something, right?

At this point, I'll take whatever Sam is willing to give me. I'm like a dog begging for scraps. And I'm not ashamed to admit it either. I fucked up. I put him and his family through hell. I'm lucky he's still willing to give me the time of day.

"Does he know that you spoke with his parents?" she asks.

I shrug. "We haven't talked about it."

Can anyone blame me for being reluctant to bring up the photo scandal situation yet again?

I think we're both trying to quietly move past it, which is difficult, since whenever we're together, it's like a two-ton elephant sitting between us.

Impossible to avoid.

What am I supposed to say?

Hey, just a little FYI—even though I fucked up, I'm trying to clean up a tiny piece of it.

Big deal. It does nothing to change the fact that there's a naked picture of Sam floating around. I passed by a girl at the library the other day who was using it as a screen saver on her computer.

That situation isn't going away any time soon.

"I don't know if his parents mentioned it to him." He hasn't spoken about it, and I'm fine with that. The sooner I can forget about the whole cringe-worthy conversation I had with the Harpers, the better off I'll be.

The memory of it flashes through my head in painful Technicolor bursts. Kind of like when you're watching a horror flick through fingers that are clapped tightly over your eyes. Every once in a while, you can't help but take a peek and catch a gruesome glimpse. Unfortunately, that one stolen glance will forever be burned into your brain.

For instance, Senator Harper glaring at me from across the highly polished kitchen table through frigid eyes. Brows drawn sharply together. Mouth carved into a deep frown that never budged from his face. Hands clenched tightly in front of him.

And then he just sat there staring at me. As if he couldn't figure out why I would do something so stupid. By the disgruntled expression that marred his face, he wasn't able to figure it out either.

Or having to face Sam's mother. The woman who gave birth to him. The woman who stepped in as a surrogate mom during my formative years. I can only speculate that she had just as difficult of a time understanding why I would feel the need to photograph her son.

Naked.

In bed.

Without his permission before allowing it to be stolen.

I have no idea how I'll ever face them again. I couldn't have felt like more of a perverted deviant if I tried. The memories alone are enough to make my cheeks burn with heat.

Would you like to guess who won't be engaging in sexy picture time ever again?

Yup, that's right—me.

This experience has turned out to be too psychologically damaging to ever engage in *that* again.

Mia polishes off her first bottle of beer before starting in on the second. Her alcohol consumption is turning out to be more of a sprint rather than a marathon. "You're just going to sit back and do absolutely nothing about this?"

I give her a blank look because yeah—that's *exactly* what the plan is. For the time being, I'm going to lay low and ride this one out. What else does she expect me to do? Haven't I singlehandedly caused enough damage to my friendship with Sam?

She scowls, looking frustrated by my lack of response before doling out more unsolicited advice. Alcohol, unfortunately, brings out the armchair therapist in Mia.

"For starters, you could pull on your big girl panties, and tell him how you really feel." When I remain stubbornly silent, her expression softens. "I can see how much the situation is tearing you apart. I get that you made a mistake. But it's not the end of the world, Violet. If you want Sam, then you need to be honest with him about your feelings. Being friends is a distant second to the kind of relationship you really want. If it doesn't work out, then at least you tried. You went after what you wanted."

As her words roll around in my head like marbles, I hoist the beer bottle to my lips and take another swig. Mia has no idea how tempted I am to follow her advice. "I'm the one who told him that we were better off as friends."

She shakes her head and huffs out a sigh before taking another pull from her drink. Bottle number two is going just as fast as bottle number one. "Of course you did. That sounds *exactly* like something you would do."

My shoulders hunch as a frown tugs at the corners of my lips. "What does that mean?"

Her eyes turn serious. "It means that not being honest with Sam about the kind of relationship you really want is *you* trying to play it safe. It's *you* being afraid to tell him that you want more than friendship even though you fucked stuff up."

My jaw goes slack. When I'm finally able to wrap my lips around the words, they're low and thick. Scraped raw. "What are you talking about? I *have* been honest with him. I just—I just..." my voice trails off.

Doesn't Mia understand that I can't live without Sam? That securing his friendship is more important than not having him in my life at all?

Her eyes fill with compassion as she leans across the table. "Honey, Sam didn't break up with you after the picture fiasco. *You're* the one who told him that you were better off as friends. *You're* the one who put the kibosh on your relationship. Not him."

No...that's not what happened. Sam was angry with me, and rightfully so. His privacy had been invaded. I hate that I'm the one who caused him pain and embarrassment. At this point, I'm not even sure if I deserve his friendship, much less his love.

"I didn't want to lose him as a friend," I whisper harshly, "he was barely talking to me. It was only a matter of time before he ended things." I suck in a ragged breath. "So what if I beat him to the punch by downgrading our relationship? It would have happened eventually. I had to salvage what I could before I lost him."

"Listen," her voice turns soft, "I understand why you did it. But you didn't give him any time to deal with the fallout. You just cut things off. You forced everything back to the way it was." Her knowing gaze stays locked on mine. "The point I'm trying to make is that *you're* the one who called it quits, not him."

"But he would have," I insist. "I violated his trust by snapping that picture and keeping it on my phone."

"You don't know that, Vi. You got scared and dumped him before he could dump you."

Her words have my throat closing up, making it painful to swallow down the thick lump of emotion sitting in the middle of it. She's right, I don't know for sure what would have happened. But still...I could see where it was heading.

The little voice inside my head reminds me that we're nowhere near the kinds of friends we used to be. That our relationship hasn't shifted back to the easy camaraderie we once took for granted. And that's a bitter pill to swallow. When it comes down to it, Sam is my everything. That week or so without him showed me just how dependent I am on him.

On his friendship.

"Well, speak of the devil...or maybe I should say *devils*."

The fine hair at the nape of my neck rises as I swivel in my seat until my gaze collides with a bright blue one. The air gets trapped in my lungs. Barely do I notice that Sam is flanked by Dylan and Liam. The three of them together—with their wide shoulders, broad chests, muscular bodies, and just general gorgeousness—turn female heads.

"Looks like company is coming our way," Mia murmurs about five seconds before they arrive at our table.

Liam treats us to a broad smile before asking, "Mind if we join you?"

Even though Liam's question is directed at me, I find myself unable to rip my gaze away from Sam. When I remain silent, Mia jumps in, waving her hand toward our table with its two extra chairs. Needing another place to sit, Liam glances around for another chair before charming a table full of girls next to us.

As Sam slides onto the seat next to me, my muscles tense, and a low hum of energy ignites in my blood. I hate it. I hate that I'm aware of him on every level. Of his sheer masculine presence. He doesn't need to do anything, and already I'm responding to him. As his knee bumps into mine beneath the table, a shiver shimmies down my spine.

His gaze ensnares mine as he closes the distance between us. "How's it going, Vi?"

The last thing I want is for Sam to see how much he affects me. I've never wanted anyone the way I want Sam Harper. The only thing I can do is attempt to salvage a shred of my pride by not allowing him to see what a pathetic mess I am.

"It's good." I'm such a liar. It's so far from good, it's not even funny.

A few short months ago, it would have never occurred to me to lie. I wouldn't have bothered to shield my true feelings from him.

He nods, taking my response at face value before flagging down a waitress. All three guys order drinks. I realize that our waitress is the same dark-haired girl who was flirting with Sam before we got together. I grit my teeth at the way her gaze strays to him as she flutters around the table.

It's on the tip of my tongue to tell her to get lost before it occurs to me that I have zero claim on Sam. He's free to hookup with whoever he wants. Unable to stomach the way she's flirting with him, I drop my gaze to the bottle in front of me.

I have to remind myself that Sam and I are nothing more than friends.

We are not getting back together again.

That thought is as painful as a gunshot wound. If I'm not mistaken, people actually die from that kind of injury. The notion isn't surprising because that's exactly how I feel. Like I'm dying a slow, painful death all the while bleeding out.

I straighten my shoulders and attempt to regroup. If the ultimate goal here is to keep Sam in my life, then I need to pull my head out of my ass and start acting like his friend instead of some hurt ex-girlfriend.

I hoist a smile and do my best to pretend that the last month was nothing more than a figment of my imagination. I never fell head over heels for Sam, we never made love to one another, and he never became my everything.

None of it happened.

I focus on the banter taking place at the table instead of the man sitting next to me.

"Whose bright idea was it for you guys to drop your drawers and have a little naked time on the field?"

Liam smirks before raising a brow in Mia's direction. "Did you see something you liked, sweetheart?"

If Liam thinks he's going to embarrass Mia, he's got another thing coming. She gives him a sly grin before leering in his direction, "Yeah, I saw a whole lot of somethings I liked."

Liam's lips quirk as the rest of the guys laugh before they talk about the newest picture to circulate around Barnett. If the women on campus were drooling over Sam's photo, they're losing their minds at seeing the hottest guys on the football team in the buff.

It doesn't matter if the view is only from the backside.

Thirty minutes slide by and the bar is packed to the gills. Several other football players have joined our group. They've pulled up chairs or stand around the table laughing and talking, swigging beer from their bottles.

Where the college athletes go, the inevitable groupies who are looking for a little hookup action at the end of the night follow. They've found laps to hang out on in tiny skirts that barely cover their asses.

Thankfully, none of them have planted themselves on Sam.

I don't think I could bear that. The facade I've donned for the evening is fragile. To sit next to him and pretend that everything is normal is more difficult than I imagined. Even though I'm having a good time, I'm unbearably aware of Sam's presence beside me. The way his knee settles against mine. The subtle touches here and there. I'm wound up so tight that it feels like I could explode from the pressure building inside me.

It's only when his fingers slip gently over mine and he drags me out of my seat, that my attention snaps back to him. The guy I've been desperately trying to ignore for the last forty-five minutes.

When my startled eyes catch his, he murmurs, "Come on, let's dance."

That doesn't necessarily sound like a good idea. In fact, it sounds more like imminent disaster waiting to happen.

One touch from him and I will shatter. There won't be a way for me to keep a tight lid on my emotions.

Sam doesn't give me a choice in the matter. Before I can refuse, my hand is secured in his larger one as he tows me onto the crowded dance floor where a slow ballad has begun to play.

Already my fingers tingle from his touch. It goes from bad to worse as he wraps his arms around me, tucking me against the solid wall of his chest.

Since I know what will happen if I allow myself to melt into him, I keep my body rigidly locked within the circle of his arms. The intimacy of the moment nearly kills me.

His lips hover near the outer shell of my ear as his warm breath feathers over my flesh. "Relax, Vi. It's just *me*. This is just *us*."

As he murmurs the words, unbidden moisture gathers in my eyes. Quickly, I blink it away.

Yes. It's just *him*. And this is just *us*.

But I don't feel like we've been *us* for a while. Not since I ruined everything. Doesn't he understand that? Can't he feel how different everything is? How stiff and uncomfortable we are now?

"Just relax and let me hold you," he says.

You know what?

Screw it. The truth of the matter is that I'm going to hurt no matter what. I might as well enjoy the feel of his arms while I can. It's as if those thoughts give my body permission to loosen as we rock steadily from side to side. The woodsy scent of his cologne has my eyes nearly crossing. I'm one massive breath away from inhaling him. But I force myself not to. That will only make everything throb and ache more than it already does.

My eyelids feather closed as I enjoy the feel of Sam's arms. Memories of what it felt like when we were wrapped around each other in bed shove in at the edges.

I've missed this so much.

I've missed being this close to Sam.

Unable to stop myself, I press my face against his chest and inhale a breath. It feels like a massive head rush. Or heart rush. Or some kind of rush as the scent of him careens through my system.

That last inhale was a mistake. One I'll end up regretting in the not-so-distant future. When I'm wrapped up in his arms like this, it's impossible to regret anything. His body is pressed deliciously close to mine. All his hard lines are perfectly aligned with my softer curves.

"You've been good?" His breath slides over the side of my face. My knees waver as if they might buckle.

"Yup." Nope.

Not by a long shot.

My life sucks right now because I miss him so damn much. But that doesn't seem like the appropriate thing to say. We need normal, and lots of pretending to get us through the moment.

"How about you?" I ask.

"I'm fine. Just getting ready for the bowl game. And then playoffs after that."

The Bulldogs ended up losing two of their conference games this season. Since they won the majority of them, they made it to the Boca Raton Bowl. Tons of students will caravan to Florida for the game.

Once the season is over, Sam will have more time to kick back and relax. Then we'll have one last semester together at Barnett. Our law school letters will roll in, and we'll find out where we've been accepted. It's a given that Sam and I won't stay together. His family wants him to attend Columbia. And hopefully, I'll continue at Barnett.

A year from now, will we be in touch?

How about in five?

Or ten?

If you had asked me a few months back, I would have laughed my ass off. Of course we would stay in touch. How could we not? We're best friends. We got through high school and college by leaning on one another.

After everything we've been through this last month, I don't know if that will be the case. Nothing between us is the same. Our relationship has changed. It's no longer easy and effortless.

I'm yanked from those thoughts when he says, "You didn't have to talk with my family." There's a pause before he adds, "I never disclosed the details of the situation."

Is it any wonder I'm so in love with him? That is exactly the kind of man Sam is. Instead of dragging me into the mess, he shouldered all the blame himself.

I turn my head and force myself to meet his gaze. "I wanted them to know that you had nothing to do with it. That you didn't even know a photograph existed until it went viral. I'm the one they should be angry with, not you."

"Thank you. I appreciate it."

"I should have done it sooner." It was cowardly not to take full responsibility for my actions. And that's not who I am. Especially when it comes to Sam. Ever since I met him, all he's done is protect me. How could I live with myself if I hadn't done the same?

As his gaze sifts through mine, a bolt of electricity snaps and sizzles between us. As much as I want to look away, I'm powerless to do so. It feels as if I'm trapped in those piercing blue depths.

The song is only midway through when he says, "Let's get out of here. We need to talk."

Instead of waiting for a response, he clasps my hand tightly in his own before maneuvering us through the thick crowd until we're pushing out the backdoor of O'Brien's and into the jam-packed parking lot. The cold slaps at me as soon as I step outside. I wrap my arm around my middle, trying to keep warm as he pulls me past rows of parked cars.

"My truck is over there. We can sit and talk inside."

As his gaze catches mine, he drapes an arm around my body, tucking me close as we continue to walk.

Every nerve ending crackles with pent-up energy and need.

When we're close enough to his pickup, Sam hits the automatic locks and opens the passenger side door. Then he's sliding in beside me and locking us inside.

It's only when he angles his body and his gaze pins me in place, that I'm slammed with the realization that this relationship isn't going to work.

No matter how much I want it to.

I can't be his friend. Not right now. Maybe not ever.

There is too much pain and regret coursing through me to pretend otherwise.

In the last week or so, I've been careful to keep my distance and hold myself back. My guess is that Sam has been doing the same. This is the first time since everything fell to shit between us that he's taken me in his arms. That I've been able to breathe in the intoxicating scent of him. That my lips have been inches away from his.

I can't do *this*.

I can't pretend that we're *just* buddies.

Friends.

Pals.

At one time, that's exactly what we were. But our relationship has changed. Morphed into something more. Only now, do I understand that there is no going back. It hurts too much to be with him, and yet, not really *be* with him. It felt like I was being eaten alive by jealousy when the waitress inside had been flirting with him. I was so afraid she would catch his eye. Or maybe it would be the next time.

Then what?

I don't think I can stand to watch it all playout, feeling the way I do. It would be like dying an excruciatingly painful death. Maybe when I have a better grip on my emotions, I'll be able to stomach it, but that's not the case right now.

As much as I want to, I can't ignore my feelings for Sam.

Chapter Thirty-Six

SAM

All I want is to grab hold of Violet and yank her into my arms. Need pounds through my body like a steady drumbeat. It's all I can think about. Dancing with her, holding her in my arms again—I couldn't do it any longer, knowing that she wasn't mine.

That I had lost her.

That she wants to be friends and nothing more.

Here's what I know—I can't go back to the way it was when Violet was oblivious to my feelings. Oblivious to the need spiking through my veins.

The distance between us is palpable. It's like a chasm. One that feels insurmountable. And that sucks. It's never been like this between us, and it scares the shit out of me. All I want is for our relationship to go back to the way it was before that fucking photograph was splashed all over social media.

I never wanted our relationship to backpedal or stall. I was thrown off by the situation. And then it spiraled out of control.

But I've had time to wade through this mess, and deal with everything hurtling at me in hyper speed. The parental bullshit has been difficult, but we're getting through it. We're moving forward. I have no idea how much damage, if any, it'll cause to my father's campaign.

In this moment, what matters is rectifying the situation with Violet before I lose her. I can see it happening already. She's distancing herself from me, throwing up walls, and I can't stand it. I want to tear them down, brick by brick with my bare hands.

I've never been happier than when I was holding Violet in my arms. When she belonged to me. She might not have realized it before, but my heart has always been hers. I'm incomplete without her.

It might be a risky move, but it's one I have to make. I reach out and cup the curve of her cheek.

Surprised by the gesture, her eyes flare.

"Vi," I rasp, "what's going on?"

Even though it's dark outside, the brightness from the parking lot illuminates her face. Light and shadow slants across her features. They're ones I've been in love with for almost a decade. The way I feel about her has never changed. And I don't think it ever will, which is why I need to do something before it's too late.

Violet shakes her head as if she doesn't understand the question. But I know that she does. I see it in the slight tightening around her lips, and in the way her pulse picks up its tempo.

"You know what I'm talking about," I murmur.

Her eyelashes feather closed before she inhales a deep breath. "I wish everything could go back to the way it was before we got together."

"Is that really what you want?" Dread curdles in the pit of my gut. "To just be friends?" Everything inside me aches for her. She's so damn close and yet...she might have already slipped through my fingers.

Almost tentatively, Violet opens her eyes before her gaze settles on mine. She nips her lower lip. "It's better that way."

"Is it?" I can't resist gently pulling her lip from between her teeth before sweeping my thumb against it. The breath catches at the back of her throat as I do.

Her nod is barely perceptible.

My hand slips around her neck before I tug her close until my lips can ghost over hers. I give her a heartbeat, maybe two, to pull away. To stop this from happening. I'm sure as hell not going to force myself on her, but I'm beginning to suspect that there might be hope for us yet.

Hope that she's not being truthful about her feelings. At the very least, her body still craves my touch. I can tell by the way she leans into me, and the way her breathing changes when I lay my hands on her.

"I can't be your friend, Vi. It's too late for that."

Sadness fills her eyes. "You can't?"

As I shake my head, my lips drift over hers. I'm dying for one damn taste. It's been too long that I've gone without. "Nope."

"I had a feeling this would happen," she whispers brokenly.

My brows slide together. At the grief that floods into her eyes. "What are you talking about?"

Emotion fills her voice. "That I would end up losing you over that picture. Not just my boyfriend, but my best friend. The one person I can count on no matter what."

The stranglehold on my heart loosens.

She glances away. "You have to know how sorry I am about what happened."

"I am." When she refuses to meet my gaze, I plead, "Look at me, baby." I wait for her to do as I've asked. Her gaze hesitantly returns to mine. "I know you would never do anything to hurt me or my family."

Emotion bleeds through every syllable. "*You* are my family. Your parents, Gavin and Ari, they mean everything to me. I hate what I've put you all through."

"I know." Violet has always been the most important person in my life. She's more important than football or school...or anything.

She needs to realize that.

I press my lips against hers and keep the pressure light. It's difficult to hold back when all I want to do is plunder her sweetness. I want to press her body against mine until she accepts once and for all that she belongs to me. That she will *always* belong to me. And there's not a damn thing she can do to change that.

Even though I haven't had my fill of her, I pull back enough to see the surprise that flickers in her eyes. Her fingers tremble as she skims them over her lips.

When I can't hold it back any longer, I tell her what's in my heart.

What has always been in my heart. "I love you, Vi. I've always loved you."

"But what about the picture?"

I shrug. "What about it?"

"Aren't you," her voice drops, "upset with me? I broke your trust and invaded your privacy." She shakes her head as if disgusted with herself. "Everyone on campus has seen your ass."

I cock a brow and attempt to lighten the mood. "Are you saying there's something wrong with my ass?"

A tiny spark of humor reluctantly flares to life in her eyes. It reminds me of the way we used to be and gives me hope for the future.

Our future.

Her teeth sink into her lower lip as she shakes her head. "Not at all." Her eyes fill with confusion. "But you were so angry with me."

She's right.

I was.

I can't deny that I was blindsided.

"I was thrown off guard, Vi. And I handled it poorly. I'm not proud of how I reacted. I'm sorry for that. Sorry for pushing you away when all I've ever wanted was to hold you close." I pause, allowing those words to sink in. "I *need* you the way I need air to breathe."

Her hand drifts to my cheek. "You don't have anything to apologize for. I'm the one who messed up." When I shake my head, she tacks on, "Unintentionally. But still, what happened was my fault. And I'm sorry. Sorry for the embarrassment it caused you and your family."

"I want to move past this. I want us to move past it together. Although, going forward, I can't be your friend. I'm not strong enough for that. I need more. I want what we had before everything fell apart. I've never been happier than when you were mine."

"Are you sure you can move past it so easily?" Hope leaps into her eyes as a smile curves her lips.

"I'm over it. Nothing is more important to me than you."

Her gaze softens. "I love you, Sam."

I drag her into my arms before wrapping them around her and pressing her close. Violet burrows against my warmth as if she needs the intimacy as much as I do. "I'm never going to let you go, baby."

She tilts her face toward mine. "I don't ever want you to."

EPILOGUE

Sam

Seven months later...

Roan—Mr. Hotshot Rookie of the Year—helps me carry the heavy couch up two flights of stairs. As we crest the landing, Violet scrambles to open the door. She slides out of our way before pointing at the far wall under the window of the tiny apartment we're now renting. "Put it down over there."

As we lower the monstrous thing to the ground, she directs, "A little more to the left, please."

Roan shoots me a look as we shuffle to the left.

"Nope, too far. Go back just a smidge."

We sidle to the right before hesitating. When she smiles, we set it down on the carpeted floor.

"Perfect!"

As I stretch my back and shoulders, my gaze strays to Violet as she fusses around the couch, adding cushions and pillows. The way she looks in those tight cutoff jean shorts—especially when she bends over to grab something off the floor—has me wishing that Roan would disappear. It also has me thinking about all the ways I plan to christen our brand-new apartment in the near future.

It's been seven months since we got back together and somehow, I'm even more in love with this woman than before. Which is seriously saying something. I've been in love with Violet Winterfield since I was fourteen years old. I can't imagine a future without her filling it. Once we were together again, it didn't take long for everything to slide back to the way it was.

And I love that.

Love that everything is so damn easy between us.

Even though I'm sweaty from moving furniture into our new place, I wrap my arms loosely around her from behind and pull her toward me. I want to feel all those delicious curves pressed against me. Only then do I bury my nose against the curve of her neck and inhale. She might be perspiring, but she still smells amazing, and it drives me out of my mind.

"You owe me a massage," I growl in her ear.

A grin spreads across her face. "I'll do you one better."

That sweet promise has a groan escaping from my lips because we still have a few more hours of crap to move. "I'm going to hold you to it."

Just thinking about sinking into her softness has my cock stiffening up with both anticipation and impatience.

Her eyes twinkle with mischief and heat. "I certainly hope so or I don't know how it'll work."

I swat her ass before releasing her. If I keep her in my arms any longer, I'm liable to carry her off to that brand-new mattress we set up in the bedroom.

"All right...enough of that, you two. There's still a shit ton of work that needs to be done before you order a few pizzas because I'm starving. So, let's get a move on it."

Roan heads back out to the truck for another load of boxes. I owe him big time for coming back to town to help us. Training camp starts in less than two weeks for the Cincinnati Bengals, so he'll be heading back this evening.

Even though I was accepted at both Columbia and Cornell, I

decided to attend Barnett Law School in the fall with Violet. After we got back together, there was no way I was leaving her. This girl is my future. She always has been. It doesn't matter where we are or what school we attend, just as long as we're together.

I knew if Violet was accepted to Barnett, she wouldn't consider any other schools. Family means everything to her. With the loss she suffered, I can't blame her for it.

As much as I would dearly love to spend the evening here, christening every damn room in this place, I've got plans.

Special plans.

————

Violet

I collapse onto the freshly made bed feeling exhausted yet oddly exhilarated at the same time. Sam and I are finally moved into our new apartment. Other than the dorms, I've never lived anywhere else on my own, so this is exciting.

As silly as it is to admit, I feel like a real adult now. I've graduated from Barnett, I'm starting law school in about a month and a half, and I'm living with the man who has always been my best friend. Life couldn't possibly get any better than it is at this moment.

If my parents were still alive, I think they would be proud of the woman I've grown into and happy with the person I've given my heart to. There is no one kinder, sweeter, more intelligent than Sam Harper.

And to think he was under my nose the entire time while I went out with guy after guy. I can't help but snort at the memory of my cock blocking best friend.

Now I'm his.

And he's mine.

Living together is just the beginning for us.

Sam walks into our bedroom with a pile of clothes before setting the stack on top of the dresser. He beelines to the bed where I'm still stretched out before settling next to me and sliding his fingers through my hair. The adoration blazing from his blue eyes is undeniable, and has the breath catching at the back of my throat.

A smile tugs at the corners of my lips. I know he mentioned heading out this evening to grab a quick bite but honestly, I'd much rather order takeout and make love all night. I've wanted to get my hands on him all day. Watching the play of his muscles under the black tank has gotten me all hot and bothered.

His mouth quirks. "What's the grin for?"

I shake my head. "No reason." Then I correct myself. "I'm just happy." Because that's the truth. I couldn't be happier with where I am in life, and the man by my side. The man who has *always* been by my side.

Even when I was too clueless to realize it.

He leans over and cages me in before pressing my body into the soft mattress. His lips sweep over mine before deepening the kiss.

Sam pulls back just enough to whisper against my lips, "I want nothing more than to make you happy. Always." And then his mouth is back to roving over mine.

After a few heated moments, he nips at my lower lip before drawing away. "Why don't you hop in the shower and then we can grab something to eat. There's a little place a few blocks away that looks good. I thought we could give it a try."

Since he's still hovering over me, I trail my fingers across his bulging muscles before arching my back until my pelvis can graze his. He's already hard. Desire leaps into his eyes. "Are you sure that you want to go out tonight?" I give him my sexiest look. "We could always eat in."

Yup, that was a total play on words.

The heat smoldering in his eyes ignites into a veritable inferno as he grinds his thick erection against me. A moan escapes from my lips. He feels so damn good.

"You're killing me, Vi," he growls.

"Hardly," I snort, "I just want to get laid."

Sam glances at the digital clock on the nightstand.

Seriously?

Here I am, pretty much offering myself up on a silver platter, and he's glancing at the clock? Have I entered a parallel universe?

The man never turns down sex.

Like ever.

"How about a quickie, and then we'll head out for dinner? Later, when we come back, I'll make slow love to you for dessert."

I suppose that works.

Barely do I open my mouth to agree before he's ripping the clothes off my body. I can't help but laugh as my black Chuck Taylors are tossed across the room. Socks, shorts, my shirt, and undergarments hastily follow suit.

"Sam," my voice simmers with barely suppressed humor, "let me take a quick show—"

Before I can blink my eyes, he's sliding deep inside me, and we're both moaning out our need. Guess I wasn't the only one who'd worked up a sexual appetite today.

Forty minutes later, and we're heading out the door. Our apartment, which is located north of campus, is about a block away from downtown. We can easily walk to stores and restaurants as well as some of the hip and trendy bars that line the street. I love that there's a totally different vibe here. It's more young professionals rather than drunken college students. We wanted to find an apartment away from the rowdy lifestyle of campus but that was still close enough to school. This works perfectly.

There's a tiny café-style restaurant with outdoor seating on the sidewalk. As we stroll closer, my eyes widen. My grandparents are sitting at one of the white cloth-covered tables. A surprised smile lights up my face as I wave.

I quicken my step and call their names, "Gran! Gramps!"

They both turn before waving back as their faces light up. It's so good to see them out, and my grandfather looking healthy again. It's been a long road to recovery but he's doing really well.

When I'm close enough, I greet them with hugs and kisses.

"We were just about to grab something to eat!" As those words slip out, I turn to Sam who wears a smug smile. His hands are stuffed into the pockets of his cargo shorts. "Oh, you arranged this!"

I can't help but laugh at the obviousness of it.

Sam is always thinking about me and my happiness. It's these thoughtful gestures that mean the world to me and deepen the love that already courses through my veins. I never imagined loving someone so completely. I was the girl who couldn't stay in a relationship for more than a week or two.

And now look at me.

I close the distance between us before kissing him gently on the mouth. "Thank you."

His lips hitch. "Anything for you, babe."

We all settle at the table. My grandparents ask about the new apartment. They're planning to stop over and see it tomorrow afternoon. We tell them about the move, and Roan driving in to help. Dylan, Lexie, Sam, and I are planning a road trip to Cincinnati for Roan's first home game.

I'm so excited for him. Roan is awesome and a really good friend to Sam. Even though I don't know his girlfriend, Ivy, I think I'm going to like her when we finally get a chance to meet. She dances for the Cincinnati Ballet and we're going to snag tickets for that as well.

We order a few appetizers to share along with a round of drinks. My grandmother orders a glass of chardonnay and my grandfather sticks to water with lemon.

Sitting here with them only reconfirms that I made the right decision to stay at Barnett. Even though I was accepted at both Loyola and Purdue, there's nowhere else I'd rather be. Barnett has a highly respected law school and being able to see my grandparents anytime I want is an added bonus.

A burst of happiness explodes in my chest as I glance around the table and realize that I'm surrounded by the people who matter most in my life.

"Violet?"

Contentment washes over me as I glance at Sam. He slips my fingers into his and gives them a squeeze. I love how open and generous he is with his affection.

It's not something I'll ever tire of.

Before I can blink, he's getting out of his seat and dropping down to one knee. My eyes snap open as I watch in stunned silence. Somewhere in the back of my brain, I understand what he's doing. Gran, who sits across from Sam, slides a little black box in his direction.

My other hand trembles as it flies to my mouth. *"Sam?"* I'm barely able to push his name out.

Oh my God, is this really happening?

Is he really doing this?

A nervous smile quirks his lips. It's an odd look on him, because Sam is never nervous. He's so strong and confident. Always in command and control. I love that about him. He's like a rock.

My rock.

"Violet, baby," he pauses, almost as if gathering himself. His eyes never falter from mine. Even though the restaurant is crowded, everyone around us fades to the background.

"The first time I laid eyes on you, I was fourteen years old. Even then, I knew that I'd found the one person who would matter more than anyone else. Loving you all these years has been as natural as breathing and just as necessary. I can't imagine my life without you in it, filling it with light and happiness. You mean everything to me, Vi. You *are* my everything, and I want you to be my wife. I want to spend the rest of my life with you."

By the end of his speech, his voice is scraped low and so full of emotion that tears of joy shimmer in my eyes. I stare at the man bent on one knee, asking for my hand in marriage. My grandparent's faces beam with happiness and I realize they were in on this as well. It makes me tumble a little bit more in love with Sam for including them in such a momentous occasion.

I will remember this moment for the rest of my life.

When he flicks open the top of the black box, there's a beautiful square-cut diamond winking back at me. I can't help but gasp at its sheer brilliance. Even though the ring is gorgeous, it's the man on his knee that has the breath catching at the back of my throat. I don't think I could love him any more than I already do.

"Vi?"

"Yes," I whisper through tears of happiness, "of course my answer is *yes!"*

A relieved grin spreads across his face before he sweeps his lips across mine. "You had me worried there for a minute."

A gurgle of laughter escapes as I shake my head. "I don't know how you could even say that. I love you so much, Samuel Joseph Harper. I can't imagine spending my life with anyone else other than you. You are my everything. You always have been."

And no matter what, he always will be.

The End

Want to read the next book in the Barnett Bulldogs Series? Buy One Night Stand here -) **https://books2read.com/jsonenightstand**

ONE NIGHT STAND

Gia

It's a little after eleven o'clock, and already this place is completely packed. It's standing room only. It might be a crappy, hole-in-the-wall dive bar, but I can't deny its popularity. Although, I suspect that has a lot to do with the cheap beer. Since it's not even half a mile away from Barnett University, and most of these people look young, my guess is that a lot of college kids have taken up residence here. I'm just thankful that Noah was able to reserve a round, high-top table for the three of us to park ourselves at.

The lights are low, drunken voices pushing in from all sides, and the music—well, it's even louder than these students cutting loose on a Saturday night. The pulsing beat practically reverberates off the walls. Even though this isn't my usual style of music or venue, my gaze is glued to the four guys performing on stage.

"I had no idea that your brother was so hot!" Harper's gaze never deviates from him. "It must be the whole musician vibe he's got going on."

Um, hello...no sister wants to hear that one of her friends is panting after her baby brother. I scrunch my nose. "*Ewwww!* You can't go around saying things like that. It's just not right."

In typical Harper fashion she grins, not taking my words seriously.

"Sorry, hon. But it's the truth. He is *definitely* looking good up there." Then she points to the horde of overzealous females who are crowded around the band, looking as if they might rush the stage before the performance is over. "And I'm obviously not the only one who thinks so either." A smirk slides its way across her pretty face. "My guess is that little Noah Monroe is going to get laid tonight. Perhaps by more than one girl."

As soon as those words are released into the atmosphere, I clap my hands over my ears before shaking my head. "That's not a mental image I want or need. So, thanks for that."

Sophie and Harper exchange knowing grins. My brother belts out another lyric, his voice soaring over the guitars and drums. The acoustics may be total crap in here, but he still sounds ridiculously amazing. Another silence falls over the three of us as our attention gets sucked back into the music.

"Hey ladies, can I buy you a drink?"

Ugh.

Not another one.

Seriously...where do these guys keep coming from? There is absolutely nothing about the three of us that screams—*trolling for dudes! Buy us a drink! We're looking to get laid! Come hit on us! Easy targets right this way!*

And yet, they keep ambling over.

One right after another.

They're a persistent bunch—I'll give them that. Why do I keep forgetting this is a crappy bar with drunken college guys who are very obviously looking to get laid?

Even if I hadn't recently extracted myself from a three-year relationship, I still wouldn't be interested in hooking up with a twenty-one or twenty-two-year-old.

I'm strictly here to watch Noah perform.

Before I'm able to cut the guy off and send him packing, like I've done four times previously, Harper gives him a quick once over before smiling prettily.

Uh-oh.

I know that look.

"Of course, you can," still smiling, her eyes turn into chips of green ice, "but understand that there's absolutely no obligation on our parts to do anything more than thank you politely for your generosity." She bats her eyelashes as if to soften the blow of her words.

The guy is momentarily surprised before an easy grin spreads its way across his handsome face. And yeah, he's definitely a cutie. But come on, he's much too young! He so boyishly adorable that I'm half tempted to reach over and pinch his cheeks with my fingers.

"You got it, sweetheart." He flags down a harassed looking waitress before whispering something in her ear and turning back to us. "This round is on me." He sends Harper a sly look and leans a bit closer to her. "Feel free to thank me once you're done enjoying your beverage."

And then he's gone.

Harper's lips tremble as she watches him disappear through the thick crowd back to wherever he came from.

When the three of us remain silent, the waitress slants a dark, uninterested brow our way. "You gonna order something or what?"

Normally, when the three of us head out for a girls night, it isn't to some low-rent college bar where the clientele barely looks to be the legal drinking age. We head downtown to the more upscale bars and clubs that line the main drag. And we stick to chardonnay and cosmos.

But here, my guess is that they don't have a good house chardonnay or make specialty martinis. Everyone seems to be drinking bottles or mugs of pale looking beer.

Well...when in Rome, right?

We order three bottles of import and go back to watching the final set.

When there's about a fourth of her beer remaining, Harper rises to her feet. "As this groups' self-appointed ambassador, I shall graciously take it upon myself to thank Mr. tall, dark, and handsome for buying us our drinks."

I give her a look rife with meaning. "Be careful how you thank him, Harp. For all you know, he's not even twenty-one."

I'm not saying that I saw peach fuzz but...

A wicked gleam fills her sparkling green eyes. "Oh, don't worry. I'm planning to do a little recon before I decide how best to express my gratitude."

With that said, she shoves her way through the rowdy crowd. Sophie and I lock gazes from across the table before bursting into laughter. "I wonder if we'll see her again."

I almost wince. "Please, these guys are like babies." They're so damn young.

Sophie makes a point of glancing around before her gaze settles on mine. "Yeah," she drawls, "most of them don't look like babies. *Like at all*."

Silently, I have to agree with her assessment. These guys may be young, but some of them are built. Not to mention ripped. I can't say that I haven't enjoyed the eye candy tonight.

But it's definitely been from afar.

I can imagine the headlines now—*Nearly thirty-year-old elementary school teacher takes advantage of barely-out-of-high-school boy*.

No, thank you.

Sophie, Harper, and I all work at North Hill Elementary School. Sometimes it's hard to believe that this is my eighth-year teaching second grade. I was fortunate enough to snag a job in this district straight out of college. And since I love where I'm at, I've never considered looking for a different position.

Since the three of us are around the same age, we naturally banded together, forming a tight trio. We eat lunch together and hang out quite a bit outside of school. Especially now that Tyler and I are no longer together.

Even though I hate to leave Sophie alone at the table—because I can practically see the sharks circling as we speak—I yell over the music, "I'm going to run to the bathroom. I'll be back in a few minutes."

With a wide smile, she waves me away before glancing around. "Don't worry, I'm a big girl. I can take care of myself."

"I never said you couldn't." As I'm about to turn away, I spin back around before adding, "Remember—these guys are like the kiosk salespeople at the mall, avoid eye contact at all costs."

She gives me a cheeky grin. "You worry too much, just go. I'll be perfectly fine on my own."

With one last nod, I push my way toward the bathroom, which is located at the far end of the bar. The crowd is packed in tight, and it takes a good five minutes to navigate my way to the restrooms. Once there, I'm horrified by what I find.

Has anyone ever cleaned this place before?

I press my fingers against my nose before inhaling another breath. The smell is enough to knock me on my ass.

I'm not going to lie—I do a little self-check and consider not using the facilities. Unfortunately, there's no way I can hold it for another hour or so. The two drinks I've consumed have run right through me.

Attempting to touch as little as possible, I squat over the toilet seat. Once I make it to the sink, I practically scrub the fingerprints off my hands before using a ripped off sheet of paper towel to open the door handle.

Once out of the bathroom, I inhale and fill my lungs with fresh— no, wait. It's definitely not fresh air, but it's a lot better than what was inside that biohazard of a ladies room.

I'm halfway to the table when someone slides in front of me, blocking my path. Since this place is packed to the gills, I don't think too much about it before attempting to step around him so I can make my way back to Sophie. Hopefully, Harper has returned to the table. She's only twenty-six, which isn't that much older than some of these college students, but I can't see her going home with someone that young. Her last boyfriend was forty.

And a stuffy lawyer, to boot.

The guy quickly sidles in the same direction, which means I find myself blocked yet again. This time, I glance at him. That's when I notice the smirk plastered across his face. It occurs to me that this little dance we're doing is intentional.

As our gazes collide, he offers me a roguish smile.

One that's meant to charm.

It falls short by a mile.

"Hey there, beautiful."

Cue the mental groaning. I am *so* not into this. All I want is to head back to the relative safety of the table. Impatiently, I give him a polite smile, hoping this won't take too long.

Even though it's been two months since Tyler and I broke up, hooking up is the last thing on my mind. When I'm finally ready to jump back into the dating pool again, it won't be with a drunk college kid who has zero idea that women have a little something called a *clit*. Let alone where one might find it.

I dealt with that in college. I'm not interested in reliving that part of the experience again.

At this stage of the game, I'm only interested in men who have, at the very least, a rudimentary understanding as to how the female orgasm is achieved. And are willing to take the time to prove it. Let's just say that Tyler had a working knowledge of female anatomy but wasn't always willing to put forth the necessary time and effort to achieve those goals.

I met Tyler about three and a half years ago through a co-worker at North Hill. We were introduced at a summer barbecue and hit it off. At the time, he ticked all the standard criteria on my mental list.

Educated—check.

Around the same age—check.

Same core values—check

Not only held down a job but was career focused—double check.

Although here's where I've learned the difference between dedicated to one's profession (me) and obsessed (Tyler). Over the last year, it became a point of contention between us, and was one of the reasons we parted ways.

Not wanting to waste this guy's time or, more importantly—mine, because what he's hoping might happen between us, is so *not* going to happen, I get right to the point. "Sorry, I'm not interested." That being said, I try to maneuver around him. Unfortunately, he shifts his body and blocks my escape.

Again.

Even though he continues to smile, my brows lower. I've just told this guy that I'm not interested in whatever he's offering. Shouldn't that be enough?

He holds up his hands in a gesture of surrender as if to show me that he's harmless.

Hey—know a better way to show me that you're not dangerous?

Accept when I tell you that I'm not interested. That would go a long way toward proving your point.

Is that concept difficult to grasp?

Apparently so.

This guy doesn't appear to be budging anytime soon, which is annoying.

"Hey, I just want the chance to get to know you."

A snort slips out. "*Riiiiiight*, I'm sure that's *exactly* what you had in mind." With a sigh, I try one more time to maneuver around him. I don't want to get nasty, but I will if I have to.

Just like before, he blocks my escape route and gives me a knowing grin. My guess is that since the first approach didn't work, he's changing tactics.

"Come on, sweetheart, you can level with me."

His gaze rakes over my body. Even though I'm not wearing anything revealing—we're talking high neck sweater and jeans—he makes me feel naked.

"You're obviously here looking to get laid. You're a little too..." he pauses.

Unconsciously, my brows wing up. I know exactly what word is about to fly out of his mouth.

"*Mature*," he says with a broad, patronizing smile. "You're a little too *mature* to be hanging out in a bar like this if you're not interested in a hookup." He shrugs as if he's doing me a favor by laying it all out on the table. "All I'm doing is offering up my services. Plus, I'm into cougars. Or MILF's. Or whatever it is that you are."

Cougar?

MILF?

I'm not even thirty! I'm twenty-nine. And some change. I'm nowhere near cougar age. Isn't that like forty or something?

Instead of going off on him, I draw in a deep, calming breath. "Exactly how old do you think I am?"

He tilts his head and scrutinizes my face. "Twenty-eight?"

Close enough.

Rather matter-of-factly, I ask, "Didn't your parents teach you that it's impolite to point out a lady's age?"

He blinks.

"Well, I'm going to do you a favor. One you don't deserve—and tell you right now that it's incredibly rude to point out a woman's age. And you certainly don't refer to her as a *cougar* or *MILF*." I shake my head. "In the future, I wouldn't open with you trying to do any female a favor by sleeping with her. That's just asinine. If you actually find a woman who is willing to climb into bed with you—especially after you've opened your mouth—she ought to be cherished and revered. Not to mention thanked." There's a pause before I tack on, "Profusely."

He shifts his stance. "So, just to be clear, you're *not* interested in hooking up with me tonight?"

My eyes widen as I shake my head. "Not even for a hot minute. I'm here to watch the band, not get laid. Now that we've cleared that up, you can kindly step aside."

When he doesn't scamper out of my way, annoyance ignites inside me. "Look, I'm not interested. I just want to get back to my friend."

He glances in Sophie's direction before returning his attention to me.

A smarmy smile settles on his lips. If he thinks that it ratchets up his cuteness factor, he's sadly mistaken. It doesn't. The only thing ratcheting up are his chances of getting smacked. I have the feeling that whatever words are on the verge of tumbling out of his mouth are going to push me over the edge.

"Hey, if it makes you more comfortable, I'm totally cool with her joining us." His gaze rakes over me again. "The more the merrier, I always say."

Ewww.

Guys like this are the absolute worst.

My eyes narrow. "Are you being serious right now?"

He looks hopeful. And oddly confident. The combination is disturbing on so many levels. Especially after everything I've said to him. "Well, that depends—are you into it?"

Um, no.

I point to all the unhappiness that has settled on my face. "Does it look like I'm remotely into *anything* you're talking about?"

He contemplates me silently.

Exactly how much has this dude had to drink tonight that he can't pick up on clear social cuing? Even my second graders understand that a frowny face aimed in their direction means that someone is unhappy with them.

Note to self—never step foot in another college bar again. No matter how much Noah begs and pleads. He'll have to step up the venues he plays at if he wants my ass in the audience.

Because *this* is not worth it.

As I open my mouth to blast him into next week, a muscular arm snakes its way around my body and I find myself hauled up against a hard male one. Knocked off guard, I blink and stare into the most gorgeous gunmetal gray eyes I've ever seen. They're crinkled around the edges with humor. He gives me a wink as if we're co-conspirators rather than perfect strangers.

Even though his comment is directed at me, he turns his attention to the idiot blocking my escape. "Hey babe, I've been looking all over for you. Where have you been?"

Want to read more of Gia and Liam's story? You can buy One Night Stand here -) **https://books2read.com/jsonenightstand**

THE GIRL NEXT DOOR

Mia

Summer before freshman year of college...

"Get your butt over here," my best friend squeals from the window where she's taken up sentinel, "you *need* to see this!"

That's a negative, Ghost Rider. I'll take a hard pass. I have zero interest in spying on a yard full of drunken classmates who are partying it up at my neighbor's house. Reluctantly, I glance up from the toes I'm painting with a pale pink polish. Coney Island Cotton Candy, to be precise.

When our gazes lock, Alyssa waves me over. She's practically vibrating with excitement. Kind of like a schnauzer.

"Everyone is over there!"

"Not true," I mutter, lacquering my baby toe with an impressively steady hand. "*We're* right here." And that's exactly where I plan to stay.

"Yeah, that's kind of the problem." She steeples her hands together before shaking them at me. "Please?" she begs. "Can't we go over there for a little bit? *Just a little*? That's all I'm asking."

That's all she's asking...ha!

I'm calling bullshit.

Alyssa knows I'd rather chew my arm off than crash one of Beck Hollingsworth's parties. I didn't mention it to her, but Beck shot me a text earlier this afternoon with all the details. If she even suspected an invitation had been issued, she would have dragged my ass across the lawn that separates our properties as soon as the first guest pulled into the drive.

No, thank you.

It's obvious from all the commotion coming from next door that the entire senior class has shown up to celebrate our newly graduated status. If we didn't live on a quiet cul-de-sac tucked away in a gated subdivision, I'd expect the police to make an unannounced visit and shut down the festivities.

Then again, no one wants to mess with Beck's father, Archibald Hollingsworth. He's a high-priced attorney with a fleet of underlings working for him. He's one of those overly tan guys with blindingly white veneers you see on television yapping about if you've been injured, you need to call them—they fight for the little guy! The dude is everywhere. Billboards. Commercials. Newspaper and magazine advertisements.

The local police have tangled with Archibald several times over the years because his son is a magnet for trouble. Let's see, there was the time (or five) when he was picked up for underage drinking. When Beck was fifteen years old, he *borrowed* his parent's brand spanking new Range Rover and did a little off-roading. And the police were involved when he super glued the locks on the high school building doors for senior prank day.

Instead of hauling Beck to the station every time he's picked up, they drop him at his front door and don't bother talking to Archibald about it. Beck is on a first-name basis with a number of guys on the force. A few showed up to his graduation party in June.

It shouldn't come as a surprise that Beck always figures out a way to circumvent the obstacles standing in his path. His parents. School. The law. It's as irritating as it is impressive. Maybe one of these days, he'll use his powers for good instead of evil.

"Come on, Mia!" Alyssa whines, all the while flashing sad puppy-dog eyes at me.

Double whammy.

My bestie knows I have a difficult time resisting puppy-dog eyes.

I wiggle my toes from the bed and grumble, "I can't go anywhere until my nails dry." I'm doing my best to prolong being anywhere near Beckett Hollingsworth. The guy drives me batshit crazy.

And that's putting it mildly.

"Great! So...five minutes?" She swings away before pressing her face against the screen as her voice turns dreamy. "I bet Colton is already there."

Ugh.

Colton Montgomery is Beck's right-hand man, so it's not a wager I'm likely to win.

Against my better advice, Alyssa has been crushing hard on Colton for more than a year. Not only is he popular, but he's a football player. Heavy emphasis on the *player* part. If Alyssa were smart, she'd find a nice guy to fall in lust with, but she has tunnel vision when it comes to the blond-haired, blue-eyed heartbreaker.

Colton has it all going on. Brains, brawn, and more than likely, a one-way ticket to the NFL after college.

The only problem is that he's aware of his own appeal.

His ego is as massive as other parts of him.

Or so I hear.

And not from Alyssa since he refuses to sleep with her. I can't decide if the situation is amusing or sad. The more Colton keeps Alyssa at a firm distance, the more determined she is to have him.

Last football season, Alyssa dragged me to every game. Even the away ones. My greatest fear was that Beck would assume my ass was there to support him. His fan club is already legendary without adding me to the ranks.

When it comes to the ladies, Beckett makes Colton look like an innocent babe. He goes through girls like most people go through underwear. Speaking of panties, the girls at our high school are always happy—hell, I'd go so far as to say thrilled—to drop theirs for him.

It's ridiculous.

He's a chronic user and abuser.

There should be a warning label slapped across his forehead.

Beware. Toxic to the female species.

But you know what?

That wouldn't stop these bubble-headed chicks from spreading their legs wide for him. I've stopped trying to figure out the appeal. All right, I'm well aware of what the attraction is. As much as I've tried to pretend I'm immune to his charms, I'm not. I just do a damn good job of burying them deep down where they never see the light of day. If I didn't, Beck would annihilate me in a heartbeat, and I have zero desire to end up a casualty on his hit list.

Given the choice, I'd rather flip through Netflix and find a movie to watch rather than be dragged over to Beck's bash.

Doesn't sitting around in pajamas and stuffing our faces with pizza sound way better than watching a bunch of our classmates get sloppy drunk, engage in way too much PDA, and puke all over the place before alcohol poisoning sets in?

I won't bother posing the question to Alyssa. There is no way she'll willingly opt for sitting home instead of stalking her crush.

Would you like to guess what Colton will be doing while I wipe the drool from Alyssa's chin?

You guessed it. He'll be flirting with every vagina he thinks he has a chance of penetrating.

Honestly, it's one of the most masochistic things Alyssa could do. I have no idea why she insists on putting herself through this kind of agony. Apparently, my job as her best friend is to support her decision to inflict untold amounts of mental anguish on to herself. I'd slap her upside the head if I thought it would knock sense into her.

My prediction for the evening goes a little something like this—Alyssa will have a few drinks, moon over Colton, before dissolving into a puddle of tears while that manwhore makes out with other girls in front of her face. Then I'll drag her home, and she'll end up knuckle-deep in a gallon of triple-chocolate ice cream.

But that's what friends are for, right?

Don't worry, I've already made my peace with it.

"Fine," I grumble with a scowl, hoping she understands the depth of my reluctance. "But let it be known that I won't be staying for more than an hour. So, you better make good use of your time, girl."

She swings around to face me, bouncing on the tips of her toes as she claps her hands together with excitement. "Yay!" As soon as she gets the affirmative, she beelines for my closet, which is half the size of my room.

I have the kind of closet most girls my age can only dream about. Shoes, purses, clothes, and jewelry. It's all there and organized.

"Cue the montage music while I find something schmexy to wear!" she squeals.

"What you have on is fine." I roll my eyes and yell, "It was good enough for me, wasn't it?"

From within the depths of my closet comes a snort.

For the next ten minutes, I'm treated to an impromptu fashion show. At the rate Alyssa is going, we won't make it to the party any time soon.

Take your time, girlfriend. I'm totally good with that.

A dozen outfit changes later, Alyssa settles on a black knit tank and white skirt that showcases her sun-kissed legs to their best advantage. Alyssa has been taking dance classes since she was three years old. She's toned with long, lean muscles.

"Damn girl, you look hot." Not that her crush will appreciate the effort. Alyssa needs to move on. I'm thinking a twelve-step program would help kick the Colton Montgomery habit.

"I would gladly live in your closet if you'd let me." She grins before doing a little twirl. "It's my happy place."

A reluctant smile quirks my lips.

My mother is a card-carrying shopaholic and has the Amex Black Card bills to prove it. She buys clothes like our house burned to the ground and nothing could be salvaged. Even with racks of space, my wardrobe is bursting at the seams. Three-quarters of the stuff has never seen the light of day. Alyssa is lucky we're roughly the same size so she can borrow whatever she wants.

Now that she's dressed and ready to mingle, her eyes narrow as she takes a hard look at me. Wordlessly, she spins around and races back inside the closet only to resurface a handful of minutes later.

"Here you go," she says, tossing two garments at the foot of my bed.

I glance at the shimmery gold tank and dark-wash jean skirt that resembles a folded-up napkin. The skirt is cute as hell, but I would strongly advise against going commando while wearing it unless you're looking to flash everyone your goodies.

Since that's not my usual style, the price tag is still dangling from the pocket. I have no idea what my mother was thinking when she picked it up.

Unsure why she's throwing clothes at me, I point to the small pile. "What's that about?"

"You need to change." She gives me a look that says—*duh* before clapping her hands together. "Chop-chop."

Changing my clothes was not part of the plan. I'm fine with going in my pajamas. It's not like I'm looking for a hookup. Or anything else, for that matter.

I shake my head and fold my arms across my chest. "No, thank you."

Her gaze rakes over me as she points to my T-shirt. "Is that a coffee stain on your boob?"

With a frown, I glance at my chest and inspect the dark spot marring the fabric of my right breast. My guess is that she's right. Caramel Macchiato, to be specific. "Possibly."

Her lips flatten. "I refuse to go anywhere with you looking like *that*."

"Great!" I stretch out before stacking my hands behind my head. "What kind of movie night does it feel like to you? Romcom? Horror? Psychological thriller? Angsty tearjerker?" A benevolent smile curves my lips. "You can choose."

Alyssa stomps her foot on the carpeted floor. "Mia!" she wails at a decibel that could shatter eardrums. A few neighborhood dogs howl in response. *"You promised!"*

Promised?

No, I don't think so.

I scrunch my nose and tap a finger against my lips. "I don't believe I ever *promised* to do anything. *Reluctantly agreed?* Yes. *Browbeaten into capitulating?* Definitely. But *promised?* Not in this lifetime."

When she straightens to her full height, I groan, knowing exactly what's about to happen. "*Mia Evelyn Stanbury*! Do I need to remind you who was there when—"

Argh.

This is the portion of the evening where Alyssa trots out every damn thing she's ever done for me until I relent. And she'll start with Harper Hastings. The girl who bullied me relentlessly in seventh grade because Xander Rossi asked me to the movies instead of her. After months of Harper's mean-spirited attacks, Alyssa waited for the girl after school. My bestie let it be known that if Harper didn't cease and desist, she'd spread the good word that the other girl was a known bra stuffer. It must have been true, since Harper immediately backed off, and I never heard a peep from her again.

"*Yes, yes, Harper Hastings*," I mutter, not appreciating the direction this conversation has swerved in.

Alyssa folds her arms across her chest as a smug smile twists her lips upward. "Harper Hastings is only the beginning, my friend." She arches a brow. "Need I continue?"

Silently we glare before I fold like a cheap house of cards. "Fine, I'll change." I straighten before scooping up the skirt and top and shaking them at her. "It's only because I love you and you're my best friend that I'm even willing to step foot next door."

An angelic smile spreads across her pretty face before she blows me a kiss. "Love you, too. Now kindly move your assets."

"An hour," I remind. "That's all you get."

Looking unconcerned, she waves a hand. "No worries, that's more than enough time to work my magic."

What she means to say is that it's more than enough time for Colton to ignore her, all the while hooking up with another girl. Part of me almost wishes he would sleep with Alyssa. Maybe then the rose-colored glasses would come off, and she would realize what a douche the guy is.

In one fluid motion, the stained T-shirt is stripped from my body and replaced with the gold tank. Then I slide off the comfy shorts I've been lounging in and yank on the tiny rectangle of material that doubles as a skirt.

I step in front of my floor-to-ceiling mirror that's propped against the wall and stare at my reflection before attempting to tug the skirt further down my thighs, but it's useless. There's not a spare inch of material to be found.

What the hell had my mother been thinking when she picked this up? Was she mistakenly shopping in the toddler section?

I turn around and bend over, touching my toes before peering over my shoulder and glancing in the mirror. It's just as I suspected. My thong is on full display. Actually, it doesn't even look like I'm wearing underwear since the material is wedged between the crack of my ass like dental floss.

Lovely.

Not to mention uncomfortable.

"Is there a second option to consider?" My gaze slides to Alyssa's in the mirror. "One where my ass isn't hanging out?"

"'Fraid not. I'm seriously loving the whole—is she or isn't she wearing panties guessing game you've got going on." She winks. "Play your cards right, and maybe you'll get lucky tonight."

I narrow my eyes as my lips thin. "Believe it or not, I'm perfectly content being unlucky."

"That, my dear, is only because you don't realize what you've been missing."

"Heartache, STIs, and the possibility of an unplanned pregnancy?" I flutter my lashes and smile. "You are so right."

Ignoring my comment, she tosses a pair of gold sandals at me before sliding her feet into black leather ones that strap up her legs, giving her that whole Grecian goddess vibe. She looks amazing. But then again, when doesn't she? Alyssa has long blond hair and dark blue eyes. Her skin has a natural sun-kissed glow that darkens under the summer sun.

It almost offends me that Colton refuses to fuck my friend.

What the hell is wrong with him?

"Ready to go?" she asks, checking her reflection in the mirror one last time.

I slip the sandals on before rising to my full height. "As I'll ever be."

Five minutes later, we've traversed the lawn and are walking around the side of the Hollingsworth mansion. All sixteen thousand square feet of it. Needless to say, Archibald has turned ambulance-chasing into a lucrative art form.

With every step we take, the sound of drunken laughter and the pulsing beat of music grows louder, assaulting our ears. As soon as the party comes into view, I wonder why I let Alyssa talk me into this.

It's complete chaos.

As much as Alyssa would like to convince you otherwise, I'm not a complete dud. I like to party as much as the next girl. But Beck enjoys taking his antics to the next level. He's not content to have a low-key get-together where people sit around and chill. This party is moments away from becoming one of those teen movies where all hell breaks loose, and the host wakes up naked the next morning in a dumpster five states away with a goat.

Over to the left, a few people are holding a guy upside down while he performs a keg stand.

Chants of—*chug, chug, chug* permeate the air.

It wouldn't surprise me if one of these drunken idiots is found floating face down in the pool come morning.

It begs the question of why Beck's parents would leave him alone without supervision. He might be eighteen-years-old and technically an adult, but he needs an adultier adult to keep him in check. Someone who can put the kibosh on his hijinks.

Good luck with that. His older brother, Ari, is out of the country for the summer.

Archibald and Caroline, his parents, must have realized this was inevitable. Every time they go out of town, Beck throws a huge bash. Depending on the amount of damage, he gets grounded anywhere from a few days to a couple of weeks. The threat of consequences— hell, actual consequences being enforced—are in no way a deterrent.

Believe it or not, before our parents left town for a long weekend in New York, Archie asked me to keep an eye on their son. His actual words were—*make sure no one dies.*

As if I exert that much control over Beck?

Yeah, right. Beck doesn't listen to anyone, let alone me.

Exactly what am I supposed to do?

Tattletale?

Facetime his parents so they can get a first-hand glimpse of the ensuing pandemonium?

As much pleasure as that would give me, it's not going to happen. I might be a lot of things (a rule follower and a goody-goody, if you listen to Beck) but there are lines that can't be crossed, and snitching is one of them.

This will be one more antic Beck gets away with. I suppose that's the beauty of being Beckett Hollingsworth. He doesn't give a shit about anything other than football.

The Neanderthal sport is his life.

By the time Beck was a freshman in high school, he'd already drawn the attention of Big Ten college coaches. They couldn't wait to get him on their roster. If he could have gone straight to the NFL after graduation, he would have. But that's not a possibility. Players aren't eligible to enter the draft until after their sophomore year of college. Beck's father has taken it one step further by insisting he wait until senior year because—and I quote—*no damn son of mine is going to be a college dropout.*

Beck will be proof positive that C's really do earn degrees.

As my gaze drifts over the thick crowd of glassy-eyed stares, it collides with bright green ones. A little zip of electricity sizzles its way through my veins as our gazes fasten. The muscles in my belly tense with awareness. Once I realize what's happening, I tamp down the reaction. My life has been filled with a thousand little moments like this one. Moments I like to pretend never transpired.

For all I know, it's gastritis from the sushi I picked up at the gas station last night.

Anything's possible, right?

Instead of glancing away, I hold his stare and scowl. What I've learned is that it's better to brazen out these situations than turn tail and run. Beck's perfect cupid's bow of a mouth lifts into a knowing grin before he crooks his finger.

A gurgle of laughter bubbles up in my throat.

I don't think so, buddy.

I'm not like the bubbleheads he usually toys with. I have a working brain, and I enjoy using it to make good decisions that won't come back to bite me in the ass. Unlike Beck, I have a healthy amount of self-preservation.

I press my lips into a tight line before emphatically shaking my head.

A wolfish grin spills across his face, giving him a boyishly handsome appearance. With dark tousled hair, sharp cheekbones that scream his Russian heritage, and thick eyebrows, he's a danger to females everywhere. I won't mention the chiseled body that looks like it was carved from stone. Broad shoulders and a tapered waist complete the package.

It's almost a relief when a bikini-clad girl steps between us, severing the connection. Now that his sharp gaze is no longer pinning me in place, I'm able to exhale all the air from my lungs.

Alyssa grabs my hand. "There he is," she whisper-yells excitedly over the babble of voices and music. "Oh my God, he's so freaking dreamy."

I regard the crowd of newly minted high school graduates before finding Colton.

Sure, I'll admit it. He's as hot as Beck. Instead of short dark hair, he's golden blond. It's buzzed on the sides and left long on top, so he's constantly pushing it away from bright blue eyes. He's tall and brawny. If I hadn't gone to school with him since elementary, I'd suspect he flunked a few grades. Even his muscles have muscles.

Girls are already circling around him, vying for his attention. The guy is like a rock star picking out groupies to sleep with at the end of the night.

"He's okay," I mutter, wanting to downplay his attractiveness.

"You're so full of shit, your eyes are turning brown. He's way better than *okay*, and you know it."

"Ewww." I scrunch my nose. "That's gross."

"Focus!" She snaps her fingers in front of my face.

I make one last-ditch effort to sway her. "You can do better than Colton. He knows exactly how hot he is and takes full advantage of it every chance he gets. Find someone like," I stand on my tiptoes and pick through the mass of bodies before zeroing in on the perfect guy for Alyssa, "Landon Mathews. Not only is he good-looking, he's a sweetheart."

Alyssa's expression turns thoughtful as she assesses the tall guy with inky-black hair and unusual blue-green eyes. He's standing around with a bunch of football players, laughing at something one of them said.

"He's definitely yummy," she admits.

For one glorious moment, my spirits soar. Maybe she'll drop this whole Colton Montgomery nonsense and go after someone more attainable. Landon is a great guy. He's as hot as his friends, but he's not a total asshat. Unfortunately, he doesn't get nearly the same amount of hype that Colton or Beck do since he's been labeled a good guy.

I mean, who wants to date a nice guy when you can have one who treats you like total crap?

Said no one ever.

Except...there seems to be way more truth to that statement than most females are comfortable acknowledging. Whether they realize it or not, these girls have been conditioned to crave unattainable jerks.

It's disturbing on so many levels.

"Added bonus," I continue, "he knows you're alive!"

"Um, excuse me, Colton knows I'm alive," she grumbles.

"Are you certain about that?"

She bites her lip as we glance at the guy in question who is—surprise-surprise—surrounded by a bevy of scantily clad girls competing for his interest.

Uh-oh.

Alyssa's got that look in her eye. The one that tells me not to bother trying to talk her out of her plans.

She confirms it by saying, "Wish me luck, I'm going in."

It was worth a try.

"Good luck."

One of Alyssa's best qualities is that she's not a quitter. That girl can be as tenacious and persistent as a terrier. And sometimes, just as yappy.

In this instance, it's a negative.

When she's a few steps away, I cup my fingers around my mouth and yell, "Maybe you should take off the panties so you can flash him your puss. That way he'll know you're a sure thing."

She whips around with a grin. "Excellent idea!"

My jaw drops when she shimmies out of her underwear and tosses it in my direction.

"Christ, girl! I was joking! That was sarcasm!" I glance at the wadded-up material I now clench in my hand. "What am I supposed to do with this?"

She shrugs. "Keep it as a souvenir?"

Gross.

"I don't think so." I stalk to a garbage can and pitch it. When I turn around, Alyssa is pushing her way through the crowd, moving steadily closer to Colton and his harem.

If nothing else, this should be entertaining. It takes a moment to realize that I'm alone at a party I didn't want to attend in the first place. I slip my phone from my back pocket and glance at it.

Fifty minutes and counting.

This is shaping up to be the longest hour of my life. Maybe I should head inside and grab a drink. By the number of drunken idiots I'm surrounded by, my guess is that the booze is flowing freely. I maneuver my way through the crowd and into the kitchen before taking in the scene.

If Beck's mom saw all these people sitting their asses on her polished-to-a-high-shine marble countertop, she would probably have a conniption. She's kind of a germ-o-phobe. There's a half-naked girl stretched out on the island with a lime clenched in her teeth as one of the football players slurps tequila from her belly button.

I'm no aficionado on hygiene, but that definitely doesn't seem sanitary.

A few people greet me as I make my way to the keg and take my place in line. I'm in the middle of chatting with a girl from my French class when she turns an unflattering shade of green and bolts to the nearest bathroom with her hands slapped over her mouth. All thoughts of a refill are abandoned as she pushes her way to the back hall. I really hope she makes it in time. Caroline will be furious if she finds out someone has thrown up on her marble floors.

Once I have a frothy cup of beer in hand, I head to the patio to check on Alyssa's progress.

Am I a terrible friend for hoping she's already been shot down and has thrown in the towel for the night?

Probably, but I can deal with that.

Instead of finding a dejected Alyssa crying in the corner, I'm amazed to discover that she's clawed her way to the front of the pack. Who knows, she may actually have a shot of getting picked from the crowd.

This could be a real game-changer for her.

Guess that means I'm stuck here. I look around the patio, searching for a place to park my ass. The Hollingsworth property is about an acre in size, which is the same as ours. The space around the pool is gated with a black-iron fence and tall arborvitae that spear into the dark night sky. Toward the back of the gate is an unoccupied lounge chair with my name on it. I'll hang out there for forty minutes before dragging Alyssa's panty-less ass back to my house.

Before I can take three steps, a deep voice cuts through the raucous noise of the party.

"Well, well, well. Look who decided to make a cameo appearance tonight."

I swing around, knowing exactly who I'll find.

Beck.

As difficult as it is, I try not to notice how delicious he looks in plaid board shorts that hang low on his hips, showing off the cut lines of his abdomen before disappearing beneath the waistband. The chiseled strength of his arms and chest are enough to bring most girls to their proverbial knees.

The operative word in that sentence being *most.*

I, however, am not one of those idiotic girls.

"Coming here tonight wasn't my idea. I was dragged under duress."

"Yeah, I figured you would have better things to do than hang around with a bunch of wasted assholes."

He's got me there.

"You know me too well." When my throat grows dry, I lift the red Solo cup to my lips. Before I can take a sip, he snatches the drink from my fingers and brings it to his mouth. I watch his throat constrict as he drains the contents.

"Rude much?" My fists go to my hips. "What did you do that for?"

He shrugs. Even though it's a slight movement, his muscles ripple, and attraction bursts to life in my core. "You shouldn't be drinking."

"Excuse me?" My eyes pop wide as laughter tumbles from my mouth. "Are you being serious right now?" I wave a hand toward the drunken mob that surrounds us. It's not even eleven, and already people are passed out on loungers. "Look around, dude, everyone is shitfaced." Hopefully, there are a few designated drivers among this group, or Uber will make a hell of a lot of money tonight.

As soon as Beck smirks, I know his answer is specifically designed to piss me off.

"That might be so, but everyone knows you're a good girl. And good girls don't drink. I wouldn't want the society to revoke your membership. You've worked so damn hard for it."

My eyes narrow to slits. The attraction that had flared to life so quickly is extinguished by his teasing.

I hate when he calls me that. And he knows it, which is precisely why he continues to do it. Beck loves nothing better than to crawl under my skin. He's like a rash I can't quite get rid of, no matter how many steroids I use.

It's irritating.

"I'm not a good girl," I growl before stabbing a finger at his ridiculously hard chest. "And *you* are not my keeper. I can drink if I want to." In a haughty voice, I remind, "I'm the one who was requested to babysit *your* ass. Not the other way around."

He crowds into my personal space. Instead of retreating, I stand my ground. I refuse to let him intimidate me.

"Babysitter, you say? Hmmm...I could definitely use one of those tonight." His fingers trace a path down the center of my chest, lingering in the valley between my breasts. "Should we take this elsewhere, and you can demonstrate everything your service entails?"

His nearness does funny things to me and clouds my better judgment. Instead of pushing him away, I'm tempted to pull him closer.

My body wavers before sanity crashes down on me, and I bat his hand away. "Go to hell."

"See?" He laughs as if I've proven his point. "A good girl through and through."

"I'm not as good as you think." The words shoot out of my mouth before I can rein them back in. To be clear, they are a total lie. I *am* as good as he thinks. Probably better. I have to be.

"Is that so?" He steps closer until the tips of my breasts brush against his bare chest. "Sweetheart, I'd love nothing better than to test that theory, but we both know you'll always be Mia Stanbury, little miss perfect."

And he'll always be Beckett Hollingsworth. The guy with little-to-no impulse control who can't walk down the school hallway without finding trouble. The same one who can't be left alone in his own house for a night without inviting a hundred of his closest friends over for an impromptu party.

We are opposites in every sense of the word.

"Shut up, Beck." I've never met anyone who has the power to turn me on and piss me off at the same time. If he ever cranked up the charm, I'd be toast. He's capable of melting the panties right off a girl with one well-aimed look. I've seen it happen with my own eyes. I refuse to be one of those ridiculous females. I won't be used and tossed aside like a dirty Kleenex.

I don't realize that I've become trapped in my own thoughts until his fingers settle under my chin, lifting it so I'm forced to meet his bright gaze. "What's the matter? Truth hurt?"

"There's nothing you can say that will hurt me." If only that were true.

His face looms closer until it fills my vision, blotting out the party. My world shrinks around us until it only encompasses Beck. My breath gets clogged in my lungs and burns like a fire before spreading to the rest of my body. Any moment I'm going to self-combust.

What am I doing?

I should pull away, but I'm powerless to do anything other than stare into his eyes and fall under his spell.

"Beck, baby!" a loud female voice booms over the rowdiness of the party, "over here!"

Even when she continues to bleat like a sheep, our gazes remain locked for several long heartbeats, and I almost wonder if he'll ignore her. But she's persistent and continues to repeat his name until he severs the connection between us and swings around.

As soon as I'm released, the air rushes from my lungs, and my body sags with relief. Or maybe it's disappointment. I tamp down the emotions so I can't inspect them too closely.

What would have happened if we hadn't been interrupted?

Nothing good.

This is *exactly* why I avoid Beck at all costs. Even though we're constantly sniping at each other, there's an undercurrent of attraction that hums beneath the surface. No other guy has ever provoked these kinds of emotions in me. I want to slap him almost as much as I want to kiss him.

Sanity returns with a rush as I focus on the statuesque blonde twenty feet away. Ava Simmons is wearing a teeny tiny bikini that leaves little to the imagination. Once she has Beck's full attention, she reaches around and unties the strings that hold the tiny triangles in place. The material floats to the cement at her feet. She lets him—and everyone else in the vicinity—ogle her perky breasts before running and jumping into the pool.

People cheer, and more girls ditch their tops, following Ava into the water.

A grin slides across Beck's face as he glances at me. A challenging light enters his eyes as he jerks his dark head toward the pool. Water sloshes over the edge of the azure-colored tile as more bodies dive in.

Oh, hell no.

My heart pounds as I throw my hands up in a *what can you do* gesture. "Sorry, didn't bring a suit."

His grin turns predatory. "Doesn't look like you need one."

Yeah...not going to happen.

"As fun as that seems, I'll pass," I wave an arm toward the pool, "but don't let that stop you from mingling with your guests. Ava's waiting." Topless. From the corner of my eye, I see her breasts bobbing like inflatable safety devices.

When his focus is drawn to the people splashing around, I follow suit. It's so much easier to stare elsewhere than hold the intensity of his gaze. Even when that option includes watching a bunch of topless girls I've known since elementary school. I don't check out the guys loitering in the area, but I'm sure most are sporting wood. Honestly, if it weren't for Alyssa, I would get the hell out of here before it turns into a raging orgy.

Beck steps closer, and my gaze snaps to his. "Sure I can't persuade you to go for a swim?"

"Nope." I shake my head.

"That's too bad. This would have gone a long way to prove that you're not the good girl I've always pegged you to be."

Before I can summon up a pithy retort, he runs and dives headfirst into the water. I catch a glimpse of plaid as he disappears beneath the surface.

A mixture of relief and disappointment bubble up inside me until I'm nearly choking on them. It's the latter emotion I'm having a hard time accepting.

With a huffed-out breath, I stalk to one of the many loungers that surround the pool and settle on top of a plush cushion. I glance around for Alyssa, hoping she's given up on Colton so we can head home. It's not too late for the evening to be salvaged with pizza and a movie. Instead, I find her in the pool.

Topless.

Sucking face with Colton.

Great.

As much as I want to take off, I can't leave her here alone. God only knows what will happen if I do.

With a groan, I squeeze my eyes tight and prepare myself for a long night.

Want to read more of Mia and Beck's story? You can buy The Girl Next Door here -) **https://books2read.com/u/4EPQPg**

ABOUT THE AUTHOR

Jennifer Sucevic is a USA Today bestselling author who has published eighteen New Adult and Mature Young Adult novels. Her work has been translated into both German (as well as audiobook format) and Dutch. She has a bachelor's degree in History and a master's degree in Educational Psychology. Both are from the University of Wisconsin-Milwaukee. Jen spent five years working as a high school counselor before relocating with her family. If you would like to receive updates regarding new releases, please contact Jennifer through email, at her website, or on Facebook. sucevicjennifer@gmail.com
Social media links-
www.jennifersucevic.com
https://www.instagram.com/jennifersucevicauthor
https://www.facebook.com/jennifer.sucevic
https://www.tumblr.com/blog/jsucevic
https://www.pinterest.com/jmolitor6/

www.ingramcontent.com/pod-product-compliance
Lightning Source LLC
Chambersburg PA
CBHW051128190726
48290CB00006B/1738